Forged in Blood

Cover Design by Carlos Quevedo

Literary Editor by Chaos Goblin Editing

www.kristinawildes.com

ISBN 979-8-9923484-0-8

FORGED IN
BLOOD

KRISTINA L. WILDES

Acknowledgements

Thank you to my grandfather, Leslie C. Wallace, for always believing in my dreams.

For telling me that no matter what stands before you, so long as you have enough desire, sheer willpower, and a community of those who love you behind you, anything is possible.
This one is for you.

I broke the mountains placed before me.

And I will continue to do so for you.

Dedication

To the mountains others created...

... and for those who broke them...

Trigger Warning

The content hereafter includes the following:
Reader discretion is advised to avoid causing any undue
memories, pain, or the like. Author Kristina Wildes wishes
all readers to feel safe in any environment, including the
world of literature.
Child Abuse
Sexual Acts
Language
Post Traumatic Stress Disorder
Violence/Gore

Chapter 1

VERENA

"Come on in, dear." Merridayn Belmont's soft voice echoed over the gate intercom before she was allowed in. She continued through, her car groaning with exhaustion. Her silver, more rust than metal, missing its rear bumper, with a significant dent on her passenger side rear door, car protested when she accelerated.

Verena sighed as her car sputtered, barely holding together as it climbed the steep, winding driveway. She rolled down her window to smack the rearview mirror back into position, muttering under her breath, "One more breakdown, and I swear I'm walking."

Something dark fluttered into the car, landing on the worn passenger seat. Verena glanced over, expecting a stray leaf, but froze when her fingers brushed the object.

A feather. Black, glossy, and unnervingly perfect, its edges shimmered faintly in the light. It felt heavier than it should, its surface oddly warm against her skin.

She shook her head and tossed it out the window. "Great. Now I'm hallucinating bird feathers. Perfect."

The feather hit the ground, vanishing the moment it touched the cobblestones.

"Just a bit longer, old girl. I need to get paid again to afford the mechanic. Hang in there." Verena patted the steering wheel as her car creaked up the winding cobble-

stone path of their drive, detailed by an expanse of shrub-
bery, various flowers, and evenly spaced trees.

Verena had worked for Elion Belmont since she received
her drivers licence at sixteen; the past two years had been
filled with numerous deliveries. Mail from their P.O. box,
groceries, clothing, and anything else which had to be
picked up from town was delivered by her. Verena's em-
ployment had been secured by proximity to the Belmont's
home while she lived in a dusty cabin a mile up the road. A
moment of chance and opportunity, Mr. Belmont waved
her down one day as she made her way home from school
and asked if she wanted a job. He was an older gentleman
with grey peppered into his dark brown hair. There was
an air about him which exuded kindness and compassion.
Verena unquestioningly accepted the offer. Anything to
help her pay for their livelihood. She felt as if nature was
whispering she could trust him, and she obliged. Luckily,
the job worked in her favour; she completed the weekly
tasks and asked no questions.

During her tenure, Verena learned the Belmonts avoided leaving their home at any cost. Every Wednesday, at
four o'clock in the afternoon, Verena arrived in her 2004
Toyota Camry filled to the brim with food for the family
of four living behind the gates. Every Wednesday, without
fail, Verena would find a way to make a fool of herself.

Every.

Single.

Wednesday.

While their home was breathtaking, wrought iron gates
loomed so high at the entry no one could view what could
be past them. The symbol of wealth in Gwendolyn could
be said to be embodied by the entryway alone. Gwendolyn was a small town at the southernmost spout of

Huntress Lake; Verena reluctantly called the place home. With its dreadful population of five thousand people, it was a town where secrets were not long kept and strangers were nonexistent. Many old decaying stone buildings with random modern eye sores were mixed in and could be seen from every angle. It was a mountain town smack in the middle of the valley. Verena dreamed about the day she could leave. She longed for the adventures she envisioned in her mind. To explore the world outside the soul-draining, always too hot or too cold, marginally colonial town of Gwendolyn, Ironia. She could not wait to leave this and every single damned person inside behind her.

At least everyone, except a lone pair of eyes she subconsciously yearned to look upon, and they were waiting for her in the entryway. His storm grey irises, always filled with mystery and dominance, stared her down as she pulled closer. His shirt was always too small, soaked in sweat, and his shorts bunched up in all the right places. His braided chestnut hair drifted down his back and ended just below his shoulder blades; a few loose strands framed his sun-kissed face. His arms and right leg were covered in ink, artwork Verena dreamed of someday inspecting up close. His eyebrow slightly cocked as she put her car in park, his full lips barely lifted in a smirk.

Aven Absolutely Gorgeous Belmont.

The second child of Elion and Merridayn Belmont, Aven was the kindest person Verena had ever met. He always tried to help others, no matter their circumstances. He made Verena's heart race whenever she saw him after a workout. The fabric of his shirt clung to him in a way the designers couldn't have intended or foreseen.

In typical Verena style, she slammed her forehead on the door frame of her car as she attempted to get out.

"Fuck, why me? Why is it always me? You can't just get out of a car without showing the world what a clutz you are?" She heard chuckles above her as she clutched her head in pain. His hand stabilised her as the other pushed her chin up. Strong fingers moved to brush her hands away, an egg on her head growing in size by the second.

"Are you alright? Do I need to call my mother out to look at you?" Contrary to appearances, Mrs. Belmont was a registered nurse who struggled to pay off her student loans before meeting Mr. Belmont. Their story was mesmerising and gave Verena hope for the future.

"I'm fine, just embarrassed, and my head hurts a tad. I'll get your groceries out and be on my way." She shook out of his grasp and fumbled to open her trunk. The embarrassment made her blush a vibrant red; getting her job done to escape his view was imperative. Verena didn't need to do anything else for him to laugh about later.

As he watched her, his arms crossed, and his veins pushed against the soft fabric. Aven couldn't help but watch the way her body moved and accentuated her ass as she strained to reach the other side of her car. Her long legs appeared slightly bruised. The bruising made him wonder if she was being abused at home. His curiosity peaked, his heart rate increased, his breathing grew heavier, and his teeth clenched. Verena was oblivious to the brewing storm as she reached for the last bag leaning against the passenger side door.

"Why not open the door to get the bag instead of crawling across the back?" His tone was strained but still curious as Verena whipped her head out of the car, this time slamming the back of her head against the door frame.

"Seriously, why? Again?" Verena clutched her head in pain as she handed the last of the bags to Aven. She looked up at him; the dreaded tunnel vision began as she gripped the door handle.

"I would have if the door would open, but once you do get it open, it won't close fully. Something about- oh my, he..." She looked up at him, worry etched across his smooth skin before everything faded.

Glass shattered as Aven dropped the bags to catch Verena as she fell. He grabbed her just before she would have slammed her head into the ground. Aven swung her quickly into his arms, cradling her body against his. His free hand moved the hair out of her face and wiped the flowing blood before it could reach her eyes. As his mother opened the front door, Aven was already carrying her inside. Mrs Belmont's shocked inhale and panic-stricken orders shouted to the others were barely audible to Verena as she fell into sleep, becoming vulnerable to a memory which kept her awake most nights.

"Verena, get off your lazy ass and go get the fucking mail! I just heard the mailman drive past, and I've been waiting all day for my paycheck!" Colin, Verena's disgusting stepfather, screamed from the recliner, where he could be found every day after his shift at the auto shop. Beer bottles were scattered around. His routine involved tearing through a case as fast as he could every evening.

"Why can't you get up and get it your damn self? I have homework to finish before Mom gets home." Verena snarled back at him while not looking away from her assigned homework for the weekend.

Colin wasn't drunk enough. He stormed out of the recliner and stumbled over to the dinner table where she sat. Verena attempted to get out of the chair to put the table between them, but she failed. Colin grabbed her by the throat, slammed her against the wall and pressed his nose against hers.

"Do I need to teach you a lesson again?" He growled in her face, saliva spraying everywhere. Verena tried to push him off her.

"No, no, I don't fucking think so. You don't need to teach me shit." She pushed back, her anger fueling her.

He was unhappy with her response as his grip tightened, and his other hand fumbled with his belt. Verena knew what he was attempting to do. He had done this before. His hand managed to rip the belt off, pulling it back and cracking it against her exposed thigh.

"Get the fuck off me, you fucking asshole." She tried to push back, tried everything to get him off her. Not this time. She was prepared since the last time he beat her, leading her to wear long sleeves at school on a hot spring day.

"Are you done back talking yet? Or do you need another whipping?" The belt raised again, threatening to come down on her.

Colin pulled her by the hair, making her look at him. Her hidden switchblade snapped open, a smile on her face. With all her strength, she reached back and struck him in the abdomen. His grip on her hair loosened, his eyes bulged in disbelief and pain. Blood ran down her hands, and something inside of her snapped. The pain in her thigh caused her to gasp, but her happiness was too overbearing. Colin would feel what she had been bottling up inside for years, ever since the first day he came into her room and beat her. He tried to fight her off, but the blood loss became too much, and he fell to his knees before her. The front door opened in the background; Verena was too engulfed to hear it.

"Colin? Verena? Are you home? The car is out front unless you went for a run. Ver... oh my Goddess, what the fuck is going on here!" Her mother, Abigail, dropped the bags she

had in her hands. Her eyes flickered between her husband, on his knees, belt in hand, blood pooling on the floor, to her daughter with her hand still wrapped around the knife. Colin held onto his abdomen, gasping for air.

"Call the police. Now, Abigail. She just stabbed me." Colin rattled out, his breathing growing increasingly unsteady.

"You stay right there, Verena, until I figure out what's happening here. What did you do?"

"What did I do? Are you asking me what I did? Is this a joke? He's been beating me for years, and you didn't care. All you cared about was the money and letting this asshole do whatever he wanted so you could live a nice life." Verena dropped the knife and began to walk away. "I'm going to go live with Nan; at least she gives a damn, unlike you."

"I should have beaten you harder then, you ungrateful bitch." Colin growled out, the statement followed by her mother gasping. The truth she had been refuting came to light.

"You've been doing what with my daughter, Colin? Have you been hurting her? All these years?"

"Someone had to teach her how to respect the man of the household. It wasn't you, now was it? You're always off spending money that doesn't belong to you." He laughed, knowing he had put her mother in a spot she couldn't escape.

Verena stopped her walk towards her room; her plans of packing her things paused as she waited to see how her mother would react to Colin's words. Would she leave him for the sake of her daughter, or would she continue to subject Verena to the abuse? In either direction, Verena was leaving. She knew, under no circumstance, she was not going to stay here any longer, even if it meant leaving her school district after she started to make friends.

"We are done, Colin. Call the damn police yourself, but I

*will happily tell them I walked in on you beating a child.
A child, Colin. Verena, grab whatever is important and get
to the car. Now."* Abigail directed her daughter, who approached Colin and crouched down to pick up the discarded
knife. *"If you ever come close to my daughter or me again, I'll
kill you myself with this same knife. Divorce papers will be in
the mail by the end of the week."* With such, she plunged the
knife into Colin again, her mother's usual blue eyes alight
with glee. Her head whipped to Verena's room to ensure she
wasn't there to see the change in her demeanour. She didn't
need Verena asking questions.

As Verena came to, she first felt the warm hands on her,
under her legs and shoulders. The next sensation was the
sound of a steady heartbeat thumping in her ears. Finally,
she felt a hot breath ghosting across her cheek. Her mind
was so foggy she couldn't remember why she was even
asleep. Was she asleep? Or was this one of her out-of-body
dreams? She mentally pinched herself, trying to startle
herself into consciousness.

Everything was dark and hazy. Conscious awareness was
slipping away. She was unaware of the havoc going on
around her.

Verena struggled to open her eyes.

The fabric moved across her skin.

"Verena, how could you be so reckless?" A sharp pitch
and the voice proceeded to drift farther away from reality.

"Aven?" His name was a whisper upon her lips, but she
felt the shiver pass through his body as it escaped her.

Verena screamed, but no one around her could hear it.

Chapter 2

VERENA

"You can't be serious, Abigail. She's not yet of age, and being away from her kind is taking a toll on her body. The poor girl looks emaciated, and let us not begin about the bags under her eyes. Have you lost your goddess-damned mind? How long has she gone without being in the presence of Fae blood? How long have you kept her away from the magic of her people? You better pray to the Goddess the infusion we gave her can give her the necessary nutrients or–"

"Or else what, Merridayn? Will you go running to the council again? Did it disappear from your precious head the last time you did?" Was that her mother's voice? How? She was supposed to be at work in the town over for the week.

Verena internally groaned. Her body was coming to. She mindlessly took in her surroundings. If voices could be believed, her mother was in the room; at least, it sounded like her. Mrs. Belmont also had to be nearby if her mother addressed the posh woman.

"One." Someone growled, and a whimper followed. "Do not ever cut my mother off. You will take what your Luna has to say, and you will sit there like the good un-grateful bitch you are. Two, you were granted custody of Verena based on her parents' belief, in which you agreed you would keep her from harm until she came of age. Do not betray their trust. Three, Verena is now gracing my bed, where she will stay until she returns to a healthy state. There is no discussion. If you wish to stay, and be here when she wakes, then you will shut the fuck up and wait like a good mutt."

Verena perked up upon hearing Aven's voice until her brain registered him saying she was in his bed. She noticed something was different. Something was on her.

For some reason, Verena felt soaked, as if someone turned on a faucet within her. She could feel herself getting worked up from just listening to the beautiful baritone voice from the other room. She outwardly stirred; her core was burning, a roaring demand to be paid attention to. She had to escape this situation before a particular need took over. As she started moving around, sheets pooled at her full hips, she realised the lilac blouse she donned this morning was missing. The sudden movement caused an aroma of old books, ocean air and a hint of evergreen to reach her nose. It was calming. Verena subconsciously leaned into it, reaching out for anything which could help calm the storm of anxiety. Rough cotton fabric brushed against her skin with faded ink around the centre. The sleeves didn't fit her arms. The material bunched up at her waist.

Aven. Her heart purred, content. Her mind compiled every time she could smell him and registered that the shirt which graced her skin was his. She pulled the sheet back slightly to see her shorts from earlier had been removed. All she wore was the black lace thong she had ordered from the internet, soaked with her arousal. A warm pool of it brushed her thighs as she shifted. Footsteps sauntered closer, heavier than the lithe steps her mother took. The door opened, and the hallway light backlit the broad frame of the entry.

"Verena?" Aven's voice was soft, so soft she barely recognised it. Until his scent slammed into her and shot right through her to her already weeping core. Aven halted his stride to her bedside and sniffed the air. She almost missed it as his eyes shifted into a feral gleam before he composed himself.

"Verena? Verena is awake?" Her mother's voice drifted behind him, and Aven's face went dark again before he moved out of Abigail's way as she pushed into the room. Abigail didn't seem to care who stood between her and her daughter. Verena vaguely heard Aven release a soft, low growl, a hint of warning to her overbearing mother now doting over her.

"Where are her clothes?" Her mother shrieked, suspiciously, too suspiciously. Abigail had never cared enough before to act hysterical. Verena put her suspicion behind her, grateful she had come despite the sudden change of heart.

"Did we not just have this conversation a few minutes ago, Abigail? Or was I dreaming? Shall we take this outside so I can remind you who I am? Again, for the third time. Because hearing you beg for mercy would tickle my ears." Aven stalked up to her mother, gripping her shoulder and forcing her to kneel. Verena couldn't bear the sight of him hurting her. The fantasy which lived in her heart was shattered. Aven had always been so nice, and this was the exact opposite of the mask he always wore. She didn't know who he was anymore, but at the same time, she had to remind herself she barely knew him at all.

"Get off my mother." Her voice was rough, parched and dry, but her tone was more commanding than she had ever heard from herself. She tried to push herself off the bed. The sheet which fell over the side provided a full view of her bruised and bare legs. Aven's breath hitched again. Abigail used it to her advantage and lowered her head in submission.

"Aven, please, please just let it go. I overreacted. I apologise for the mistake. It will not happen again. Please, let her lay back down. She's not strong enough. She's not ready. It's not time." Abigail's words confused her more as Verena's strength faltered, and she plopped back down on the bed. Verena's breath laboured, her eyes solely focused on Aven's hand, which still gripped her mother. Verena didn't see Merridayn coming up on her other side with a needle in hand. Verena felt the soft pinprick of the needle break the skin and slide into her muscles.

Her eyelids grew heavy, and Verena's head spun. She was losing consciousness again. She fought to stay awake as hard as she could. One of her hands reached out for someone, anyone at all. As her head hit the silk pillows, Aven brushed the hair from her face and covered her back up.

"You are safe now, my sweet Verena." He kissed her brow, and the world went dark for the second time.

Red eyes peered at her, confused but curious. Only the eyes were seen. Verena couldn't make out anything else in the darkness. She'd have thought she was hallucinating if not for the hair on her arm standing straight up. Her pulse raced, ready to fight or flee.

"Your heartbeat races in fear. But the aroma between your delicious legs smells even more decadent than I ever imagined. Oh, my sweet, how I have waited for your return just to hear the sound of your heart under my lips." Verena shivered, terrified yet surprisingly aroused. Those red eyes

sparkled in amusement.

Then they vanished—here one moment and gone the next. Verena panicked, her heart racing even faster. She didn't know why she was afraid, why she was petrified of those eyes. This must be a dream, right? She remembered being in bed, Aven's bed—the soft green sheets and dominating grey eyes—until a sharp pain in her arm, and the light winked away.

So, who was this? Was this some sort of trick of her mind? A fantasy tucked away in her subconscious? Perhaps one of those frisky yet mouth-watering characters from her romance novels, her mind projected. She wouldn't mind if her dream went like it did in her books. The damsel in need of aid but doesn't find her knight in shining armour. Instead, he's decked out in leather and screams bad boy. Books where the hungry predator devours the main character. It made her shiver with expectations of debauchery.

"Is it what you want, my sweet? To have me devour you whole? I had other plans for you, but if that is what you want..." those red eyes appeared again right next to her ear, cold breath ghosted her neck *"...I could be convinced you're a good girl. Are you a good girl, darling? Only then would you be bent over and railed into deep, rough and mine. You will be soaking when I do, otherwise, you'll be in for a delightfully harsh awakening."* A dominating laugh breached her ears. She was already heavily aroused by her imagination of who could possess those glaring red eyes.

She pictured a man with broad shoulders, wide enough her hips could sit comfortably while she rode his lips. Rough hands from working all day whose callouses gripped her ass. Rock-hard abdominal muscles delectable enough to lick chocolate off of. It all made her whimper with need. The need to be fucked into oblivion by this red-eyed spectre, to

plead with him she could be a good girl. She would be the
best girl if only to feel him subdue her so sweetly.

"*As much as I am enjoying myself, you need to wake up,*
my love. The time for us to meet is neither here or now."
She swore she could feel a ghosted kiss upon her neck and a
deep inhale before the dream shifted into nothing. Was this
a dream? It felt all too real. The need for him raged inside
of her. A ghost of a man she didn't even know. She knew
she could never have forgotten those eyes if she had met him
before. Her thoughts churned inside, bursting at the seams
to become reality before her mind settled. She drifted into a
deep slumber filled with images of the moon at its peak.

Chapter 3

VERENA

A droplet of water hit her lips. Just the smallest of sensations stirred her from her drug-induced sleep. Her eyes fluttered back and forth, struggling to open. Had her eyes been stuck shut for days? How long had she been asleep? Question after question crossed her mind as she fought the anaesthetic to move. Any part of her would do at this moment. Her body refused the slightest twitch, but her heart rate increased enough.

"Verena? Verena, can you hear me?" The voice was deep, not high-pitched like her mother's, but not as deep in her dream. Who was speaking to her? Why could she not recognise the voice?

"Verena, don't fight. It is wearing off. You should be able to open your eyes in a few minutes. Stay calm, dear; it will pass soon." Merridayn Belmont, Verena recognised her soft, windy, almost breathless voice. It was as if the woman had practised at a young age how to sound graceful even in the smallest of moments.

As much as she would have preferred not to, Verena obeyed. She waited for the medication to pass through her system; the medication was like fire in her veins, and her body was actively extinguishing it. It was a strange sensation, one she had never experienced before in her short-lived life, but it was there. As her feelings came back, the first thing she noticed was the state of arousal she was in again. The smell of her arousal wafted heavily to her nostrils. Her face flushed as she was able to open her eyes. She was immediately panicked as a blinding white light assaulted her eyes.

"Turn the light off, Cavanaugh; she must be blinded now. Let her adjust to the room, considering the infusion is running its course." Merridayn spoke, but to whom? Who was Cavanaugh?

"Yes, of course. I apologise for my thoughtlessness, Mother." Her mind raced, trying to place the voice. It was male, submissive, and must have come from Cavanaugh. Was he their oldest son? Verena had yet to meet him. His voice sounded like rough sandpaper on a chalkboard. She wagered it could sound like honey when, and if, he wanted. If he did, Verena wouldn't have been surprised. The whole family was mouthwatering. Come to think of it, Verena had yet to meet their daughter, Vivianne. She'd been told Vivianne was at a private school due to reckless behaviour early on. Still, she had never seen a photograph of her anywhere. No one mentioned Vivianne. Each time she was mentioned, the topic was hastily changed.

"Verena, listen to me carefully; do not question me, dear, and do not give me the face you are making either. I am going to walk you through the process, alright?" Verena regained her attention as she tried to blink the white light away. It was no use as the world faded to black. Verena felt herself becoming more and more frustrated with her ability to be a hindrance. "First, I need you to close your eyes. Keep them closed. We must work on regaining your mobility before we attempt to regain your eyesight. First, try to move your toes. I need to ensure your nervous system has regained its connection to your limbs. Can you do this with me?" Verena could feel Merridayn's hand on her feet as she struggled to move anything. Her brain was firing off signals intensely, attempting to connect with her nervous system. She breathed heavily, trying to move like she was asked.

"It is quite alright, darling. We can return to it if you cannot do it yet." Merridayn removed her hand, sighing softly. No other instruction came, and Verena struggled against the anxiety of the situation. "Cav, Love, please go get your father. Be mindful not to alert Aven. I would like to keep him away from her for the time being. It will not help the situation if we have to restrain him from his more primal desires, if you will."

"Of course, Mother. I understand. I find it difficult to restrain myself, too. I can theorise what would come if we let Aven near her in her state." Cavanaugh's voice dropped, her body quivered, and she could hear him inhaling deeply. *What the fuck was going on?*

"I know, my lion, I know. You have a better sense of control than Aven, with the wolf clashing against his self-control." Merridayn's weight shifted from the side of the bed as she got up and stepped away. Verena was still preoccupied with trying to get up, to open her eyes, to do anything at all. Her back was arched, her stomach did backflips like an Olympic gymnast, and her vision burned. She was on fire but was shivering. Her legs quivered, and with each passing second, her arousal hit her nose. Verena was embarrassed; Cavanaugh's words had her needy, and she knew the man knew what he was doing when he spoke.

The door opened and closed softly. Cavanaugh must have left. His footsteps faded into the hallway, farther and farther. He was light on his feet. The taps resembled those of a ballet dancer en pointe. The bed shifted again as Merridayn returned to her side. Cool fingers brushed Verena's face. Verena sighed happily as she was able to move her toes.

"I'm doing it. Oh, thank the stars, I am doing it." Merridayn chuckled as if she could hear Verena's thoughts. The same cool fingers brushed hair from her face.

"Good, now, Love. Try moving your hands. Can you? Try lifting them off the bed. Then we will open your eyes. Does that sound like a good plan?"

Verena internally agreed. She was ready to get up and go home, maybe splurge on a hot bath and some bath salts she bought last week.

"Okay, on the count of three, I want you to attempt picking your hand up. I'll be right here with you." Verena breathed in, calming her nerves. "One." She tried moving her fingers. "Two." She could do it. She was going to do it. "Three."

Verena's hand shot up into the air, and she yelped with shock.

"I did it! Oh heavens, I just want to go home. Mrs. Belmont, please, I just want to leave." She was shocked to find her voice at the same time. The same hoarse sound came from her as the night before, or at least what Verena had thought was the night before. Verena tried opening her eyes again. Everything was dark, but she could see outlines. She couldn't tell if it was night or day. But it was progress, and Verena would take it. Progress was progress; if the heavens willed it, she would leave shortly.

"You did indeed. Let's get you sat up, and we will see how to get your eyes to focus. You've been asleep for almost a week. It might take longer than you want to regain your vision."

"A week! I've been asleep for a week! What about

school? My mother? I had a test on Friday that I couldn't afford to miss. Oh heavens, I'm going to fail. I'll never get into Heaven Sight now." Verena could feel her eyes tearing up as her anxiety became overbearing. "I had so many plans, Mrs. Belmont. I wanted to leave. To get out of Gwen, attend speciality school and help provide for my mother."

"You will, dear, you will. Have faith." Merridayn's arms moved behind Verena to help bring her to a sitting position. "What do you want to specialise in? As you know, I went to Xavier for nursing." Verena looked in Merridayn's general direction, and a smile formed on her lips.

"I enjoy my molecular engineering classes. I was hoping to specialise in it. If I can get into the school. I also enjoy statistics, so maybe a speciality in arithmetics would be helpful."

"Cavanaugh is attending Theron for arithmetics. You might ask him for advice sometime." A deeper voice came from the doorway. Verena's head turned towards the intruding sound. She hadn't heard the door open or the footsteps approaching. "You're safe, Princess; it's just me, Elion. Cavanaugh caught me as a meeting was ending. I came straight here when I received the message." Verena relaxed. She recognised the voice. Though the driveway speaker distorted it slightly, his voice sounded the same. "What seems to be the problem, Merr?"

"She is having a hard time with her vision. We turned the lights out a while ago. Verena, what do you see now?"

"Shapes, mostly. They are blurry, but I can mostly see shapes. It has been getting better with time." Verena confirmed Merridayn's theory.

"Elion, I think it's time we wake Abigail. They need to talk, and I do not feel comfortable being the one to do it. The transfusion is too much. Her body has been without for too long. I'm not sure how much longer she can be hidden away. Look at her. Her skin was glowing from the fusion. Her body is burning through it faster than we expected it to." Verena was puzzled. Transfusion? Did she lose blood? How did she lose blood? The last she knew, she hit her head on her car door.

"I understand. I will wake her. But I will warn. If Aven wakes and finds he wasn't told the second Verena woke up, he might need to be tranquilised again." Elion was disappointed in his son, and his tone said it all. As he left, Verena tried to devise why Aven would need to be tranquilised—again, of all things. Had this happened before?

"Why was Aven tranquilised?"

"Oh, sweetheart, it's not to worry about. He will be fine in a few hours." Merridayn patted her hand. "Let's try blinking and see if we can reactivate your nerves to regain your eyesight."

"Okay." Verena followed Merridayn's instructions and blinked her eyes repeatedly. They were dry as if she were walking in a sandstorm. The irritating scratching tore at her corneas with each blink. Even through the pain, her vision was returning.

"Goddess, forgive me. Verena, darling, I'm sorry, but this might be uncomfortable."

Something wet and gritty ran over her neck, then her wrists.

"What are you doing?!? How disgusting." Verena's tone conveyed a sense of repulsion at what she had just experienced.

"Aven is awake, and he is furious. He's coming down the hall now. I had to scent mark you to cover up yours, hopefully."

"Excuse me? Scent mark?"

"It means I used my saliva to cover up your scenting glands. I'll have to explain later. For now, try not to move, dear. Stay still. Only speak when spoken to. We do not want to anger Aven when he is in this sort of mental state." Merridayn turned around, facing the door and shifting her body to cover more of Verena's body from view. She prayed to the Goddess, and her scent marking worked. Merridayn didn't know if she could fight Aven off from Verena if his wolf demanded his mate.

Aven was out of his temporary room for half a second when he caught wind of her arousal. His wolf tore through his control and bolted towards her room. Elion prayed witness to the mayhem and was intimately aware of the signs. He managed to hold Aven back, if just barely, until Cavanaugh could sedate him. Merridayn had been sedating him since. She hated doing it, but Verena hardly survived the infusion. There was not a chance in hell she would be able to withstand a mating bond.

"Where is she!?" Aven roared, his demanding tone sending chills straight to Verena's core. She was almost panting in need but could not see beyond blurred outlines. "Damnit, Father, where is my mate? I can smell her. So help me, Goddess, if you do not get out of my way. I am not sure how much more I can hold him back." Verena subconsciously whimpered.

"What the fuck? Did I do this?" She forgot Merridayn's words a few moments earlier.

"Here we go." Merridayn's voice was soft, almost inaudible.

Verena looked towards the other woman's voice, her vision focusing a bit more. She could see the woman's black hair cascading haphazardly around her face. Her grey eyes were identical to Aven's, indicating who had given them to him. Her face was blemish-free with hardly any wrinkles. She was beautiful. Perfectly shaped eyebrows, high cheekbones, and an angular jawline with a button nose. The shape of her fingers gripping the bed sheets. Verena reached towards her hand as if her mind was playing tricks on her. Was Merridayn afraid? Of Aven?

Wait.

Did he say-

Mate?

Verena's brow furrowed in confusion. She never considered herself to be friends with Aven. On a good day, maybe, they were more like acquaintances or employees and employers on a bad day. She had only been a girl with a crush on a man entirely out of her league.

"Son, you cannot go in there right now. Let's get you back to the room. Perhaps a bit of hibiscus rum will do you well?" Elion's voice trembled, but he was holding his ground. Verena couldn't understand why both parents seemed terrified. Aven had been nothing but a sweetheart to everyone. He held his parents with so much respect. Everyone could tell, even without adequately meeting the family.

"I'm losing control, Father. I need you to move. Please." Aven groaned. A thud came from the hallway. Verena suspected Aven fell to his knees. Pleading. "I-i need her, Father. My blood is burning. My head is seconds from ripping itself into two, and my heart is hurting so much. Please. Father. I need to be with her. I am unsure how much more I can fight being away from her." Verena whimpered again. Hearing Aven plead with Elion made her chest hurt. She cried out, damn the words Merridayn said. Her heart ached like she was about to have a stroke.

"Verena! Verena, my Princess, I can hear you. Please, please, just let me in. Just let me in." Aven stood; he would get in the room one way or another. "Father, I am going in. You can let me by, or I will go through you. One way or another, I am getting in." His voice dropped significantly, and Merridayn shuddered.

"Elion, Love, let him pass. We are not doing either of them credit to their health. Perhaps being together will assist Verena in healing. Only the Goddess knows why this poor child is burning through the infusion faster than she should be." Merridayn spoke up, her hand still gripped the sheets tightly. Verena could make out more of the fair woman. A blue blouse graced her slight frame while a strange tattoo peaked at the collar along her spine, but Verena couldn't tell what it was yet.

"Very well. Go on, son, but know I will remove you should you be anything other than a gentleman towards Miss Nightingale."

"Nightingale? Who is she? My name is Verena Saxon."

"All in due time, dear. All in due time."

The door opened, pulling Verena's attention to it. She could make out Aven's broad form. A rust-coloured v-neck adorned his frame. It hugged all the right spots. Verena had to refrain from drooling consciously. The man just walked around looking like a sex god without even trying. She could only imagine the results if he put even an ounce of effort in. *I wonder if he'd take the shirt off. Maybe add a little spin.*

"Oh, my darling, all you needed was to ask."

"Did I say it out loud?"

"Obviously."

"Of course I did."

Aven chuckled, coming closer to the bed. His mother

shifted in her chair as he approached.

"How is she doing? What is the wretched smell coming off her?" Aven paused, sniffed the air and then glared at his mother. His nostrils were immediately assaulted by the scent of his mother coming off of Verena in waves. He gagged, disgusted at the thought of his mother on his mate. "Did you scent mark her? For Goddess' sake, I won't just go into a rut at the sight of her mother. Will you please just wipe it off?" Knowing his mate was covered in anyone else's scent but his was angering him.

Merridayn cocked an eyebrow at her son but didn't move.

"Mother?" Aven challenged her, his anger rising with each passing second she didn't answer.

"No. Absolutely not. Just because you claim you won't do anything to her does not mean she is not safer smelling like me. You know this."

"Fine, please just move back and let me see her."

Merridayn looked at her son momentarily, then relented and agreed that the best option was for Aven to be close to Verena. As she moved, Aven exhaled heavily. Verena shivered again, and Merridayn could see the second the girl's arousal hit his nose. She watched her son fight against his wolf, her heart breaking for him and the wolf for being unable to begin the mating ritual. Merridayn stood her ground in front of Verena. She would not let him push Verena into something her body could not handle at this moment.

"I'm fine, mother. I can handle it. I need her. I need to be next to her. I just need to hold her. I am banking that having her in our arms could calm him down."

Merridayn was exhausted from the continuous back and forth. She was getting a headache, rubbing circles on the sides of her temples. Aven groaned, causing Verena to whimper again. Merridayn finally caved, allowing her son to pass. He hadn't seen Verena in days, and the infusion had worked wonders on the girl's complexion. Her hazel eyes shifted to a vibrant green. Her mousy light brown hair became a lively chestnut. Her skin glowed like she was constantly being illuminated by ice. Her round ears had changed to high points. She looked like the earth breathed life into her with each passing second. The transformation began on the fourth day of her slumber. Merridayn and Elion watched, astounded, as glimmers of light would rise from the floor and seep into her skin each time the moon passed the room. It was magical and wondrous to behold as if Verena's soul called out to the Moon Goddess, and she answered.

"Verena? Verena!" Aven was breathless. His wolf was howling in his head at his ethereal mate. She was a beauty before, but now. Now? She was empyreal. "Verena, how are you feeling?"

"I've been better. You know, I knocked my fucking head around. Got a transfusion. Who would have guessed? I didn't know I lost any blood. Sign me up for the 'Clutz of the Year Award'. I've been asleep for almost a week. I missed an important exam, so Heaven Sight is out of the question. I've been sequestered to this damned bed for days. Whose bed is this even? It doesn't matter. I want to go home. My mother has to be worried - if she has even realised I am gone." Verena rambled off, working herself up. "Oh, let's not forget I was just licked - let me repeat - licked by your mother. I'm allegedly your mate. Whatever the hell that means. Your father called me 'Princess.' I mean, Nan used to call me princess all the time, but it is completely different. She's family, you're not. I have no idea whose shirt I am in, but I know damn well they aren't mine. I've got a splitting headache. My stomach has been growling this entire time you all have been going at it. Let's also not forget I was INFUSED with whatever the fuck without my permission. I digress. How do *you* think I am?" The way she addressed him was laced with venom, yet somehow sweet to his ears.

Aven laughed—a whole-body, hearty laugh. He moved to the edge of the bed. He was running his fingertips along Verena's jaw, softening as she leaned into his touch subconsciously.

"I figured you were just waiting for your knight to wake you from your slumber, Princess," Aven whispered. "I cannot help myself when a damsel in distress needs to be saved."

"News flash, I am not a damsel. But I am in distress." Aven's lips curled as he picked her petite frame up so he could sit behind her. "If I could see right now, I cannot guarantee your face would not be my punching bag." Verena continued to protest and tugged at what she believed was him. "Put me down. Now. This is not up for negotiation."

"Everything is for negotiation, love. But I think I'll decline. Thanks for the offer, though. I might take you up on it later." He settled her down between his legs. Wrapping his arms around her abdomen, she fought herself to keep from getting comfortable. "You meant don't put you in between my legs? Could have fooled me, Princess." Aven leaned closer, his lips brushing her ear. "Do continue squirming, my love, your moist pussy smells divine every time you fight against me."

Verena bristled, "Excuse you? I'll have you know it is certainly not because of you."

"Keep saying it. Maybe if you say it enough, you'll believe it."

"Ahem." Merridayn cleared her throat. Verena blushed deeply while Aven grinned at his mate's innocence. "If you two are quite done, we need to alert Abigail that Verena is awake and notify the council of the update on this situation. Get comfortable, dears. This is sure to be a rough night. I will have Cav go pick up some takeout from town. Is there anything in particular you want, Verena?"

"Greens. Please. Anything with bacon sounds good, too. Anything. I'm starving." Aven smirked at his Princess. She was so damn adorable when she rambled.

"To be expected, of course; you've been surviving off the infusion and an IV of liquids for quite some time. How does Kingmans sound?" "Ravishing," Verena begged.

"Fabulous. Aven, do not do anything unbecoming toward her." Merridayn left the room, and the door closed behind her.

Chapter 4

VERENA

"Now that I have you to myself, how about we get you a bit more relaxed?"

"Your mother just left seconds ago, mind you, and you've got sex in your forefront? We hardly even know each other. I'm just your delivery girl. In any other damn situation, I would have ridden you like a bitch in heat. But last I heard, you were still hooking up with Kessa. On second thought, I don't even know why you are still holding me."

"Kessa? Goddess, we haven't been anything in quite some time. Yeah, we hooked up a few times here and there, but it will never be anything else. Certainly not even a hook-up now."

"Ah, the fuck and duck. I pegged you for the stable type. I've never had an issue admitting I was wrong, and you won't be the one to break it. Now, if you please, detangle from me, we can forget that this conversation began. Yes?" Verena attempted to break free of him. Needless to say, it didn't work. Shocker.

"Don't," Aven whispered, his face in her neck. "I can only hold back so much from marking you right here and now. Stop fighting me. I'm trying not to do anything I would regret later." His hands wandered to her waistline. Verena became acutely aware of the state of undress she was in. She found herself there with only her underwear. Her anger rose to a level which would make the Devil blush in embarrassment.

"I will say it again, which is saying something as I never repeat myself. Get. Off. Me." Her teeth ground together, her nails dug into his forearms. A wet, sticky substance could be felt dripping over her palms. She desperately wished she could see correctly to check if she had caused him to bleed. It would have served him right; maybe he should have taken her seriously.

Aven groaned, but not from the pain - it was arousing him even more. His groan stemmed from the overwhelming need, the primal desire, to mark her. To bite down on her mating gland hard enough to mix his blood with hers. A signal to everyone stating this woman - no, this Goddess - was claimed and protected by him, Aven Nathaniel Belmont. His wolf pleaded with him to do it, to claim his eternal mate, his future Luna to the Bluraine Pack. But he shouldn't; he couldn't if he was honest with himself. She had no idea there were other worlds hidden from her due to a centuries-old prophecy fulfilled the second her true parents were slaughtered. Everyone knew about the prophecy, everyone except Verena, for the Prophetess never spoke another word in her thousand years of service. A grand total of four prophecies remained in the Hall of Stars, with one stamped Verena Halliwen Nightingale. The others had no names, no titles; it was rumoured they were all conjoined to Verena's.

"As much as I enjoy this whole 'stubborn, I can handle it myself. I'm an independent woman' type of attitude. You'll realise I am more stubborn, more persistent, and more patient, so sit back and let me fucking hold you. You don't realise why now, but you will in time." Aven growled, the sound laced with authority. "I swear to the Goddess, Verena, I just need you to stay with me for a while. Please?"

"Fine, fine, damn, don't get your panties twisted. This is weird, but it ranks about number three of the weird shit which has happened to me in the last twenty-four hours." She grumbled, unhappy but resolved to deal with her situation. Her grandmother's treadmill would be putting in some work after all this nonsense was said and done.

"Number three on your list? What are numbers one and two?"

"Are you thick-headed enough to have missed the entire external monologue I gave when you asked how I was?" Verena hated repeating herself—a trait stemming from years of being ignored by her mother when she was begging for her help. "Don't answer, it was rhetorical. I don't care to hear the excuse. You can figure out for yourself what number one and two on my list of 'crazy shit to happen to Verena in the day.' Let me know what you think, and we can compare notes."

"You are such a smartass when you want to be. You devilish little thing. I like it. Not what I expected when I met you, though."

"Oh? What did you expect? A dainty woman willing to bend to your whim? Someone who would do what you said when you said it? To fill whatever burning need you have to protect? Or was it more someone who would forgo speciality schooling, stay at home, pop out a few of your kids, and be the ever-loving housewife? Because neither of those options is me, pal. You must update your hard drives and catch up with the century here." She scoffed, almost vomiting in her mouth. "Granted, there is nothing wrong with being a housewife. However, listen to me closely here;

if you take anything out of this conversation, please, for my fucking sanity, let it be this. Being a housewife is not and will never be an option I will take. You would have to break every single bone in my body and physically drag me to hell before I would ever need a man to 'defend my honour.' I learned how to defend it years ago."

She was ribbing him, hopefully making him feel as uncomfortable with this situation as she. Holding her breath and hoping he would find her tainted, disgusting even, and leave her alone. She wasn't looking for a relationship in any actual capacity. She was pretty happy being a loner. She had always been alone since she started school in Gwendolyn. She had no one to give the title of best friend, so her options were limited. Everyone else seemed to ignore or taunt her. They were taunting to the extent she detested going to school. She certainly didn't need to be associated with Aven Belmont anymore than she had been. Thankfully, nobody at school knew she was the family's errand girl, and she planned on keeping it quiet.

"What do you mean you learned how to defend your honour?" Aven's heart beat faster. His wolf was roaring in his head at the implication she just made. "Verena, what the fuck do you mean?"

"That's exactly what I said, Aven. I can repeat it if you want, but I'd rather not. You would have to ask nicely, though."

"Woman, I am not in the mood to play this mental parlay with you anymore. Tell me what the fuck happened, or so help me, Goddess, the ending to this will be brutal for everyone."

"I'm not telling you. I don't want to. I don't owe you a damn thing. Did we already forget all the crazy shit I have been put through at the expense of bringing you your weekly milk and eggs?"

"Verena."

"Aven."

"Verena."

"Verena is indeed my name, congratulations."

"What happened?"

"I was beaten. By my mother's husband, Colin Saxon. I was thirteen when it started, and it didn't stop until I was sixteen when my mom walked in on it."

Verena hated talking about the past. She'd seen so many therapists and spoken with so many police officers, and still, there was a part of her screaming for revenge. Her current therapist was fantastic. She specialised in physical assault and Cognitive Processing Therapy. Verena switched to Dr. Romano when her previous therapist moved out of town. At this moment, to this day, Verena idolised the doctor and confided everything with her. Verena could proudly say she started to move on from the memories and looked forward to her future.

"I am so sorry, Verena. I just-"

"I don't want or need your apologies, Aven. It's my past to bear, and there is absolutely nothing you can do about it now."

"Hold on, did you say, Colin Saxon?"

"Yeah? Why?"

"No reason. No reason at all." Aven pulled her in tighter, his breath ghosting against her ear. "Let's change the subject. You smell amazing. Have I mentioned it recently? If not, I really should have said it sooner. Like pine needles, cardamon, star anise and chocolate." He hummed softly, inhaling even more of her. "I don't want to make you uncomfortable, Verena. I'm sorry."

"I thought you needed to hold me, but now you're

second-guessing it? Can you be any more temperamental? And I thought I was bad about changing my mind." Verena raised her eyebrow, trying to look back at him. Her vision had been clearing as they talked. She could see the ink of his tattoos with almost crystal clarity. "If I had a problem with it, I would have been free well before I even asked you to let me go."

"I do not want to do anything you do not want, Verena. I apologise if I overstepped my bounds in the last few moments. I would not be put upon if you decided you wanted nothing to do with me or my family after today." His manners were hounded into him, and came to the surface at the realisation his mate had been brutalised by someone who was tasked to protect her.

"I just got comfortable and do not plan to become uncomfortable at your whim again. Looks like you're stuck here until your brother returns with food." Verena meant every single word she said. He was built, yes, but the muscle felt comforting. The way his hardened chest felt under her shoulders, she was swooning. He was rock solid in all the right places, the epitome of a masculine protector. His forearms were the same size as her calves. The tattoos gracing his body just added to the ensemble. They seemed to breathe life into him as they decorated his skin, like the kiss of a lover's lipstick, something belonging solely to him and meant for him and him alone. Verena blushed as she realised she was checking him out, and her body reacted accordingly.

She wasn't sure how yet, but she knew Aven was acutely aware of the roaring rapids growing between her legs because of him.

"Is this because of me? Did I cause you to become aroused, my Princess?" He part moaned in her ear.

"No. Not at all. I haven't the slightest what you are even referring to."

"Playing games again, are we?" His hands slid down her abdomen. Teasing. "Does the Princess want to play with the big, bad wolf? I'm sure if you asked nicely, he would."

"Pardon you, you stole my line."

"Not anymore, Princess."

Verena was intensely aware of the way his hands crept downwards towards her thighs. She wondered if he thought he was being sneaky about it.

Cocky bastard.

"I'll have you know I do take offence to you utilising my phrases without proper attributes. You didn't even say it in the right context!" Verena threw her hands in the air, emphasising her bafflement.

Inch by inch, those lethal fingers drifted over her navel, ever downwards.

His lips nipped at her ear, causing her to jump.

"Would you like me to try again?"

Well hell-fucking-o to you, too. Repeat it. Maybe slower. With a bit more "I am going to rail into you so damn hard you'll think other men are pathetic" attitude.

"Would." Nip.

"You."

Breathe, Verena, breathe.

"Verena?"

Yes. "No." *Hell. Way to go, Verena, you are your own cock block.*

"If you're so sure, then I'll stop." His hands were so bloody close to her thighs that she almost cried when he lifted them off her. Her legs rubbed together subconsciously in an attempt to find some sort of relief.

"You smug ass. Why are you so damn hot and cold?

First, you want to hold me, then you turn me on, and now you want to walk away from what you started acting like you were innocent the whole time?" *This man.*

"I can return if you want me to." Aven's hands hovered an inch over her thighs. "But you'll have to beg me for it."

"Hard pass, thanks. I beg for no man."

Verena rolled her eyes before turning her face and blowing in his ear. His eyes narrowed. She could feel his erection at her back.

"You devilish woman. Don't start something you can't handle."

"Whoever told you you were so difficult to handle? They lied to you." Aven's hands slammed back onto her thighs, reaching boldly to her core.

"You'll be in for a rude awakening then, Princess."

"I highly doubt it." Her left hand gripped his wrist, bringing it to her pussy as she leaned back again. Bringing her right arm up, she grabbed at Aven to keep him close. He shuddered. His breath came sporadically. "I bet you'll be so eager to please me."

Where the fuck?

Aven ground his teeth. His wolf howled at his mate's defiance. They enjoyed her spitfire, her ability to keep him on his toes.

"I warned you."

Chapter 5

VERENA

His hand had found the edge of her shirt. Was it his shirt? His skilled fingers slid under the soft fabric. She could not help arching upwards at the touch. A spot in her abdomen was now lit aflame as one hand teasingly followed the path of her body downwards. Her breath caught in her throat as Aven ran his forefinger over her nipple before rolling it gently between his finger and thumb.

This tease.

She was a heap of breathy moans. He laughed into her ear when he pinched down on her nipple and earned a wailing moan. His hand between her legs was the sweetest torture. He broke his torment for a moment to trail his lips down her neck. Her hands gripped his arms, pleading with him to continue. He let out a small moan as her nails scratched pleasantly against his skin, a growl of possessive lust ripped out of him.

"Fuck me." She gasped when his hand moved without hesitation, setting a torturous pace against her bundle of nerves.

"Patience, Princess."

"I'll grow old and die before you do." She knew it would make him laugh again, and it did. He dropped a few kisses to the back of her head.

"Are you sure you don't need -" He ran his hand down

her slit, brows raised with amusement. "-never mind, have you been soaking this entire time, Princess?"

Such a bastard.

She groaned with relief when his finger pressed inside her, his thumb rubbing her clit. It didn't take long for her to climax like this; Aven was relentless. Only when her orgasm had passed did he slow but did not remove his fingers. His controlled expression was long gone; he was feral and wanting. She already learned scratching him and digging her nails into him would make him go wild and could get her more of what she wanted. His lazy stroking turned into a jackhammer. His finger slid in and out of her at a harsh pace. A second digit joined the first, and the onslaught began. She mewled softly, her leg quivering and her thighs slicked from her first orgasm. Rougher, harder, faster. She loved every second of it.

"Oh hell, keep going." Breathless moans erupted from her. "Yes, right there. Keep going. Oh yes, Aven..."

"Repeat it. It sounded delightful, Princess."

"Gods, Aven, what do you want me to say?" Verena bit her lip, and her teeth punctured her skin. She wanted more, needed more, and there he was, dangling her release in her face. If he didn't move in the next few seconds, she would take matters into her own hands.

"Tell me how you want it. Tell me what you want me to do with these fingers of mine. Demand what you want from me, Verena. I will give you anything."

"Anything?"

"Anything, Princess. You name it, and I will bend hell to my will to obtain it for you."

I am hell, and I will not bend to you.

What the fuck?

"I want it so rough I won't be able to walk," Verena

demanded. She did not know where this unbridled desire came from, but she did not question it. Her previous partners left much to be desired.

"As you demand, Princess."

His hand returned to her centre and began to finger her. He internally wished it was his head in between those creamy thighs lapping at her like a starved man. In, out, in, out. He pinched her clit roughly, and she screamed. He clamped down on her mouth.

"As much as I want to hear your screaming, Love, my family is right down the hallway." He whispered into her ear. "Once we are mated, though, I am going to make you scream so loud the whelps across the pond can hear you."

His fingers continued in their pursuit of her orgasm. She was so close, so damn close, her legs were on the brink of giving out.

Oh, hell yes.

Not even close, my love. A strange voice whispered in her mind.

What?

Come, Verena. Come for me, my sweet girl. Let me hear your screams from there.

Verena moaned; Aven's fingers were not relenting as her body started to demand her attention.

Am I crazy? Since when does my subconscious start talking to me?

You are not delusional, Verena. I am real, and I can feel your body on the cusp of an orgasm. Come. Now. The voice inside her head demanded. The control the voice had over her body sent her over the edge. Her orgasm flooded through her as it pooled between her thighs and soaked Aven's hand.

"You-" Aven cut himself off "-you are exquisite."

"Tell me something you haven't said to somebody else after you have fucked them. I'll give you a minute to try again." *If only he knew someone's voice in my head dominated my body with two simple words.*

"Still so damn feisty after it was my fingers bringing you to orgasm. Twice."

His right hand left her, coming to grip her by the throat without her seeing the movement. He brushed her cheek with his thumb before pushing her neck to the side, giving him full access to her mating gland. Her sweet, sweet aroma invaded his nose, a loud melody in his ears. He flicked his tongue out, licking the right side of her neck. Cinnamon bursting on his tongue as the beads of sweat came crashing into his senses. He growled, instinctively curling his fingers around her covered mound. Verena's eyes rolled into her head, and she fell back into his shoulders. The sensations were overwhelming. He was everywhere. A fire burned through her veins and lit a torch she didn't know existed.

"This is not something I have ever done with anybody else, my sarcastic mate."

"I don't believe you, but keep trying."

Aven sighed, content with the outcome of his actions. The wolf inside him closed his eyes and fell asleep with her aroma filling their nostrils. Aven was also on the brink of falling asleep but wasn't happy with his scent marking. Verena hummed happily, her head resting on his chest. He swelled with pride; despite everything she had been through in her short life, she felt safe enough to be so vulnerable with him. The thought caused his perpetually aching erection to remind Aven he was still there. So, Aven did the one thing he could think of to settle his arousal down. He leaned in. He wanted to scent mark Verena again. Praying to the Goddess, just the motion of claiming her would give him release. He didn't care at this point if he soiled his trousers. His cock was throbbing with need.

"Verena..."

"Yes?"

Aven didn't say a word as his tongue lapsed over her neck for the second time. He was sending shivers through both of them. He went to do it again. She was on the cusp of release. He was so close, she was flooding his nose with her pent-up arousal.

"What the absolute fuck are you doing?"

Mom?

"Verena Halliwen Saxon, you have three seconds to explain to me what in the absolute fuck you are doing with a boy in the bed! Speaking of, where the fuck are your parents, Aven." Sure enough, Abigail Saxon was standing in the doorway. The anger caused her cheeks to inflame, a colour covering her face which could easily be compared to a tomato.

"Nightingale."

"Excuse you? What did you say?"

Aven growled. Abigail's disrespect to his mother had already worn thin his patience. His wolf was stomping around in his head. He was waiting for the moment she disrespected his rank again to put her in her place.

"You heard exactly what I said, Abigail. Her name is Verena Nightingale. I will not repeat it, and you would do well to start calling her by her actual name."

"I don't care for your tone, *pup.*"

"Poor me, I'm shivering in my socks. Oh, sorry, I'm not wearing socks." Aven howled with laughter, looking at Verena, who was cowering. Her body was pressed against his as far as she could manage. She was terrified but could not for the life of her understand why she would be. "Verena, did you think I had a tone?"

"Do not bring her into this."

"I'll bring my mate into this if I damn well please, considering when my father steps down, she will be your Luna."

"Luna?" Verena whispered.

"I forgot. I'm sorry, your *mother.*" He spit out, disgusted. "She has made you oblivious to everything. We will get it situated soon, Princess."

"What I tell her is my business and mine alone. You will not tell me how to raise my child."

"News flash, Abigail, she is not your child. You knew what you were getting into and failed to keep her healthy. I should have you skinned for this."

"What did I say about your tone, *whelp?*"

"Is this how you want it to go?" Aven glared at Abigail before turning his attention away. The disrespect he showed Abigail by metaphorically turning his back to her was evident as he picked Verena up. Gently placed her down where he previously was, kissed her forehead and tucked her under the blankets. "I am sorry to have to let you go, Princess. There are some pressing matters I need to deal with. I will return as soon as I am able." Aven kissed her forehead again before turning around.

He stalked up to Abigail, his height giving him a foot and a half over her. Abigail puffed her chest out, challenging him, unlike most wolves who would recoil at the closeness. Aven smirked, knowing full well what was about to come. He relaxed his shoulders, then his neck and looked down to meet Abigail's eyes. Abigail was furious, the anger rolling off her in waves. His eyebrow cocked as he awaited the words.

"I, Abigail Loraine Saxon, challenge you, Aven Nathaniel Belmont, to a warrior's trial."

"Mother, stop." Verena squeaked. She didn't know what it meant but didn't want anyone to get hurt, especially Aven. Her childhood crush seated into carnal lust.

"Shut up, Verena. We wouldn't be in this predicament without you."

"You. Will. Not. Disrespect. Her." Aven growled loudly. The commotion caused footsteps to come pounding down the hall.

"How many times do I have to tell you, I will do what I want with my fucking child."

Aven stepped closer again; inches remained between him and Abigail. The power emanating from him caused Verena to whimper with need.

Fucking hell, hormones. Wrong place, wrong time. Get a grip on yourself, Verena.

The footsteps got closer and closer.

"I have repeated myself too many times today and will not do it again. So hear me closely, you daft bint. Disrespect her, and you will regret it."

"I do not fear you."

"You should, Abigail." Elion's voice sounded from the doorframe, announcing who the footsteps belonged to.

"For what, *alpha?*" Abigail spat out, her attention not leaving Aven, saliva hitting him in the face.

"I, Aven Nathaniel Belmont, accept your, Abigail Loraine Saxon, challenge to a warrior's trial."

The room swarmed with a blinding blue light. Verena watched as it dissipated, and matching illuminated blue bands surrounded the wrists of her mother and Aven.

Curious.

"Son, you do not need to do this. She is not worth the

trouble."

"You are right, this bitch is not worth my attention. Yet she issued the challenge, and I will not be known as the alpha who refuted a beta's measly attempt to humiliate me." Aven spits out, disgusted with the entire situation.

A beta believing they would win against him? His entire bloodline produced irrefutably strong alphas. The entirety of the situation was laughable at best and boring at worst. He would finish the childish challenge and then return to everyday life. Abigail bristled at the insult. Aven and Elion paid her no attention, another show of power by ignoring her. It was confusing to Verena at the blatant disrespect the men showed her mom, and she didn't like it.

"Do not disrespect my mother, Aven." Verena levelled him with her best attempt at a glare, her head swarming and legs shaking. She turned to Elion, and the respect she had for him faded. "I expected better from you, Mr. Belmont. You have never once shown anyone anything but proper manners. Yet, you have disrespected my mother and have allowed your son to do the same."

"Verena, I will take your words this one time as you are unaware of the situation, but do not misjudge my actions when you are oblivious to the world surrounding you. By any means of no fault of your own. Once everything has been explained, and after your questions are answered, I hope you will see it differently."

"Who is to say I will see it any differently? A duck is still a duck no matter the colour of its feathers."

"Yet a duck could be a goose depending on its parents."

Verena had nothing to say as she looked on at the situation. Her mother boldly stood between the two large men, glaring at the both of them.

Mom has some balls. God damn.

"Verena, stay out of this. You are the reason this is happening in the first place. Do you not think you have caused enough trouble?" Abigail crossed her arms over her puffed-out chest, trying to show impatience.

Verena was a mess of emotions; they all flooded her rapidly. She landed on feeling disgusted—disgust she directed at herself for putting them in this situation and disgust at her mother for continuously antagonising her.

"Do not blame your ego on me, mother. I was not the one who challenged someone else. Challenged, do you hear how crazy you sound? Is this the medieval times where two fight for the hand of a maiden? Because if so, I'll have you know I cannot be won. I am not a broodmare being fought over for the chance to breed with. Let us not forget, according to many today, are you even my mother?" Verena almost screamed out. She had enough of her 'mother's' misguided love. A laughable reality, her love was what her therapist stated was abuse. Abuse Verena was beginning to see for herself.

"We are not speaking of this right now, Verena. I will talk to you when we get home. Now, if you'll excuse us." Abigail attempted to push Aven out of the way. The brick house of a man did not move a centimetre. "I am taking Verena home, and you will not stop me."

"You will not stop me," Aven mocked. "I just did. You're welcome to try again, perhaps with a different stance. I could show you if you'd like me to." Verena snorted, slamming her hand over her mouth to stop the oncoming laughter.

"Do I amuse you, Aven?" Abigail sneered at him, causing another outburst from Verena.

"Very much so."

"Verena, get up. We are going."

"No, she is not." Elion intervened, moving around Abigail to stand next to his son. A united front they portrayed.

"No, I'm not going with you. I do not wish you any harm, but I'm done playing the obedient daughter if all I will get from you is lies."

Abigail's head whipped to Verena in shock. Verena had never disobeyed; she had always done what Abigail said, when she said it. Verena lifted her head, defiant. She was eighteen now and could make her own choices. She did not want to return to a house where she would continue being lied to by someone she thought she could trust.

"You spoiled fucking brat. No wonder Colin beat you if you had a mouth with him."

Aven surged towards Abigail, almost reaching her before his father pulled him back roughly. He struggled to keep his son in his arms.

"Cavanaugh!" Elion yelled out, veins pulsing in his forearms against the sheer strength Aven was fighting against him. "You have gone too far, Abigail."

"You think I give a shit anymore, *alpha*." Abigail sneered. "I've been harbouring her for years. Having to play the nice parent. Having to give up my life to raise a child who isn't even mine."

"Woe is me, you bitch. You and the disgusting cunt you called *husband* deserved each other." Aven struggled against his father. Desperate to murder the whelp in front of him.

"I do not care, Abigail. They were your friends! Jerifeyn trusted you out of everyone else! You! For fucks sake!" Elion yelled. Cavanaugh's shadow loomed in the doorway, unsure what was going on. Verena didn't even hear him coming down the hall. Her cheeks flushed with the amount of drama she unintentionally caused. "Cavanaugh, escort this beta out of my home and into the holding bay. She can wait there until the challenge proceeds tomorrow."

"Challenge, Father?"

"Yes, she has issued a warrior's trial to Aven."

"Did I hear you right? A warrior's trial? Her?" Cavanaugh pointed at Abigail and then to Aven. "Against Aven?" He snorted, looking at Abigail. "Are you dumb?"

"Evidently." Aven piped in.

"She challenged you, brother?" Cavanaugh raised an eyebrow, pointing back at Abigail while looking at Aven.

"She did."

"I'm going to need a lawn chair, popcorn and maybe a beer for this show." Cavanaugh snorted, his lips curling upwards.

"Save me one?" Aven grappled with his brother, amused.

"Obviously. What do you bet? Five minutes?" Cavanaugh placed one hand under his chin, a questioning look on his face as he appraised each contestant.

"Five minutes? You give her too much confidence. I'd say two, at most." Aven held up his thumb and forefinger to indicate the maximum amount of time he reckoned Abigail would withstand against him.

"I'm right here, assholes," Abigail growled.

"Cavanaugh, take her out of here. I'm unsure I can restrain Aven if she repeats something malicious." Elion told his oldest for a second time, his strength depleting faster than he wished.

Cavanaugh winked at Aven, bowing to Verena and gripping Abigail's wrist so hard Verena could have sworn she heard it break. Verena watched as he dragged her mother out.

Wait, no, she's not my mother. But if she isn't my mother, who is? Who is Jerifeyn?

"Wait," Verena commanded; the command fell from her lips faster than she had anticipated.

"Yes, Princess?" Cavanaugh paused at the doorway.

"Where are you taking her?"

"She's going to a holding cell on the outskirts of the property. She will wait until someone escorts her to the trial grounds tomorrow morning."

"Okay." Verena gulped, watching Abigail's failed struggle against him. "Thank you."

"Anytime, Princess."

She watched them walk away before resting her gaze on Aven. Her heart thumped loudly at the sight of him. The sizzling anger coming off him gave her chills.

For fucks sake, get a grip. She mentally slapped herself in the face, trying to regain control over her arousal. *Do I have a thing for anger? What kind of fucking kink?*

Aven's lips curled slightly, hearing her heart beat quicker when she looked at him. He tapped his father's arm, signalling he was good to be released. Elion squeezed once in reassurance before letting him go.

"Are you going to be okay, Verena?" Elion asked her.

"I've been suspecting something was off for years, Mr. Belmont. This revelation does not come as much of a surprise for me as it probably should."

"Even so, child, it is difficult to look at your parents in a different light. Regardless if they are your actual parents or not." He walked over and touched her shoulder, attempting to offer comfort. Straightening up, he stepped back. "I will check to see where supper is and inform Merridayn of the situation." He took leave, closing the door behind him. Aven and Verena were, once again, alone.

Chapter 6

VERENA

"Aven?" Verena tilted her head, her eyes glancing at his wrist. A look of confusion splashed across her face.

"Yes, Princess?" Aven glanced at her, hoping to continue their earlier escapades.

"What are those blue bands on your wrists?"

"Blue bands?"

Aven looked at her, at his wrists, back at her, then back down again. Over and over again, as if he would suddenly see the invisible magic bonding him to the deal he'd made. Verena watched in amusement, her lips curling upwards as she attempted to contain her laughter. It was adorable. The motion of being caught unaware of everything warmed her heart. It helped her forget, even momentarily, the information she received from her mother. No. Not her mother. Her guardian?

Was she a guardian, though? She admitted she didn't want to take care of you, Verena.

Verena regarded the information for a few before being interrupted.

"What do you mean, blue bands, Verena?"

"The blue bands around your wrists, Aven. What do you mean, 'What do I mean?' They are right there!" She pointed at the bright glowing bands.

"Princess—" Aven paused. "Verena, there isn't anything on my wrists but my tattoos."

"Yes, there is. They are right here!" She tapped at the spot they were on her wrists.

Why was he playing dumb?

"Okay, let's try this again." Aven sat down on the edge of the bed. "Show me where you see these 'blue bands'?"

"I'm not sure why you are playing ignorant. It doesn't become you." Verena rolled her eyes, grabbing his wrist. "I suppose I can, though." Verena looked at him curiously.

"Anytime, Princess." He brushed his thumb over the back of her dainty hands, caressing her silky skin.

"They are right here." Her finger hovered over the bands.

The logical part of her screamed not to touch them.

"What do they look like exactly?"

The minor part, the part telling her to touch it, won. She knew she shouldn't, knew in her head she should avoid it, but the voices told her to do it, touch them. Everything would be fine.

Verena screamed, her vision fading to black, then rapidly moved into a memory not of her own.

"Jer, we need to go."

"Not yet, Francis. I just need a little bit more time."

"My love, there is no more time!"

Verena's head whipped around to face a man she had never seen before. He was beautiful in a way she didn't know could be possible—eternally beautiful. Like the sun had never touched his skin, a faint iridescent glow came behind him. She felt like she was staring at the moon's peak, his awe-inspiring beauty. Green eyes met hers as he reached out to touch her cheek, wiping the tears off her face.

"Jerifeyn, my heart, we need to go. We will start over. In

a new city. Somewhere where the Mordinian's cannot find us." He was saddened, one might say even depressed. *The thought of having to continue running made his heart heavy with disdain. He was tired of running, tired of it all.*

Jerifeyn? Who was Jerifeyn? Francis?

"I cannot, Francis. I cannot keep doing this, my love. Every time, it shatters a piece of my soul." Verena - Jerifeyn? - said to Francis. "How do they keep finding us, Francis? We've moved so many times, and yet they keep coming. They keep searching."

Is she Jerifeyn?

Pain erupted in her knees, and Jerifeyn slammed to the floor. Her head was thrown back, and she screamed—a scream which shook the walls of the room. A scream echoed through time.

"What do they want!" Jerifeyn wailed. "What do they WANT!?"

"I do not know." He was discouraged. The unknown was draining him as well.

Jerifeyn slammed her hands onto the floor. The ground was trembling as if poised to answer her call.

"I will not continue running, Francis." She stood. Energy crackled around her. "They will tell me what they want, so help me, Goddess. Are you with me or not, my love?"

"I am always with you, my Queen. Through life and death."

Jerifeyn smiled, looking back at the beautiful white claw-foot tub.

A tub which contained the bloodied remains of a child born too soon.

Chapter 7

VERENA

Aven rocked her softly. His arms cradled her to him as he whispered words Verena couldn't understand.

"What happened?" She whispered. Her eyes sprang open to look at him.

He was pale, worry was etched on his face. His hands gripped her roughly as if he would lose her any second. Verena could hear his heart pounding.

"Aven?"

"You fainted, Verena. You screamed after touching these alleged blue bands on my wrists, and then, next thing, it was lights out." He bit his lip, looking at her again. "Are you sure you aren't a damsel needing to be rescued?"

"Absolutely not." Her face scrunched as if she had eaten something she didn't like.

"Could have fooled me," Aven smirked, wanting to smooth the wrinkles out of her cheeks.

"Moving on. What happened after?" Her eyes narrowed, levelling him with a look of discontent.

"Why are you asking me? Verena, you've been out for an hour. Everyone came running in after they heard you. I told them what I just told you. They left about 20 minutes ago to eat. I've heard their phones ring consistently since you screamed. It was terrifying."

"The phone ringing was terrifying?" She was confused,

her tone incredulous.

"No, Verena. You were terrifying." Aven pointed at her in emphasis, one hand placed upon his hip. "The room got so cold and dark. Like the sun was blocked out. The atmosphere was off-putting. Every inch of me wanted to run. As if you walked back in time to the Mordinian War. It was-"

"Stop." Verena held a hand out, stopping him mid-sentence.

"What is wrong?" Aven reached out for her, concerned something terrible was wrong.

"You said Mordinian. I know the name." Verena's head tilted again, as it usually does when something confused her.

"How?"

"I'll answer in a moment. What is the Mordinian?"

"Answer me first, Verena. How do you know the name?"

"Fine." *Stubborn asshole.* "When I touched your bands, it took me back. I'm not sure where. I'm not even sure I was me. There was a man." Verena shook her head. "No, not a man. More like something immortal. He was glowing. The not-me-me said his name was Francis. I think."

"Francis? Are you sure?"

"Yes, Francis. He had green eyes and pale skin like the sun never tanned him. And when he spoke, he called me 'Jer'? It might be short for Jerifeyn because he called me Jerifeyn later."

"Jerifeyn?"

"For the second time, yes. Are you paying attention?"

"I am. I am." He held his hands up as much as he could while cradling her. "I'm just making sure I heard you right. Continue. I won't interrupt again."

"See to it." She huffed, irritated. "As I was saying. He called me Jerifeyn. I tried telling him my name was Verena, but nothing happened. It was like I was there, in the moment, feeling the memory as if it were reality, but I couldn't do anything. I could only watch the scene unfold. She started crying, and he kept telling her they needed to go. They had to leave. They could start over someplace else. Someplace the Mordinian's cannot find them. She told him it wouldn't help. They've moved so many times. So many, many times, yet they kept coming. They continued to find them. She was done running." Verena paused. Tears flooded her vision for people she didn't know. She didn't understand the calamity of the dream.

"And then?" Aven said softly, bringing her closer to him.

"She fell to the ground, Aven. Hard. I could feel the pain in my body as if I lived it myself. She told him she couldn't keep leaving. She could not keep doing it. Then she screamed. It was so heartbreaking. The windows rattled, and the air crackled with electricity. She was asking what they wanted and telling Francis she would not keep running. They would tell her what they wanted, or else. But before I woke up, Aven. Before I came back from whatever the hell this-" Verena waved her hands in the air. "-was, I saw a white bathtub." Verena couldn't finish the rest. Her heart broke for the person she didn't know.

"Ok? What does the bathtub have to do with anything?" Aven coaxed.

"I can't, Aven. I can't say. Don't make me tell you." Verena panicked; she did not want to relive the moment again.

"I need to know, Verena." He leaned down to kiss her forehead. "I cannot help you if I do not know. What was in the tub?" *How had he guessed it so easily? How had he known?*

"The remains of a child." She whispered so softly Aven almost missed it.

"As in murdered?" Aven's eyes looked over hers, searching for clues in the depths of the green staring back at him.

"No. As in, the baby was born too early. As in, she suffered a miscarriage."

"Are you sure?" Aven choked, coughing roughly.

"I'm sure. It is not like I can forget it." She felt offended as if she couldn't be trusted to recall what she had seen.

"Goddess."

"What?"

"I'm not sure yet, Verena. But I am sure it will not be easy from today forward." Aven wanted to take her memories away. He wanted to help her forget what she had seen. It was too late; they had opened this door and were now facing the consequences.

"It's your turn now. What is the Mordinian?"

"Verena, I think you need to hear it from my parents. Based on what you told me, this is a conversation we need to involve them in."

"Excuse me? You swore you would tell me." Verena whipped her head and body around to stare at him.

"I know, I did, but it is a promise I must break—no matter the pain it causes me to misplace your trust in me. I cannot be the one to take you down this path. You need to hear it from them."

"Of course you would. You males are all the damn same. You get what you want from me, and damn all the consequences I have to deal with later. Clearly, I have a type. A type I never asked for." Verena tore herself from his arms. Struggling to stand on weak and shaking legs. Immobility and extended time in bed did her no favours.

"Verena, please don't do this. Let's go and find my parents. Please? They will explain everything better than I can anyway." Aven stood up, reaching out to her as she wobbled around. "I do not mean to upset you. I honestly believe the information they can give you is tenfold better than I can.""You can go to hell, Aven." She snarled at him, irritated he would break his promise so quickly.

"At least I'll be warm."

This fucking smartass.

"Where are your parents?" Verena started towards the door. Having to brace herself on the furniture littering the room, she felt like she was walking on pins and needles.

"They are most likely in the dining room. At least let me help you walk before you fall." He reached out again, and she nodded her acceptance.

"Fine. But only because my legs cannot do it at the moment and not because I need you."

"Whatever helps you sleep at night, Princess." He snickered, knowing he would make her legs feel the same way repeatedly.

"I sleep just fine, thank you for asking." Aven chuckled but kept quiet.

He understands to shut up and look pretty.

The duo walked in silence down the expansive hallway. Verena held onto Aven fiercely as he guided her. The off-white coloured hallway with chair rail moulding held paintings on the right and picture windows on the left. Little lights hung above them, casting their hue onto the delicate paints. She could not see a placard indicating who had painted them anywhere. She stopped at one painting in particular.

In the frame was a woman, half turned to the right

with her eyes closed, draped in purple and gold. At her back was the outline of pitch-black wings. Feathered wings draped to the ground, the tips dipped in gold. Around her neck, a massive sapphire encased in yellow gold. The stone nested at the top of the Angel's breasts. Defined tattoos encased her left arm, outlines of the duplicates on the right. Those tattoos spread up her shoulders and were lost under her hair. Verena could faintly see the same ink on the Angel's partially exposed left leg. A beautifully intricate crown of gold with the matching purple sapphire in her left hand. It reminded Verena of crowns she had seen in history books. In the Angel's right hand was a black carved sword. Strange symbols lined the forte, and a large red ruby adorned the pommel. Blood dripped off the foible to pool at the ground and stained the bottom edges of the Angel's garment.

Aven beheld her as she studied the painting, pulling her closer to him to keep her steady. Her chest rose, brows furrowed in concentration. He wondered which part of the painting had her confused or startled. What could she have been thinking? He knew it was a lot to take in all at once and was a point of contention in his household. Aven argued it was disturbing, while everyone else had differing opinions.

"Who is she?" Verena pointed at the Angel, cautious not to touch the canvas.

"I don't know. In one of his insomniac phases, Cavanaugh painted it a few years back."

"Cavanaugh painted it?" Verena looked at the painting from a new perspective, hoping to see what Cavanaugh wanted to portray.

"Yes."

"Hmm." Verena looked at him. "Did he name the

painting?"

"He did. I do not remember what it was, but you can ask him about it at dinner."

"What time is it anyway?"

"It is about three o'clock, Verena. You woke up around ten o'clock this morning."

"We are already having dinner?" Aven shrugged.

"It'll be an early dinner. We can have supper later if you are still hungry."

They continued onward, the painting taking harbour in Verena's mind. Her eyes drifted outward toward the windows. They breathed life into the house with their view of the beautiful mountainous landscape. Further down the hall, a well-maintained yard with an Olympic-sized pool could be seen through the windows, with the corners of an outdoor kitchen mostly blocked by a wall of vines. A tennis court was in the lower section of the yard. If one squinted just right, one could see the outline of a lake in the forest line, which could also be seen from a different location.

"Is there anything you don't have access to?" Verena was jealous, plain and simple. She envied him for the luxurious lifestyle he had grown up in.

"No, not really. Mom and Dad's contractors were generous when they built this house. My parents' highest priority was to provide an area where their children could be outside without needing to leave the property." Aven grimaced, seeing the jealousy in her posture. She was farther from him than he would like and starkly rigid like she was beating herself up for jealousy.

"I wish."

"Why?" It was his turn to be confused, to wonder.

"You just don't get it, Aven, do you?"

"No, I understand I have been given every privilege available to which most do not have access. I just don't understand what you wish for."

"I wish I had even a minuscule amount of things you have been given in your life. Any of the opportunities you've received. Hell, I would be fine with not worrying if we have enough money for food every week."

"Verena, I don't understand. The council gave Abigail money every month to ensure your upbringing was exceptional."

"Aven, you won't understand, so just stop trying." Verena paused, blinking slowly, her eyesight unfocused as she processed what he had just said. "Hold on, what did you say? Did you just say this strange council or whatever gave money to my mom to take care of me?"

"Yes."

"How much money?"

"I am not sure. My parents might know, though."

"You're telling me I didn't have to grow up struggling?" Verena's breath hitched. "I didn't have to be abused by a piece of shit because she never would have had to move in with him?" She fought the tears threatening to spill over. Verena was done crying over them.

"Yes." He said softly, unable to find anything else to say.

Verena didn't say anything else. She nudged her shoulder into him to signal she was ready to continue walking. At some point, they stopped, and Verena's stomach announced itself loudly. Aven chuckled but obliged as he took a step forward. Her hand gripped his right shoulder tightly for a few seconds. They walked in silence. Verena kept her head forward as stairs came into view on the right.

"Just these stairs, and then we will go to the left. Everyone should be in the dining room already, but if they aren't, I will get you a chair before going to find them."

"Alright." She nodded, following him down their seemingly floating stairs and glass bannisters.

Chapter 8

VERENA

Their dining room came into view faster than she expected. It was just as luxurious as the rest of the house, the white oak wooden floors accented by lush beige velvet high-back chairs, a plain white marble table and a few pieces of green vinery acting as a centrepiece. There was nothing significant except one item commanding Verena's attention: an overbearing mountain range painting. The range looked identical to what could be seen outside. Though the mountains didn't yell for her attention, the painting held the upper half of a wolf with striking blue eyes in the forefront. Verena's focus shifted to the same painted Angel from earlier. This time, the Angel was garbed in black leather, an assassin's armour. Her sword, encased in its sheath, strapped to her back. Red irises stared back at her. Verena shivered, her mind returning to her dream of the man with the same red irises.

"How are you feeling, Verena?" Merridayn's voice startled Verena out of her trance-like stare at the painting. "We were waiting for you to feel up to dinner, but I planned to bring it to you. It is a warming sight to see you here instead."

"I have felt better, thank you."

"To be expected, dear. Everyone has had a go-around with concussions. Your particular injury was just a tad bit more ostentatious. I will have the boys bring dinner here then, don't worry."

Verena couldn't express her appreciation in time as Merridayn swept from the room.

"Thank you." She said to nobody in particular.

Verena's attention remained steadfast on the Angel painting. An eerie feeling sank in as the hair on her arms tickled. Something about the Angel trapped her gaze, keeping Verena from looking away. Her subconscious screamed, even in painting form. The wolf was dwarfed by the predator standing next to it.

"Be careful, Cavanaugh. Why don't you put some of the boxes down and go back for them?" Elion's voice carried closer, hinting at him holding back a chuckle.

"I've got it.""I'm sure you do, son." Elion jested, rolling his eyes at his oldest.

Aven strolled into the room, his arms carrying multiple bags of takeout from Kingmans. Verena's stomach growled again. Cavanaugh burst out laughing as he rounded the corner into the room. His arms laden with cardboard boxes.

"Quick, get the beast something to eat before she goes rabid." Cavanaugh dropped the boxes on the table, darting behind a chair. His head popped up now and then.

"Hey!" Verena was taken aback, offended.

"What? The sound your stomach made probably woke the vampyres in the basement." Cavanaugh looked between her and the direction Verena assumed was their basement.

"There's vampyres in the basement?" Verena stepped backwards, terrified.

"No. Don't be ridiculous." He waved his hand, brushing off her question as he finally sat.

"You just said there was."

"I was wrong. She already went rabid." Cavanaugh threw his hands up.

Aven bit his cheeks to hold back his laughter. His brother's amusement was spreading like a disease.

"Maybe we should check her gums to see if she is foaming yet." Aven piped in.

"If this were the case, son, she'd already be dead," Merridayn chimed in, helping to lighten the room's atmosphere.

"Call the doctor! Get the shaman!" Cavanaugh dropped the boxes with a thud, throwing his hands in the air in false panic.

"Ignore them, Verena. They get their humour from their mother." Elion patted her on the shoulder before sitting down at the far left of the table.

"I can tell. I find it amusing."

"You can always ignore them. It is what I do most of the time."

"Excuse me, father, for failing to appreciate a good sense of humour." Cavanaugh feigned insult.

Elion's eyes flicked towards his son and back, his head tilting in his son's direction as if silently saying, *'See what I have to deal with?'* The corners of Verena's lips curled upward.

"Alright, boys. Enough. Let us put the food down so we can eat." Merridayn placed the bowls she had brought in on the table before taking her seat to the right of Elion. Cavanaugh followed suit, taking the chair on his father's left. Aven sat to Verena's left and his mother's right. Verena's eyes scanned the remaining five chairs at the table, wondering who they were for with such a small family.

"Good, good. Now, can we eat? I'm starved." Cavanaugh looked at his parents, begging to be given permission.

"Very well. Verena, please help yourself first." Elion swept his hand to Verena.

"Are we going to talk after dinner then?"

"Of course, dear. Let us get you fed first, and then we can move on to other matters." Merridayn smiled at her.

Verena filled her plate with a little bit of everything, from a vegetable salad to pasta, steak fillet to fruit, and a slice of chocolate pie. Aven filled her glass with sparkling water. She grinned at him. Once she was satisfied with her plate, the rest of the Belmont's took what they wanted. The conversation began effortlessly; Cavanaugh talked of college, and Aven would throw sarcastic comments out in inopportune moments. Elion listened attentively to both sons while scolding Aven occasionally. Merridayn sat in silence, her eyes flicking between Verena and Aven. Verena's heart clenched at the ease between the family, and jealousy reared its ugly head. She had only ever seen the amount of love they had for each other in movies. Verena's dark memories flipped through her head. A single tear ran down her face, and she hastily wiped it away before anyone could notice.

"Ah, right, Cavanaugh, I have a question." Verena held her hand over her mouth to finish chewing.

"I might have an answer, Verena." Cavanaugh looked at her, waiting for her question.

"Did you paint this painting here and the one of the Angel in the hallway?"

Merridayn looked sharply at Verena, her hand reaching for Elion's under the table.

"Yes, I did."

"Who is she?"

"I don't know."

"What do you mean 'you don't know?'"

"Exactly, I don't know who she is. She came to me in a dream; all I remember was painting. The next thing I knew, sitting on my easel, was the painting of her, which is now hanging in the hallway."

"I see." Verena looked up at the painting. "Did you name them?"

"Did I name them?"

"Yes, did you name your paintings? I heard most artists do."

A deafening silence filled the room. The tension was so thick it could be cut with a knife. Cavanaugh was unsure how to respond to Verena's questions.

"I did." He said after an eternity. Verena could feel his reluctance to answer her from the way he hesitated.

"Can you tell me the names?" Verena was getting increasingly curious, as if he was trying to avoid her questions.

"The one in the hallway I named '*Daybreaker*' and this one I named '*Predator in Waiting.*'"

"It suits them."

"Yes, it does, doesn't it?" Merridayn offered her in an attempt to ease their tension.

"Well, shall we retire to the sitting room for the evening?" Elion stood, offering his hand to his wife. He was prim and proper, contrasting his earlier easy-going demeanour with his family.

"I am ready when you are." Verena pitched in, taking a last bite before they could begin the needed conversation.

"We shall, then. I will help you, Princess." Aven got up, offering his hand to Verena as his father did. She scoffed but took the appendage. She would need to repeat to him later that she could stand on her own.

The sitting room held a beautiful, lit obsidian fireplace with a massive brown leather sectional facing it. A concrete round coffee table with beautiful white lilies sat in a vase atop it. Throw pillows of green, white and beige were unceremoniously thrown. The light brown plank tiling, which covered the entire home, was covered with an emerald green rug. Verena estimated it to be at least twenty feet by ten feet. The fire crackled softly in the background as everyone sat on the couch. Verena's perusal of the room was interrupted by Elion clearing his throat.

"Let us start from the beginning then, yes?" He asked. Merridayn folded her hands in her lap as Elion reached over to sit one of his atop hers.

"I have something to say first before we start."

"The floor is yours, dear." Merridayn smiled at her again.

"When Aven made the- what was it called?" Verena looked at Aven for help answering her question.

"The warriors challenge?" He offered.

"Yes, thank you. When Aven made the warriors challenge, blue bands appeared on his wrists." Verena pointed at the blue bands still adjoining his wrists. "When I touched them-"

"You touched them!" Merridayn's voice rose an octave. "Why in the Goddess would you touch something you didn't know?"

"My love, let her finish. There is plenty of time later to educate her." Elion patted her hands in an attempt to calm Merridayn down.

"I'm sorry." Verena looked down, embarrassed for a second before continuing. "When I touched them, I was transported into some sort of vision, maybe? A memory? I don't know what it was."

"She was also the one who let out the scream." Aven pitched in.

"Oh, right, I did." Verena blushed. "How embarrassing. But as I was saying. I saw someone. Two someones, actually. One named Francis and the other named Jerifeyn, I believe." Both adults gasped in shock, giving Verena a hearty pause. "Francis was telling her they needed to leave. Something called the 'Mordinians' were coming after them. Jerifeyn didn't want to keep running. She wanted to stay and fight. To figure out what they wanted from her. She fell to the ground and screamed. When she did, I could feel the air around her. It felt like an electric storm. Like she could control the energy around her. Before I woke up, I saw a white tub and inside-" Verena choked, trying to tell them what she saw. "-inside-" Verena faltered again."It's fine, dear. Take your time." Merridayn offered the poor girl softly.

"It's not what you expect, mother. What she saw was horrible." Aven grabbed Verena's hand. "Do you want me to tell them, Love?"

"Yes, please." Verena sobbed. She could no longer hold back the wave of emotions as tears streamed down her face.

Aven's heart clenched at his mate's tears before looking at his parents and addressing them.

"Inside the bathtub, Verena saw the remains of a miscarriage."

"Oh, Goddess." One of Merridayn's hands flew to her mouth while the other gripped her husband's. "Are you sure, son?"

"Yes, Father and I believe her."

"I will need to inform the council." Elion looked at the young girl sobbing into her hands and watched his son offer a tissue. He was proud of raising such a gentleman.

"Verena, I need you to know what you saw was real. It was real, and it is acceptable to grieve. No one should have to bear witness to what you saw. I cannot comprehend how you must feel right now."

"I understand." Verena looked between the family. "Who are they?"

Elion sighed loudly; Merridayn looked at Verena with something akin to sorrow and regret, while Aven and Cavanaugh couldn't bear to look at her. Verena knew something was wrong, something they didn't want to tell her. It was unsettling.

"Verena-"

"Yes?" She interrupted him, tired of people hiding things from her.

"Are you sure you are ready to go through this?"

"Yes."

"You might want to get comfortable because this story is not short. However, once I start, Verena, I expect you to listen to me carefully and keep your questions until later."

"Ok." Verena looked at him before nodding her head. She was ready. Almost.

"First, is there a blanket anywhere? It is a tad cold." Verena shivered, rubbing her hands over her arms. Aven burst out laughing while handing her the blanket his body was covering.

"To start, Jerifeyn and Francis Nightingale are Fae. They were given life by the Archangel Ariel and taught the ways of the affinity they were assigned. The Archangel Ariel, with the help of her sister, Archangel Haniel, and brother, Archangel Uriel, the Angels gifted four of the Fae families with higher abilities to lead the rest. Each family was given a specific affinity: Moon, Sun, Soul and Blood. The only intention of these families was to help teach others and guide them towards complete perfection. The Archangels could not understand that nobody but the Angels were perfect or designed in the Goddess' image. Only the Goddess was able to create beings of perfection." A pause came, Elion's eyes exploring Verena's face to assess whether he should continue. There was much to explain, and he was confident she wouldn't understand it all in one night.

"The Archangels only could grant magic to the races they created. Not the ability to create an image of the Goddess. This was acceptable, as the other Archangels began creating in their own ways. Archangel Ariel created animals as she is the Angel of Nature. While her sister, Archangel Azrael, the Angel of Death, created Demons. Werewolves, what we are-" He waved his hand between himself and his sons as emphasis. "-we were created by accident. The story has it that the Archangel Orion desired Ariel. When she turned him down, Orion unleashed his rage on Ariel's prized wolf, Kaulron. Kaulron was the only one we know of, unable to control his bloodlust. Orion cursed Kaulron to attack humans once a month to anger the Goddess. We believe he did this to gain the Goddess' attention, as Ariel's wolf was the one killing the Goddess' creation of humans. Perhaps in an attempt to force the Goddess' to give him the hand of Ariel. I will let Merridayn explain from here as she better understands the werewolf genetic process."

"Kaulron had attempted to kill a human, but the human was able to escape before he succeeded. It is said that Ariel took pity on the human and bound his soul to the moon to save him with the help of Archangel Haniel. However, the human had Kaulron's blood in him, which reacted to being bound as Haniel is the Angel of the Moon. The binding process forced moon magic into the human. This merging of genetics caused the human to shift into a wolf during the full moon when the moon is at its peak." Merridayn's soft-spoken voice held no room for discussion.

"Thank you, my love." Elion smiled at his wife, then turned back to Verena. "Those are just a few of the races we know of. Jerifeyn Naedian and Francis Nightingale were from two families the Archangels were blessed to lead. The Nightingales, Ice Fae, had telepathic magic. The Naedians, Earth Fae, were gifted with the ability of premonition. The other two families, the Mordinian's, Fire Fae, and the Sinclaves, Sky Fae, were given strength and healing, respectively. All four families were supposed to work together in harmony."

"The elder Nightingales, Sinclaves and Naedians disagreed with the Archangels cursing of the wolf. They believed it was a disgrace to the Nightingales. This reproach was heightened more when the wolf started killing humans—only the Mordinian's approved of the bloodshed. From journals left by Jerifeyn, we know she was engaged to Torvan Mordinian. Unbeknownst to anyone, Torvan died, causing their engagement to end. The Mordinian's expected Jerifeyn to accept their younger son, Caine. Jerifeyn's family refuted their claim as Torvan had passed, therefore annulling the contract they held. This angered the Mordinian's but was miniscule compared to the feud they ignited when Jerifeyn married Francis. Marrying Francis had caused the Fae to go to war with each other. Sinclaves were forced to side with the Mordinian's as the eldest daughter of the Sinclave family was the mother of Torvan and Caine." Elion paused, ensuring everybody in the room was keeping up with the plethora of information he was giving. When he was satisfied with their attention, he continued.

"It was an unfair battle, leaving the Nightingales and Naedians to side together without the support of healers. The Nightingale family could not win if their wounded or sick couldn't be healed. While the Nightingales could perform extraordinary feats of magic, they had no chance in combat. Naedians weren't warriors; eventually, we believed they were wiped out completely. Francis had dragged Jerifeyn across the world, trying to hide her as she was who the Mordinians wanted. Jerifeyn was a Prophetess, a unique gift the Naedians hid from the world. She could not only see the future but bend it to her own will, changing fate whenever she saw fit."

"I'm sorry to interrupt. I know you said to wait. But what about the dream I had?" Verena felt horrid about interrupting them, but they had yet to answer her.

"I believe what you experienced was not a dream but a memory of the past. I do not believe anyone was aware Jerifeyn experienced miscarriages. The information must have been left out of her journals intentionally." Elion smiled; he knew Verena would hyper-fixate on one portion of his history lesson and could not move past it until it was answered.

"Why?"

"I'm not sure, Verena. I can only imagine it must be embarrassing and painful to think about. The Fae were not known for being unable to produce children. Quite the opposite. They had a plethora of children." Elion chuckled, remembering his parents telling him about the invites to welcomings their grandparents had received when the Fae were at peace.

"Why did I see it then?"

"I am speculating here; don't take my word as final.

These 'blue bands' you see, when did they appear?"

"Immediately after Aven accepted my mother's challenge." Verena paused, clearing her throat. "I'm sorry, *Abigail's* challenge." The name alone made Verena's stomach lurch like acid on her tongue.

"Interesting." Elion paused, leaving Verena almost bouncing in her seat with nerves. "If we speculate these bands are physical presentations of the challenge, we can assume they are pure magic."

"I see where you are going, Love." Merridayn squeezed Elion's hand. "With Verena's background, we should assume she could see magic in its purest forms. When she touched the bands, she could see she was taking in magic. At some point, she should be able to control it. Assuming we are correct, we could potentially have an understanding of her abilities."

"We could presume she might have either telepathic or seer abilities. Unless there is something within the two bloodlines we are unaware of."

"You might be onto something. Would either of the families have been able to wipe records?"

"If anyone could, I suspect it would be the Naedians. According to the books in the council library, they were the closest thing to record keepers."

"Theoretically, they could then, yes?"

"Theoretically."

"Excuse me, could anyone explain what is going on here?" Verena announced loudly, exhausted from watching the two argue.

"I apologise, Verena. Let us explain." Merridayn shrugged apologetically. "Theoretically, you would be able to see magic due to your heritage. What is confusing is how you were able to traverse back in time to a memory that was not even yours. I would reckon it was pareidolia if you didn't use specific names. As it is not, we are not able to explain how. What we can explain is that your blood has magic in it because of who you are."

"So, who am I?"

"You are an Ice Fae, Verena." Elion looked at her as if it should have been obvious.

"Okay, let's say I believe you. My question remains unanswered as to who Abigail is to me."

"Abigail is a werewolf. We believed she was good friends with your mother. When your parents passed away, she stepped up to become your guardian. The council believed you would be safest there as werewolf scent could hide you away. We didn't expect that Abigail was using you for her gain and didn't actually care for you. This was news to us." Elion looked at Merridayn, and she nodded. "We offered to become your guardians, but Abigail was given the responsibility due to her alleged connection to your family. We are deeply sorry things turned out horribly. I can only imagine the things you should never have been subjected to."

"I don't blame you, Mr. Belmont. If what you say is true, there is nothing you could have done then and nothing you can do about it now." Verena wiped a tear from her face when she realised the woman she thought was her mother was a fraud. "Aven mentioned that some council had given her money to support me and give me a better lifestyle. Do you know how much she was given?" "Are you saying you didn't know?" Merridayn questioned.

"Yes. All I have known my entire life is hardship and financial struggles. It got to the point where Abigail moved us in with Colin. The rest I would rather not talk about."

"Another day, Mom," Aven added, knowing what had

happened. His and his wolf's anger was brimming.

"Alright then." Merridayn looked at her son, questioning. "Yes, Verena, you were supposed to be given a large sum to cover your expenses, schooling, and any other things you wanted. The sum was substantial, but the exact amount was never shared at the hearings."

"I am not surprised," Verena muttered.

Chapter 9

VERENA

*S*elfish bitch.

"You did not know, Princess. Nobody could have known. She fooled us all." Aven stroked Verena's cheek, attempting to reassure her.

"I am nonplussed, but it leaves me with one question." Verena tapped her foot, irritated but collected.

"Go on, dear." Merridayn smiled at her.

"You gave me history but didn't answer the main question." Yet again, she was left with her questions unanswered, which was genuinely annoying.

"Which is?"

"Who are my parents?" For the last time, Verena swore it would not be a pretty spectacle if she had to ask again.

"They are your parents, Verena," Merridayn said softly, unable to form the words any louder. The heartbreak sank in as the older woman realised she was still mourning over the couple.

"Not a chance." Verena raged. She couldn't believe the words they said. "There is not a chance those two are my parents. I'm just a regular person—a human, if you will. They aren't."

"Verena, Princess, you are not human." Aven looked at her, his brows scrunched, his lips pursed. He was trying to convince her, but the classic puppy dog face was too bad for him; it wasn't working.

"Yes, I am. I don't have any special powers or look any different from the likes of you." Verena swept her hands downwards, over herself, and then pointed to them. They looked identical to her, yet they were trying to tell her she wasn't human. Lunatics, the whole lot of them.

"We are werewolves, Verena," Elion said matter of factly.

"And I'm the tooth fairy. What are you all on? What drug?"

"I will not argue with you, Verena; your birth name is Verena Halliwen Nightingale. You are the daughter of Francis Pierre Nightingale, the Crown Prince of the Nightingale Family and Jerifeyn Amelia Nightingale, the Crown Princess of the Naedian Family. You are the current Crown Princess of the Nightingale and Naedian Families, as the council is unaware of anyone else in your two families surviving the war." Elion stared at her, his face laced with no-nonsense. "You are old enough to understand when someone is telling you the truth; start acting like it. If you still decide you cannot believe the words coming out of my mouth, I hope you have your eyes wide open tonight at the challenge." Elion got up and left. Merridayn looked at Verena willfully before following him but not before stopping to give Verena much needed reassurance.

"I hope you find the answers you seek tonight, Verena. There will be many things which will make sense when you see them." Merridayn squeezed Aven's shoulder.

"I wish I could believe you," Verena whispered.

"It'll be alright; you'll see tonight. Let's find you some different clothes, and then we can start going to the ring." Aven held his hand out for hers, hoping she would accept his good-natured gesture.

"Where is this ring?" She pushed his hand away and stood on her own, determined not to be helpless again.

"It'll take us about an hour on foot. Typically, we ride out there, but I'm unsure how you feel about riding." Aven smirked. Her resilience was adorable.

"Riding?" Verena questioned. Did she hear him correctly? He surely did not expect her to ride anything at this moment, especially not with the crazy smirk growing on his too-perfect lips.

"Yes. Riding."

"I get it, smartass. What kind of riding?" Verena rolled her eyes. Somebody needed to help this man because he was seconds from getting slapped.

"Horseback, what else?" Aven looked at her, amused. He knew exactly how to get a rise out of her and exploited every chance he had.

"Oh, I don't know, sir rich parents. Motorcycle riding, ATV riding, car riding, bike riding—there could be many different types of riding." Verena glared at him.

"Most definitely horseback riding. Have you met my mother?"

"Yes, I have. What does it have to do with this?"

"Do you honestly believe she would allow me to be on a motorcycle or ATV? She would call them a deathtrap and lock me in my room like I was five again. Absolutely not." Aven faced her. "Are you ready, or will you stand dumbfounded all day, Princess?" Aven changed his mind, taking three steps to her before he swung her into his arms, bridal style.

"What are you doing?"

"What does it look like? Carrying you. You were not moving. I got impatient." Aven shrugged, moving Verena with the movement.

"I can do it on my own."

Aven didn't listen but continued towards the opposite side of the house, a portion Verena hadn't seen before. 'Where are we going?" Verena looked up at him, subject to being in his arms.

"My sister's room," Aven said gruffly as if he didn't want to go there yet and had no choice.

"Is she going to mind us going in there?"

"She isn't home. The two of you are roughly the same size." He was curt, to the point, solidifying her suspicions.

Verena didn't respond but watched as he walked, passing two massive doors on the left and another wall of paintings on the right. The hallway veered right, and a dark green door was at the end. The name 'Vivianne' was embossed in gold near the top. Verena knew Aven and Cavanaugh had a sister but never met her.

"Where is she?" Verena's curiosity peaked hard.

"I don't want to talk about it." Aven bit out. "Can you walk, Princess?" He looked down, his tone changing.

"Yes. I could have walked here, but someone was impatient." She poked him in the chest as he gently set her down.

"Semantics. Let us find you something appropriate to wear." Aven looked her up and down, raising an eyebrow as he appraised her. "Granted, I do not mind seeing you in my clothes."

"Oh hell, I left the bedroom without pants on." Verena flushed in embarrassment.

"Nudity in this house is typical. Nudity in our community is pretty normal. Nobody cares." Aven reached forward and opened the door. A beautiful evergreen zephyr emitted from the room. Her senses vaulted with glee. The interior of the room was gorgeous. From the doorway, Verena was spellbound. A splendiferous-sized bed sat comfortably in the centre of the room. The windows held grandiose drapes of feldgrau, an obsidian chandelier hung from the ceiling. Muted grey closet sets lined two walls while an extensive desk faced the drapes.

"Why is it so obscure here? Can we turn on a light?" Verena quipped.

"We can; Vivianne typically keeps them closed." Aven fiddled with light switches until he found the one to open the drapes. Verena was atingle. The scenery presented to her from their opening showcased a pulchritudinous viewpoint. Edges of the lake could be viewed from here, and Verena was astounded in wonder.

"Was the house built around the lake specifically?" Verena mused.

"Yes, I believe it was the selling point." Aven rummaged around in the closets behind her.

"What are you looking for?" Verena turned to witness him throwing clothes asunder. "Honestly, the blatant disrespect to the clothes."

"I am attempting to find you something to cover up when we venture outside later today. Your outfit must cover your scent glands, or the unmated males could become distracted." Aven mused. He was focused diligently on his task, not a care in the world where his thrown garments landed.

"Why do my scent glands need to be covered? And why does it matter to unmated males?" She asked while ducking for the trousers bounding towards her.

"Your scent could cause issues with the males during the challenge. Many cannot contain their wolves in an atmosphere so high in pheromones." Aven dismissed her questions, continuing his search.

Verena held her hands up by default, turning around to explore the room more. Her eyes landed on the pristine xyloid desk. She was curious about the virtuoso display of art from such a master, a white oak base with the appearance of a river through the middle. The craftsmanship was outstanding. A picture of a black-haired woman surrounded by Aven and Cavanaugh was on the desk. The two men dwarfed her, but the group appeared happy and loving. Verena became curious as to the superstitious behaviour of the family concerning their daughter.

"This should do," Aven called out triumphantly while holding up a pair of brown leather trousers, a chiffon silk bodice, a brown leather belt with a gold buckle, knee-high leather boots, and an aegean shawl. Verena looked at him in dismay, his taste in clothes shocking.

"There is no chance I can pull this off, Aven," Verena exclaimed upon being presented with the clothing, her affinity for accïsmus openly presenting. The clothing was astounding and otherworldly.

"You can and you will." Aven thrust the clothes at her. "Besides, Viviane will not miss these. Goddess knows the woman acquires clothes like candy just because she can." Aven dumped the items on the bed impatiently.

"If you are sure." Verena plucked them up, waiting for him to give her privacy.

"Right then, I will be outside the door." He promptly absconded.

Men and their perpetualism to entertain sexual ideas at all waking moments.

When Aven knocked, Verena struggled to lace up the boots, pecking his head in the door.

"Are you modest?"

"I am, thank you." Verena finished lacing the boots.

She stood after, rocking on her feet to test them. The silk blouse brushed against her skin nicely. She could get used to the quality of life Aven grew up with.

"You look—" Aven swallowed hard. Verena noticed the way his throat moved. The movement gave her a jolt of confidence. She felt powerful in her ability to stun him. "There are not enough words to describe how beautiful you are." He crossed the room, cupping her face and kissing her forehead.

Verena blushed, leaning into his kiss.

"Let's get going. The sun is due to crest within the hour. It would bode well to arrive beforehand." Aven took her hand, pulling her out of the room.

A cacophony of sounds came from the speakers lined up on the ceiling. Verena couldn't quite put her finger on its meaning, though it must have meant something from Aven's growl in discontent.

"What is this sound?" Verena looked up towards him.

"It means the challenge is to start within a few hours. I was hoping it would not be broadcast to the entire pack. Alas, here we are." Aven's lip curled.

"What do you mean 'broadcasted to the entire pack.'" Verena looked at him. He needed to learn how to get his point across without her having to drag the answers out of him.

"It means the whole pack will be there." Aven rubbed his temple, and Goddess help him. He did not want it to go this way. Now, it seems he had no choice, he would have to abide by the rules to the letter.

"Is this a bad thing?" Verena couldn't see how everyone knew, though she did not know who exactly he meant. She still couldn't see it being a problem.

"No, not exactly. It just causes a few complications."

More than a few if his blank expression was to be believed. He was trying so hard not to worry her.

"Do I need to keep pulling teeth, or will you tell me everything in one go?" Verena was beginning to lose her patience.

"I apologise. Yes, I will." Aven rubbed his face. "If the pack shows up to the challenge, it will lead to the old rites being followed. Meaning, if Abigail loses, she will either be exiled from the pack or killed. There are no other options." He fixed her with an unsettled gaze.

"Exiled?"

"Yes. She would have to continue travelling. She cannot settle down in one spot for long due to all the land being claimed. She would be a vagabond. A nomad of sorts." Aven looked down, torn between completing his challenge and breaking Verena's heart.

"I do not know what to say."

"I am unsure as well. I wished they had allowed the challenge to be kept private if only to keep you from losing the only mother figure you have had." Verena pulled him closer and then sank into his chest. Her arms wrapped around his upper abdomen, her head pressing against his heart. She wanted to help him, the need growing with each passing second. Some unexplainable portion of her cried out for him.

"I do not blame you for what will come. She caused her problems and needs to take responsibility for her actions. These choices are hers and hers alone. Nobody forced her to make them." Verena whispered to him. Aven wrapped his arms around her, taking comfort in her closeness.

"I will remain vigilant to uphold your honour." Aven pulled her chin up to look at him. "I will do anything you ask of me, Princess. I want you to know, no. I need you to know how genuine my words are."

"I am beginning to understand, Aven. I am still having trouble with the why, though."

"Everything will make sense in time. Now, shall we continue our journey?"

"I suppose we should, at least if the sound is anything to go by." Verena waved him forward. "How long did you say the trip would take us?"

"If we can keep a canter for the majority of the time, it should only take about twenty minutes." Aven began walking back where they had come, the massive double doors reappearing on their right.

"What is behind those doors?" Verena asked him curiously as the doors faded from view.

"The doors? Oh, the library." He said nonchalantly, waving his hand towards them as if it were an everyday household staple.

"Of course, you have a library. Do you have an indoor pool and bar, too?" She quipped.

"Indoor pool, no. Bar, yes."

"Of course you do."

Aven's eyebrow quivered in amusement. Their continued path led them through the back doors of the house, entering the beautiful outdoor kitchen she had seen earlier. The pair did not stop moving, bypassing everything and heading straight to the barn. She made a mental note to come back later to explore the grounds. Upon entering the stables, Verena lost all sense of reality. The interior was beyond her imagination. Stunning saddles lined a wall, all black concrete flooring, shower stalls and gorgeous black walls.

"I will assume you do not know how to ride, so we shall ride pillion." Aven tugged her towards the back of the stables, where an oversized silver dapple horse stood proud. "This is Markanith; he has been my horse since I was born," Markanith whined, answering his partner.

"How exactly do you plan to go about this?" Verena peeked at the horse curiously, slightly terrified.

"I can fetch a pillow for you to sit on, and you will ride behind me." Aven patted Markanith's neck as the horse blew into Aven's face. "Or, if you are up to it, we can put you on a horse and ride slower."

"Yes. The second option. Please." Verena trembled, her fear overweighting her verbal courage.

"Alright." Aven looked around, contemplating. "But which to put you on." He let go of her hand and began to pace in front of the other stalls. He stopped before a stall holding a giant, liver chestnut stallion. The horse stomped his feet; he wanted to run, wanted to feel the wind in his mane, but not for Aven. "Orivan is too bold; he probably won't listen." Aven approached the stall opposite Orivan and appraised a lanky blue dapple stallion. He was standing near the back of his stall, almost glaring at Aven. Aven shook his head at the horse; the beast had not been the same since his sister disappeared. "Tefillyn is the epitome of Vivianne. It just won't do. Ah, I got it." Aven looked back at Verena, a smile gracing his face.

"You've got it?" Verena's curiosity peaked again.

"Yes, you will ride my mother's horse, Isaya. She is younger but is well-mannered compared to the rest. Though she is the tallest one here, I hope you don't mind heights." Aven walked over to the larger stall opposite Markanith. Verena had not noticed a horse there as her focus had been entirely on the gusto of the building.

"Isaya, this is Verena. We need to go to the ring, and Verena has never ridden before. Do you think you will be nice to her?" Aven called out to a massive cream-looking horse. "Isaya is a three-year-old saddlebred horse; she is gaited. Your ride should be smoother because of it."

"She is beautiful." Verena unconsciously reached out to touch the mare.

"Easy, let Isaya come to you first." Aven cautioned, holding his hand out to Isaya in respect.

"Oh, I'm sorry. I didn't know." Verena stepped back, nervous.

"It is quite alright. While she is not known to anger, she is still a horse and deserves respect. Especially as you are not my mother, she will need to come to you on her terms." Aven gave her a weak smile. "Come, stand closer, but do not move. Let her take the first step."

Verena obeyed cautiously, sitting still and allowing Isaya to move first. It felt as if an eternity flew by before the imposing horse came to her. Aven had already saddled Markanith, leading the horse to a tie-off point. Markanith stomped his feet impatiently, causing Aven to chuckle. While Verena was paying attention to the two of them, Isaya had moved behind her to push her muzzle into her back.

"It looks like Isaya accepts you; she should let you ride her now." Aven kissed Verena's forehead before walking to grab a saddle.

"She should?" Verena squeaked. "What do you mean she should?"

"Unless you royally piss her off somehow, she should be fine. Just listen to my instructions, and you will be fine." Aven threw a pad over the horse and followed with a brown leather saddle. His muscular body can hoist the saddle onto Isaya without struggle. His biceps bulged against his smaller shirt, causing vivid memories of earlier to appear.

"Do not anger the horse. Easy enough." Verena held her hand up in an imitation salute.

"Come over here, and let's get you mounted up." Aven held his hand out for her to take. "Put your left foot in the stirrup, and then on the count of three, we will hoist you up." Aven watched her as she followed his instructions. "Alright, here we go." Aven placed his hand under her thigh. "One." He looked at her. "Two." He bent his knees slightly for the kinetic energy. "Three." He pushed her up, and she mounted with ease. He could tell she was uncomfortable and suspected Isaya knew it, too.

"I'm up, now what?" Verena's voice was laced with a tinge of fear.

"Let me mount my horse, and we will get a move on," Aven replied while walking towards Markanith, removing his tether and mounting him easily. "Let me lead, and then tell her to lead on. She will follow Markanith."

"Sounds easy enough. Lead the way." Verena gripped the reins, waiting for Aven.

"Let's go, Markanith. You know the way, buddy." Aven held his reins loosely.

"Lead on, Isaya." Verena mimicked Aven's lead and loosened her reins. Isaya moved onwards, with Markanith leading them out the front door.

Chapter 10

VERENA

"You said it'll take us about an hour to get there, correct?" Verena yelled out to Aven, who was already a reasonable distance away.

"It will probably take us the better part of an hour if we set off on a walk. The time will decrease if we can get you up to a trot. It typically takes about twenty minutes if we reach a canter or sprint." Aven looked over his shoulder at a nervous Verena. The way she gripped her reins gave it away: tight, close to her hips, and shaking. Isaya's head was held proudly as if she knew the poor human was terrified.

"We can work up to whatever you say. I cannot make any promises as I have never done this before." Verena's shaky voice betrayed her nerves, and she blushed.

"Whenever you feel ready, you let me know," Aven reassured her. "For now, why not just take it slow and enjoy the process." Verena hummed her agreement, unwilling to inform Aven he was right. Riding Isaya was exceptionally smooth. She hardly felt anything as they walked on. Aven took her to a grass-laden trail she couldn't see until they were right upon it. The mountainous range loomed before their way, and the overbearing Douglas Firs surrounded her. Verena's nostrils flourished with moss, fresh rain and pine needles. She could hear birds singing, and her heartbeat sang with happiness. Being in the presence of nature was relaxing. The rise and fall of Isaya's breathing created a soothing presence against the rising anxiety.

Verena lost track of the time they had spent in the forest. She grew accustomed to the scent of the forest, feeling at home there. In the distance, she thought she noticed a smaller lake, much smaller than the one their house was built next to. Perhaps it was more a pond than a lake if she thought about it. Something she made a note to ask Aven about later when there were fewer pressing matters to attend to. The steady sound of Isaya's steps changed, drawing Verena's gaze back to her surroundings. They were going over a bridge; the stream beneath seemed calm and wild simultaneously. There was an unmistakable energy in the air calling to Verena. She couldn't place it but felt drawn in all the same. Verena looked up from the water beneath her. She opened her mouth to speak, but the words were lost in the sight of the cabin before her.

Eclipsed between the mountains and surrounded by trees, a modern white-toned cabin overshadowed everything else. Massive floor-to-ceiling picture windows dominated each side. Accented with black steel siding and a black roof, the cabin looked out of place in the mountain range. Many bodies could be seen through the windows, but the pair was too far away for Verena to tell who they were. A few off-road vehicles lined the front of the drive.

"Aven?" Verena hesitated. She did not like what she was seeing.

"Yes?"

"Why is there a cabin in the woods, and who lives here?" Verena tilted her head towards the offending property.

"This is the pack house. All our unmated pack members live here while the mated ones live in their houses nearby." Aven's response sounded as if this should have been obvious.

"Un-mated?" She questioned the word.

"Yes, all wolves have a mate. A person who is meant to be their equal in every aspect and balance them. Our pack members who have not found their mate live together here. Our mated pack members live in their houses about four miles north of here."

"Do they have to live here together, then?

"No, it is not forced, but many find they want to stay because of the safety it provides. We are essentially on our own out here."

Upon getting closer, Verena could begin to see the formation of faces. Men, women and children running about. She would have thought they were going inside, but Aven led them directly past the cabin, following the sun, which continued to dip closer to the tree line. Verena knew they must have been getting closer to what the family had called the ring.

An obsidian ring, approximately fifty feet in diameter and four feet deep, was presented below. As the name suggested, it was a legitimate ring. Stairs led down into the pit from each cardinal direction, and torches sporadically lined the border. Verena didn't have a good feeling about this place. The entire thing felt off as if her body was warning her.

"I'm just going to throw this out there, but this must be the ring. I could be wrong, but it is a massive circle."

"It is." Aven's voice sounded tight, strained.

"It feels-" Verena cut off, trying to find a word to describe her feelings. Her right hand bobbed up and down. She tried to force herself to remember the word from motion. "-dark, like someone has been hurt here. Like we shouldn't be here."

"People have been hurt here, Verena." Aven looked at her. "People have been killed here."

"Killed?"

"Verena, what have you gathered from today's conversation about this challenge?"

"Abigail issued the challenge, and you accepted the challenge. You said you both would fight until the other either dies or loses. If the party does not die, they get exiled and become a nomad. Am I correct so far?"

"So far, yes. With the potential of everyone being here, I suspect the challenge will follow the old rules where both parties will fight until the other dies. I don't believe there will be a possibility of exile. The parties must stay within the confines of this ring or risk being disembowelled by the spectators. Any party entering the ring who is not a part of the challenge can also be killed. For example, if my brother came in to assist me, Abigail would also be entitled to attack him."

"Do you think you will have to kill her? She might not have been my mother; however, she was the only parent I knew as I grew up." Verena's voice softened, and tears started to build against her will.

"If the old rules are called, I will have to. I have alpha blood. Abigail made a mistake in challenging me."

"Why?"

"Alpha blood makes us stronger, faster, more lethal. It is so we can more effectively defend our pack. Abigail is only a beta, and historically, they have been weaker. Female betas tend to be working wolves, while male betas lean towards protection." Aven reached out to her but could not reach her due to the size of their horses. "I cannot promise I won't be forced to kill her, but I will try to reason with everyone."

"Thank you." Verena felt a tear fall down her cheeks. "I appreciate it. I know she doesn't deserve any kindness, but I cannot bring myself to watch her die either."

Aven directed Markanith back towards the cabin to introduce Verena to his packmates, prepare for the challenge, and perhaps enjoy a few moments alone with his mate. He thought about the empty words he had told Verena, and his wolf howled in anger for lying. Aven meant what he said about not being able to promise he wouldn't kill Abigail.

"When we get to the cabin, dismount and let the reins go. Isaya and Markanith will walk home." Aven threw over his shoulder. "A bit of warning; the pack house can get rowdy."

Chapter 11

VERENA

A ven was far from exaggerating when he said the house was rowdy. Verena could only imagine what it would look like with a party in full swing. Men, women, children, and even a few elderly patrons were in attendance. The moment Aven opened the door, all eyes were on them. Verena half-heartedly wished she could be in the saddle heading back to the house with Isaya. She resolved to stand interminably close to Aven, or at least as close as she physically could.

"Aven! Where have you been, mate?" A man with sandy blonde hair, green eyes and tan skin came rushing up.

"I've been around." Aven half-clapped the man on the back. "Holden, let me introduce you to Verena Nightingale." Aven stepped away, holding his hand out in Verena's direction.

This egotistical, self-righteous, pompous di-

"Miss Nightingale, it is a pleasure to meet you." Holden gave Verena a suggestive look as he appraised her attire. Verena consciously yearned to be anywhere but there.

"Nice to meet you." Verena quipped, taking him in with disgust written across her face.

"Now, son, will you introduce everyone to this beautiful young lady?" An older woman smiled up at Aven before pulling him into a hug. The woman's smaller size was dwarfed in comparison.

"Pardon my manners, grandmother." Aven hugged his grandmother back and then released her to stand taller, addressing the room. "Everyone, I would like to proudly introduce you to Miss Verena Nightingale. Please, make her feel welcome as she will become a permanent fixture in our lives."

Whispers erupted around the room, making Verena blush. Aven's grandmother fixed her with a curious look before coming over and pulling Verena into a hug.

"It is nice to meet you," Aven's grandmother said before dropping her voice "*Princess.*"

"How did you-"

"I knew about your parents, my dear. My Andrew and I fought hard against the council many times to let my son, Elion, and Merridayn take you in." The elderly woman rubbed her back softly. "But I can see it would not have mattered, as mates always find their way to one another."

"Grandmother..." Clearly, Aven was eavesdropping as he was startled by his grandmother's words.

"Do not fret, my boy. Though you have not completed the mating bond, I can see it between you." She reached out to pat his arm, releasing Verena in the process. "Now, I believe others are requesting your attention. I shall see you both later." Verena watched as the woman walked away gracefully despite her age.

"Who was she?"

"She is my father's mother, Katherine Belmont. She married my grandfather, Andrew Belmont, and they were the previous Alpha and Luna of the Bluraine Clan before my grandfather stepped down." Aven's face turned south. "My grandfather passed away a few years back. We never found out why."

"I'm sorry, Aven." Verena reached out for him, Aven gave her a weak smile.

"It is alright." Aven's gaze wandered around the room. "Let's continue mingling. I'll introduce you to the rest."

For the next twenty minutes, Verena was introduced to every member within the cabin. She was beginning to become so overwhelmed the names were starting to mix together. She needed to rest; her feet and legs were already burning from the ride over and the continuous standing. Aven must have sensed her growing distress as he guided them towards the kitchen bar stools.

"Would you like something to drink?"

"Yes, please." Verena's mouth was dry, and she realised how hungry she was when they approached the kitchen. "Actually, can you point me toward a bathroom?"

"Up the stairs, at the end and the last door on the left. The bathroom is the right door when you enter."

Verena rushed up the stairs. While she didn't actually need the bathroom, she would still use it for both physical and mental relief. Trudging up the stairs, she quickly found Aven's room. Unsurprisingly, it mimicked his room at the main house. His bathroom here was still more luxurious than where she lived, and jealousy peaked slightly. The noise level was significantly reduced in his room compared to the hallway.

Do they have noise cancelling panels in the wall?

Verena scoffed.

Of course, they do, idiot. The whole damn family screams money.

Verena went to wash her hands, her eyes catching a glimpse in the mirror. She dropped the hand soap and fell backwards into the wall. Her normal green eyes glowed brightly, white peaking between the green. Her occasionally acne riddled face was flawless. Her typical inordinately tanned skin was paler. Her hair was no longer in a rattled state of affairs. The strands gracefully framed her face and appeared to have grown at least a foot and a half in a week. Verena moved to pull her hair into a pony and her ears were proudly at a point. The longer she looked in the mirror, the more she felt she was losing her mind. Tears formed in her eyes and began to fall down her cheeks.

What the absolute fuck did they do to me?

"I suspected you were in here, dear." Merridayn's soft voice came from the bedroom.

"Did you do this to me?" Verena's voice cracked, "I don't even know why I am crying."

"I did not intentionally do this to you, dear. When we gave you the infusion of Fae blood, your dominant genetics reacted to it." Merridayn sat gracefully on the edge of an armchair. "You were so starved of magic your body shut down. Your blood activated with the infusion, causing these drastic changes. Elion and I could only assume what they would be as we are not Fae. The most noticeable was your appearance. The night we gave you the infusion, you lit up brightly. Your hair and nails grew longer and stronger, your skin glowed, the acne went away, and your ears went from round to a point. While the Fae could not fly, they were stronger, faster, and most were apt at physical magic. We will have to see if we can find you some books, as we cannot openly announce your return." Merridayn spoke with sympathy but was still authoritative.

"Basically, you're saying I am a freak?" Verena panicked. Her plans for the future vanished.

"No, darling." Merridayn gave a soft grimace. "I am saying you are becoming who you were meant to be. A woman I know your parents would be proud of." Her words caused Verena to cry harder, coming from the woman who had been nothing but kind to her. Merridayn patted the seat she was perched on, which Verena took. The woman's hands nimbly pleated Verena's hair into a crown. Her pointed ears were on display for the world to see. "Do not hide who you are. You are beautiful, and the world deserves to see it."

"Who am I if not myself?" Verena was confused. Everything she had known about herself was a lie. Who was this new person? Who was she supposed to be now?

"You are Verena Halliwen Nightingale, Princess of House Nightingale and House Naedian, the only daughter of Prince Francis Pierre Nightingale of House Nightingale and Princess Jerifeyn Amelia Nightingale of House Naedian. You, dear, are fated to change everything. You already have my son's heart wrapped around your finger, and I plead with you not to break it." Merridayn leaned over to kiss Verena's hair, giving Verena a quick squeeze as she got up.

"I can only hope to believe you one day, Mrs. Belmont."

"Please, dear, call me Merridayn."

"Very well..." Verena hesitated. "Merridayn."

"Now, we have guests to corral, and Aven will need you there while he prepares. I believe he has some things he wishes to explain to you before the challenge commences. Last I saw him, he was headed outside." Merridayn left the room, the door hanging open.

Here we go.

Verena descended the stairs, watchful of all the eyes on her. The whispers began again with renewed vigour.

"Are her ears... pointed?" "Do you see her ears?"

"Is she a Fae?"

"I thought they were extinct."

"Who is she?"

"She is absolutely stunning."

"Why is she here?"

Verena ignored the crowd for the most part. She headed towards the exterior door she had seen earlier near the kitchen. The cool mountain air brushed her face as soon as she breached the threshold. She just now registered that she hadn't felt the cold on the ride up here. Her brain knew it was chilly outside, but her body was not responding.

What an odd development, but I like it.

Verena's ears picked up a seductive laugh coming from the backside of the house. She followed it, hoping it would lead her to someone who could point her toward Aven. Her heart thumped loudly in anticipation. Rounding the corner, said heart slammed into her stomach.

"Aven! I haven't seen you in forever. Where have you been?" A woman's voice squealed.

"Around." Aven snapped. "What are you doing?"

"I've missed you. What else, dummy?" Verena could barely see the silhouettes of the pair but did not miss how the woman attempted to sit on Aven's lap as he was lounging on a wood log.

"Get off me, Kessa." Aven tried pushing the woman, Kessa, off him.

"What is the matter with you, Aven? You've never been this way with me." Kessa snuggled closer, dipping her nose into his neck. "Why the fuck do you smell different, Aven!" Kessa recoiled from him.

"I said get off, Kessa." Aven tossed her off him. Verena could see him shudder. He was furious. The vein in his forehead pulsed, and she could hear him clench his teeth together. The grinding of bone on bone rang in her head.

"Answer me, Aven." Kessa moved, trying to stand over

him. Her meagre attempt at dominating him was laughable. "Why do you smell different?"

"Probably because I found my *mate*, Kessa. It does not take a genius to figure it out." Aven gripped his thighs, his fingernails dug into the expanse of them. Verena smirked, wiping it off her face. She was supposed to still be mad at him, not ogling how he defended their, not official, official relationship.

"Still does not explain why you smell like *her*." Kessa spit out. "I can tell you have not completed the mating bond, so why do you smell like her?"

"Again, an answer you could easily figure out on your own. Why do I smell like her? Because I had my fingers so far in her, she had forgotten her name. Why else?" Aven stood up. His height towered the infuriating bitch.

"I do not agree with this at all, Aven." Kessa crossed her arms. "I forbid it, actually."

"You-" Aven stumbled over his words. "You forbid it?" He let out a loud laugh. The amusement didn't reach his face. "You forbid it? Oh man, I might need to change my boxers. How hilarious, thanks. I needed a laugh today."

"I am serious, Aven." Kessa stomped her foot as if she were a five-year-old again. "You are engaged to me, not her."

"No, Kessa. Our parents engaged us as I had yet to find my mate." Aven stepped toward her. "We were engaged because everyone thought my mate had died when I couldn't feel the mating at eighteen." Aven stepped closer again, inches away from her. "We got engaged when I turned eighteen because I had to do something for my pack to show I would be a great alpha." He took the last step, dominating Kessa's space. "I know why I could not feel her, Kessa." He looked down. Disgust adorned his features. "Because my mate is not a werewolf, but a Fae. A beautiful, fiery, sometimes irritating, but I like it, Fae."

"B-but" Kessa stuttered. "But it is unheard of!"

"Unheard of but not impossible." Aven snapped; he was getting impatient with the audacity.

"You cannot be mated to her!" Kessa stomped her foot; Verena thought she was dreaming.

"I can, and I am." Aven sighed, his patience gone, and he was holding on by a thread not to explode.

"I won't allow it." She was about to stomp her foot again, like a bratty child being told no for the first time. Verena grasped the moment to leave the shadows where she had been listening.

"It's a damn good thing I do not need your permission then, isn't it?" Both heads snapped towards Verena.

"Verena..." Aven trailed off, a blush forming on his cheeks.

"I heard the entire thing, Aven. While I am not impressed by your lack of informing me you were *engaged* before your fingers brought me to orgasm. I can overlook the infraction after a bit of grovelling. Considering what you all have said is true, I will be marrying you. Mated to you?" Verena moved her attention from Aven to Kessa. "Regardless, I would like to know why you believe you can tell Aven what he can or cannot do. He just told you he is mated to me, and yet you continued to act like a petulant child about it."

"I know you are not talking to me in any sort of way." Kessa fixed her with a stare.

"Cute." Verena rolled her eyes. "You might want to fix your face. It looks like you are about to shit yourself."

Aven slapped a hand over his mouth in a meagre attempt to control his laughter, and Verena pressed her lips together. Kessa turned red with anger.

"Now you look like a tomato. Are you injured? Do I need to call someone over?"

"You are lucky, bitch. You are not a werewolf, or I would admit my own challenge. As it is, Aven is already having to fight your whore of a mother to defend you." Kessa spit.

"My mother is dead, cunt. The whore you are referring to deserves every inkling of what is coming for her." Verena turned to walk back into the house.

"If you ever call her a bitch again, Kessa, it will be the last time you ever utter another word." Aven's voice was laced with venom, his wolf demanding to put the omega in her place.

"But Aven."

"No, Kessa. She is my mate and the future Luna of this pack. You will respect her because, help me, Goddess. I will let her do whatever she feels necessary." Aven absquatted towards Verena; his need to explain overwhelmed him.

Aven found Verena curled up in his bed; tears streaked her face, and he knew she tried to hide them. He didn't have to say anything. He knew what would come if he tried. Instead, he crawled into bed behind her, pulling her to him. She weakly fought against him, but gave up in the end. Aven sat there patiently, waiting for her to say something, yell at him, cry, or do anything at this rate. It felt like an eternity had gone by, the light outside signalling he needed to prepare for the challenge.

"Aven?"

"Yes, Princess?" His heart thumped loudly.

"Did she mean anything to you?"

Aven knew who she was referring to, and the shame floored him.

"She did, Verena." Aven took a deep breath, trying to

calm himself. He looked down. He couldn't face her right now. He couldn't see the way Verena looked at him with distrust in her eyes. "I believed she would have become my mate at one point. I do not believe I would have fallen in love with her. It would have been a necessary transaction to ensure my pack's and my family's safety. So yes, a part of her used to mean a lot to me."

"Does she still mean anything to you?"

Aven's wolf howled, his heart breaking at the idea his mate was about to refuse him.

"No, not anymore." Aven pulled her closer, leaning into her hair. "We consider wolves to be adults when they turn eighteen. When they can weakly feel a mating bond, letting them know their mate is out there, somewhere. The bond gets stronger as the two get closer to each other."

"And you couldn't feel me because I am not a wolf, right?"

"Clever girl." Aven kissed her neck. "Correct. When I turned eighteen, I couldn't feel my mating bond. Everyone assumed it was because you had died. We didn't expect the reason I couldn't feel it was because you were not even a wolf."

"Is it uncommon to be mated to someone who is not a wolf?" Verena

"No, it is not. My mother is not a wolf either, love." Aven

"She's not?" Verena

"No, Merridayn is a Huntress. A human who, at one point, had a wolf ancestor. They have no wolf spirit, but with scientific help, they can gain small percentages of our abilities."

"I don't think I can handle any more information today. Can we talk about what it means later?" Verena squirmed around until she was facing him.

"Of course, Princess."

Verena didn't respond but chose to snuggle into Aven's broad chest. Her every dream of being here, with him, flocked to the forefront of her mind. A blush began creeping up her cheeks as the memory of them earlier came rushing back. The way he felt inside her, the sounds he made, and the way he made her climax caused a shudder to flow through her.

"Aven?" She whispered.

"Yes?"

"Can you promise me one thing tonight?" If she could only have one thing, and one thing, it would be for this very moment.

"I can do my best to uphold anything you ask of me, but Verena, I cannot make a promise I cannot morally keep."

"I understand." Verena looked up at him.

"What is it you want me to promise, love?"

"Can you promise to let me ask her why before you kill her?"

"Why?" Aven looked startled, not expecting this question to grace her lips. He was expecting Verena to beg him to spare Abigail. A promise he knew he would not be able to keep.

"I want to know why she treated me like she did. Why did she act like she cared when he abused me? Just to turn around and be completely indifferent." A tear ran down her cheeks. "Why didn't she love me when all I tried to do was make her proud."

"I promise, Verena. I promise you I will get you the time you need to ask her what you need to." Aven wiped the tear away. "But I cannot promise you I will not kill her." He growled, his wolf trying to rip the chains Aven kept on him to defend his crying mate.

"Thank you." She meekly said.

"Verena, I need to get ready. It is almost time, and I am running behind."

"Oh." Verena shot up. "I'm sorry, I didn't know."

"Do not be sorry. Before we do this, I must impress upon you that no matter what you see or hear, you cannot—" Aven pulled her chin up to look into her eyes. "You cannot enter the ring. Under no circumstances, Princess. Promise me you will listen."

"But-"

"Promise me, Verena. I cannot risk your life. If I have to, I will have someone restrain you, but you cannot enter the ring."

"I promise, Aven."

Aven untangled them, placing Verena back on the bed and standing beside it.

"Good." He began undressing, starting with his shirt.

"Aven!" Verena blushed, quickly looking away.

"What?" He looked around, searching for the trouble before looking back at her.

"What are you doing!"

"Getting ready?" He was confused.

"By taking your shirt off?" Verena peeked up at him, her body already reacting to the sight of his chiselled chest.

Am I sure this isn't some sort of sick dream?

Verena pinched herself secretly as Aven smirked.

Nope, not a dream.

"Yes? Verena, what did you think we meant when we said we are wolves?" Aven shook his head. "Did you think we were having a laugh?"

"Yeah, maybe a bit." Verena's blush increased. "I don't know what I thought, but it wasn't this."

"Let me explain it to you again." Aven sauntered over to her, knowing she was checking him out. "I am a werewolf, Princess. I can turn into a wolf." He gripped her legs and pulled her to the edge of the bed. "I will demonstrate it to you in a few minutes." Leaning over her, he caged her in with his arms. His breath faintly touched her flushed cheeks.

"Then what are you doing now?"

"Making sure my mate is hot and bothered before she watches me take my pants off." Aven nipped her earlobe and promptly stood back up.

Tease.

"I'll have you know. I am not bothered." Verena lied straight through her teeth, and Aven knew it.

"If you say so." He raised an eyebrow and then tugged his pants down his hips, boxers and all.

Verena let out a loud groan, struggling to keep her eyes from surveying his now naked body.

"Like what you see?"

"No. I've seen better."

"Liar." Aven leaned back over her, his unnaturally large cock brushing against Verena's thigh. "You have yet to even look at me, Princess."

"Because I am being respectful, unlike some who believe it is perfectly adequate to strip in front of someone they hardly know." Verena blushed, and it spread across her shoulders. The heat she knew well grew at her core, need.

"Not what you were saying when I was pounding your g-spot with my fingers earlier." Aven grabbed hold of her hand, placing it on his dick. Her smaller fingers were cool against his warm appendage. He watched her blush creep farther down her neck as she took hold of him entirely.

"I most definitely was not." Verena lied through her

teeth as her hand stroked him.

"Don't start what you cannot finish, Princess."

"I am positive we've been here before, and if memory serves," Verena gripped him harder, stroking him earnestly. "I handled it just fine this morning."

Aven opened his mouth to respond when light knocks on his door sounded.

"Aven? You need to get a move on, my dear. We will meet you outside to walk Verena down." Katherine's raspy voice alerted the two that they were there for a reason.

"Coming, grandmother!" Aven hollered back as he untangled himself from Verena. "As much as I want to fuck you until you're screaming, Princess, it will have to wait."

"I'm not a screamer." Verena squeaked.

"You will be." He growled.

Verena tutted as she moved to the edge of the bed, watching Aven intently.

"Don't panic, okay?" Worry etched Aven's face.

Verena nodded, unable to make any promises as she was unsure what would come next. Aven hunched over and groaned. Within seconds, a massive light-brown wolf stood in his place. Verena scuttled backwards. Logically, she knew it was Aven. Illogically, she saw an enormous wolf standing in the room.

"Aven?"

The wolf nodded, pawing at the ground.

"You're not going to kill me or anything, right?"

The wolf snorted, sitting on its haunches.

"I'm really talking to a wolf." Verena shook her head, standing up. "Verena, you might as well check yourself into a psych ward." Tentatively walking towards the wolf, her hand stretched out. "Nobody would believe anything I said, anyway."

The wolf snorted again; if Verena were asked later, she would have said the wolf was laughing.

"I kid you not, if you bite me, I-" Verena looked around in panic, not noticing anything to defend herself. "I don't know what I'll do, but it'll be something."

The wolf stood up and sauntered over to her.

"Aven, this is not funny." Verena covered her eyes with her free hand, barely peeking out from the space between her fingers. Soft fur brushed against her hands, and her breath hitched.

"You aren't going to kill me?" She dropped her hand from her face and squinted at the wolf, rubbing his head on her hand.

The wolf looked at her, head aslant, expression indignant, as if saying: *obviously not.*

"I need to get my head checked." Verena looked at the wolf. "Damn it all." She stepped closer and buried both hands in his fur.

The wolf growled softly before moving towards the door, looking back at her. "Right, no hands. I'll get it. Let me use the bathroom first." Verena ran off to the restroom and was back in record time. Her face was slightly damp, and the wolf barked, laughing at her.

"Did you just laugh at me?"

Nod.

"Asshole."

The wolf nudged the door again ardently.

"I'm going, hell, eat a plant or something." Verena opened the bedroom door and proceeded to walk through it first.

The wolf followed after, nipping softly at her hands.

"Do you eat when you're like this? Ow, you ass. What did I tell you about biting?" She flicked his ear.

Verena walked down the stairs and paused at the bottom. Watching the wolf Aven come down was the highlight of her night. His paws were too big for the steps, almost missing a few and jumping the last handful. He nudged her toward the back of the house before leading her to the backdoor.

"Are you nervous?"

He snorted.

"I will take your snort as a no." Verena rolled her eyes. "You are quite big, though." Verena wasn't lying this time. Aven, in human form, was well over six foot five. Verena estimated he was closer to four and a half feet in wolf form, from the ground to the top of his shoulders. Verena made a note to find a measuring tape and determine how large he was later. He was even wide in wolf form; his muscles moved with purpose as if Gods had sculpted his body. His human silver-grey eyes carried over into his wolf form, reminding Verena of molten silver.

They continued outside in silence, Verena opening the back door for him as he steered them towards his family. Merridayn, Elion, Cavanaugh and Katherine all stood in a circle, their hushed voices registered to Verena's newfound hearing.

"Do you think this was a wise choice, Elion?" Katherine asked.

"I'm not sure, mother. I can only hope Aven prepared her for what she will see tonight."

"Let us hope, dear. I have confidence in our son." Merridayn reassured them.

"And if she doesn't listen? He will be forced to choose between protecting her and completing his challenge." Katherine hissed.

"I will hold her back if I need to, grandmother." Cavanaugh, the voice of reason.

"Enough, they just walked outside." Elion snipped as quietly as he could.

"We are much too far for his ears to pick up what we are saying, son."

"We are for him, mother. But I am unsure about her since we gave her the infusion." Elion chastised his mother. "You know the stories. They are stronger and faster. We can only assume her eyesight is better, her hearing is elite, and she is staring right at us."

Verena and Aven strolled up to the group, Verena looked at each one of them individually. Merridayn glanced at her husband, Elion bristled. Verena knew they realised she could hear them and had listened to every word. One eyebrow raised in defiance as if she was confirming their suspicions.

"Are you ready, dear?" Katherine broke the silence, looking at her grandson and Verena.

Aven nodded, shaking his fur out.

"Verena, I believe we forgot to introduce you to Jasper, Aven's wolf." Merridayn entwined her hands together, the picture of etiquette.

"Jasper?" Verena questioned.

The wolf, Jasper, looked up at Verena.

"Yes, his name is Jasper. While Aven and Jasper share the same life, Aven is human while Jasper is the wolf. They are much alike but do have their differences." Cavanaugh offered Verena his arm.

"How does it work?" Verena wrapped her arm around the offered limb. The group walked towards the ring.

"The easiest way I can explain it is that when Aven is in human form, Jasper can talk to him through his mind. Jasper can feel, hear, and smell everything Aven does, but it feels dull. It is the same when Jasper is present. Aven is there, just in his mind." Cavanaugh walked leisurely, the ring less than two hundred yards from the cabin.

"So it is like an out-of-body experience? Where you can be present but not completely."

"In some ways, yes. What a great explanation." Cavanaugh beamed at her, pleased she could keep up with him.

"Interesting. How do you know his name is Jasper?" Verena was staring off into space in Aven's general direction.

"Because he told Aven when he shifted for the first time at eight. Aven then told everyone." Cavanaugh's tone remained patient, allowing Verena comfort in her questions.

Verena didn't have any other questions, so she looked forward, the ring coming closer and closer. Jasper padded up to her, rubbing his head against her legs. Verena rubbed his head; he essentially acted like a massive puppy. The thought made her heart skip. She had always wanted a dog as a child, but Abigail always said she couldn't have one because she was allergic.

What horse shit, isn't it? Can't have a dog because you're allergic, but your mate...

Still so strange.

Mate.

Verena shivered involuntarily at the thought.

Your mate turns into a massive dog.

"Jasper is about to go into the ring, Love. Did Aven tell you the rules?" Merridayn's voice snapped Verena out of her internal rage.

"Yes, he did, but he also promised I could talk to her first."

Merridayn looked at her, understanding washed

through her eyes, her features twisting into sorrow and regret.

"Very well." Merridayn smiled at her. "But do remember not to enter the ring. Even when you are questioning her."

"I won't." Verena bristled, already having been warned many times by Aven.

"Get your filthy hands off me, you bitch. I can walk by myself." Verena rolled her eyes. She knew the shrill voice. The voice she used to recognise was her mother.

Some mother, huh? Went right out the window, didn't it?

"I don't give two flying fucks if you can walk by yourself. Alpha told us to escort you to the ring. Mutt." A male she had yet to meet threw her into the pit.

"Fucking pigs." Abigail spat.

"The only one here who is a pig is you, *Mother.*" Verena stepped into the torches' light, her voice dripped with venom. "Pardon me, you aren't my mother, right?"

Abigail went to speak, and Jasper growled loudly.

"I didn't need an answer. It was rhetorical, but you wouldn't know what it meant, would you? I am curious about a few things." Verena crouched near the edge, not daring to enter. "One, why would you voluntarily take me in if you couldn't give a damn about me? Two, why would you pretend to care when your *husband* hit me, day after day, for years?" The crowd visibly grew angry at the revelation. "Three, did my parents ever mean anything to you, or was it just a means to an end?"

Abigail blanched, knowing every scheme she had planned was coming unravelled.

"Oh yes, I know about the money my parents left for me to be given a wonderful life. The trust my parents put in you to keep me safe, and all you saw were dollar signs."

Verena looked at her nails. They were deadly as is. She flicked dirt out from under them. "I was dying, Abigail. Dying. I was supposed to be around my kind, so the magic in my blood didn't go dormant. But you sure fucked it up, didn't you? Where's my money, Abigail? We lived like shit, less than shit. So, where is it, *Abigail?*"

"You want honesty? Fine." Abigail started to stalk towards Verena. Jasper let out a low growl in warning.

"I want honesty, yet I expect nothing but lies from you anymore. Give it your best shot. Impress me."

"First, I took you in because of the money. That should have been easy to figure out. You were my cash cow, my ticket to getting anything I wanted. My entire life was nothing but a struggle while you were sent here with enough money to feed the country. When Heathrow came stumbling in with the Belmont's in tow, holding you in his arms. Our plan was formed. You weren't yet a handful of days old and already filthy rich. Second, I didn't give a shit about Colin beating you. I knew the whole time and voluntarily looked away. Because if he was hitting you, he wasn't beating me. Again, another means to an end. He paid for everything while we lived with him." Abigail took another step towards Verena.

"I figured you knew; it was obvious. How could you not? It happened for years unless you really are oblivious." Verena flicked her hair over her shoulder. "I wouldn't put it past you, though, to be stupid."

"Third, your parents didn't mean a damn thing, little girl. They gave their lives up for what? They didn't end the war. They didn't change anything. They died because they were too fucking selfish to fight back."

"Selfish! Francis and Jerifeyn Nightingale died to protect everyone after the Mordinians *bound him*, releasing

him from Dremora! And you fucking know it, Abigail."
Elion yelled, furious Abigail would disrespect the two
bravest people the world had ever met.

"Yes, selfish, *alpha*. Because if they weren't, they would
still be here taking care of their fucking brat instead of
everyone else." Abigail took another step toward where
Verena crouched. Jasper moved to stand between Abigail
and Verena. "Lastly, your money is long gone. I spent it the
second it hit the bank accounts on things I wanted. I let
you starve, hoping you would just die from malnutrition.
Little did I know you'd survive like the roach you are. If I
had my way, I'd have let Colin continue."

"Thank you, Abigail, for giving my son full reason to kill
you." Merridayn stepped forward.

"The little bitch son of yours won't even come close."
Abigail stripped out of her clothes, shifting into her wolf
seconds later.

"If he fails, Abigail, there are plenty of other wolves
here waiting for the signal after hearing what you did to
a child." Merridayn's voice echoed through the ring, and
the spectators yelled words of acknowledgement.

Chapter 12

VERENA

Verena watched as Jasper began to circle Abigail. She deliberately positioned herself at the edge of the ring in a subtle attempt to assess her options. Her judgement was machiavellian at best, deceitful at worst. Inner turmoil fought against the promise she made to Aven. Verena wanted her revenge. The deafening crowd immediately silenced. Jasper covertly shortened the radius around Abigail. Verena's attention switched from Jasper to Abigail, gauging her. Abigail was significantly smaller than Jasper. While Jasper was quickly pushing over four and a half feet, Abigail could be estimated at about three foot eight. She found herself embittered at how immensely impressed she was as Abigail had the nerve to reveal all the information she had. The more Verena assessed Abigail, the more she realised she was someone who only cared about herself and had no regard for others. A sense of nausea settled in Verena's body as she surmised she had fallen victim to a narcissist and sociopath.

"Come stand by the fire, Verena." Cavanaugh brushed her shoulder, warning Verena she was standing too close to the ring for his comfort.

"I'm fine here, Cavanaugh. Thank you, though." Verena refused to move from her crouched position. She wanted to see every inkling of the fight without hindrance. She tried to be as close as possible if she could not join the fight.

"Jasper said he would feel safer if you were further away, so there is no risk of Abigail pulling you in." Verena's face shot up to meet Cavanaugh's.

"Jasper?" She pointed to the massive wolf in emphasis. "Jasper said he would...excuse me?"

"I see Aven failed to tell you everything werewolves are capable of. I will let him explain the rest, but we can communicate through our minds. It is easier to do so when you are family, but all wolves in a bonded pack can talk to each other telepathically."

"Are you having a laugh?"

"No, this time, I am serious."

"It sure seems like you are having a laugh. You are trying to tell me you can talk to him through your mind."

"Verena, it is true. I promise you."

Verena could see the truth in his eyes, and she acquiesced. She didn't have the energy to contemplate his words at the moment. Adding another bullet on the list of things she needed clarification from Aven later.

"I want to stay here, Cavanaugh. I need it." Her eyes were pleading, and she bared her soul to him for a split second.

"Fine, just don't do anything dumb." Cavanaugh relented and walked back to where his family stood.

Verena watched on as the two continued to circle each other. Neither Jasper nor Abigail had feigned an attack. She assumed this would continue until one could find the other's weak points or simply got bored. Considering how cavalier she knew she could be, Verena secretly hoped Abigail would launch first. Verena noted she could hear both heartbeats. It surprised her. Abigail's was rapid, while Jasper's maintained a steady rhythm. It was as if signalling to the world that Jasper was collected, halcyonic in battle, a sign of confidence. While Abigail's outward arrogance was nothing more than a false bravado, Verena laughed. The woman she knew for so long was terrified, exposed by her own heart. The crowd began to get restless.

"Finish this, Aven!"

"Come on, she's nothing compared to you!"

Verena ignored most of the comments, finding them irritating, but focused on one in particular, a whisper under their breath.

"The wench doesn't deserve him."

She knew who it belonged to and smirked at the ignorance. Verena had not entirely grasped the situation she was in, but she had grasped enough. She knew that no matter the circumstances, Aven was hers.

"Did you not learn from earlier?" Verena mocked, hoping the werewolves had as sensitive hearing as she had.

"I could help you get what you wanted." Verena whipped her head around, trying to locate the speaker. Her soul knew who was speaking, and the memories of him rushed to the forefront again. "Just say the word, darlin'."

Where are you, scum?

"What could you even do about it?" Kessa asked him.

Abigail and Jasper were still circling. Verena watched as a few members drifted back towards the cabin. The cat-and-mouse game was becoming tiresome. Abigail stepped towards Jasper, and he took the opportunity to lunge. Teeth bared, paws gripped, and body wound tightly. Verena observed Abigail feigning right, making a meagre attempt to move out of the way. Jasper predicted the movement, angling his body in her new direction. His teeth scraped her occiput, then made a purchase in her left shoulder. Abigail ripped away, skin tearing open as she scurried opposite of Jasper. Verena curiously wondered if Jasper would kill her. He pivoted around her again, pushing her towards the area near Verena—a silent offering to his mate.

Fat chance, I deserve to be the one to end this.

Verena stood up, cracked her neck and stretched her limbs out. Her body felt powerful, her limits unfounded. She was eager to test them and hoped her prey took the bait Jasper had positioned for her.

"Verena, dear, are you o-" Merridayn was cut off as Verena stepped forward and jumped into the ring behind Abigail. The six-foot plummet rolled through her body, energising her.

"Verena!" Cavanaugh yelled, rushing forward before his father pulled him back. Abigail was oblivious to the predator who dropped in behind her.

"Stop, son. You know the consequences." Elion held on tightly, and Cavanaugh sank into his father's hold. His promise to keep Verena safe vanished into the air.

"How could she!" Cavanaugh cried. "She knew! Father, she *knew!*"

"She made her choice." Merridayn reached for her son.

"I never thought I'd see the day I would kneel to a Fae." Katherine grinned, appreciative. "This damn woman is going to make a fine Luna for this pack and an even greater Fae Queen."

"Luna?" Elion asked his mother.

"My boy, you are still oblivious after all these years." Katherine cupped Elion's cheek. "Yes, she and Aven are mates. Their bond has yet to be sealed but is already strong."

Verena was clueless about the goings behind her; her

only focus was the small brown wolf in front of her. Aven watched as she fell into the ring, silently cursing Jasper for putting Abigail into a position benefitting Verena. Looking between his family and his mate, he howled. Panic struck him hard. An insignificant part of him knew Verena was going to be stubborn. Aven wondered if Jasper had done so intentionally; he raged mentally. He found himself shocked as he realised most of him was weeping with pride. His Verena wanted to defend her own honour.

Verena snuck up behind the wolf, whispering into her ear.

"I see you."

Abigail jumped at Verena's admission. Verena dug her nails into both sides of the wolf's neck, piercing the thick skin. Blood dripped down her fingers and coated her fur. Abigail yelped, jerking herself free and stumbled into Jasper. Her shoulder wound exsanguinated, draining profusely to be joined by the new punctures Verena gifted her.

"Oh no, did I hurt you?" Verena let her hands hang. The blood dripped towards the ground. Her honeyed voice falsely layed on the concern. "Fantastic." She shifted her weight back, getting ready to strike. "Let's do it again."

Jasper took the opportunity of Abigail's distraction to sink his teeth into Abigail's flank. Verena's ears ignored the screams, concluding anything remotely small could make the woman howl. Verena grinned; her heart soared with the pain being inflicted.

"This," Verena yelled at Abigail, pointing towards the open wounds she sported. "This does not even come close to the amount of pain you have subjected me to over the course of my life." Verena bolted towards Abigail, crashing into the wolf and slamming her into the wall behind Jasper.

"What do you know?" Verena praised her body. "Didn't know I could do that."

Jasper circled around, pacing in a line behind Verena in case Abigail tried to run for it. His haunches lowered, his teeth dripping red. Jasper was delighted with the outcome of his mate's attack. His heart soared as he observed her. Aven and Jasper agreed Verena was perfect.

"You want to hear something fucked up?" Verena's hands pushed harder. "Granted, you can't respond, but I will say it anyway."

Abigail whimpered pathetically.

"There is a tiny voice in my brain screaming at me to kill you slowly, but I am not sure I want the therapy bill later." Verena forcefully pushed harder, a loud crack rang through.

Abigail screamed; she knew her ribs were broken. Using the distraction from her scream, Abigail surged forward, using the wall she was pinned against as leverage, barreling into Verena and knocking her onto the ground. What Abigail didn't expect was Jasper laying in wait for the moment she escaped to grip her by the neck again with his teeth. As if she was a ragdoll, he shook Abigail around violently while Verena stumbled to her feet.

"Fuck the therapy bill." Verena leapt atop Abigail, gripping her into a bear hug.

Spectators watched on as the wolf and Fae tumbled to the opposite wall. Abigail tried vigilantly to shake Verena off, unsuccessfully, as Verena punctured her fur again with fingernails. Freeing her right hand, Verena grasped Abigail at her elbow and pushed inwards. The crowd could hear a loud snap followed by another scream, Abigail's leg bent at an odd angle. Verena chuckled, her body vibrated with adrenaline.

"This is for the years you let him take advantage of me."

Verena's right hand found purchase again in Abigail's shoulder. Her legs gripped tightly around Abigail's flank. Verena let her left hand go as she grabbed Abigail's left leg. The next moment, Verena sent a powerful force at the arm, snapping it in two as well. Abigail fell onto the floor on her front two stumps, howling. Verena dismounted the wolf gracefully, leaving her back turned to Abigail. The crowd hooted at Verena's show of dominance, to turn her back towards an opponent.

"Enough yelling, you sound pathetic." Verena's haughty laugh came out in parts. "This is for me and my parents."

"Enough, little bitch." Verena's head lashed around, noticing Colin standing by the opposite edge of the ring.

"Or else what, *Colin.*" Verena's rage was overwhelming; she picked Abigail up and threw her into the wall he stood by. "Are you going to come in and *save your little wife?*"

Having watched the scene unfold at a safe distance, Jasper took a moment to lunge at Abigail. He had decided he was tired of waiting and wanted to enact his revenge. Verena watched as Jasper ripped Abigail's throat out with his teeth in her peripheral vision. Her focus was entirely in front of her. She was moderately irritated; he took her chance at complete revenge away. At the same time, another opportunity awaited in the form of the scum before her.

"Come on then." Verena held her hands out, an invitation.

Jasper, covered in blood and gore, pawed back behind her, baring his teeth. He had been hoping Colin would be ignorant enough to show up today. He sent a silent prayer to the Goddess for answering his request. Jasper promised himself this bottom feeder would suffer for every vile act he'd put Verena through. He only wished Verena could convince Colin to get into the ring; otherwise, he would need to find a different route to accomplishing his goal.

"Why should I give you the pleasure?" Colin sneered.

"Because we were betting you'd show up." Elion's voice came from behind Colin; having snuck up behind him, the two in the ring had not noticed. Elion's words were immediately followed by a shove, launching Colin into the ring. The crowd jeered. "Oops. Sorry, sleight of hand."

Jasper nodded towards his father, grateful the old laws now bound Colin. Jasper watched as his mate shook and tried not to double over in laughter.

"Oh, how the tables have turned, right, Colin?" Verena looked Colin in the eyes, visibly amused. "Did you know who I was too?"

"Of course I did; everyone did." Colin took a step towards Verena, and Jasper roared. "Every single person here knew about you, but nobody offered to take you in except her." He pointed towards the dead wolf, and his eyes glazed over in sorrow.

"You best watch your tone, beta." Elion's voice boomed. "We offered to raise Verena but were overruled by the council because everyone believed your wife meant more to Jerifeyn than us."

"Or else what, *alpha?* I am already here. In this ring." Colin seethed.

"While this is fun and all. Your voice is irritating." Verena interrupted. "It might be fun to watch Jasper rip you to shreds, so you can join your wife."

Jasper growled in answer, waiting for Verena to give him the signal.

"But this is my revenge." Verena bolted forward, her

body becoming more attuned to her newfound abilities. Even then, her legs burned from the previous fight.

"You won't win, cunt. I have years over you." Colin braced himself for her onslaught.

"It's a great thing you still have no idea what I am capable of." Verena adjusted her trajectory, slamming her body into the ground to slide into his legs. "Remember when I stabbed you while you were trying to beat me?"

The crowd roared; their anger was palpable.

"I'd do it again in a heartbeat." Colin tried to scramble away from her.

Verena reached out as she slid past him, burying her blood-soaked fingernails into his ankle, pulling him towards her. She heard a loud crack as Colin's nose broke against the ground with his impact. She watched the foul git begin to shake, his transformation beginning.

"Oh no, you don't." Verena swung her body around, using the momentum to push herself to her knees. "You're not allowed to get off easily. When I kill you, you will look me in the eyes and die knowing you were bested."

Colin let out a pained groan. His body was taking longer to shift.

"Oh, lucky me. You're drunk, aren't you? Don't answer. You are always drunk. I bet your wolf is hating it, isn't he?" Verena stood up, her hands covered in dirt as she pushed her boot into his upper thigh. "Is he screaming at you for hindering him? Didn't you know alcohol is a poison? Silly me, I forgot, you're too dumb to know a damn thing about biochemistry."

The crowd burst into laughter, and Verena chuckled. Verena looked down at the man hunched over on the ground. She leaned to grab hold of his ankle. With one hard tug, she ripped his leg off at the hip. Blood sprayed across her face, her stomach recoiled in disgust. Ripped flesh and a protruding femur dragged across the floor. Colin screamed belatedly, as if his muddled brain couldn't comprehend what happened. Verena toyed with the removed appendage, throwing it at his head.

"I'm going to need at least three showers, but it is completely worth it." Verena watched as Colin still attempted to shift through the pain and loss of limb. He crawled forward, a pool of blood beneath him. The ground lapped it up greedily.

"How captivating to watch you debase yourself and comprehend the magnitude of disgrace you are." Verena languidly kept pace with him, entertained with the notion he could escape her.

Jasper circled around, watching with pride as his mate enacted her revenge. His only wish was to be able to do it himself. He watched Verena stroll away from taunting her prey to the edge of the ring. As she stretched, reaching for one of the torches, Jasper tilted his head, confused. Her plan of action escaped him while the crowd was contemptuous.

"Does it hurt?" Verena feigned apprehension.

Colin groaned, unable to form words of any calibre. He spit out blood in vile discontent.

"Oh no, I'm shaking in these Jimmy Choo's. Whoever will come to my rescue?" Verena pressed one hand to her head, a mocking sign of being a damsel in distress.

Jasper snorted, thinking back to their earlier conversations. The crowd laughed, her theatrics not lost on the company. He scrutinised her actions as she snapped a torch off at the base and walked towards Colin with the flame brushing the ground. She looked like a vengeful Angel, her pale skin outlined by the hue of fire. The dragged torch licked at the spilt blood, leaving small pools of flames behind—a trail of retribution left in her wake. Jasper observed with satisfaction as he figured out Verena's plan. Colin was ignorant of the woman approaching him, and the crowd gave nothing away. Jasper could see his packmates looking on, some with horror but many laced with admiration. His heart swelled with love for his mate.

Burn it, my love.

Red eyes?

Tell me you are not referring to me as 'red eyes.'

What else am I to call you? You still haven't told me a name.

Verena leaned down, dragging Colin back to her by his remaining leg.

"Where are you going to go, Colin? You have nowhere to run to now." Verena brought the torch to his bleeding stump, relishing in the scream he released. "No one to help you."

Burning flesh seared through the air, Jasper revolted backwards. His nostrils were overwhelmed. He could sparsely make out what Verena was saying to him over the accolade from the crowd.

"This is for all the times you hit me. All the seconds I spent crying out for someone to help me. Someone to make it stop." Verena slammed the torch back against the bloody stub. "Every moment you made me regret ever being born. This is for all the pain, all the nightmares, all the disappointment I have faced. Because of you."

Verena launched the torch away, her face laced with tears. Her hands were shaking, and she could not hold the torch steady. She looked down, her reflection showing in the pool she stood in. In the moment, she bared her soul for the world to witness. But now, she was disgusted with what she saw looking back at her.

Rip the other one off, love. Make it to where he can't run from you again.

Verena watched as Colin completed his shift. A mangy brown wolf half stood in his place. His hind leg, still missing, caused him to wobble. She reached out to grip his other leg when the wolf turned far too quickly for an animal with three legs to bite into her arm, drawing blood and ripping tendons. Verena screamed, and Jasper bolted towards her.

"You little shit." Verena bit out.

Jasper brushed up against her back. Verena listened to the scream of agony in her mind, her uninjured hand weakly coming up to her head—a meagre attempt to drown out the screaming.

Am I the one screaming?

Verena!

Red?

Verena watched Colin bolt up the stairs, barreling into the few people standing there, vanishing into the forest. Nobody around them moved, too focused on the woman leaning heavily against Jasper, who protectively curled around her. She looked down as her blood pooled out of the wound, an odd red glow coming from the drops.

How the tables have turned.

Verena? Are you hurt?

Red?

Talk to me, Verena.

Can you hear me?

"Verena!" Merridayn rushed towards the ring.

I cannot lose you too...

"Stop!" Katherine bellowed.

"She's hurt, and you want me to stop?" Merridayn

yelled back at her mother-in-law.

"Don't enter the ring." Katherine pointed towards the pair. "Watch."

Merridayn focused her attention on the wound, on Verena, and her son. Her worry amplified as she was sidelined. Her training as a nurse caused everything in her to protest as the need to assist forcefully reared its head. She gasped, her hands coming to cover her mouth. The crowd mimicked her notion as they all watched on. Verena's body began to glow, a bright white light emitted from her.

"What's happening, mother?" Elion questioned. "You know something, I am sure."

"I've heard whispers of this, but nobody has been able to confirm it. Look at where Verena and Jasper meet. The light being emitted is strongest there, right?"

"Yes, I see it," Elion murmured.

"Verena is not a wolf, so it should not be possible..." Katherine trailed off. "If what I know is true, Jasper and Verena are true soulmates."

"Soulmates? Mother, what a fairytale. A children's story you told us at bedtime."

"It's not, son. If the recorded history is correct, it has happened a few times."

"What does it mean for what is occurring now?"

"Jasper is healing Verena, unintentionally, I suspect." Katherin nodded towards the pair.

"Elion, it's true. Look." Merridayn moved closer, watching as Verena's wounds began to close.

"By Goddess." Elion was stunned. "Though nothing comes for free, does it, Mother?"

"No, son, it does not. The texts state Jasper can only do it a handful of times before it could kill him."

"How?" Elion questioned.

"How what, son? You must be more specific." Katherine chastised.

"How will it kill him?"

"I'm not sure. We will need to ask the council."

"Look, there's a faint trail leaving Verena." Merridayn interrupted. "To where?"

"Interesting." Katherine looked on.

Verena was bewildered as her arm pierced itself together, slightly panicking about the situation. She gripped Jasper fiercely, not wanting to let him go. Her heart filled with increasing ire as she realised Colin had run off. She vowed to herself she would hunt him down, no matter where he was and finish what she started.

"Keep running, Colin. Don't ever stop. Because once you do, I will find you. And when I find you, I will rip you apart." Verena's voice dripped with venom. Her vow to find Colin filled her with motivation. Unbeknownst to her, a small blue tattoo marked her shoulder. The vanishing pain in her arm masked the pain of the burn.

She needed a shower, a nap, and maybe a stiff drink after this whole ordeal was done. She shuddered at the thought of the dreams she would be having from this occasion, her mind questioning who she would need to contact to find a therapist.

"Verena?" Aven's naked body pulled her into him. She was unaware that Aven had shifted back, lost in her thoughts. "Let's return to the cabin and get you washed off."

"Are we allowed to?"

"I hope someone tries to stop me."

"I love this idea." Verena blushed when she came to the realisation Aven was naked. "Aven!"

"What?"

"You're naked!"

"Your point?"

"There are people around! Your parents!" Verena blushed harder. "Your grandma!" Verena tried covering him up with her body.

"Are you enjoying the show?" Aven threw his hands out wide as he addressed the crowd, his hard cock saluting everyone. The crowd jeered.

"Oh my," Verena whispered.

"Fantastic." He mockingly bowed. "We will bid you adieu. I have a mate to clean and fuck into oblivion. Good-night."

Chapter 13

VERENA

"Verena..." Aven pressed Verena against his bedroom wall, his member dug into her stomach.

"Aven!" Verena squeaked, surprised yet exhilarated.

"I have waited to do this all goddamn day, woman." He ran his hands across her arms, his fingertips sent shivers down her spine. His heartbeat was the sound of war drums to her ears. His hips ground into hers, and the moan slipped from her lips. The verbal confirmation she was acceptable to his ministrations encouraged him to continue his purview of her. The wall became enticing as he pushed her farther in.

"Aven." Verena rested her hands upon his chest, her heart swooned at the firm muscle she suspected from earlier but could not determine with certainty.

He didn't move, his attention elsewhere as she tried pushing him off her again. Her self-consciousness flared up, not wanting him to think she was disgusting. The years of bullying over her appearance from her classmates wore her down. Her tendency to believe she was less than reared its ugly head. She pushed against him again. Her need to escape and prepare for their combining was pounding. She knew it was an unreasonable self-doubt. Aven already told her she was beautiful. She just could not escape the urge to look and be better. Considering everything he had done for her today, he deserved the best, standing up for her against Abigail and allowing her to enact her revenge against the woman. However, her self-conscious awareness taunted any viable thought she had about her appearance. She was covered in blood, potentially skin and other parts of Abigail. Her stomach rolls in disgust with every passing second of knowing what she was covered in.

"Hmm?" He hummed, bringing his head down to her shoulder and leaving soft kisses along her trapezius.

"I need a shower." She protested, but her body defied her words. "I feel disgusting, and every second, I feel as if I will vomit if I linger on the thought for too long."

Aven mumbled something incoherent. Verena struggled against him, her heart begging her to give in while her nostrils were repulsed by her own scent.

"Aven Belmont!" Verena said with ferocity, commanding his attention.

"What?" He looked at her, lust coated her eyes.

"I need a fucking shower." Verena pushed against him again, harder. She watched as he stumbled backwards, her strength was more than she intended. Her tone left her reeling in shame. "You can join me if you want, but I am taking a shower first."

"Okay, okay." Aven held his hands up in surrender with a devilish smirk. "I'll be good."

Verena nodded her head in gratitude, sashaying off towards the bathroom. She was immensely grateful for the opportunity to get clean. Not wanting to face what she knew would be a gruesome visage, she avoided looking at herself in the mirror. Divesting herself of her clothes as Aven whistled from the doorway, she blushed, not being used to someone believing she was beautiful.

"Stop looking at me all lovey-dovey. I just tortured people." Verena attempted modesty by covering herself up, losing her confidence from earlier when she invited him to join her.

"He does not deserve to be called a man. He is nothing more than a cockroach. The same could be said about Abigail, she earned her death." Aven stalked her, grabbing her chin to force her to look at him. "I thought you were the Goddess in human form when I watched you." He slammed their lips together, using his hands to grip her sides, pulling her closer.

He could smell how soaked she was, it filled him with primal need. Jasper howled in his head, demanding to seal the bond. Aven wanted nothing more than to do so but would settle with pounding into her delicious cunt until she couldn't walk straight for a week. He proceeded to tell her such. As he watched her cheeks turn brighter, his balls tightened.

"If we don't stop now." Aven rasped between kissing her. "I am going to bend you over the counter and slam my dick into you until you scream my name."

"What's stopping you?" Verena was breathless.

"A Princess I know stated she wanted a shower. I am attempting to give her what she wants." Aven groaned from Verena palming his erection. Her small, warm hands wrapped around him felt heavenly.

"The Princess best continue with her plans of showering then, wouldn't you say?" Verena backed away. He moaned, and she dragged her hand down him again before releasing him.

"You little minx."

"Am I?" She said as she turned around, stepping into the shower.

"You are going to be the death of me." He mumbled

under his breath, believing she couldn't hear him.

"Most definitely," Verena replied to him, smirking.

"Of course, you can hear me. Goddess damned Fae hearing." He stepped in after her, the water at his feet ran red with the blood she was shedding.

Aven reached around her and maintained eye contact as he grabbed hold of his loofah. He took the soap bottle she held, putting some on the instrument in his hand and rubbing the soap around to make it sudsy. Wordlessly, Verena understood what he was asking. She lifted her arms up a smidge, giving him access to her. He diligently scrubbed the blood and dirt off her. The drain eagerly devoured the vile remnants.

"Does this not disgust you?" She asked, borderline heaving from the scene.

"Not even remotely." Aven shrugged, humming to himself as he inspected her for any spots he had missed.

"How?" Verena's eyebrows furrowed in confusion at the expression. Any reasonable person should have been repulsed by her state of being.

"I suppose it is because I grew up a werewolf." He signalled for her to turn around. "Being one shaped my outlook on blood and gore. The community has many challenges all the time, such as wolves fighting amongst each other for ranking in the pack. Typically, I do not participate in these events as I am an alpha's son, but I have participated in a few for propriety's sake."

"This whole." Verena paused, her hands waving around the air. "Charade still doesn't make sense. Logically, I know you are not lying to me. I watched you change into a massive wolf in front of me. You were here one second, and a wolf stood in your place the next. However, there is still so much to wrap my head around mentally."

Aven had nothing to say to her. Instead, he wrapped his hands around her waist, pulling her closer. His gaze brushed hers, and she held it. Deviance smelted in her eyes as he leaned down to capture her lips in a bruising kiss. Their mouths moved on their own accord, hands exploring. Her skin felt heavenly, otherworldly even. His fingertips brushed her spine, trailing down each vertebrae. He purred as she shivered in excitement. His right hand cupped the bottom of her plump ass, his hand covered the entirety of her cheek. He imagined the view he would receive as he fucked into her from behind. Gripping her cheeks, using them to pound into her harder. Her small hands brushed against his pecs, stopping to pinch his nipples. He yelped loudly at the unanticipated retaliation she gave him, breaking their lips apart.

"Devilish woman." His left hand gripped her other cheek as he picked her up and slammed her against the tiled wall. His mouth captured hers again as his cock brushed against her cunt.

"God, fuck me already." She dug her nails into his shoulders. The elevation change no longer startled her.

"God isn't here, Princess." He murmured against her lips. "Aven will have to do, I'm afraid."

Dropping her back onto the ground, he sank to his knees. He was palming her thick thighs and pushing them apart. She stared down at him, curious as to his expectations.

"What are you doing?"

He refused to answer her, choosing to forcefully push her thighs farther, his nose coming up to meet the apex of her legs. He breathed in her sweet musk; the dormant predator in his mind momentarily took control, demanding to take her into his mouth immediately. Aven could not find it in him to argue, surrendering to his base instincts. He growled imminently as his mouth made contact with her. His tongue flicked out, and he was floored with awareness. She tasted delightful, her smell was identical to her taste: peaches, honey and a hint of cinnamon. His hands gripped her thighs harder as he licked her from base to clit. Her folds parted for him, her nectar flowed without hindrance. She quipped slightly as his tongue circled her clit, shrouded by a hood, he used his hand to expose her nub. Taking her between his teeth, her moans gained strength with his small nibbles on her exposed nerve.

"Oh yes." Verena groaned, her hips bucking into him. "Oh fuck."

"Do you want me to stop?" His eyes flicked up to her, his tongue continuing his onslaught on her pussy between words.

She grumbled something unintelligible, incapable of cognitive thought. He chuckled against her, the vibrations sending her over the edge. Her climax sent her body into the wall behind her, her knees buckled, and her orgasm coated his lips.

"I'm not done with you yet," Aven whispered into her thighs, her eyes rolled.

"Can't wait." She managed between breaths. Her body was shaking profusely.

Aven managed to turn the water off blindly as he rose from his knees. He pulled her back into his arms with ease. Their bodies were soaked, his cock didn't care. He needed her, all of her. Using his elbow to slide open the shower door, he shifted her weight to free a hand to open the bathroom door. The last blockade before his bed, when he could thrust into her. She mewled into his ear, his heart swelled knowing she made those sounds for him.

"The things I want to do to you."

"So do them." She lifted her head defiantly.

"I will."

As Aven slammed her onto the end of the bed, her body gave a slight bounce. An overwhelming sense of lust filled his senses as he watched her breasts move as she fell onto the bed. He was sceptical if his dick could get any harder from her and concluded he probably could. As her legs fell open, baring herself to him, Aven's blood ran hot and a growl ripped from his chest while the knowledge she was his mate burned into his soul. He sent a silent thank you to the Goddess for giving him a perfect mate. Aven reached for her ankles to drag her closer, as he draped her knees over the edge of the mattress.

"Do you trust me?" Aven's tone held a hint of mystique, a tinge of seduction. Every particle of her purred in contempt, begging for attention.

"Yes." She breathlessly moaned.

He pulled cuffs from beneath the bed and shackled her to the posts. Her legs kept wide from the position she was in. She squealed, the tone of consternation unable to be determined for confusion, awe, or possibly anxiety.

"Aven!"

Aven ignored her protests, choosing to lick her from knee to hip. A shiver floored through them both, her attempts to break free, placated by the one simple action. A loud thud and a crack sounded in the room as Aven fell to the floor, hard. He didn't care for anything but the sight in front of him. The image of Verena earlier pressed against his shower walls, his face between her legs and her hands gripped in his hair, shattered all conscious thought.

"Aven?" Verena squirmed, wondering what was going

through his mind as silence filled the room.

"You are absolutely gorgeous, Verena." Aven looked up at her, meeting her eyes. "Has anybody told you?"

" N-not really." She blushed, self-conscious of herself.

Aven kissed the inside of her thigh, his fingers trailing over her soft skin as it erupted into goosebumps. One hand slid upwards, reaching for her glistening cunt. He gently stroked her, groaning as his lips met her skin when his finger circled the sensitive nerves of her clit. Her back arched, bringing her closer to his coquetting, while every part of her burned with desire. He locked eyes with her, taking in her flushed cheeks with a devilish grin. He slid one finger inside her, coating it in her juices. Her moans were delicious, he wished he could record them for later. Her hips bucked against him, impatient in her longing. Using his free hand, he pressed Verena's pelvis down, holding her in place. As she was held still, Aven added a second finger, stretching her wider.

"Goddess, you're so wet for me! "

He pulled his fingers out, watching in awe as they glistened. Bringing them to his lips, he sucked his fingers clean. The sight caused her blush to spread to her chest in embarrassment.

"Exquisite, but I am a hungry man." Aven wasted no more time teasing her as he dove in, his tongue flicking her bundle of nerves, earning a loud moan reverberating through the room.

He savoured her cunt like a man taking in his last meal. His lips closed around her clit. A vibrant cry tumbled from her lips, and she gripped the bed sheets as he sucked at her. Drinking in every ounce of her desire, his senses delighted in her reactions. A new sense of enlightenment came from the excitement coursing through his body. He pushed two fingers back into her, finding her spot, embedding stars in her vision.

"Aven." She moaned, his name falling from her lips as little more than a breath. Her head spun as she lost herself in his actions.

Aven's grey eyes filled with searing heat as they glanced up to catch the green of Verena's for a small fraction of a second. Every part of her tightened and tensed around his fingers. It was clear Verena was close to the edge of another orgasm. Aven could feel her attempts to withhold it from him. He increased his pace, growling into her folds, a demanding effort to bring her to completion. The sensations were too much for her to handle as she crested and her orgasm rocked her. A cry escaped her lips as his tongue found her clit once more. Long moments passed before she could do anything but gasp for breath; her mind was improvident, and her body was twitching from the aftermath of her climax.

Aven chuckled, licking his lips and fingers, then proceeding to press lazy kisses to her inner thighs. A sly grin spread across his face, and his eyes sparkled as he took in Verena, his mate. Her flushed skin and twitching body, knowing he was the reason for her reactions. As Verena's breath returned to her, she lifted her hand to beckon him to her. He acquiesced this unspoken request, his mouth finding hers in an instant. She could taste herself on his tongue as he shifted his body weight, resting most of it on top of her. She reached for him, her hand dragging down the length of him, savouring the low groan against his lips. Desire and arousal heated her blood again, anticipation swelled as the two both imagined him buried inside of her.

"I need you." Not a request but a demand, one Aven was eager to follow.

Without a word, Aven wrapped his hand around hers, halting her teasing strokes. He laced their hands together and dragged her hands above her head. He was acutely aware of her body arcing and her pussy brushing against him, every new sensation was driving Aven mad with need. He couldn't wait any longer as he gripped the base of his cock, rubbing it up and down her lips, gathering any moisture she had to help ease the size of him in.

"Aven, please." She begged.

With one thrust, he buried himself inside her to the hilt. Her core strained against his girth, pain initially flared but dissolved as fast as it came, turning to bliss. He stilled, allowing her time to adjust to his size before he began pounding into her at a frenzied pace. She cried out, his voice joining hers, as she tightened around him. It was invigorating the way her cunt clenched down on him. Her body melted into the bed, and her legs ached to wrap around him.

"Fuck these." He heard her whisper, followed by a loud snap as she broke the cuffs locking her ankles in place.

The cool metal dug into his hips as Verena's legs wrapped around him. Aven used the leverage her legs gave him to pull her against him, sliding his arm under her back as he moved into a kneeling position. New sensations came crashing into her as he was pushed further into her. Verena's head pressed against Aven's chest as he haphazardly moved them higher up on the bed, stopping to lay her against the pillows. He wanted their first time to be unique, a memory to remember. She wasn't just some quick romp in the sheets to be forgotten about the next day. She was the woman he was meant to be with for the rest of his life. A woman he wanted to cherish, love, and grow old with.

"Are you sure you want to do this now? Do you not want to wait for a better time?" Aven searched her face for any sign of apprehension or regret.

"Yes." She met his eyes, determined to make him understand she wanted this.

"You realise, Verena, you're mine. I won't ever let you go." His hair fell into his eyes, his gaze smouldering. "So, tell me right now if you still want this."

"I want this, Aven."

Her answer was enough for him; he moved his body to hover over hers. Aven's large hands encompassed her shoulders, his body taut, as he gave her one last longing look. He pulled out of her slightly, only leaving the tip of his bulbous head inside her. Pushing his restraint as far as he could before he bottomed out in her, his testicles slammed against her ass. The sudden clenching he felt around him made him delirious.

"Baby girl, I will not last long if you continue squeezing me," Aven growled as his body begged him for release.

He watched her pick her head up slightly to watch him disappear into her. His pride blossomed at Verena's silent admission of being intrigued. Sinking back into her inch by inch, he watched as her expressions detailed every ounce of pleasure she took from him. His face contorted in pleasure; his abs strained against his need. Every cell in him yelled to fuck her into the following year, to ensure her every need was met while simultaneously guaranteeing she would long for him.

Her moans set him aflame, and his need for her increased with each sound he earned. Verena reached up, gripping his back and digging into the skin beneath her fingers. As Aven let out a growl, Verena was riled up to continue. Her nails cut skin, the flesh tore under her fingertips. Ecstasy overtook her, she threw her head back and screamed. His pace quickened, each thrust harder and longer than the one before. Verena's legs tightened around his hips, squeezing hard against him before her body clamped down on him, seconds from another orgasm.

"Yes, baby girl, let go for me." He nuzzled her neck, wanting to feel her release.

"F-fuck, Aven." Verena's yells echoed throughout the house.

Aven continued, relentlessly pounding into her. He could feel her pulsing and then he felt the well burst. Her orgasm flushed through her harder than the first or second, her eyes rolled back in pleasure. His own were howling in need, but he wouldn't budge. Without warning, he flipped her over to her hands and knees and wasted no time before he slammed back into her. Aven intended to work her up again for a fourth time.

"Aven!" Verena groaned. "I'm not going to be able to walk tomorrow at this rate."

"My point, exactly." Each word was enunciated by his hips bouncing against her ass.

His balls were tight, threatening to spill any second. A luxury he would not give them until she climaxed another time. The sound of slapping pulsed through the room, his testicles brushing against her oversensitive nub. Aven reached around her and fondled the bundle of nerves just how she loved. Her cries joined the sound of his balls slapping against her.

"Aven..." She gasped. "I-I can't. Fuck, I can't."

"Yes, you can." His pace impossibly quickened again.

"A-Aven..." Her orgasm rocked through her before she could finish her sentence.

"Verena!" Aven roared, his climax unleashed as stream after stream pushed into her.

Verena collapsed into bed, exhaustion rearing. Aven rolled off and joined her other side. His eyes searched the room for water, locating a bottle on the dresser. Forcing himself up, his legs almost giving up as he braced himself against the wall.

"Are you good?" Verena held her chuckle as she witnessed him almost fall.

"Fine. I'm fine." Aven tried hiding his dilemma.

Struggling to reach the dresser, Aven was oblivious to Verena covering her mouth as she watched his legs shake uncontrollably.

"You don't look so well there." Verena pitched. "Legs a bit jell-o, hmm?"

"Oh, because you could do it any better, Princess."

"I could." Verena moved to the edge of the bed.

Aven watched as she stood up gracefully, her legs not buckling under her weight. Reaching the dresser quicker than he had been able to and took a long drink from the bottle of water presented.

"How?" Aven was dumbstruck.

"How the fuck have you forgotten you all gave me some sort of infusion?" Verena chucked the bottle at his head, watching his reflexes still able to catch it. "Since I woke, I have noticed many changes in my body. Namely, physically. My legs do not feel the strain as they should right now. I am chalking it up to the infusion."

"You have a point." Aven mused, his ego deflated a bit.

"I know I do." She returned to the bed, moving the blankets and curling underneath them.

"So." Aven began, looking sheepish. "Round two?"

Aven looked over at her when she didn't respond to him

to find her sound asleep, her body shutting down after the day's excitement had worn down. Smiling, he joined her in bed. He ran his hands over her face to smooth out the pooled hair.

"Thank you, Goddess, for sending me an amazing mate." Aven kissed her forehead. "I will protect her with everything I have."

Chapter 14

VERENA

Verena awoke to a darkened room. The outlines of what appeared to be furniture were blurry. She stood in the middle of the large room. She stepped back after hearing someone on her left. She hit a hard surface. Her hand shot out to feel for her surroundings. Rough stones greeted her on both sides. She could hear her heartbeat echo in the room. She inhaled, cardamon and a hint of salt flooded her nostrils.

Thinking upon it, Verena had a nebulous memory of grabbing the water from the dresser. Taunting Aven with her ability to get up without a struggle, and snuggling under the blankets. She faintly remembered his room having wood floors with a rug covering a more significant portion. The walls were painted, not rough or stone. Her senses were filled with the smell of soft vanilla and pine trees. Her face pressed against the hardened muscle of Aven, and his heartbeat flitted in and out of her sensitive ears.

Afterwards, there was nothing. She could vaguely remember them conversing and a wisp of voices from the halls. She braced herself against the wall she unintentionally found earlier. Her heart was racing, strangely not from fear but more so in anticipation.

The same footsteps from earlier came closer, and the outline of a body began to clear.

"I can feel you there." A deep timbre, the same tones she associated with the red-eyed man.

"Hello?" Verena voiced out. Hopefully, she wouldn't come to regret making her presence known.

"Verena?" He sounded worried.

"Red eyes?" Verena could see him searching for where she was. "Oh, Devil, it is. What's going on? Where am I?" Verena stepped out of the darkened area, which obscured her from view. Her eyesight was acclimating to the dim lighting.

"I should ask the same question." As he approached, she could see the key features of the man who stood before her. "Are you alright?"

"What do you mean, 'Am I alright?'" Verena scoffed. "I'm right here unless this is the afterlife. Then no, I would not be 'alright.'"

Always the theatrics with him. We can't just cut to the chase, can we? She thought, letting her guard down from watching the male before her.

He surged forward, sensing the distraction, not giving Verena adequate time to prepare, and pulled her into his arms. He was noticeably taller than she and Aven. Height was not the only difference, though; as far as she could tell, he was bigger, much bigger, in every aspect. His hand cupped her chin, forcing her to look up at him as his beautiful red eyes scanned her face. As he moved to look over the rest of her, she began to feel embarrassed.

"Thank the Demons." He pulled her closer again, enveloping her in his arms. Her cheeks flushed, her hands flew to his chest. Verena's head barely reached his abdomen, her hands cupped the ripples under his shirt. Her face flushed and heated more than she thought possible as she tried to look in any direction, but to him, a feat which proved impossible. She was a mere fraction of his size, a blade of grass compared to an oak tree.

"What the hell are you doing?" Her temper rose.

Who does he think he is?

I can hear you.

"What the hell! Get out of my head!" Verena tried pushing him off her but he persisted. "This is all a dream, right? A hallucination of all the stress I faced today. Yeah, makes sense. All I need to do is just wake up."

"You're in my head, sweetheart. Not the other way around." He continued checking over her, his hands seemed to grip tighter so she could not pull away. "I am so relieved to see you are not injured."

"Pause. We are not going to move past what you just said as if you didn't just say it." Verena pressed her hands against his sinfully toned chest. "I am in your dream?"

"My head, but yes."

"Obviously, smart ass. How the fuck am I-" She pointed at herself. "-in your head." She took the finger she used and poked him in the abs to enunciate her point.

"The same way you were in my head a few days ago," Kieran smirked. He was toying with her, learning all the buttons to push to raise her ire, learning how to rile her up.

"You are insufferable." Verena snarked, her eyes narrowing. She knew he was attempting to get a reaction out of her. She refused to give in to him, to give him what he wanted.

"Have you looked in a mirror lately?" He bit out, nodding in her direction.

"At least I am not some perverted menace who gets off on murder and pain." Verena huffed, trying to pull away from him. She was losing the game between them; he was pushing all the right buttons, and she was struggling to control her irritation.

"Are you sure, darling? You seemed pretty excited to partake in murder earlier today." He walked her backwards, feeling her body press against the wall. Leaning down sensually, his words licked her newly pointed ear. "Don't try throwing insults if you, too, are guilty."

"Whatever, red."

"My name is Kieran."

"Kieran?" The name felt sinful coming off her tongue.

"Kieran. Kieran Dremorta."

Verena's head tilted slightly, she felt she had heard the name before but could not remember from where. A nagging sensation in her brain irritated her, trying to recall the specifics. It was as if her innermost self couldn't let the mystery go; if she couldn't figure it out, her life could be on the line.

"Why am I here, Kieran?"

"I am not sure, I was going to ask you the same question. I can only presume you are asleep, which is the means by which you came. But the reasoning behind it eludes me."

"If my body is asleep right now, is yours as well?"

"Not necessarily, no; on the contrary, I am currently in weapons training while we speak."

"Should you not be paying attention? Sounds like an activity you'd want your full attention on." She looked up at him, and her stomach flipped. "On the off chance you get hurt, you know."

"It is not necessary. My body is capable of multitasking. I have lived long enough to be able to do both." He let her go, but not before squeezing her into him one last time.

She watched him fight within himself. Obviously, he wanted more, but he knew she wanted him away. The conflict seemed to flow from him into her. As much as she wanted him away, her own body seemed to betray her by the way her pants felt. In the short time they were together, despite the mental connection from the time of the infusion, at least this was her assumption since she'd first seen his eyes then. She couldn't believe she was this needy. Verena's face flushed again, wondering if he knew it as well. She couldn't believe he would be oblivious to such from how he acted.

"You've lived long enough?" Verena moved to perch on the edge of what appeared to be a chair. Crossing her legs in an attempt to hide her arousal. She was seeing Aven, or at least she thought she was. She would not allow herself to give in to the desire she felt for Kieran, she would not be known as a cheater.

"Yes, Verena Nightingale, I have lived."

"I did not tell you my name." Her eyes narrowed at him.

"You telling me your name is irrelevant. I already knew the moment you entered my mind the first time."

Verena watched as he strolled over to the opposite chair, gracefully lounging upon it. She came to the conclusion that this man could be in rags and still cease her heart from beating. The epitome of a King in front of his netizens. She momentarily envied his ability to embody class with ease.

"Also, you can cross and uncross your legs, my love. I could smell the need flooding the air the second your delectable pussy started begging to be filled."

Verena's brain chose to ignore his comment but her body betrayed her again by flooding her thong again. A wave of embarrassment hit her as she questioned her choice of panties. She watched him take in a deep breath, his eyes murderous for a flash of a second.

Perhaps I can use this to my advantage.

Perhaps I will let you, my little dove.

Perhaps you should stay out of my head.

You are in mine, your thoughts are subjective to my domain. And there is nothing in this room which isn't mine already.

"Who are you? And who am I to you?" Verena tapped her fingers against her thigh.

"I am Kieran, and you are my Verena." He seemed amused.

"I know my own name, thanks. You already told me your name; therefore, your entire sentence was irrelevant. Secondly, I am not a pawn you can own. I already have a partner, thank you." Verena held up two fingers, a physical count of the points she had made. He smirked at her. "You find this so damn amusing, don't you. You think you are so funny, huh?"

"Obviously." He leaned forward, his breath brushing her cheeks. "I will not deign to give you an answer about your pathetic little wolf you call 'partner.' The idea is insulting enough. Your dog is a flicker of dust in comparison." His ego was bruised, a flicker of flames in his red eyes at the mention of another. His barely contained growl shook through his chest, the vibrations felt in his feet.

"Are we going to get anywhere here at some point, or will you continue insulting me and Aven?" Verena flicked her eyebrow up.

"Ah, so the pup has a name? Aven?" He growled. "Cute."

"You are insufferable!"

"Do you know you are utterly marvellous when you get angry?" He shifted in his seat, the movement highlighting the growing tent in his slacks. She looked down at the bulge, her breath skipping. He was definitely bigger than

Aven, if the strain of his slacks were any indication. She shook her head, reminding herself she was with Aven.

"For the love of- will you answer my questions or not?" She watched him raise his hands, a sign of surrender.

"I yield, I yield." She raised an eyebrow at him. "For now." Verena barely caught his added jest towards the end. Her temper rose again as he let out a hearty laugh.

"Come closer so I can slap the arrogance out of you."

"Don't tempt me, darling." His voice deepened, her body shivered at the sound.

"You are unbearable." Verena rolled her eyes, gritting her teeth as they barred in a snarl.

"I can be helpful, if you ask the right questions." Kieran started, enunciating his words seductively. The way he curled them sent shivers down her spine. "Or if you were to strip naked and beg for it. I prefer a beautiful woman on her knees before me." Verena watched him shrug, insinuating there was something more to him than the words he was spilling.

"Fine, I can play your game." Verena glared at him. "For now." Taking a page out of his book from earlier.

"How exciting." He tapped his fingers on the armrest. The sensation sent ideas about what those fingers could do to her.

"Is this a duplicate of your bedroom?" Verena waved her hands around the room, indicating towards the entirety of it.

"Yes."

"How did this link between us come to being?"

"I cannot answer."

"Cannot or will not?"

"They are one and the same, are they not?"

Verena rolled her eyes, sliding over to sit in the chair

instead of perching on it. Her knees brushed against his; she did not remember the chairs being close enough together to brush against each other. Looking up at him, she noticed he was smirking.

"You moved the chairs closer together."

"Obviously."

"Why?"

"Why else?" He leaned forward, his shirt pulled against his muscles shifting. "To feel you against me again. To hear your heart flutter and to see you flush. It is intoxicating."

"Why do you care so much?"

He fixed her with a smelting gaze, his eyes burned with lust. Kieran's hands gripped the arms of his chair harder, the veins in his arm bulged.

"There are things better left unsaid but all will be explained in time."

"What can you tell me then because this is getting exhausting."

"Everything but nothing. Choose your poison correctly and you might walk away with knowledge."

"How old are you?" Verena leaned forward, her hair draped over her shoulders. She caught his gaze flicking towards the tops of her exposed breasts but he rapidly regained his composure.

"Nine hundred and seventy." He paused, bringing his hand up to his chin. "Or was it seventy-one? Semantics, I suppose."

Verena blinked at him, her brain attempting to comprehend someone his age and if he was jesting.

"Are you serious?" She looked at him, deadpanned.

"Depends. Is it winter on Alusso yet?" Kieran tapped his fingers against the fabric, looking away as if trying to remember what day it was.

"No, it's not." She said it as a statement, but it should have been a question. Why does it matter if it was winter or not?

"Then I am nine hundred and seventy."

"Is this some sort of joke?"

"Would you like it to be?"

Verena stood, the chair moving backwards slightly. The surprise did not faze Kieran in the slightest. If she could put a word to the action, she would say it turned him on because of the way he licked his lips and clenched his hands tighter.

"Oh darling, release the anger you carry. It is delicious." He crooked a finger at her, beckoning her to come to him. "Come now, let us see this righteous anger I have had many centuries to hear about. The power wafting off you in waves excites me."

"Centuries? I'm eighteen, I have not been alive long enough for your statement to be correct." Verena inched closer to him, her body moving without thinking.

"Mmm." Kieran released a low rumble. "You are mistaken, Princess."

"Mistaken?" She was even closer now. "Princess? You're on this too?"

Kieran spread his arms out wide, a mischievous grin on his gorgeous face. He scooped Verena into his arms in moments, settling her into his lap. The wind lapsed from her lungs, hair littered her face, and her hands gripped him. Every inch was toned, hardened and felt delicious against her. Kieran smirked, knowing if the tiny Fae moved slightly, she would feel the raging erection he held just for her.

"Yes, Princess Verena Halliwen Nightingale, I know exactly who you are, my love."

"Who am I to you, Kieran?"

"A person who was fated to be my equal in every way since the beginning of time."

Verena wiggled, her ass feeling every inch of his erection. A deep blush garnered on her face, her hands fidgeted, not knowing what to do. Her mind said she should feel offended as he did what he wanted. But her centre said she should feel excited and proud she had caught the attention of such a man. She looked to notice his deep red eyes were focused on her, his expression mixed with lust and something she couldn't quite place. His hand stroked her cheek, pushing the hair out of her face, thumb brushing over her lips. He looked conflicted, as if he wanted to kiss her, but couldn't decide if it would be worth it as it was only a dream.

"You don't make any damn sense." Her voice held little ire, her heart pounding harder and harder.

"Has anyone told you how beautiful you are?"

"I-i-i, what?" Verena stuttered over her words as her heart stuttered in her chest.

"You were made for me, Verena. In every aspect of the way, in every lifetime, you were made to be my perfect half."

"Were you made for me then?" Her hands sprawled against his chest, her fingernails digging in.

"I was." He leaned down to kiss the crown of her head, his lips lingered. "I was born to be yours, in every sense of the meaning. I have trained every waking second of every day to protect you. I have become a living weapon to ensure you are never harmed. I was raised to lead but I was born to kneel. And to whom, my love, is you. You say the word, and I will destroy the heavens and hells for you. Every inch of me belongs to you just as every inch of you was born for me." His words ghosted over her skin, shivering down her spine, igniting a fire she wasn't sure was there.

"Who am I, Kieran?"

"You, my dear, are the one they write stories about. You are my salvation, but..."

"But what?"

Kieran stared down at her, his plush lips turned downwards. He met her gaze; a single red tear fell down his cheek. His mouth opened in response, but no sound came through to her ears. Light filled the room, and Verena closed her eyes from the pain. Her hand came to rest over her face as the light began to burn.

"You are destined to destroy the world," Kieran whispered to the fading image of her. His hands gripped the chair roughly, and the wood cracked from the force.

Chapter 15

MERRIDAYN

"If I understand you correctly, Princess Verena was given one litre of blood approximately thirty-seven hours ago. When she was given the transfusion and now, you stated there were visible changes in her appearance while she was unconscious, such as hair growth, skin, nails, ears, and eyes. Shortly after becoming conscious, your son, Aven, reacted violently to her as the mating bond awoke. The Princess did not verbally accept or reject Aven. Still, she seemed to be accepting of the predicament she was put in. She became more agitated as time passed due to a lack of explanation of what was happening to her in a timely manner. An altercation between Abigail and the Princess resulted in a warrior's challenge. Abigail is now deceased, and Colin Saxon has gone rogue and has no current known location. You explained the circumstances to the Princess in moderation. Everything was fine; she was recovering in Aven's room, and now she will not wake." The elder looked between the four Belmont's, all four heads bowed down. "Am I missing anything?"

"Sir, there is-" Elion began to speak when Merridayn shot him a quick glare.

"What my mate is trying to say, sir, is there is something we would like to discuss with the elders privately?" Merridayn looked up, meeting each of the elders' eyes to show the importance of discretion. "I believe it would be in the Princess' best interest to keep the matter within a limited number of minds at the current time. As it pertains to the Princess, who is currently unable to speak for herself. In the short time I have known her, it is in my professional opinion she would prefer to keep the rest of her medical information to a small amount of personnel." Merridayn bowed her head again in respect.

A scoff was heard behind the group, indicating indignation and irritation. Elion clenched his jaw, knowing who was emitting the sound.

"What bullshit, Merridayn." Venom laced the speaker's words. "'In my professional opinion... What a mockery! The pointed ear freak show is in our territory. Far from her kind, and here you are, trying to 'keep her medical information to a small number of people.' At the same time, begging the elders to give over our resources to help her! You are part of the reason our numbers are dwindling with your inability to provide adequate pups. Or shall we forget when you were on your knees begging the elders to save your daughter? What-"

"Alexandar, you are dismissed." The elder's tone held no room for questioning.

"Sir, you cannot possibly-"

"I said you are dismissed, Alexandar Romanti."

Alexandar levelled the Belmont's with a stare which could rival the High Priestess when she was giving birth to Verena. The woman could stare into your soul without so much a glance. She knew everything about someone and their future with one look. Merridayn shuddered, shooting her mate a worried glance. They were not making any alliances with the Romanti's pack anytime soon.

Elion exhaled, saying a quick prayer to the Moon Goddess for allowing the council to hear his wife before subjecting judgment. Verena's predicament was not her fault. This fell directly on his and Merridayn's own laziness. They hadn't checked in on her well-being, hadn't been there when he saw the horror in her eyes every time she would come by. His own ignorance when he saw all the signs the girl was being abused. He should have opened his eyes and prayed the Goddess would judge him rightly for his ignorance when the time came. He would accept his punishments for putting the Fae Princess through so many hardships in his ignorance to protect his blood.

"This meeting is now at the end. The council will see the Belmont family in the sanctum. You are all dismissed."

Murmurs came from the rounds, the room emptying. The remaining pack leaders all mimicked Alexandar's disapproval. Their judgement of being dismissed as a potential safety concern was brought to their front door. The whole of werewolves have had seclusion for the past two centuries and were on the verge of shattering. All safety and peace potentially collapsed because Verena Nightingale showed up on their front steps, unconscious to boot. The blame rested on the Belmont's and each knew it. Merridayn watched her husband and son's expressions change from dreary to fatal. Her heart broke as she recognised what their face would not betray, but their body language did. She knew a war could be on their hands the second they walked out of the council's chambers—a war they had caused. The Belmont's followed as the council filled through the mahogany french doors behind the round high table.

The half-circle room they were just in merged into a large chamber. Bookshelves lined two sides of the room, and a large moss wall on the back wall emitted a soft rainforest feel. Wolves were nothing if not connected to the nature that created them. The centre of the room featured black granite tables, and eight high-backed wood seats sat behind them. Council members each took their place while the Belmont's came to stand before them.

"What is it you wanted to discuss in private, Merridayn?"

Merridayn looked up at elder Armand. He had changed minutely over the last few years. The laugh lines around his eyes were dominant. His hair had a few more greys than before. His hands started to thin, and more wrinkles had formed. His eyes, though, had changed the most. The eyes held so much love for his surroundings, so much compassion for his appointed role. Those eyes had dulled to ones filled with sadness and sorrow. It was as if the weight of the role had become too much to bear anymore.

"Elder Armand-"

"Speak freely, Merridayn. There do not need to be honorifics here." Armand held a hand up, gesturing towards the rest of the council. Their heads nodded in agreement, and they all bore the same look of exhaustion.

"Very well. Armand, Verena is soulmated with Aven."

The chorus of gasps was instantaneous. A few of the elders gripped onto one another while some leaned back in their chairs.

"Child, you do not mean what I believe you mean. It was a trick of the light, yes?" The soft-spoken man spoke outwards, the blindness he suffered from left him to speak in the direction he believed Elion was in.

"No, Hansen, it is not." Elion stepped forward. "I saw it as well during the challenge. They shared the light, which was visible to the whole pack. It was hard to miss from how blindingly bright it was."

"Why was it not reported immediately?! The blatant ignorance of the bylaws will not go unnoticed."

"Islabell, let them speak." Armand shot the outburst down.

"We are aware it was to be reported immediately, Islabell. We were doing such when Aven stormed out of his room in a panic, which is when we began the process of getting here. While our pack was with us at the cabin, my beta was not. He had been assigned to negotiate with the neighbouring pack." Merridayn could tell her husband was beginning to lose his patience. She knew she needed to wrap this up before something was to unfold negatively. She owed it to her son and Verena, her heart clenched thinking about her.

"When we were informed of her comatose state by Aven, I immediately began medical protocol. Her vitals were stable, and her appearance showed no distress. During the transfer, we noted she was moving a lot more. Her vitals spiked once during the transport and stayed elevated for approximately five minutes. She spoke three times in her state, but it was in Fae or Draconic. Nobody around could understand. We could not get a recording as she stopped by the time we could start recording."

"Does she respond to anything at all?"

"No, she does not. We have all tried to get her to respond with touch, sound, pain, and everything else we can think of. Aven tried holding her to get any sort of reaction, but she did not respond."

"Strange." Armand was pacing, emotions flickered across his face.

"There was one other thing, Mother," Cavanaugh spoke up from the doorway. "The golden light was highly visible between Aven and Verena, but there was another going in a different direction. It was faint, but it was still there."

"You are right. I had completely forgotten about the second." Merridayn smiled fondly at her boy.

"What bullshit!" High pitched and angry, a tone standard from Islabell. Her voice alone could wake the dead.

"A second?" Their voices whispered, shocked but curious. One could tell by the way their lilt increased near the end, a question needing to be answered. "How?"

"Where does it lead?" Armand asked, nearly drowned out by the others.

"Poor child." A softer woman's voice snaked around the rest, saddened by the circumstances.

"Interesting." Elder Heathrow voiced, he was known to speak only when necessary.

Everyone in the room stopped to look at the man who had led the pack for the last forty years. They were all expecting an answer in any capacity, holding their breath in anxiety. Armand met each and every eye, his expression turning grim with each passing head.

"I do not know." Elion let out, answering Armand's question, the one almost lost to the commotion of the room.

"A soulmate bond can be seen only under intense emotions between both parties—for example, stress, love, sadness or death. The soulmate bond can be seen shattering when one of the bonded passes. The bond, when visible, has more intensity the closer the pair are together. You stated it was blinding, which would make logical sense as they were in close proximity. However, with the addition of a secondary line going in the opposite direction of Aven and Verena." Heathrow left no room for anyone to interrupt him, though nobody would. The elder hardly spoke as is, and when he did, everyone listened. "You could theorise Verena is soulmated to a second person."

Everyone was silent. The only sound echoing through the room was the heartbeats pounding with the sheer amount of conflicting stances.

"Heathrow's statement is close to verbatim on the definition of soulmates. With the definition in mind, his theory would align. Verena could be soulmated with another, though never heard of in history, we could only assume it to be true until further information is gathered." Armand sat back in his chair, leaning heavily against the armrests. "For now, we need to gather more information on soulmates. Scavenge every pack library, the council's library, everything. Islabell, do you still have your contacts within the Mordinian's?"

"I do."

"Contact them discreetly and request a wide range of books, including any information they have on Fae mates. Remind them of the need for discretion."

"Very well."

"It will do none of us any good if their leaders find out we have been hiding the Nightingale Princess all these centuries. Especially in her current condition." Armand sat straight, his expression becoming more in tone with his position as he gave orders. "Merridayn, I am assigning you to the team to oversee Verena's healthcare while she is under these walls. We will keep her here until she wakes."

"I would be delighted, Armand." Merridayn smiled, grateful she could stay with Verena. She nodded towards the rest, looking back at her husband.

"Elion, Cavanaugh, return to your pack tomorrow. Give strict orders. Nobody is to speak a word of Verena, Aven, or what they saw. As far as they are concerned, Verena was never there. Aven was challenged by Abigail over pack drama and lost. Make something up if you have to. Come up with an excuse for why your Luna is not with you. Report back to me this evening what excuses you have come up with so the council can provide assistance confirming your claims."

"Understood." Both Elion and Cavanaugh echoed.

"Orla, do you continue your monthly communication with the Dremortas?" Armand turned to his left to face the petite black haired woman.

"Yes." Orla nodded, her gaze never leaving the Belmont's. She was watching them for something Merridayn couldn't quite put her finger on.

"Good. Fantastic." Armand stopped, looking at his hands. "I hate to put you in this position, Orla..."

"What is it you need, Armand?" Orla's heavy accent floated across the table.

"We need the Dremorta's information on mates as well." Armand looked up after the request left his lips, his face scrunched in worry. Was he afraid of angering the woman, or was it something else? What could there be to be scared of?

"This will not be an easy price to pay, Armand." Orla sighed, her eyes finally leaving the Belmont's to look towards Armand. She was biting her lip, flicking her attention between Armand and Islabell.

"I know, and I do not wish to pay it, but it must be done." Armand looked conflicted. He knew it was not the right time to ask, but he had already opened the door. He would now have to face the consequences.

"I will find a volunteer." Orla nodded her head again, affirmation she would carry out the order.

"Volunteer for what?" Islabell blurted, one could say she

nearly screamed it with how loud her voice was. Merridayn surmised this was a detail not all of the elder's knew about.

"The Demons trade slaves for information," Orla responded before Armand had a chance to break it to Islabell softly. "We will send a volunteer to be their slave in whatever capacity they require for a month. If they return, we give them enough funds and a home so they will not have work for the rest of their natural life." Orla was blunt, her hands crossed delicately behind her back. Merridayn knew the stance, the one where the player held all the cards.

"What do you mean, 'if they return?' How many times have you done this to our wolves?" Islabell slammed her hands on the table, standing up from her chair and the wood cracking under the force.

"One a month for the last twenty years." Orla recounted precisely, Merridayn suspected she could remember the names of every person she had recruited for their trade.

"One a month." Islabell sat down again, almost faint. "For twenty years."

"Yes."

"Two hundred and forty wolves. You have sent two hundred and forty wolves to become slaves to the Demons." Islabell looked between the others, gauging their reaction. Her anger returned as she noticed the rest had not reacted the same as she.

"Yes." Orla was losing her patience, her eyes narrowed in irritation. How long was this facade going to take before the infamous anger showed itself?

"How many have returned home?" Islabell eyed Orla, her lips curling to show off her elongating canines.

"One hundred and three." Merridayn could hear the sadness in Orla's voice, the despair for what she had done under the pretence of gaining information.

.

"One hundred and three?" Islabell repeated softly, shocked at the number.

"Yes." Orla's hand clenched together, the cracking of her knuckles as she tightened her hold, even Merridayn's hearing picked it up.

"YOU SENT TWO HUNDRED AND FORTY WOLVES, AND ONLY ONE HUNDRED AND THREE RETURNED HOME!" Islabell screamed. There was the infamous anger Merridayn had heard rumours of, her ears rang from the aftermath.

"Correct." Orla nodded again, another finger cracked. Merridayn wondered now if the cracking was standard knuckles popping or if she was breaking her fingers.

"And you have no remorse about it?" Islabell pointed at Orla, accusatory.

"No." Another crack, Orla did not flinch. Merridayn shared a look with Elion; his eyes widened momentarily.

"Over half of the wolves sent did not return home," Islabell whispered, her head dropping to look at the table. Were those tears coming to her eyes, or was Merridayn imagining things?

"Correct." Orla looked towards Armand for assistance. Their alpha shrugged. Merridayn knew he couldn't involve himself, though she suspected Orla operated under Armand's orders.

"Why?" Islabell spoke to the table, her head yet to rise.

"We do not know." Another crack, Merridayn knew now Orla was breaking her fingers to remain calm. A painful technique, Merridayn wondered when Orla began resorting to self harm to not lose control.

"Are they dead?" Islabell stuttered out, slowly raising her head to look at Orla. Malice and murder were present in her eyes. Merridayn moved closer to Elion. Should the elder lose control, she wanted as far away and behind her husband who she knew would get her out of the way.

"Again, we do not know." Orla bit out, her teeth nipping at her lower lip. Merridayn witnessed a droplet of blood pooling on her lips. She also noticed how Heathrow inched his way closer to Orla.

"So they are alive." Islabell leaned forward over the table, her teeth now fully elongated, causing a lisp.

"For the last time, we do not know." Crack, Merridayn shivered. She had counted five in the last few minutes. If she was correct, Orla had now broken five of her fingers. Heathrow was growing angrier, inching closer to Orla faster than before. His subtle movements now openly shown.

"What the fuck do you know then, Orla?" Islabell snapped, her fingers digging into the table, cracking it some more.

"Demons will not talk unless a bargain is made." Orla shrugged. The volunteers knew what they were risking when they signed up. "How do you think we have survived without a Demon army raiding our borders, Islabell?" She mocked.

Islabell rushed around the table towards Orla, hellbent on attacking. A loud, aggressive growl sounded from the centre of the room. The sound coming from Heathrow stopped everyone in their place, including Armand.

"Heathrow?" Armand walked towards him. "Is everything alright?"

"Get away from my mate, Islabell." Heathrow ground out. The remaining elders, including Orla, gasped.

"Heath..." Orla started. "I thought we would not tell them until later?"

"I cannot stand here and watch my colleague threaten

to attack you, flower." Heathrow walked over to cup his mate's face between his burly hands. The delicacy shown made Merridayn's heart stutter in remembrance of her own love.

"What an interesting turn of events. Though I cannot say, I am shocked." Armand clapped, embracing Heathrow's shoulder from across the table. "This will be something to celebrate once our sleeping Fae Princess awakens. For now, we must continue the path the Goddess has made for us. Let us return to our duties and meet again in a few days' time."

Everyone nodded before heading back out the door. Nobody said a word, and each kept their heads down. Merridayn kissed her husband on the cheek and hugged him goodbye. He looked at her longingly but pressed his head against hers. Merridayn knew the time apart would be hard but necessary. If only to protect the society they had all come to know. The peace they each fought tooth and nail for. All to ensure the sacrifices the previous generations had made were not in vain.

"I will see you in a few days, darling," Elion whispered against her forehead. His heart broke at the thought of leaving her behind.

"Protect our boys, Elion. I will be here for Verena. When she wakes, we tell her the truth and let her decide if we have damned ourselves to Hell for neglecting our promise to Jerifeyn." Merridayn stepped away from him, pressing her hands against his chest to push him into motion. She knew the feeling of watching him walk away would break her. She turned away first.

Chapter 16

MERRIDAYN

Merridayn walked towards the room they had placed Verena in earlier. Determined not to look back, one step after the other. Verena's room came into view as if time slowed to torture her. She knew she deserved the pain. Double checking the door tag on the right, her heart rate slowed momentarily.

Princess Verena Nightingale
Healer Gracella Joplin
Druid Nora Greenhaven

Her anxiety dulled in comparison to the pain and suffering Verena went through at the expense of her choices. Merridayn took a moment to observe her surroundings. Verena's door was white, almost pearlescent in colour. A gold tag placed near the top centre stated *'Iris'*, and the walls were porous and surrounded by moss as if the walls were a part of a tree. Entering the room, Merridayn noted the ground covered with sedum moss. A white plush bed graced the middle of the room, appearing to be made of clouds. Merridayn smiled, sending a silent prayer to the Goddess. Her heart swelled with relief, knowing Verena would be comfortable as her body adjusted to her new state. If she ever awoke from whatever plagued her.

Not if, Merr. When.

Birds chipped from the tree branches above, leaves

drooping downwards towards the ground. Reminding Merridayn of a willow tree, the sway of the branches moving softly to and fro. Small balls of light floated, adding a soft tone to the room. Soft echoes of water ran through the room. Merridayn looked around her, her eyes catching on a stream near the back of the room. Spotting a cavern opening at both ends of the room, she noted the stream did not have an ending. Darkness alluded from both openings. Her human eyes failed to see if the stream led to the next room.

Striding over and keeping as silent as possible, she adjusted her skirt and kneeled. Reaching a hand into the stream, the water was cool but not frigid. Merridayn looked around the room once more. A rouge smile played on her lips as she found what she needed. Bundled together by the sink were white hand towels. Collecting one, she dipped it into the stream. She wrung out the excess water, she strode to the bed. Her petite adopted Fae, eerily still in her bed of clouds, only her chest rising and falling, showing her still alive.

Heart Rate stands at 20 beats per minute. Breathing rate at two breaths per minute.

Perched on the side of the bed, Merridayn struggled to stay upright. Exhaustion slammed into her consciousness, her body fighting to stay awake. She patted the light perspiration on Verena's forehead using the towel she had dampened earlier. Instinct took over as she pulled the blankets closer around Verena. She wracked her brain on her knowledge of Fae anatomy, knowing they could slow their hearts to protect their bodies. Merridayn wondered if Verena's body forced the poor girl into a coma due to the infusion. She couldn't help but fear the overload of magic infused blood was too much for the malnourished child to handle. Merridayn's body went into autopilot, her brain shutting down as she went through coma protocols.

Ensure the patient's head is elevated in case of perspiration. Utilise a foam tongue depressor to wet the patient's mouth and lips to ensure the patient does not incur xerostomia. Maintain average body temperature, removing or adding blankets as needed. Intravenous fluids and nutrition. Potential catheter should it prove necessary. Roll every two hours to reduce the possibility of bed sores. Merridayn began the steps she could without requiring assistance from healers or medical equipment. She questioned how the Druids would go about Verena's treatment. She couldn't imagine Druids had IV equipment, blood pressure and heart monitors or anything of the like she would find in her department. With such, Merridayn resolved to do what she could and wait to see what Verena's healer's treatment plan included.

Limited precautions were completed, and Merridayn took up residence in the sole wood chair in the room. Exhaustion caught up with her as she proceeded to get comfortable. Hours could have passed without knowing the time in the room. There was no visible window to the outside, only having her phone clock to keep track of the seconds. Her screen was bright in contrast to the soft lighting in the room. The time blinked at her, ten o'clock pm, and her phone, which presently dinged, was at five percent. She rubbed her eyes and stifled a yawn. Curiosity peaked at how easily time flowed.

Merridayn compared her notes from before Verena's infusion to the present. Her ears grew long and pointed rather than rounded as a human's. Her big round eyes had merged into almonds, the innocence be damned. Her hair had gone from mid length to nearly her hips. The strands were much healthier, and Merridayn lifted a section closer. Taking a dagger out of the sheath at her leg, she tried to cut off a small section. The hair stood firm, confirming the suspicion Merridayn heard rumour of.

Hair cannot be cut by normal means. Withstood being damaged by a blade.

"Goddess, forgive me for forcing her into a role she should have had the option to choose." Merridayn wiped the tear falling down her cheek, electing to return to her notes. These notes could be used to update werewolf knowledge on the Fae for future reference. Fae were fantastic magical healers, but wolves outpaced everyone in holistic healing. Werewolves had never been surpassed by any species due to their innate connection to the earth.

Verena's skin was lighter; her minorly sun-kissed flesh paled significantly after the infusion. Her nails had extended, filing into a sharp point naturally. Merridayn lifted Verena's index, took a paper from her notebook, and dragged the nail down the paper. Stunned to see the piece was split in two. She thought about what else the child's nails alone could puncture. Merridayn's mind returned to the challenge between her son and the wretch, her eyes widening as she remembered. The alleged claw marks she believed were given by Aven at the time were actually nail marks. It all made sense; the fur tearing was too small, shallow, and close together to be from a werewolf. Merridayn has seen the work of a wolf's nails, the skin torn in a multitude of directions from the curved, ragged shape of a wolf's claw. The occasional large chunk of fur torn off completely. Abigail's skin was cut with precision, and no error was to be found. No excessive skin tearing or jagged wounds. Five clean cuts.

Nails as sharp as daggers - caution.

Merridayn circled her statement a handful of times, the information being the most exciting find yet. She fought internally against attempting her subsequent trial. Her heart screamed against it while her brain raged to do it. To see what the Fae could do and what wolves would be up against should the Fae attack again. Curiosity outweighed logic. The tip of her blade hovered above Verena's arm. Without giving herself a chance to change her mind, she dragged the blade down her arm. Shock struck, and the dagger fell to the ground with a loud clunk. The noise echoed across the chamber, and Merridayn's heart raced. Verena's skin remained unmarked, undamaged. One of Merridayn's sharpest knives did nothing to Verena.

Skin is unable to be punctured with steel weapons. We need to follow up with what can. Iron? Find the section on this in the archives. Skin can be penetrated by transformed werewolves. Make a note of whether they need to be transformed or if being partially transformed can cause penetration.

Merridayn lost herself in her notes, scribbling down everything she had noted about Verena's transformation over the short period, underlining and circling anything with significance. She was so consumed with her notebook that she almost missed it when Verena twitched. Before Merridayn could nicely set her belongings on the ground, Verena's body contorted at an odd angle. Her back nearly came entirely off the bed she was resting on. Merridayn dropped everything, shooting out of her chair like a lightning bolt. Not knowing what to do to help, she grabbed hold of Verena. Bringing Verena to her and holding her close like her own daughter. Hoping the contact of another human would help.

"Ma'am? Is everything alright? I heard the commotion

while doing rounds." A wolf nurse popped her head into the doorway. Shock littered her face upon seeing the situation.

What was her name? Rosie?

"I am not sure. She-" Merridayn paused. *Lacy?* "I'm not actually sure what happened. Her torso had lifted off the bed as if floating."

Wendy? Merridayn tried to picture the woman before her as a Wendy, striking the name from her list of possible names.

Nope.

Jenny? Merridayn tilted her head, looking over the woman. Unaware her face gave away her forgetfulness, Gracie chuckled at the look.

"Ah." The nurse sat in the vacant chair previously held by Merridayn. "I am Gracella, or Gracie, by the way."

Gracie... Merridayn internally chastised herself for forgetting it, her focus on Verena so intense she managed to block out anything anyone else had said to her in the last ten minutes.

"Hello, Gracie." Merridayn offered the nurse - Gracie - a weak smile, silently hoping she could mask forgetting Gracie's name.

"You looked as if you couldn't remember" Merridayn offered her a weak, guilt-ridden smile in response. "It's fine by the way. I'm sure your mind is circling with other things. All things considered, you know." Gracie waved at Verena. "With a transforming High Fae in the sanctum and all it entails."

"Pardon? High Fae?"

"Yes, ma'am." Gracie leaned forward, intention unknown, before shooting her hand back. A red mark appeared on her fingertips.

"What do you know about High Fae, Gracie?" Merridayn absently brushed Verena's hair. Her hands acted on their own accord, the action giving her a hint of comfort. She watched Gracie sit up straighter, her legs crossing over and tucking under the chair. Merridayn did not need to be a wolf to know this child was nervous. "It is just us, Gracie. I am not versed in the Fae as wolves are, having grown as a normal human."

"The High Fae-" Gracie gestured toward Verena. "Verena here is an evolved sub-species of Fae. According to the books, the High Fae were chosen by the Archangel Haniel for their actions and were gifted relative to their type. The Sinclairs, Mordinians, Naedians and Nightingales were the original High Fae for their contributions during the Red Gaylewen War. This is all speculation, though, as the Fae, in general, are a secretive species. All the information is what the archivists have gleaned over many years. High Fae could only have children with other High Fae as their bodies were no longer compatible with normal Fae. The body violently refuses any child not of the same calibre. It created a low genetic population as the years went on. Causing some of the High Fae to intermarry, namely the Mordinians." Gracie paused, looking towards Merridayn to ensure she was keeping up. When she was satisfied Merridayn was on track to understanding, Gracie continued.

"One could speculate that the High Fae population was headed towards extinction. Knowing what we do about genetics and inbreeding from modern technology, you could figure the High Fae had possibly one or two more generations after the Princess here before the incest caused infertility or worse. According to speculation, there is a fifth house, but nobody knows anything about it or has confirmed the rumours." Gracie rattled on as if she was reciting from a textbook or perhaps attempting to impress Merridayn with her sheer knowledge.

"Let me stop you there, Gracie. Are you saying Verena is not an Ice Fae but a Moon High Fae?" Merridayn held her hand up, a physical sign asking Gracie to hold the thought she had.

"Verena is from House Nightingale, right?" Gracie pointed towards the sleeping Fae child.

"Correct." Merridayn was unsure where this was leading, she knew Verena's house. This knowledge was not uncommon.

"Then yes, Verena is a High Fae," Gracie said matter-of-factly. There was no room for debate in her tone.

"Goddess, help me." Merridayn's face blanched, looking between Verena and Gracie.

"Why?" Drug out and pronounced, Gracie showed her confusion all too easily.

"Elion and I understood Verena was an Ice Fae. We were unaware of High Fae entirely. We told her she was an Ice Fae." Merridayn dipped her head low, a silent curse slipping her lips. "Is there a difference between the two?"

"There is a significant difference, Merridayn." Gracie clasped her hands together in front of her. "Significant."

"Goddess."

"Were you not taught this by the previous Luna? Even your mate himself should have known. All pack leaders have to learn the other species' bloodlines."

"I was not. I was barely accepted as Luna due to my own circumstances." Merridayn looked down at Verena; the girl's gown had moved off her shoulder. A twinkle caught Merridayn's eye, causing a pause to what she would say. "Gracie, can you grab my notebook? I just noticed something on Verena's shoulder and would like to investigate.

As you are evidently unable to touch her, if the red marks still present on your hands are any indication. It would help me if you could write down what is seen. It could lead us in the right direction as to why she is still comatose. At this point, any lead is better than none."

Merridayn did not wait to see if Gracie obeyed. Moving the gown lower on Verena's shoulder, she couldn't hold back her shock. Standing stark against her unblemished, paler flesh were multiple intricate white lines of various degrees of thickness leading towards her spine. Merridayn shifted Verena to open the back of her gown.

"Goddess..." Gracie's hand flew to her mouth, the pen dropping to the ground again.

Staring back at the two women, the complete moon cycle in white ink traced down Verena's spine. The intricate white marks Merridayn saw gracing Verena's shoulder were stars. Constellations were thrown in, and little filled-in circles flittered between the blank spaces. The entirety of the ink filled Verena's back in white. Merridayn made a note of the ink expanding lower down, past the waistline of the pants Verena had on.

If she is not awake soon, I need to explore the markings down her waistline upon giving her a shower, attempt to get a sketch down before she wakes. Hopefully, the archives will have something on this.

Merridayn pulled Verena's gown back in place when her eyes were caught by a slight blue runic marking on her right shoulder. She didn't know how she missed it. The marking contrasted drastically with the white ink on Verena's pale skin. Searching her brain, Merridayn came up blank on what the rune could mean.

"Gracie?" Merridayn said over her shoulder, not looking towards the woman she was speaking to but instead looking at the oddity presented before her.

"Yes, ma'am?"

"Have you seen this rune before?" Merridayn pointed out the rune on Verena.

Gracie scooted as close as she dared to the edge of the bed, careful not to touch Verena for fear of being shocked again. Merridayn watched the young wolf. A part of her itched as if questioning the integrity of the nurse. Her instincts had not led her wrong before; she would not let it start today. Not with the safety of Verena on the playing field. To a lesser trained person, one who had not studied medicine for as long as she has. Training taught her to detect when people are in pain or lying to her. Merridayn would have missed the quick twisting of Gracie's expression. She would have missed the look of recognition and rapidly swapped to confusion. An act many would have missed had Merridayn not been so studiously trained in the art of composure through vigorous hours in A&E.

"I cannot say I have." Gracie paused, looking at Merridayn. "I feel as if I should recognise the rune as all wolves are taught them. At least to the extent of the ones we know. But this one exudes my memory." Gracie doodled the rune in Merridayn's notebook. "If you take away this line here." Pointing towards a lower line extending outwards to the right at a curved angle. "And if you make it a straight line. Then the rune means 'Promise.'" Merridayn watched as Gracie drew a small arrow from the original rune present on Verena to the rune Gracie had mentioned.

"The attention to detail has been extremely insignificant; many might have pre-emptively guessed it to be the one I just mentioned. However, due to this line here..." Gracie pointed at the top line. "This one here I've never seen used in any rune. I'm not sure what this line means.

Suppose the line was curved downwards in an extremely elongated 'U' shape with the straight bottom line from before. The rune would then mean 'Marked.'" Gracie doodled the new rune she had mentioned. Merridayn was soaking up all the information eagerly, the subject being reasonably new. "This rune is said to have been created when the Morningstar led the rebellion against The Creators. All those who fought against The Creators were given the rune, depicting them as never able to return home again. Legend has it, those with this rune are here in Alusso."

"The Morningstar? As in, Luc-"

"Don't say his name." Gracie harshly interrupted her. "We do not say his name here. Or anywhere, for that matter. Legend states those who call upon the Morningstar do not make it to the next day. You are correct, though. The one you were about to mention is the Morningstar of legend."

"Why would it matter whether his name is stated? There is no way wolves are afraid of a fairytale."

"At one point, Luna Merridayn, did you, too, not believe in werewolves?"

Merridayn opened her mouth to respond before promptly closing it. Gracie had a point, and she knew it. Before meeting the love of her life, Merridayn was oblivious to the supernatural, hidden amongst the rest of the world. With the occasional confusing training regime her parents forced on her before she fled to school to become a nurse. She was ignorant of the comings and goings of reality. Believing humans were the only intellectual beings around. Until Elion was rolled in on a stretcher to her A&E department from a forty-car pile-up on Kiteway Artenia, Merridayn's life was flipped upside down and shaken said day. She had not looked back or regretted it since then.

"Exactly what I thought, Luna." Gracie reached out to take Merridayn's hand but pulled back as if she remembered Verena could shock her again.

"Please call me Merridayn. I assume you were assigned to the Princess' care while we were here, or are you only here for today?"

"I am assigned to her, as well as Healer Jorhenna. When one of us is not on duty, they could be found in the healers' quarters. Feel free to come find us for anything you or the Princess might need."

"I do have one request at the current time. Is it not too much to ask, Gracie?" Merridayn stroked Verena's hair out of her face, absently fixing the gown for the millionth time.

"Anything, Merridayn."

"When are you going to tell me what you actually know about the rune?"

Gracie was startled, her eyes flickering between Verena, Merridayn and the doorway. Regaining her composure quicker than any actress Merridayn had seen, Gracie sat up straighter. Her fingers tapping the notebook anxiously, a slight sheen formed on her forehead.

"I do not know what you are talking about, Merridayn." Gracie panicked, her fingers gripping the paper roughly. "I told you everything I knew about them."

Merridayn's head tilted to the right, her eyes inquisitive. Any of her children would recognise the look effortlessly. The same head tilt she would get when she knew they were lying. Even for being human, she had an innate ability to detect even the slightest of lies. Merridayn chalked it up to her countless years of giving people false hope as their loved ones fought for their lives. Sitting through innumerable meetings with board members all while they laid claim to the nursing department's achievements, though none had a licence. Merridayn wondered if they held a degree at countless points in her career. Gracie had yet to learn her lie had been caught. It wouldn't be long before this would be revealed to her.

Unless...

No, surely not.

What an absurd thought, Merr. Merridayn mentally scoffed, a chuckle close to escaping her lips. She rapidly composed herself, not wanting to give Gracie a second to believe Merridayn was mental.

Right?

Flicking her eyes at Verena, the way her chest softly rose and fell. Her breathing was even, with no signs of stress. Remembering how Gracie could not touch Verena nor herself without some sort of backlash. Merridayn remembered how red Gracie's fingers had gotten from it. Curiosity peaked, but she squashed it into a box to investigate at a later time. She glanced at Gracie. Her breathing was even, but her posture was stiff. She looked between the doorway, the bed, and the notebook. Merridayn could tell something was wrong, or someone. She did not know the extent of wolf abilities, but it would not surpass her surprise if wolves could bend nature to them.

They wouldn't send someone here to kill Verena while she was comatose. Not with the council having given explicit permission for Verena to be here.

Would they?

Merridayn had a handful of seconds before whoever, or whatever, was scaring the nurse took liberties. She needed to make a choice, and quickly.

Do I believe the girl or not? Damnit, Merr, why did you agree to allow your children and husband to leave you alone in the wolf pit?

"I believe you, Gracie." Merridayn squeezed Verena tighter to her, keeping her focus on the doorway. She was unsure what she expected to see as her human eyes were subpar. Gracie let out the air in her lungs. Merridayn didn't know she was hiding. "If it's too much to ask, will you sit with Verena while I use the restroom to freshen up? It has been a few hours, and I feel like I stepped into a bin." Gracie offered Merridayn a small smile, nodding her head while loosening her posture.

"I would be happy to! Were you shown the way to your quarters earlier?"

"I was not, no. I came right to Verena after the council meeting. Could you give me verbal directions?"

"Certainly." Gracie shifted in the seat to face towards the doorway. "Once you leave the door, you'll turn right. Pass the next five doorways on both sides, and you'll see a large circular desk where the other healers are. I would check with them to be safe in case your quarters were reassigned. However, if you weren't reassigned, you'll take a left at the station and be in the room labelled '*Lapis*'. I do not believe you would be reassigned, though; we do not have many rooms equipped for humans." Merridayn vaguely noticed the malice Gracie laced in her words when she spoke the word 'human.' Rolling her eyes at the wolf's discrimination against the human race. Merridayn knew she would face racism for being human, but she never expected it to encompass her entire life span.

"Thank you, I should not take more than an hour." Merridayn exited the room, following the directions until she reached the alleged desk. She noticed the tree-like texture of the walls as she passed door after door. "Oh my…"

Chapter 17

MERRIDAYN

B efore her stood an enormous willow tree, one so tall Merridayn could hardly see the top branches. A stained glass dome erected above it poured a rainbow upon the room. Someone had delicately strewn strands of lights to dangle downwards in various places as if they were part of the branches themselves. A cacophony of birds sang above her, and a few could be seen flying around in play. The desk appeared to be a section of the tree's root, which had shaped into a flattened surface.

Behind the other staff members was a secondary root, which formed another flat workspace. One which played host to variable cages and glass domes. The cage doors were ajar; Merridayn assumed the cages were a safe haven for the birds she saw above. Inside the glass domes were various flowers of all shapes and colours, but one stood out above the rest. A black-petaled, black-stemmed flower which seemed to ooze a silver-flecked mist. The stunning flower drew her attention away from the staff members attempting to gain it. The flower seemed to get none even in the bask of many lights. Acting in favour of the shadows, the beams of light violated all known physics. Bending around the pocket of the dome, which held the flower, and permitting it on the other side, it acted as if the spot was a black hole.

"Luna Merridayn!" A staff member exclaimed irritably, shaking Merridayn out of her odd trance.

"Pardon?" Merridayn met the ice blue eyes of the staff, grabbing her attention.

"It's about damn time." The girl whispered under her breath.

"I'm sorry, I did not catch what you said."

"Can I help you with something? If you must request anything for the Princess, ask her assigned healers first. Gracie is still in the Princess' room where you had just come from, last I was aware." The girl's tone clipped as if she was annoyed having to address a human with respect garnered from being a pack Luna.

"I see. I do not need assistance, thank you. Verena does not have any current needs. I will be sure to remember to ask *her* healers should she require anything. I *was* headed to my quarters. However, Healer Gracie stated I should check to ensure they were not reassigned." Merridayn cocked an eyebrow, a silent challenge towards the impudent child's disrespect. She had many years of dealing with disrespectful co-workers and knew precisely how to get under their skin.

"You were not reassigned; the elders were strict with your room assignment, and we were told under no circumstances should you be moved." Her head tilted back, a silent challenge to argue with her. "If you do not require anything else, I have others which need my attention. I'm sure you understand." Without waiting for Merridayn to respond, she turned away.

Cute.

Merridayn rolled her eyes, stepping back from the counter towards the direction Gracie mentioned. Her room door came into view, and a silver cutout of *'Lapis'* graced the dark blue door. The walls, which should have the same bark texture as the rest, were covered in blue star columbines instead. Gorgeous white petals with a layer of blue sepals, the area reflecting a blue hue against the moss covered floor. Merridayn caught herself sighing happily, the aroma of the flowers filling her nostrils. Her mind flicked back to the black flower in the jar, and her curiosity peaked. Determined to figure out what it was, she pushed her door open to be struck in awe by her room. The same river feature of Verena's ran through her room, only a few feet away from the door. Merridayn noted a stone footpath running through the water, evidently a bridge to her elevated bedroom. Covering three-quarters on the left following the stream hung a curtain of vines. Little blue columbines speckled here and there. Merridayn peaked at the edge of a stone basin, assuming behind the curtain was her washing area.

Ding

Her phone ringing in her pocket reminded her it was close to shutting off. Frantically searching the area with her eyes, she located her bag atop her bed. She vaguely took a moment to appreciate the masonry of the bed frame. A smooth white marble shaped in a wave formation, creating a pitched head of the bed with a downward slope at the end. Soft white sheets donned the mattress, starkly contrasting her brown leather luggage. Merridayn sat on the edge, annotating the depth of which the mattress bowed to her weight, a calm feeling settling on her. Rummaging through her bag to find the pesky charger, she prayed she remembered to pack it in their frenzied rush out of their home.

"Please do not be at the bottom of the bag." Merridayn softly prayed to any deity who would listen at this point.

Pulling out anything and everything, she tore through her items, decorating the lush bed with her clothes in search of the black charger cord. Alas, the deities ignored her prayer, as she found it located at the bottom. "Of course it was."

Ding

"I know, I know." Merridayn inspected the area around her, her eyes spotting an outlet near the head of her bed.

Plugging her device in, she pressed her palm against the back insignia. Her palm tingled as her phone scanned it to unlock. Setting the phone down, she turned on the off screen keyboard. The projection of her home screen appeared above her lap, the ethereal keyboard flickering into existence in her hands. She had a few missed messages, one missed call and various notifications from pack members. Tapping on the projected inbox, her eyes scanned the room once in search of anything looking out of place before opening her husband's messages.

[Text]: The boys and I are almost at the airport. Let me know when you get to Verena.

[Text]: We just reached the airport. Have you seen Verena yet, my love?

[Text]: Boarding now. I will let you know when we return to the ground.

[Text]: Landed, awaiting Conroy to get here.

[Text]: Merr?

[Text]: I think someone is going to attempt to kill Verena, Eli.

[Text]: I found a rune on Verena, one I didn't recognise. Her Healer, Gracie, I'm almost positive, knew what it meant. But E, when I asked her about it, she hesitated, looked out the door, and then lied to my face.

[Text]: Are you alone?

[Text]: Yes, but I cannot talk. I don't know who may be

listening.

[Text]: Is Verena with you, Merr?

[Text]: No. I am in my assigned quarters. I needed to shower and a reason to message you.

[Text]: They can't touch her, E. Gracie tried, and something happened when she did. I'm not sure what, but she jerked her hand back. A massive red mark appeared on her fingertips where she attempted. It's as if Verena's body put up some sort of protection warding around her.

[Text]: But here's the thing, E. I can touch her. I held her while Gracie took notes in my book.

[Text]: Notes! Why didn't I think of it first?

[Text]: Merr, love, I'm not following.

[Text]: Of course, why did I not think of it? E, I will send you a photo of the rune I found on Verena. Can you search our archives to see if they have information on it?

[Text]: Merr... darling. I need you to slow down and explain what is happening.

[Text]: Photograph Attachment

[Text]: I will check our archives, my love, but I still do not follow.

[Text]: The rune above is inked onto Verena's skin; her Healer knows what it is, but she won't tell me. She kept looking back at the doorway when I asked her when she would tell me the truth about what she knew. As if someone was watching her, listening to our conversation. Gracie tried to touch Verena but couldn't. She got hurt in the process, but I could. I was holding Verena when I found the marking. She's also got a lot of white ink covering her back. I'm unsure how far down it goes or how intricate it is. I am going to explore it later when we are alone. But E, I'm almost positive someone is trying to kill her. Why would her Healer get nervous about a marking? She knows something, E. I just know it.

[Text]: It does err on the side of suspicion. Keep close to Verena, love. Just because one got hurt when trying to touch her doesn't mean others will. They will not hurt you, and so long as you are near Verena, they will not touch her in fear of the elders.

[Text]: I will, dear. I need to wash and change, and then I will return to her room to rest.

Chapter 18

VERENA

Bright white light filled Verena's eyes, her eyelids heavy, and her brain foggy. She was lying down; the area was soft but prickly. She rubbed her eyes, hoping to clear her vision and gain more awareness of her surroundings. Her ears picked up the sound of running water, the droplets crashing against each other. The sound of a soft breeze picking up strands of her hair. Wisps of feathers brushing against one another and an unnaturally slow, steady heartbeat.

Where am I?

Her eyesight cleared, a hue of colours becoming more pronounced as each second passed. She dug her hands into the ground she was laid upon, her fingernails cutting through the soft material, and she felt the dirt move beneath her.

Dirt?

Sitting up, her right hand came to rest above her brow, blocking out the light beating down on her. Her vision was clearer but not wholly restored; Verena could make out shapes and their colour. Looking around, she took in what appeared to be a forest clearing. Tall, strong trees smelling like pine and cedar surrounded the circular opening. Their branches filled with various hues of green leaves. Little green blotches littered the ground around her, some jutting out towards her as if trying to reach her. Verena looked forward, her eyes clearing gradually, spotting a minor waterfall cascading over moss-covered obsidian boulders, droplets of water splashing against the darkness of the rocks. Tiny rainbows glittered over the falls, casting a folly of colour over the stark contrast of the black backdrop they fell over. The falls confirmed the sounds of water she heard earlier. The beads of water fell into the crystalline pool beneath. The colour reminded her of a frozen lake, only the ripples from the falls causing any movement in the surface, as if frozen.

She continued to look around, noticing a fallen trunk closest to her. Moss-covered and roots decaying, various bugs skittering about the nook of the tree. Someone sat upon it, and Verena jumped slightly. Unsure how long they were there for, her fight or flight instinct kicked into overdrive. Every centimetre of her body screamed to run. Silent words yelling at her, telling her the person in front of her was exuberantly more powerful than anyone else she had ever met. Verena studied them, taking in their slender shoulders partially covered in an almost translucent silver fabric reflecting the downpour of sunlit strands parting the heavy tree foliage. Their long golden hair, laid in an immaculate braid, descended towards her hips, filled with tiny twinkling lights that reminded Verena of falling stars. Her silver draped tunic was tucked into a pair of dark-coloured leather-like trousers. The most notable feature was their massive tucked-in pair of silver-hued feathery wings.

Wings?

Verena heard a chuckle come from the person, startling her immensely. She thought her ears deceived her as no movement came from them. Only the unbelievably slow, steady heartbeat reminded her she was not imagining things. She watched as the winged person moved to place their hand on the right of the trunk. Long fingers tapped the trunk softly, their pointed fingernails gentle against the wood.

"Come, child." Their soft, melodic voice filled Verena's ears, pushing her to get to her feet.

"I am not a child." Verena huffed, closer to the trunk than previously, as if her body acted on its own accord.

"When you are as old as I, have seen many millennia pass in the span of a single breath, everyone else is a child, my dear Verena." They tapped the trunk again, an indication. "Come, sit with me. We have much to discuss and little time."

Much to her confusion, Verena obeyed, her mind still trying to grasp who was before her. Stepping over the trunk, she sat down where they pointed. Her feet planted in the soft moss, and a gentle sigh escaped her. Verena hesitated, unaware of how the other occupant watched her with interest. Gathering her courage, Verena turned her head to her left, her hands gripping the tree to keep her grounded at what she saw.

"Who are you?" She asked again, before her sat a beautiful woman. Their face was angular, mouth voluminous, nose pointed elegantly and a set of the most gorgeous silver eyes she had ever seen. The same eyes stared into hers, seemingly reading her soul through hers. Those silver irises reminded Verena of constellations, the colours vibrant and ethereal.

"I have held many names of your kind." They looked up at the sky. "Between the Moon Goddess, Venus, and the Rose of Venus. Though in truth, my name is Haniel, the Archangel of the Moon." Haniel looked back at Verena, a smile gracing her features.

An Angel? I'm in the presence of an Angel!

Yes, my child, you are.

"You do it too!" Verena almost screamed. Her eyes widened as she recognised she disrespected an Angel, her head lowered to the ground, and her hand came to cover her mouth.

"Do not fret, dear. I find no disrespect from your actions. I apologise for the intrusion you must feel. I often forget your species finds it to be an invasion of privacy. It is hard to remember such things when I am not often found in your company." Haniel reached out, her fingers gently pushing Verena's face upwards and towards her. "I can hear your thoughts, my child. I will attempt to refrain from listening while we speak. Is this acceptable to you?"

Verena nodded, tears coming to her eyes. Haniel swiped her thumb across the falling drops across Verena's cheeks. The water gathered on Haniel's fingers; Verena watched in awe as Haniel brought her hand to her lips and blew softly. The two teardrops froze instantly against her breath, sparkling against the moonlight. Haniel cupped the drops carefully, reaching towards Verena's hands. Recognising the gesture, Verena opened her palm as the Angel dropped two teardrop-shaped gems in her hand.

"They are beautiful..." Verena trailed off, bringing them closer to her face to inspect. "Thank you." Verena knew there was a point to Haniel handing her the stones, but she couldn't put her finger on why. Her knowledge of gemology was subpar.

"They are moonstones, symbolised for new beginnings. Fitting, don't you think?" Haniel's lilt of her words held an air of mystery; the probability of Verena understanding the minds of these celestial beings went negative.

"New beginnings," Verena repeated, attempting to understand how the stones fit within Verena's life.

"I am aware you were given a transfusion of blood, were you not?" Haniel asked, looking at the child knowingly. Verena suspected it was more of an observation stated as a question to gauge Verena's knowledge of her circumstances.

"I was, yes, ma'am." There was no point in lying to her. Verena suspected Haniel could tell if she did.

"This transfusion caused your blood to begin your transformation into your true form years too early." Haniel waved at the moonstones in Verena's hand. "Hence, the moonstones are fitting. Though you should have been properly prepared for what is to come, the subject of your birth does not change. This was always meant to happen, Verena." Haniel let out a delicate flutter of her wings, stirring up the air around them. Verena felt as the wind her wings brought up pushed her hair out of the way, showcasing her pointed ears to them both.

"What do you mean?" Verena was unprepared for her life to be shaken any more than it already was. If what the Angel was about to tell her was what she knew, subconsciously, Verena wasn't ready to hear it. Her entire life was already upended as it stood; Haniel seemed to sense her distress. Verena felt the cold, soft skin of the Angel's hand brush against her shoulder. An ominous sign if Verena had ever seen one. She has read enough books to know that lousy news always follows when physical contact is initiated.

"You were never meant to be human, dear." Haniel broke the news to her softly, or as softly as Verena could expect from an immortal celestial.

"I wasn't?" Verena did not know why the question fell

from her lips. Her brain shut down the moment Haniel confirmed her suspicions.

"No, you were born a child of the High Fae." Haniel used her thumb to brush away another lone tear streaking down Verena's cheek for the second time in a short period. A gentle smile graced her ethereal features. "How much do you know about your history?"

"Not much, honestly." Verena sniffled, looking up at the Angel finally. Unaware when her head dropped to look at the ground. She was crying again, she knew it, though this time, no memory of when it started came to mind. "I was told I am an Ice Fae, about you and the rest of the Angel's who created the four Fae houses." Verena felt an eerie calm settle over her, wondering if it was a type of magic protruding from Haniel. Was the Angel trying to calm her?

"Let us start at the beginning, shall we?" Haniel leaned back on her delicate hands, spreading her wings wide in a stretch. "You may as well get comfortable. This conversation could prove to be lengthy."

Verena did as told, sliding back to lean on her hands and digging her feet into the moss-covered ground, tilting her head to look up at the darkening sky. The moon peeked behind clouds as if shy to present itself to the Archangel of the Moon. Verena watched as the Angel wove her hand in front of her, palm opening in the middle. A light mist ghosted above the eerie pond.

Woah.

"You, dear one, are a child of Prophetess Jerifeyn Amelia Naedian and Prince Francis Pierre Nightingale." Verena watched as the mist took the form of her parents, almost identical to what she had seen in the memory. "Many centuries ago, your kind, the Fae, were created by Ariel. Ariel had initially created four different types of Fae, each with an ability to coincide with the elements: Fire, Ice, Earth and Sky. These Fae were responsible for preserving peace throughout your world and always living in the shadows of humans, clearing messes and preventing the destruction of the ecosystem. It was efficient, the Archangel's way of giving humans their best chance of survival without stepping in, without angering our Creators. Peace was a falsity, and humans began to outpace the Fae with curiosity and technological advancements. The Fae began to struggle to maintain equilibrium, being outmanoeuvred by humans and their bloodlust." Verena watched as the mist continued to produce a moving picture. The Angel continued talking, sliding down the side of the trunk to rest her torso against it. She got comfortable; the soft hum of the water and the almost theatre-like motion of the mist-formed people reminded her of a film.

I know most of this already.

Verena had forgotten the Angel could hear her thoughts, blushing at the faux pas she had committed.

"Seeing her sister's creation becoming obsolete in the face of humans, Azrael created what you know as Demons. Demonic beings with the sole intention of creating bargains with humans, those bargains ended in the loss of the humans' life within a short span. Humans were seduced with promises of fortune, fame, and the like, but ultimately, Demons created loopholes in their contracts. Unbeknownst to their prey, to collect years before the contract was set to expire. Demons were effective, precise and calculating. Their ability to control the human population is second only to the Angel of Death herself. Peace was well within grasp again-" Haniel slowed, her wings stretching out, fluttering rapidly. "-or so we believed."

Kaulron...

Verena shivered at the memory, her heart stuttering in contempt. Her subconscious movement was not lost upon Haniel as Verena felt the Angel drape a wing over her. Soft feathers curled around Verena's small frame, eyes widening at the sheer size of one. More prominent than she expected, Verena hesitated before reaching with her right hand to gently hover her palm next to one in comparison. Her, albeit small, palm, about four inches in width, only covered a third of the width of a singular feather.

"Thank you," Verena whispered, leaning into the warmth of the wing while looking back towards the pond.

"It was common knowledge to all Angels, Orion lusted after Ariel, as was the knowledge of her persistent rejection of him. To his chagrin, he could not accept her refusal with elegance, swearing he would win her hand regardless of her wishes. We had all but forgotten his sworn oath until Azrael stumbled upon him attempting to drug Ariel. This angered Azrael-"

"Rightfully so, the slimy bastard," Verena muttered to herself, believing Haniel could not hear her until the Angel chuckled.

"You are correct, child. He was definitely a, how did you put it, a slimy bastard and thus angered one of the most deadly Angels in creation. Azrael is unparalleled in combat, only being bested by our parents, The Creators, or, on occasion, her partner, the Morningstar." The picture of an Angel with pitch black wings and waist-length black hair appeared before Verena, and she shot up from her slouched position.

"I know her!" Verena exclaimed excitedly, leaning forward to get a better look at the Angel she knew.

"Pardon?" Haniel's silver irises stared down at Verena,

her perfectly shaped eyebrows almost disappearing behind her hair.

"I've seen her before, in Aven's house." Verena stood, striding towards the pool. "I'm sure of it." She could barely make out any other details. The fog was unable to create colours beyond monochromatic. "Does she have red eyes?"

"How do you know this?"

"Cavanaugh has painted her many times, and they are hung up throughout their home." Verena subtly moved away from the Angel, fearing she had angered the benevolent being.

"I see." Haniel shifted positions, electing to stand with her. A massive shadow encased Verena's; she saw Haniel towering over her. "I can see your face, child. Do not be afraid. I am relatively shorter than most of my brethren."

"Um." Verena cleared her throat. "How tall are you, if it's not disrespectful for me to ask?"

"I am around three hundred and sixteen plumes. Acutriel-nove, your kind uses, feet? Yes?" Verena nodded. "I am approximately eight feet then."

"Eight feet. Holy Hell." Verena's eyes widened, her face paling. "I'm sorry."

"Do not be. I have been around long enough to watch your language evolve. The human tongue amuses us all sometimes." Waving her hand towards the pool again, the stagnating mist form of Azrael shifted towards another angle of the deadly Angel. "When Azrael stumbled upon his attempt to kidnap Ariel, the rest of us were later informed of the wreckage she made of Orion. Blood was splattered on every surface but Ariel. Azrael's skin was coated in the same colour as her eyes; it dripped from every feather, so much so that an entire team had to help her wash them."

Verena shrank back as the mist depicted the sight she was being told, wondering how grotesque the scene was in reality.

"What did she do to cause so much carnage?" Verena subconsciously reached out towards the fog, her mind going back towards her memories of being covered in gore to a lesser extent.

"She ripped off his wings with her hands. Once she shredded through them, she dug her nails into the cartilage. Ensuring his wings would not repair for centuries, it is one of the most painful subjections for any Angel." Stretching her wings out wide, her deltoid muscles rippled in a shiver from the thought. "After, we are not sure of the timeline of events. However, we do know Orion is now permanently scarred from head to toe. A long serrated scar runs the length of his eyebrow to his lips, perpetually inflamed and will not heal properly. Occasionally, it re-opens, and he must undergo major healing sessions. The sessions are quite painful in their own right."

"I thought Angels could not be injured due to their resemblance to God?" Verena heard the rumour somewhere: Angels were meant to be invulnerable. Staring at Haniel's skin, she wondered what could puncture it to cause enough damage for an Angel to receive continuous healing.

"Yes and no, dear. However, we must continue onwards before I must return to my duties." Haniel was patient, gently reminding Verena to stay on topic.

"Yes, ma'am." She winced, embarrassment coursing through her again. A familiar feeling as of late, especially in the presence of Haniel.

"We all believed that Orion had learned his lesson, that nobody crossed the Archangel of Death twice in fear of her." Haniel flicked her hair over her shoulder, pausing. "We were wrong." Her voice darkened, hatred nearly visible. Verena watched as her nails curled inward, the only physical sign of anger from the perpetually stoic Angel.

"He created werewolves, right?" Verena remembered the information she was told about werewolf creation from Elion and Merridayn. Though, she wondered if there was more to the story even the wolves did not know about.

"Not exactly. Orion waited and watched for decades, healing and plotting. In all those decades of wait, he watched Ariel grow closer and closer to her creations. Her most prized accomplishment being wolves; they reminded her of her sister. They had family-oriented traits and were fiercely protective of those they loved. Ariel adored them because of it, having spent many moons in her human form to frolic with the packs. Orion noticed, and he envied it; he wanted the attention she gave to what he saw beneath us. He believed she was soiling herself by spending time with these 'abominations.' We were too late to see it, too late to stop him. And because of it, a creature none had planned was created, humans doomed to a curse we couldn't stop. Couldn't reverse." Haniel let loose a beat of her wings, forcing the mist above the lake to diminish before Verena watched it shift into the scene she had just said.

"Because Angel's cannot interfere, right?" Verena was confident she was correct, a marginal piece of information from the bible so many at school lectured about.

"Correct, we cannot. We can only watch as life unfolds. When Orion cursed Kaulron, he violated our customs and etiquette. For which he was punished, though many believe it was not adequate. The Curse of Carnage ravaged Kaulron, an established blood-seeking wolf. This caused

Kaulron to seek out and slaughter villages at a time, reeling in the bloodshed his teeth and claws generated." Haniel's lip curled upward in disgust, a human emotion on an inhuman being. It was surprising, to say the least, one Verena would remember for eternity. "After a handful of months, our Creators sanctioned Ariel to step in. Kaulron's actions violated the natural order of the cycle, and many humans, slotted to live a long and healthy life, were demised from a curse Orion had created. Ariel sought my aid, seeking to bind Kaulron to the cycles of the moon. His curse would break free of confinement only once a month, a temporary reprieve to an otherwise difficult predicament. When the binding failed, we retreated to devise a different option." Haniel looked down at her. Verena could see the Angel grimace as if she was in pain.

Does this hurt her? Speaking to me?

"It wasn't until Kaulron was in the midst of shredding a human apart that he was distracted by a brave soul seeking to help the pinned-down victim. The victim, a human named Calvix, shredded apart, blood seeping into the earth, had crawled his way into a temple of Azrael. Seeking protection and aid, he cried out to her, praying for a miracle to end his suffering. Azrael created a barrier outside the temple doors without fearing the consequences she knew would happen. A passage Kaulron could not penetrate; confusion laced his snout as he paced the outside walls. Azrael summoned us both, Ariel and I, offering a solution to our problems. Can you guess the solution, child?" Haniel spread her right hand out, a small moon appeared in her palm. A tiny replica of the larger one in the sky, Verena wanted to reach out and see if it was real.

"Bind Calvix to the moon?" Verena pointed at the moon in her palm, an obvious sign Haniel had given.

"Partially." Haniel smiled. "Ariel could bind Kaulron to the body of Calvix whilst I bound his soul to the moon. Azrael theorised the bindings would limit the threat of Kaulron's bloodshed to the cycles of the moon. While the human side of him, Calvix, might temper his bloodlust. As his curse could not be removed, it could be altered. Calvix was dying, his heart slowing with each passing second. We were not able to confirm our theory, or else we would lose our chance. Another opportunity might not have presented itself later if we passed on the one we were given." Within the confines of Haniel's palm, Verena witnessed the picture of a human man and a bloodied wolf being bound together with a black thread between them.

"Because of the person who interrupted Kaulron while he was killing Calvix," Verena remembered Haniel telling her about another human who sacrificed their own life to distract the wolf tearing into Calvix.

"Precisely, we were unsure if the same situation would happen again. We witnessed Kaulron's higher intelligence and ability to learn. We had to act and do it right then. While we were busy with the bindings, Azrael was keeping Kaulron busy. She kept him running in circles and kept him close for when we were ready. She violated the divine laws because of it, yet..." Haniel gracefully wiped away a tear, a smile coming to her beautiful face. "Yet she didn't care. She knew she would be punished for it but continued regardless." There was something about the way Haniel revered Azrael which made Verena wonder what happened to the Angel.

"Punished? For what?" The question slipped out of her mouth before she could stop it.

"We were allowed to contain Kaulron, but Azrael intervened by keeping him from killing others. By running

him around, she distracted him from other prey nearby.
By erecting the wards around her temple to keep Kaulron
out, she hindered him from finishing what he started with
Calvix. We were only allowed to stop Kaulron, not involve
another. Azrael took the blame for the entirety of it, stating
she thought of the plan and executed it." Haniel shivered,
Verena reached out to place her hand within the Angel's. A
human comfort she was not sure the Angel would accept,
but she hoped she wasn't out of bounds by doing so.

"I assume the bindings worked if there were werewolves
now?" Haniel squeezed Verena's hand, her eyes bulging as
she looked up at Haniel.

"They did indeed with unexpected results. Instead of
binding Kaulron to Calvix, we bound Calvix to Kaulron.
The wolf turned into a human, and Calvix's body disappeared. Once a month, Kaulron would return to his
wolf form. His bloodlust was dulled, dampened by the
humanity of his human side. We did not expect that he
would pass his genetics on to a child when he mated. The
curse flowed to them, forcing these children to shift into a
wolf when their human bodies reached an age of maturity.
Their first shift is said to be extremely painful." Another
wave of Haniel's free hand and the images shifted.

Verena watched teenage children being forced into a
wolf, their skin ripping as fur sprouted in its place. The
agony shown on their tiny faces made her weep for them,
and knowing the pain Aven was subjected to made her
heart hurt.

"Where does this lead to me, though?" Verena understood how Wolves, Fae, and even Demons came to be, but
she felt she was not classified as any of them.

"Ever perceptive, dear." Haniel chuckled, running her
fingernails through Verena's hair. "Life demands a balance,

an equilibrium of power. With the creation of werewolves, the power was at an imbalance. Ariel, Uriel, Azrael, and I came together to infuse Fae with additional power. Ariel gave blood to the Naedians; her blood caused them to shift from Earth Fae to Soul Fae. Azrael gave it to the Mordinians, causing them to become Blood Fae from Fire Fae. Uriel gave it to the Sinclaves, and they went from Sky to Sun Fae. I gave it to the Nightingales, and they turned from Ice to Moon Fae. We designed these Fae to balance the power within the Wolves. Everything was in equilibrium again."

"I see, but I still do not understand where it leads me." Verena could see herself as a Moon Fae. Her skin was pale enough to almost be iridescent, relative to Haniel's own flesh.

"You, child, are a Moon High Fae with Soul Fae abilities. While your body showcases the descendants of the Moon, your magic is attuned to both parents. An odd combination of the two creates a child who can see magic in its purest forms—those pesky blue bands, as you like to call them." Verena's head snapped to Haniel, then to her wrist, where the two thin blue tattooed bands glimmered in the moonlight. She hadn't realised how much time had passed in this world between worlds. Entering from the moon's peak to now, the moon slinking away.

"You can see them?" She whispered, shocked she found someone who didn't think she was going crazy.

"Of course, I can, dear, all Angels can. We were created from the same magic which flows through those bands on your wrists." Haniel turned around, flexing her wings and moving her silver gown out of the way. Verena peered on, watching as white shimmering ink revealed on the Angel's spine. The phases of the moon aligned perfectly between the bases of her wings, running down the length of her vertebrae. "Do not be surprised. You will now bear the same on your spine. A gift from me to you, of sorts."

"I have one!" Verena tried moving her head to peer over her shoulder, struggling to see anything but her scapula. Fingers clawing at her shirt to move it out of the way. "I cannot see it."

"You will, in time." Haniel returned to face the pond, her fingers waving over it again as the mist cleared in command. "We have little left to discuss before I must return to my realm, child. Shall we return?"

"Yes, please." Verena's disappointment showed on her face before she could hide it. She was amassing a slight smirk from Haniel as they returned to their fallen trunk.

"I know your question remains, but I will not ruin your genuine reaction to seeing your own for the first time. Humour me, will you? These days, we rarely get entertainment that is not our kind. Now, back to our conversation." Haniel turned her body, her leg draping over the side, her entire attention focused on Verena. "Verena, you were not meant to be born. However, because you are, you were never human. Your body was only put into stasis until you were old enough to handle the transformation. You were not supposed to come out of stasis for another few years when your body had matured to its peak. I am not aware of the circumstances of why this process happened earlier, and the reason is of no consequence now. But, Verena, I should warn you, everything you see and hear from now on, you need to be the judge of who is telling you the truth and who is not. Many will try to use you for their gain. Sell you or offer you up as some prize to be won. Trust yourself and your body. You were designed to be superior to humans but equal to Wolves."

"Are you saying people I know might not be who they say they are? Because if so, I already know. It's why I am in this predicament." Verena huffed, memories about Abigail coming to the forefront.

"Not just her, dear. Others would wish to own you, control you, and some would rather see you dead." Haniel reached out to cup Verena's cheek, the Angel's hand much softer than Verena had thought. She leaned into the feeling, her body registering she was safe here. "I believe I have left you with enough to consider for now. I must return before I am missed. Sleep well, my child."

Verena pulled back as she watched Haniel stand, the Angel's wings flared out, beating the air softly once, twice, three times as if testing. Haniel looked back and smiled again at her, those pearly white teeth reflecting the moonlight. She was entranced as Haniel bent her knees slightly and pushed off the ground. Mighty wings threw solid gusts of wind downward, throwing Verena's hair all over. Small pieces of moss sprayed from the ground, and the leaves shook from the force. Leaning her head against the trunk, she watched her fly off until Haniel was but another star in the sky. Whispers of their conversation replayed in Verena's mind as her eyes drifted to a close. Sounds of water lulled her back to sleep in the haven she had found with dreams of white wings and pale silver eyes.

Chapter 19

KIERAN

"You again? Either I need to get my eyesight checked, or are you here right now?" Kieran sighed. His patience had already hit its limit today. He rubbed his eyes, hoping it was a trick of the light and the old wolf was not in front of him. "You are actually here again, aren't you, Orla?" Her name was heavy on his tongue.

"I am." Orla's stout height barely cast a shadow on him from the burning torches behind her.

"What is it this time?" Kieran strode to his receiving room, knowing the wolf would follow.

"I have come for information." Her heavy footsteps followed behind him, down the dark panelled walls lit by sporadically placed torches. Her gaze swept past the familiar portraits of infamous Demons, battles and various scenic places she had not seen before. Her feet knew the way as Kieran wound through the halls from the portal. Having been here many times, she knew the path and areas to avoid.

"How bewildering, Orla. You never come bearing gifts or just to chat." He was exhausted, and his body ached for rest. Yet it seemed the day had continued to deny him his desires at his expense.

Having reached his receiving room after a handful of

twists and turns, his chair beckoned for him. His body reared for his bed just a handful of steps away. He could be laid up and dreaming about Verena's bodacious curves by now, except for the stench of the wet dog clouding his nostrils from the maker itself, trailing closely behind him. A foul sigh escaped him as his knees bent to lounge upon the ebony leather seat with its mahogany wood accents and legs. Cool to the touch and plush enough to cushion his weight without feeling like sitting on a tree.

It would be a sight to see Verena sitting upon my lap here, naked...

The thought alone made him shiver, and it did not go unnoticed by Orla. Her brows raised as she sat in the duplicate chair opposite him. Kieran levelled her with his best unamusing glare, a challenge in silence, daring her to say anything about his reaction. She knew better, though, the sly pup. Her knowledge of Demon law astounded him. Knowing had she so much as chuckled, he could have her bound to slavery for the rest of her miserably long life. He perused his room, taking in the chosen decor and making mental notes on things he wished to change. His decor taste changed quicker than a slattern changed underwear. His assigned room attendants were most assuredly going to be irritated, though they seemed to realise he didn't care in any capacity about their irritations. Dark green, almost black, walls littered with silver framed photographs and portraits. A grand mahogany desk on the backside of Orla's chair and various knickknacks cluttered his desktop. High-pitched doors behind him opened to let the cool breeze in, which smelled suspiciously like pine trees and tobacco. His silver curtains fluttered in the breeze, casting shadows on lighted torches, keeping the room bright. He smirked; wolf eyesight was abysmal compared to Demons.

He could snuff the lanterns out in a flick of his wrist and tear the old cow limb from limb before dinner rang.

An amusing thought. I could make it quick. Nobody would know.

Kieran studied Orla; the pungent smell of decaying and drowned rabid dog wafted off her in waves. His stomach rolled at the scent. He'd need to keep the doors open for weeks after her visit if he ever wanted to step in the room again. Perhaps he should invest in a nose clamp for her inevitable return. Orla shuffled in her chair impatiently, her brown turtleneck raised high towards the lobes of her ears. A pearl strand decorated her throat with the matching earrings peeking between her curled, short, shoulder length hair. Kieran would bet his left testicle she had an identical bracelet gracing one of her tiny wrists. Most likely, the right was traditional, but she didn't give off typical traditional vibes. She might have been an exceptional beauty when she was younger had she not been born a wolf. Her foetid stench filled his senses and overtook any sort of affection he may have developed for her. One he might have even taken as a concubine to pass the time.

Orla huffed, her patience wearing thin as the minutes passed. Kieran held back the vomit collecting in his mouth when her breath reached his nostrils. He looked up, examining the cathedral ceilings draped in swaying, diversified green silks. Lanterns floated intermittently, each exuding a soft light from the captured Sargynx. His lips curled at the memories of capturing them, the lure of fresh bleeding meat on a disguised silver plate. Deciding enough time had passed, he settled his eyes on Orla. He debated how he wished to proceed with the conversation and concluded he would listen to her requests and decide accordingly.

"What is it you want this time, Orla?" Kieran was

bored—bored of the conversation, bored of the interaction—and, deep down, he was truthfully exhausted. Exhaustion likely drove his complete indifference to her, but boredom in his station certainly did not help matters.

"I need information." She sat up straight, her odour wafting to his nose more so from her movements. The overwhelming sensation caused his face to twist slightly in disgust. Lacing him with a disappointed stare, Orla rapidly realised her disapproval did not affect him as it might with her species.

"So you said earlier." He leaned forward, a sign of irritation. Kieran clasped his hands toward his face, his weight resting on his elbows pressed against his knees as he brushed his lips with his fingertips. It was as if he was contemplating what his following statement would bring, not that he cared what the female really needed. "You have failed to specify what information you need."

"I need reassurance that you will listen to my proposal before rejecting me outright."

Demanding little thing. Reminds me of my little Fae Princess.

"I can assure you I will give you an adequate answer should the proposal be worthy."

"Very well." Orla knew the deals Demons made suited their own needs before anything else. She was quick to take Kieran's statement before he decided to change it. Meeting his eyes, she proceeded. "I need all the information on the High Fae the Demons possess."

Intriguing.

"Why?"

"I cannot reveal why." Her gaze lowered to her lap. Orla knew she could easily have pushed him past his limits should she have continued the back and forth.

"Cannot or will not?"

"Take it in either direction you want. But I need this quickly. It is a life-or-death situation. The Wolves are willing to negotiate any price you set within-"

"No." Kieran interrupted her sentence, only to be ignored as Orla continued.

"-reason. We have prepared an assortment of options but are willing to change them to your liking. I am aware of the boundaries this may cross, but as I said before, we could be on the precipice of life or death." Orla rushed the words out of her mouth, purposefully ignoring the glare Kieran levelled her way by occupying her attention observing the oddities of his room.

"Orla." Kieran lowered his tone, commanding. She was ignoring him, intentionally. Kieran felt his ire rise again.

"Please, Kieran. We are desperate." Orla never begged. In the years he had known her, Kieran had never heard her beg for anything. It was an odd sensation of sorts, the feeling of power over someone when you have something they want.

"Orla." He dropped his tone again, leaving no room for her to mistake his intent.

She looked up at him. His posture had changed. His hand gripped his knees, and acute nails needled his trousers. His blackened blood pooled around the punctures, and drops ran down his leg. His usually bored eyes transposed into anger, his expression tensed, on the brink of what she anticipated could be an incoming attack. She whimpered, attempting to show submission in the way she knew how her neck bared. Pearl earrings swung, hair covering her face. She didn't dare move in fear of the Demon ripping her to shreds. Orla knew she did not stand a chance against him in her human form, calculating he would tear her to pieces before she had a chance of shifting into her wolf. Her body shook; what had been a minute movement increased with each second as the terror of what could be overtook her. Orla awaited his next move, her mind raced as she considered each option and its potential chance to make it from her location and back to the portal. The portal, her beacon to safety, was the only thing she could focus on now.

"I said no, Orla." The male snapped, his tone clipped, and he could feel his control slipping. "If you cannot tell me why you need the information, you will receive nothing, regardless of your proposition. I couldn't care less if you handed me a squadron of virgin slaves. You will not get anything without revealing who you are trying to protect."

"Kieran," she partially cried. The old wolf had succumbed to such a deplorable level. "I cannot tell you."

"Let us partake in a game, shall we?" Kieran smirked at her low whimper. He enjoyed the power he had over her, how he could make her cower and beg. She was nothing more to him than a wretched whelp, and his behaviour toward her clearly showed his disdain.

"As you wish."

"A guessing game, if you will?" Kieran leaned back in his chair, releasing his hands from his legs. His blood dripped off his manicured nails and onto the leather of his seat. "If I guess correctly, within three attempts, you will tell me everything you know."

Orla waited for the punchline and the reward if he couldn't guess correctly within his allotted attempts. She stared at him, curiosity outweighing her training when dealing with Demons. He said nothing in return, and his sentence ended. There was no continuation to be seen, as she concluded.

"And if you don't?" Curiosity won; she tensed as she anticipated the reprimand she was bound to receive.

"I do not intend on losing, Orla. There is no need for theatrics. You have known me long enough to summarise that you will not succeed in this game." She was trapped in a corner with no path towards success. Kieran could have laughed as he noticed her shaking hands while she fidgeted with her blouse.

"I do." Her voice quivered. She was terrified of disappointing the council and her mate and, mostly, of what Kieran would do if he found out who they were harbouring.

"Now, you tell me you need information on High Fae. This leads me to believe you, or someone you know is researching them. Correct?"

"Yes. Two attempts left."

"You aren't as daft as you appear, good girl." His tone is low, sensual, almost a caress. He witnessed her shivering, unable to resist the incubus blood coursing through his veins from two generations ago. "If you are researching them, you must be in close contact with a High Fae. And as everyone knows, they are reclusive. They stay in their realm and never venture far from their meagre portals to steal supplies, children, and even adults. So, this means there is a High Fae in your realm, correct?"

Orla hesitated, her body trying to reject answering, but her brain compelled her. She knew fighting was futile when she agreed to a Demon's deal. Even verbalising the words of agreement bound one to their terms until the contract was finished.

"Correct?" Kieran insisted again, with a slight growl in his tone. He was close to getting the answer from her, having already figured out who she was trying to save days ago. At this moment, he just wanted to toy with her—make her believe she could win in his game of charades, give her hope that she could walk away without losing her dignity.

I will find you, Verena. It matters not if I have to traverse through blood and bones to get to you.

"You are correct." Orla's fidgeting worsened, her hands white as she gripped the edges of her chair. "One attempt left."

"Fabulous." Kieran got out of his seat forcefully, the chair tipping backwards, on the edge of falling. He didn't care if his back faced the wolf. He was confident he could kill her even if he had a disability. His arrogant saunter took him to the open balcony doors, where he braced his broad shoulder against the window pane. He stared out at the expanse of the city below him, taking in the sounds of life occurring. His spine shivered in ecstasy at the faint sounds of screams coming from those being tortured.

"Let us put together what we have learned, shall we?" He didn't wait for her to respond, his long fingers tapping the sill excitedly. "You want information on High Fae because you, or someone you know, is in close contact with one. A High Fae trapped, or left intentionally, in Alusso. One who cannot return to their home due to some circumstance or another, or else you wouldn't be here. Here, begging for information from Demons. Now, we all know High Fae rarely leave Lothaire. Their population has been too low and too spread out since the start of the war. A war they are still fighting to this day. A war where a certain babe was put into stasis when they were born, and sent to Alusso for protection until the war was deemed close to the end, or so the rumours state."

Kieran turned to look towards Orla; his broad shoulders encompassed the entire window frame. Orla's heart skipped a beat; he listened to the blood flow into her cheeks. She whispered under her breath, chastising herself for finding him attractive. She told herself she was too old to think such things, entirely in love with her mate. Her pleas to her Goddess to give her strength for what was to come.

"Now, I have one last attempt. One meagre attempt to guess correctly who you wolves are hiding, or else you walk away with what you want scot-free." He stalked towards her, a cheshire cat grin bearing his perfect teeth. He backed her into the corner he wanted and was about to take his prize. The closer he got to her, the farther she slid into her seat. Fear wafted off her in waves, causing his loins to tingle. Craving the fear, the aroma it put off, the screams people give when faced with the inevitable.

"Yes." She whimpered as far back into her seat as she could go. Not daring to flee, to try getting to safety. Her legs quivered, her wolf screamed at her, unable to determine if they should fight or run.

He continued, even closer than before, until he was almost on top of her. Leaning down to brace his hands against her chair's armrests, his face inches from hers. Kieran held his breath, not wanting to ruin the moment by vomiting on her from the stench. His afternoon indulgence threatened to make a reappearance.

"I only have one question left, *pup.*" He leaned in even closer, his eyes bore into hers. Where is Verena?" Each word was accented with deadly intent. While it was a question, it was clear that this was a demand—a demand for information that sent Orla's heart racing and her lungs screaming as she forgot to breathe.

Her fidgeting stopped, her fingers clenched around her

thighs. Digging into the soft material of the trousers she elected to wear. He waged imprints would be left for quite some time, a memory of this moment seared into physicality by nail marks washing away.

"I'm-" She gulped, air racing into her burning lungs. "-I'm not sure who you are referring to, Kieran."

His right hand moved to her throat before she had time to register what was happening or take another breath, his weight solely resting on his left. Anger flowed from him in palpable waves, a burning ocean awaiting release. She squealed, unable to track his movements. Werewolf eyesight may have been far superior to humans but was woefully subpar to his own. Her small, frail and wrinkled hands gripped his arm. A plea to release her, a pathetic attempt to fight back. Her grip tightened around his forearm, comparable to a babe's wrapped around her father's finger for the first time. Ignorable.

"Do not lie to me, wolf." His face was inches from hers, and he could see sweat pooling above her brow. The way her lips quivered, and her eyes flicked back and forth.

"Kieran..." She whimpered.

Pathetic rodents.

"I can smell her on you, divinity amongst the garbage. Underneath the horrid stench of shit, you animals sweat, and the barest hint of flower and spice lays. I will ask again, and you will answer as the deal dictates. Should you refuse, I will enjoy the screams you give me as I take what I want from your pesky little mind instead."

"*Please.* Kieran. I really-"

"Where is she?" Each word was clipped, poised to strike should she answer incorrectly. He increased the pressure on her fragile throat, her blood roaring against his fingertips. "Answer correctly this time, Orla."

She struggled against him, fighting for control of the situation. Kieran laughed a cold yet sultry sound. Enjoying the fear coursing through her, her rage against her bindings. He knew about her contract, having made the contract himself with her decades ago. He knew about the poison she had running through her veins, a scant attempt to control the vicious side of her wolf. The struggle was a humerable attempt to control the consequences she alone had asked for, nee practically begged for. The whole thing is just to lose everything in the end. She tapped at his arms, her voice unable to sound as his grip gradually increased in pressure. She was surrendering, adhering to their contract obligations as her life started to fade. He would have been disappointed to end his fun so early, but there were no lines he wouldn't cross for Verena.

"Speak, Orla. You know I have no morality; I will kill you should it resort to such dramatics." He released her partially, enough to allow her to croak out words but not enough for her to become confident she could claw her way free.

"We have her." Orla gurgled out, her mouth filled with saliva as her body was able to breathe. "She's with the council, the others."

"Why?" It wasn't a question; he demanded answers. A possessive wave rushed over him; his mate was in the hands of animals.

"Kieran, I'll honour the deal, but please let me go," Orla begged, looking up at him sincerely. "Please."

He raged with himself, wanting to rip the information from her quickly. Plan a raid against their sanctuary and bring Verena home. But the little spot in his heart, the spot Verena opened when she first stepped into his mind, unconsciously reminded him of the virtue of patience.

He knew it was foolish to attempt a raiding party against their sanctum, the imprudent wolves having made a deal with Druids. Their inner areas were unable to be accessed by anyone with the same blood as him, unless invited in. A pact the Angel's who created them had made to keep peace between the species. Asinine as it was, he knew he would never be able to cross an Angel. Their pacts were impenetrable, and their consequences were severe, should one try. He released Orla entirely, electing to sit on the table and dividing the two chairs instead. She was farther away than before but close enough to rip her intestines out should she try something idiotic. "Go on." He motioned with his hand for her to continue, his impatience rising steadily. "Do not leave even a single detail out."

"She was brought to us a handful of days ago, unconscious and carried. The Belmont's brought her in, worried as she went to sleep normally then never woke up." Orla related to him the proceedings of Verena's circumstances, from her transfusion to the challenge. His pride soared when hearing how beautifully she slaughtered, his mind latching onto every second of the telling gloriously. Imagining her on the battlefield with his crest on her shoulders and crown on her head. She would rip through their enemies as the epitome of beauty and the picture of chaos while the blood dripped down her magnificently.

Kieran shifted in his position, hiding the raging erection he boasted from his musings of her in war. His High Fae Queen, a sight to be seen with her pointed ears and golden hair stained from the bloodshed she would bring. His body hummed at the many ways he would take her, how he would pull those pretty little orgasms from her. How she would look naked and tied to his bed or how she would moan his name to the balcony doors wide. The entirety of their city would hear the cries of their Queen being pleasured. Orla interrupted his thoughts, and he recognised she kept going on about how Verena came to be in their sanctum until the aggravating pup said the words his heart did not want to hear.

"What did you say?" He snapped back to reality.

"She might be dying," Orla whispered, knowing the direction the Demon Prince would take at the news.

Anxious and angry, his powerful body shattered the table he was residing on in his scramble to stand. Blue flames licked at every inch of him, his control over them loosening in his anger. He had yet to see her physically. Their trysts, in his mind, are enjoyable but not comparable to reality. He had yet to hold her, share life with her and now he's being told he could lose her based on some *human* miscalculation? In his state, he hadn't noticed the wolf attempting to sneak her way to the portal. Her end of the bargain was completed. A pallid attempt to flee while he was distracted, a deadly miscalculation on her part. Blue fire soared towards her, the wolf ducked in the knick of time. He watched as a favourite portrait he had painted of the Kiltrend Mountains a handful of decades prior went up in flames. Screams sounded from the hallway, the raging bell alarm ringing in his ears, and the pathetic whimpers of the old wolf near the burning painting fueled his anger more.

"Where is she, Orla?!" He bellowed, racing towards her as she scrambled on her hands to back away down the hall.

"Kieran..." She began, trying to catch her breath and run simultaneously. "It will do... neither of us any good... if you murder me here today." She choked out the words, pausing every few to take deep breaths as she tried to escape Kieran's ire. "You and I both know this. How about...

we take a step back?" More gasping breaths came before she tried to continue, still attempting to dodge the fire's heat emanating from his raging emotions. "We can work together... the wolves with you. We can... save her, but we need... the information your kind may possess." She found space beyond a column where she thought she could buy herself a little time, the physical barrier bringing her a sense of ease while she wheezed out her last request. "Your mother worked closely with them before, Kieran. She might know something. Something which can help us bring her out of her unconscious state." Orla desperately wanted to de-escalate the situation and calm Kieran. She stepped from behind the column, her hands coming up and opening in front of her, bracing for his wrath but hoping she would be seen as harmless.

"First, you come here, uninvited and unannounced. Expecting to make a deal for information regarding High Fae. Second, you tell me Verena might be dying, and you have *no idea why*." Sarcasm dripped off his tongue viciously at the last part. "Now, you want me to calm down? You cannot be this daft, Orla. After our decades of partnership, I had begun to believe you were one of the more intelligent of your kind. I can regretfully say, I fooled myself. And I do not take kindly to being fooled."

"I apologise for your feeling of being fooled. I do. But Kieran, I have not acted to deceive." She continued backing up, hands in front of her. Aware she only needed to take a right and then a handful more feet where she could bolt towards the portal. "I will admit it was a slight oversight to give Verena the transfusion. However, we didn't know it would cause this reaction to her. How could we have? What they did and tried, they were acting with the information they had and what could only have been assumed was in her best interest, we swear it! Please, Kieran, help us. Help her. You could hold the information we need to keep her alive."

"A slight oversight!" His boisterous laugh filled the corridors, his eyes catching the guards lining the halls. Weapons in hand and confusion on their faces. They were ready for a fight and didn't know the reason for it, but their training dictated that they ask no questions. "A slight oversight is giving a puppy a ball when it should be given a bone. A slight oversight is teaching a child to run before they can walk. A slight oversight is impatiently killing someone who holds necessary information." With each sentence, he stalked closer towards her, his anger rising again.

She said nothing, having nothing to say as she continued backing away. Her back brushed the tip of a sword as she realised guards blocked her only path towards her portal, her only path back to Alusso and the safety of their sanctum. The Ancient Willow naturally ward against those not welcome by the Druids. She began to panic, feeling Heathrow's worry caressing her mind through their bond. Cohesive thoughts were unable to transverse dimensions, but feelings could. She knew he could feel something was wrong. Could feel her panic and anxiety but could not place the cause. Orla would need to figure out a way to rectify the situation before Heathrow did something crazy, like come through the portal. She might have been uninvited, but he would be slaughtered on sight. A vision she would not be able to live through twice, having watched her first mate rip himself to shreds in his blood craze.

"A slight oversight is not giving a High Fae, having spent over a century away from her realm, her people, a transfusion of regular Fae blood. Do you not recognise the dangers you have put her in? The dangers she is now suffering from because of what you consider a slight oversight?"

"We know, Kieran. That is exactly why I am here." Orla gulped, her brain trying to figure out a plan. "We need help." She admitted, throwing her pride out the window and hoping it would shock him enough to see reason. To calm him to a point where they could collectively come up with a solution.

"Why should I help you, Orla? Why should I help you and not raid your precious sanctum altogether? Why should I not bring her home, where she would at least not be subjected to idiocy? Hmm? Tell me why." He cocked an eyebrow, the flames dwindling from a roar to embers.

"Because Kieran, you know there are no better healers than the Druids. No one is better than them—not even the Fae and especially not Demons. She's safe in their protection, safe under their care, but even they do not know how to bring her out of her coma." Orla took a brave step forward, reaching her hand out. "Will you help her or not?"

"Of course, I am going to help her, you daft bint!" Kieran roared, his anger breaking the seal. "Now get out before I kill you for just existing." His guards parted, allowing her access to the portal.

"When shall we expect to hear from you?" Orla yelled at him, scrambling to get to the portal home before Kieran decided against not killing her. The temperature increased as the seconds passed, and her legs burned. What felt like an eternity trickled by, feeling as if she would never reach it in time before he exploded. Taking everyone not of Demon blood down with him.

"Just go. We will calm him. You have mere seconds before he reaches a point where we all might not survive."

A strong feminine voice sounded behind her, cold hands pushing her towards her destination.

Orla looked back to catch a glimpse of long white hair and the tips of black flesh-like jagged wings barreling towards the room she just left. As she ran headlong into the portal, the all familiar feeling of a rapid pull and drop took over. Her stomach seemed to rise into her throat, and her heart felt like it couldn't beat. The feeling of free fall consumed her, but a tether around her midsection pulled her back to the world where she belonged. She would soon face the interrogation of her peers, something her head already pounded from in anticipation. She could feel the headache coming, her head splitting in two as dizziness and disorientation soon took over. As quickly as it began, she felt herself slam back into reality.

Chapter 20

KIERAN

B lue hot fire suffocated Kieran, the loud screams of
orders rushing to his ears. His body moved on its
own accord, throwing flame after flame, ember after ember. He began collecting his anger and fear, funnelling
the emotions into his hands. His power was unparalleled,
Dremorta Flames, named after him when he started showing signs of this new type of Demonic fire. His officers
surrounded him, and chaos continuously erupted as the
constant barking of updates and status reports added to
his ringing ears. The information was still necessary. He
needed the updates from the battlefront and status reports
for the soldiers, this did nothing to calm his nerves and
added to his angst and ire.

Heavy wings and dying screams never stopped from
above him. Regardless of how many his flames slaughtered, more kept coming, replacing their fallen brethren.
He was on the brink of burning, his body heavy and
breathing harder. Delaney, Kieran's previous lover, a
woman he still respected and needed, noticed his state, and
her hand rested on his shoulder. Her more petite frame
pressed into him, a bow in her hand, and her quiver peeking behind her wings. She was speaking to him or someone
else, Kieran didn't know. He only knew her mouth moved;
her breath caressed his skin, but there was no sound.

It was too loud for Kieran to hear her; there were too many sounds, such as yelling, agonising screams, and barked orders elsewhere. He couldn't tell where to focus his attention, his head constantly on a swivel, attempting to locate the source of all the noise. The main sound flooding his head was a mournful howl. Something in him wanted to comfort the source, end their misery, anything to stop the haunting echo in his head.

"Kieran, my darling, you're safe. You're home." Whispers in the wind, seemingly coming from nowhere and everywhere.

"Safe? How could we be safe in the midst of this?" He raged, unable to find the speaker. His hands gripped the spear.

"Get down!" Someone else screamed from his left.

"My Lord!" Delaney's seductress tone was laced with worry.

He reacted without thought, gripping Delaney and pulling her into him, using his free hand to tuck her wings in tight before slamming them to the ground. He knew they would both feel it later, and he would suffer the consequences, but until the moment arose, he didn't care. Her breathing laboured, or was it his? He looked down at her under him, her wings sprawled in the dirt, hair tousled, and blood covered her face in splotches. She was beautiful, an avenging Demon in her black armour and dark red wings. She smiled at him, her fangs bloodied, and her lips split. The light of her smile reached her eyes. Those ethereal white irises he could get lost in for centuries. She whispered something, her armoured hands resting on his cheek. He was lost in her, he couldn't feel the blood seeping into the creases of his own set of blackened armour.

"My love, come back to us." He closed his eyes as her

words reached his ears. Her smile was ingrained in his memory.

"I am right here, beautiful." He looked upon her again, her silver irises closed and the smile fading on her lips. "I have not left. I will not. Ever." Her hand fell from his face, clattering on the ground beside them. He startled, shifting his weight to bring his hand to her cheek.

"Delaney?" He shook her softly, unresponsive.

"Delaney!" He repeated her name, his voice increasing in pitch until he was eventually screaming out for her.

"Kieran..." The sound again from behind him was so faint he thought he imagined it.

"DELANEY!" He broke, tears running down and splashing against her paling flesh.

He pulled them up into a sitting position. His knees haphazardly under them, her wings lifeless under his arm, her blood-matted hair whispering in the breeze, and her head had to be supported by his hand. He noticed the gaping wound in her abdomen, a fatality he could only assume was meant for him. A fatality she earned from stepping in front of him to protect him, save him, keep him alive and fighting. Kieran's heart shattered. The well of tears he fought viciously against broke as he screamed. A roar of heartbreak unleashed upon the battlefield, so loud the fighting stopped, staring at the direction it came from. All his subjects, comrades, and Demons stopped at once and dropped to a knee. Their heads lowered, weapons buried in the ground, and fists closed over their heart. Their Prince's screams echoed through their core. The battle was forgotten as if one they shared in his grief.

Kieran raged, his head thrown back as he screamed to the Heavens above. He was cursing the Gods, the Angel's, the damn maids, everyone. He howled and shook as hands gripped him harshly, trying to tear her away from him. To take her away, away from where she should be, alive and breathing, firing her Daedalic Bow into the hearts of their foes. Each arrow notched fueled with her green fire, releasing a bright green path as it struck true.

"Let her go!" He snapped at the attendant, trying to take her to be placed in stasis until they could return to Borraine. "No! No, please. Please. I can't. I can't let her go." He sobbed, his broken state leaving no dry eyes in the vicinity.

"Sir, I'll keep her safe. I swear it. I'll bring her home." They convinced him as he released her limp, lifeless body. "I'll bring her home."

Kieran's hands stayed steady in the same position he had held her, her warmth fading from his arms. His tears dried up, anger took over, and his body began to ignite. Sparks of blue crackled and burned away the memory of her blood dripping down his armour. Tips of her waist-length black hair flew in the breeze, covered in his blue fire. His hands fell to his knees, armour clanking and sparks flying around to sizzle the pool of blood he was knelt in.

"She's gone." He whispered to nobody in particular. "She's gone."

"She is gone, darling. But you are here. You are here, but her memory is never gone. I've got you, my little flame. Come back to us." The blasted voice in his head sounded again. He wanted to claw his brain out, look at it, and ask why it would be taunting him. After everything he had gone through, was it not enough? Could it not leave him alone? Let him mourn in peace?

He looked down around him, surrounded by a high wall of fire. Crackling and angry, he watched as it licked at anyone who dared come near. His brethren were doing everything they could on the opposite side to gain his attention, trying to bring their commander back as the temporary peace ended. His Demons needed him, needed his help, and here they were, stuck on the other side without any clue how to bring him back. Kieran took in a deep breath, looking up at the sky. The clear green skies and mountainous terrain in the Fae realm of Lothaire were exceptionally different to the red skies back in Borraine. He wondered if Delaney would have enjoyed a mountain house somewhere in Lothaire, a getaway to escape when life became too much.

"You would have loved it here, Del. We could have bought a mountain home near the water. I know how much you loved water, even though you couldn't swim." He laughed, tears coming back to his face as his rage-fuelled his flames higher and higher. "We could have taught the Fae children how to speak Axani." A language familiar to the Demon lords of old which allowed them to stand out above the lesser. "But these egotistical idiots couldn't live in fucking peace, could they?" Kieran got to his feet, completely encased in fire at this point. Not a single inch of him was safe.

"You just couldn't be fucking peaceful, could you!" He screamed into the air, his face streaked with drying tears and eyes closing.

A loud crack sounded above him, and shadows eclipsed the sunlight on his face. Had his eyes been open, he would have watched ally and foe drop to the ground. Their heads bowed, and weapons were discarded as the shadow that eclipsed the sun fell out of the sky. Slamming into the ground, not but a hundred feet away from him. The earth shook from the impact, causing him to stumble. His eyes rapidly opened, and his gaze landed on the ten-foot-tall woman with black wings held proud and high. Heavily armoured in her own set of black, her waist-length hair in a neat braid swayed on her back. Steel-dipped feather tips, every inch of this female oozed deadly as if she was created to kill mercilessly. Bright red eyes on a pale, angular face met him. Even across the length of distance between them, he could see them. On her hip, a longsword, a glowing red gem on the hilt and the tip of a longbow hiding on her spine, taunting with each other step. Compulsion washed over him. He knew her from somewhere. He couldn't put a name to the face, his grief clouding his memory.

"My lord, get down." His mates hissed at him from outside his fire ring.

Kieran refused, and his anger was the cause of his reckless behaviour. He couldn't be bothered. His heart felt miles away, and if this winged person would kill him for his lack of courtesies, it would be better. She continued her trek towards him, and those in her way parted before her. As she passed, their bodies lowered significantly. Whispers and murmurs spread rapidly, too many for him to understand. The flame's roar clogged his ears as they crackled and popped angrily, begging to be unleashed. He watched her, feet away now from his fire. Where many stepped back, she continued head-on. He hesitated, battling himself on whether he should warn her to stay away. Not capable of watching another die so close to losing Delaney. He didn't, his curiosity capturing the best of him as he wondered if she would attempt to get closer.

"Kieran Dremorta, Prince of Borraine." He recognised her tone, authority.

He said nothing, obviously this winged person knew him, yet he still had yet to remember who she was. His mind ravaged every memory of every lecture he had been forced to attend. His mother's nagging at him to pay attention played on repeat in his head, an irritating reminder of his failure. His distraction broke as his breath caught in his throat. He watched her step close to his flames and then step over it. Unharmed. No screams of pain were coming from her. His mouth dropped, flames stuttering as she was now in front of him. She was perfect, beautiful in ways he could have never imagined. His heart felt disgusted, having just lost his first love mere minutes before.

"Kieran... my little flame, everything is alright. Come back to us."

"What?" He looked at the beauty before him, and surely she had not said what he believed she did?

"Get up, Kieran." She reached her hand out towards him, clad in black clawed armoured gloves.

Reality came into shape around him, and battlefields faded to the dark green walls of his home. The silver-framed portraits came into focus, screaming agony turned to light ringing and from light ringing to the regular bustle of his home. The woman's tall frame in front of him dwarfed his relatively larger size for a Demon, and he wondered if he could blush. Would he have? He accepted her offer, his hand reaching for hers as his temper lowered. Fire cooling down from a raging volcano to a campfire, his soldiers' faces became more apparent as the wall came down. He squinted; their faces morphed into those of his guards, attendants, and servants. He looked up at the winged woman, her wings transitioning from black feathers to black flesh, her face from angular to heart-shaped. Her long black hair faded to white, and her red eyes changed into black.

"Mother?" He whispered weakly, his throat sore and scratchy.

"Oh, my little flame." She wept, her arms crashing around him fiercely and swaying them back and forth on the ground where she held them.

His body felt heavy, and his eyes burned as he closed them. Resting his head against his mother's shoulder, he smelled soot and ashes. His body tensed. He wondered how badly he burned the room this time. A singular tear dropped down his cheek, one not missed by her as she whispered sweet nothings while wiping the tear away. His mother had always been his biggest supporter, the one who would ground him during his episodes. Having found him hiding away after his first. Years had passed since the war. Attempting to lock himself in his bath, believing the water around him could keep him from burning his surroundings. She happened to walk by his room, hearing his screams and the sizzling of water. Barging in, regardless of propriety and etiquette, she didn't hesitate to climb in after him. His clothing was soaked, and his hair was ruined; his mother didn't care. She held him as he sobbed, as he screamed and thrashed against her. Begging her to end his misery, to stop the memories from tormenting him day in and out. Ever since, she had an obscene sense of knowing when he was on the precipice of breaking. Always rushing to his side, holding him, grounding him, enduring the fire his body released uncontrollably.

"Talk to me, dear. What happened?" She stroked his hair, cradling him close. Her wings curled in on them. A visage of privacy as she subtly nodded to release the bystanders. The silent order to leave them understood as fabric and metal rustled out.

"She's dying, Mother." His voice cracked, sobbing. The feeling of disappointment washed over him. He gripped her to him tighter, needing the physical reassurance to calm him.

"Who is dying?" Sylvia ran her manicured nails down his cheek, urging him to let out the pain he was feeling. She would keep him safe, she swore it when he came back from losing Delaney.

"Verena," Kieran whispered, his tears drying up as his body began to shut down.

"Jerifeyn's daughter?" Her curiosity peaked; she had yet to hear the name of the High Fae's offspring.

"The very same." He yawned, exhausted.

"She's alive? How?" Her hands faltered momentarily before returning to stroke his hair. "Was she not the same person rumoured to be lost over a century ago?"

"She was, now allegedly, she is in Alusso. She's been so close this whole damn time, and now she's fucking dying." He croaked, his head pounding. "I have yet to even meet her in person, and I might never get the chance to meet her now." Pushing himself to his knees in preparation to get up.

"One step at a time, dear. Tell me what happened." She let him go, unfolding herself from her position on the floor. Electing to stand with him, her wings marginally flapped to stabilise her as she gracefully got to her feet.

Kieran stalked towards his sitting room, not wanting to see the damage he caused, as he kept his head up. Knowing his mother would follow, he refused to wait any longer in the room he destroyed. Pausing in front of his reception room, he tossed around the idea of burning the entire room. His anger residual from the news Orla gave him. He could re-decorate once Verena was home, where she should have been decades ago. He cursed Francis' grave, promising himself he would stop by the old oak tree he was buried under to do so. His mother's light footsteps behind him motivated him to continue on. His lips curled at the thought of telling her she could decorate, one of her favourite pastimes.

"Shall I request some tea, Mother?" He threw over his shoulder, knowing her devious mind was already at work. It would be a long afternoon and his head pounded from his episode.

She hummed, her acknowledgement silent, her thoughts flying, scheming. Their footsteps slowed as Kieran reached the double-arched doors, his numerous Sargynx filled lanterns floating above. Skylights, the span of his ceiling, highlighted the sunken onyx furniture, and red blossomed trees petaled the glass. The back wall features a waterfall cascading into the live koi pond at the base. On the left were three doors: his bedroom, private study, and bathroom. The right side was pure glass, and a double door located in the middle opened to a large mahogany balcony overlooking the Hellsdusk lake. This room was one of Kieran's favourites; the serenity of the waterfall and the red blossom trees created the perfect place for him to relax after a long day. They proceeded towards the sofa, his entire body collapsing onto the soft onyx cushions as his mother perched on the edge of the opposite. Ever poised and proper, he blamed the succubus side of her for it.

"Now, tell me everything." Her eyes met his, settling into the mischievous woman he knew she was. Her delicate hands wrapped around the teacup, delivered minutes after they entered the room.

Kieran explained everything, from his episode, Delaney dying, seeing *her* again, to what Orla told him about what happened to Verena. He refused to leave a single detail out, knowing they would need every piece of information to plan. Kieran's temper raised again at the thought of the

Wolves' ignorance. Though the information did not shock him, previous experience with them had shown him their intelligence. Their tendency to not ensure the outcome of their plans would be beneficial has landed them in dire need. Much to the Demons' benefit, having granted many deals in the past centuries. He wrecked his brain, mentally going through the information they knew on High Fae. His mother's expression turned from unamused, to anger, and exhaustion. At least Kieran was grateful she was on the same wavelength as he, his irritation for their stupidity palatable.

"Fools, the whole lot of them." Surprising them both, she rolled her eyes. "In what mindset would you inject someone having been raised around Wolves the entirety of their life and expect them to be acceptable the next day?"

"I questioned this as well." Kieran agreed with her, having the same questions arise when he learned of Verena's upbringing.

"It has been at least a century since she was born, has it not?" Sylvia spoke out loud, perhaps asking nobody and everybody all at once. Her mind surprised him at times, her ability to perceive details those else would have missed.

"Indeed, at least. Perhaps a bit more." Kieran was unsure if she was asking him or hypothetically, erring on the side of answering in either case.

"Where has she been all this time?" Sylia hummed her confusion, tapping her nails rhythmically.

"I am not sure, and she vanished almost directly after her birth." Kieran understood where Sylvia was going with her trail of thought. Putting together the pieces she laid out in front of him.

"I would presume—this is just my assumption—that Jerifeyn would put her daughter in stasis. This would allow Verena to stay a babe until a later time, though we know the process to do such is costly. She must have been passed to a caretaker, someone the Nightingales trusted, someone who could live an exceptionally long time." Her inquisitive mind spelled everything out, every possibility Kieran had thought about was presented to him by the very woman who knew him the best.

"There are not many species with long life spans, however." Kieran supplemented. He only knew of a handful of species capable of surviving the longevity of the Fae, leaving them with a short list of potential candidates.

"No, it does narrow it down, though. If she is in Alusso, we could assume she has never left. I would expect the stasis to only be able to handle planer teleportation once. This limits us to the Vampyres and Elves as beings with near immortality." The moment the two species left her tongue, Kieran watched Sylvia's face scrunch in distaste. As per typical with Demon kind, they hated the thought of the spawn known as Vampyre. Yet to speak it usually left a bad taste in ones mouth.

"I could not see her being given to a bloodsucker; they would have drained her dry the moment she reached them." His lips curled in disgust. The Vampyre was a spawn of Daerkyn Demon and Blood Elves—beautiful creatures, taking the beauty of Elves but the bloodlust of Daer.

Should have been put down the moment the spawn was born. Fucking disgusting beings.

A regret he has been unable to live with for millennia when a Daer Demon mated with the seductress. He crossed the possibility out of his mental list, focusing on the elves. Running through all known clans, he selected three possibilities for caretakers among them.

"What about the Draecon, Ambrose, or Galent Clans?" Kieran supplied three possible Elf clans who could have taken in a comatose baby. They had the longevity and were, albeit distant, cousins of the Fae.

"No, I do not believe so. She should not have had such a dramatic reaction to a transfusion had she been exposed to magic for a majority of his life." Kieran did not think about the reaction, Sylvia was right. The Elves carry magic within themselves as well, Verena would not have a severe reaction had she been raised by them.

"What are you thinking then, Mother?" Kieran had exhausted all possibilities; his shortlist was depleted.

Her eyes brightened, a wicked smile growing on her lips. He knew she had figured it out, the woman with a penchant for rumours. He surmised when he became as old as she, he would use all resources of information he could grasp his hands on as well. The truth was at the base of all rumours if one knew how to discern the lie. He watched her gently set her teacup down, ironing out the invisible wrinkles in her gown and then fixing him with a knowing smile. He sighed, dragging a pillow over his face. Knowing she would make him wait, she collected her thoughts and organised them into a cohesive statement. An eternity passed, his body creeping towards sleep. Having exhausted his energy stores with his episode, on the brink of slumber, his mother gently cleared her throat. Kieran rolled his eyes, moving the pillow slightly, just enough to uncover one eye. Just enough to see her poised perfectly, her wings neatly tucked behind her, and her feet delicately crossed to the side. "Do go on, Mother. I was almost asleep and would greatly appreciate the opportunity to think of anything but this." Kieran yawned, his hand came to cover it as etiquette dictated.

"She wasn't housed with the Elves, my son. Not in the slightest." She paused for dramatic effect, his accompanying sigh making her chuckle. "She was housed with a hybrid."

Chapter 21

ORLA

Taking in a deep breath, the clean and crisp air of the inner sanctum met her. Her hands shook as she came down from her adrenaline rush. Heathrow's callous, ravaged hands pulled her to his chest. Her wolf howling in her head for him, her body shaking uncontrollably. She laid her forehead on his chest, her arms coming to circle her. She could hear his heartbeat ravaging, his anger gravitating out of him. She softly moaned, grateful to have escaped Borraine before Kieran's anger could be unleashed. Her body shook at the idea of what could have happened had his mother not pushed her forward. Orla knew she owed Sylvia her life because of it, silently acknowledging their life pact.

"Talk to me, petal," Heathrow murmured in her hair, having not let her go since she came through the portal. Her shaking had diminished over the previous minutes. "What happened? I could feel you but couldn't hear you."

"We had to restrain him physically, Orla. He was seconds from jumping through the portal." Armand sighed, his exhaustion palpable from the sound.

"Do tell, Orla. I almost broke a nail trying to keep him in check." Islabell huffed, checking her manicure, and Orla's irritation skyrocketed.

"You did nothing, Islabell, but sit on your ass watching

the rest of us struggle to keep him from doing anything he would regret later." Hansen snapped back, the blind man tapping his way towards the couple. "Orla, what happened?"

Heathrow surprised her, swooping her up and taking her over to sit in a chair. Not wanting to let her go as she curled into his arms. Taking in a deep breath, she looked at her companions. Their eyes are all on her, awaiting her answer, impatiently for some.

"I had asked to make a deal, to trade anything for information on High Fae. What I had not expected was the deal to go south." Orla leaned her head against Heathrow's broad chest, fighting the urge to fall asleep in the safety of his arms.

"What do you mean?" Hansen's cane tapped again, she watched him reach the centre of the room and turned in the direction he believed she was in.

"Prince Kieran was already in a foul mood, perhaps from a previous engagement before I arrived. He did not seem amicable in making a deal, which is where I possibly should have left to try again later. However, knowing the subject's time sensitivity, I elected to stay and attempt. I did not expect him to counter with a deal of his own." Orla stifled a yawn, her head pounded after being subjected to disorientation from the portal and the Prince of Hell's moodswing.

"What deal?" Hansen asked her, a smile crept on Orla's face as he was faced the opposite way of where she was.

"If he managed to guess why we needed the information, I had to tell him everything on why."

"And?" Armand's voice was laced with worry, and he braced himself against the table.

"He guessed it correctly." Orla was exhausted and knew

the reaction she would receive, though she could not hide it any longer.

"He guessed correctly?" Islabell demanded, the exact reaction Orla knew would come, came.

Orla placed her hands on Heath's chest in an attempt to keep him calm in the face of what she was about to say. She could feel his heart beating, his hands gripping her tighter. She knew he would do something irrational had she not been in his lap. She watched as they all looked at her, waiting for her answer.

"He knows we have Verena." Orla clarified, seemingly useless, as they all knew where she had been. It should have been obvious to her, though Orla chastised herself for assuming.

Everyone stopped moving, heartbeats quickened, and Heathrow's arms tightened around her. The silence was deafening. Orla's anxiety was reaching heights she hadn't been to since her youth. Her breathing quickened, her body tensed, and her grip on Heath tightened. She waited for the ensuing response she knew would come. Seconds turned into minutes. The time carried onwards before everything burst into chaos, everyone talking over the other. Orla's head swam with the heightened emotions overwhelming her. Heathrow pulled her closer to him, almost smothering her with his more oversized frame. His lips came to touch her forehead, his breathing heavy.

"Everything is going to be alright, flower," Heath whispered against her hair, his voice overpowering the chaotic surroundings.

"How can it be, Heath? I was meant to gain information, and now I might have started a war we do not have the resources to win."

Orla placed a hand over his lips, listening to Armand

give orders. Tension rose between the others, all awaiting their directives. Islabell locked eyes with her. Animosity laced her pupils. Orla shivered, and everything within her screamed for her to run. Intuitively, she knew Islabell couldn't be trusted.

"Islabell, secure the Willow and inform the Druids of the impending attack. Ensure all active patients can be stabilised should an attack occur and we lose the ability to leave for some time."

"Understood." Islabell curtly answered, glaring at Orla again before stalking out of the room. Her stilettos clacked against the ground loudly.

"Heathrow, prepare our Elites. Have them stationed outside Verena's room and as close to the portals as possible within the wards. So long as we are within them, Kieran and his Demons should not be able to cross them."

"Should not?" Heathrow questioned.

"Theoretically." Armand clarified.

"*Theoretically.*" Heath mocked, his tongue dripping with sarcasm.

"It has not yet been tested, but yes, theoretically, the Demons should not be able to get past the wards." Armand sighed, knowing his answer was bound to anger the giant wolf.

"Brilliant. We are putting stock into untested bounds with our lives." Heathrow stood up, Orla in his arms. "I can cross off 'test ward boundaries against Demons' from my bucket list."

"Orla-" Armand started.

"No, whatever you are about to say to her, Armand, the answer is no." Heathrow bit out, pressing Orla into his chest.

"Heathrow..."

"Do you want to go toe to toe with me right now, Armand?" Heathrow asked as he set her down in the seat he had vacated earlier.

Orla watched Armand weigh the options presented to him, his face blanching as he recognised Heathrow was far from jesting. She buried her face into his neck, nuzzling him, her hands coming to grip his shoulders. "Heath, don't." She whispered.

"Very well, flower." He proceeded to pick her back up, his eyes locking with Armand's in a challenge. Orla assumed Armand had backed down, as he refrained from saying anything else instead. He elected to move on.

Armand's voice faded rapidly as Heathrow took her from the meeting room. She could hear the loud beating of boots against the ground as people rushed around her. The clanking of heavy armour being rustled around as Elites moved to post. Ripping and tearing as some shifted into their wolf form. Sounds of wolves being armoured reached her ears before the final order Armand gave, a whisper now from the distance Heathrow had gotten in the seconds from leaving. A final direction before the peaceful sanctum turned into a battleground, awaiting the inevitable.

"Hansen, inform the sanctum; code Asmodeus."

Chapter 22

MERRIDAYN

"Can I get you anything else, Luna Merridayn?" Gracie spoke without knocking, her head suddenly appearing in the doorway, startling Merridayn.

"What?" Merridayn straightened up in the chair she resided in, her spine screaming. She did not know when she must have dozed off but knew how she slept was not kind to her body. She looked around, meeting Gracie's smile. "I must have closed my eyes for too long and succumbed to sleep."

"Quite alright. It's been about an hour since you returned from your shower and changed your clothing." Gracie's movement, ever graceful, as she strode further into the room, a little clipboard in her hands and her pockets stuffed to the brim.

"Actually, can you sit with Verena for a few? I want to go through the archive but don't want to leave her alone should she wake." Merridayn portrayed her worry through the wringing of her hands, a silent plea for the healer to sit with Verena.

"I'd be delighted, Luna." Gracie stepped to put her clipboard onto a hidden slot near the door, overlooked by Merridayn when she first came in. The oversight was understandable, the file holder blended into the moss-covered wall. Merridayn caught a glimpse of Gracie tying her

hair into a messy bun, the action reminding her of someone. She couldn't figure out who it reminded her of, but
the feeling of recognition flooded her.

"Oh, before I forget, can I get a change of clothes for her
and a wash basin? I'd like to get her changed and clean so
she doesn't feel dirty when she wakes." Verena had been
sweating profusely the last few hours when Merridayn
dozed off. Feeling guilty, she wanted to adjudicate herself
by changing Verena as she failed her job to watch over the
child.

"Certainly, they will be waiting when you return." Gracie came to stand at the end of Verena's bed, tilting her
head as she took note of her charge.

"Thank you. I'll be off now." Merridayn hurriedly collected her things, stuffed them into her bag, and headed
off. Pausing at the doorway, she looked back at Verena. A
pang of guilt hit her again for the trouble she had caused
the girl. Merridayn vowed she would find a way to wake
her. She had to, or she felt as if the guilt would eat at her as
it had with her daughter.

The way Gracie interacted with Verena brought waves
of emotion to Merridayn. Her brain attempted to figure
out why she thought she knew the healer. Having met a
plethora of healers before, Merridayn grew irritated with
her inability to appease the feeling. She scoffed at herself,
shaking the eerie feeling off as her feet took her towards
the archives. Soft moss turned to hard dirt as she neared
the entrance to the sanctum. The hallways, busy with the
comings and goings of others, headed in a multitude of
directions; from the soft steps of Druids, to the clanking
of guards' armour. Merridayn was silently thankful she did
not have the advanced hearing of the wolves. She knew
her head would have been a raging battlefield of migraines

had she been born with such. As she walked further and further, the noises faded to nothing. Her feet came back into contact with the soft moss she knew.

Sizeable white oak doors came into view. The intricate swirls and knotwork one would find in a Druid dwelling stood tall and proud. Small bird perches carved into the wood held a multitude of avian species, all stopping as she approached, their beady eyes glaring at her for interrupting them. Their gaze felt as if they were judging if she was worthy enough to pass by them without harm. Merridayn took a frightened step back. She had not been warned of any guardians in any of her lectures. Searching for the handle, she was left to ascertain there was not one, at least not a physical one she could see. Now, Merridayn was left without any idea of how to get inside. The thought of leaving and returning later crossed her mind. Returning with a companion better equipped to open the door may be best. Just as she had almost made her mind up, she recognised a soft tapping coming from behind her.

"I was wondering when you would arrive, Merridayn." Hansen chuckled, his white cane coming into view before he rounded the corner.

She listened as the canaries chirped excitedly, their eyes landed on the elder. The sing-song voice sang their praise to him as he came near. His uncanny ability to stop right before hitting anyone did not fail. His cane was centimetres from her feet, and his hand outstretched for her to take. Without looking a gift horse in the mouth, she took his invitation as a means to pass the unsettling birds. A smug look crossed her face as the feathered animals moved to reveal the black wrought iron handles they had been hiding. Merridayn questioned if the little nuisances could speak. She garnered they would be cursing her profusely if they had the ability. Their little eyes rested on her in irritation, a silent pass only because their master had granted her permission.

"Ignore them, Merridayn. They tend to hold grudges against others who are not myself and a very, very select few. Even Armand cannot pass a fair selection of time, while Heathrow once threatened to pluck every feather to turn it into a coat should they try stopping him." Hansen chuckled to himself, perhaps at the memory of Heathrow yelling at cognizant canaries.

"I feel so much better, Hansen." Merridayn jested, still apprehensive of them. "Honest."

"Come, child, what brings you here at this hour?" Hansen pushed the doors open, the dim lighting of the archives flaring to life as he stepped through. Rows and rows of books lined shelves at least ten feet tall, covered in vines, branches and flora. Besides, from the doorway, no birds were seen flying around. The books somehow shimmered as if something was reflecting the sunlight. Hansen took a deep breath, his face relaxing as the scent of earth and parchment filled their nostrils. Merridayn took in how the branches curved to form dome peaks, glass framed between the hollows in various shades of greens. Trails of sparkles bounced between shelves, high and low, before fading into nothing. Books floated as if being carried by nothing, trails being left as they soared across the space.

Curious...

"Those are imgrids, Merridayn. Obsessive little creatures, they frock to knowledge like lifelines. Think of them as if they were hoarders, collectors if you will. They make some of the best keepers of books alive, keeping them immaculate." Hansen reached out, patiently waiting.

"Hoarders?" Merridayn repeated. "What do they look

like, elder?"

"Hansen is fine, child. I am fairly young to be considered an elder. The task bestowed on me only due to my blindness." He chuckled, grinning at her. "I would make a terrible warrior. The whole inability to determine ally or foe. I can't protect someone I cannot see." He used his free hand to wave it in front of his face, indicating there was no sight between his eyes. There was laughter aplenty coming from him, he had come to terms with his circumstances.

Merridayn let out a small laugh with him, her nerves rising as she couldn't determine if laughing was an acceptable answer to his jest. Her anxiety vanished as a creature, no bigger than a softball, landed in his hands. She stepped closer, trying to understand better what she was seeing. Before her was the body and tail of a fox, light and fluffy; however, they had the feet of a long and pointy crow filing into claws. Their face was angular and furry, but instead of a nose and mouth, Merridayn saw a beak. Ears of a fox but snout of a crow. The imgrid looked at her, and soft blue eyes stared into hers. She watched as the creature tilted its head, tapping its front claw on Hansen's palm.

"Hansen?" Merridayn startled, looking at the elder for direction. She did not know what to do or say.

"Hold your hand out, she wants to come to you." He was serious, Merridayn was sure. Though, she wondered if it would be much too disrespectful to say no.

Merridayn obeyed, her hand shakily rising from her side as her eyes closed. Her fear caused her to be unable to watch as the imgrid sprang off Hansen's palm, jumping to her outstretched one. Merridayn gasped, the imgrid's fur was softer than she expected as the creature nuzzled into her fingers. Sharp little points dug into her hand, rougher than expected but not hard enough to hurt. She

opened her eyes, trying her hardest not to insult the creature by dropping her. The same blue eyes stared back, and
a slight sound came from the imgrid. Tail swishing and ears
perked, Merridayn wondered if the imgrid wanted something. She looked to Hansen for guidance. Panic filled
her as she noticed Hansen had walked away towards the
centre of the room. Looking between her palm, which the
imgrid perched upon, and Hansen getting farther away,
Merridayn began to stress. Choosing the safest option, she
held her hand close to her chest as she sprinted towards
Hansen. Her secondary hand came to clutch the imgrid
closer to keep the creature from stumbling off her.

"Hansen!" Merridayn whispered, yelling at the elder
wolf, the imgrid snuggling into her breasts. She looked
down, panic apparent on her face, before morphing into
fear. Merridayn was afraid of the creature she clutched to
her as if it were a baby, uncertain if the imgrid would bite
or worse.

"She likes you, Merridayn," Hansen called out, his cane
tapping against the floor as he walked closer towards the
steps near the centre of the room.

"You put this, this thing in my hand and ran off. Now
you tell me she likes me?" Merridayn grumbled to herself.

"You keep speaking to her like you are, and I would not
blame her should she bite you." Hansen laughed, his cane
bouncing off the steps as he ascended them.

Merridayn looked down at the imgrid, their blue eyes
looking at her in defiance. A chill ran down her spine,
knowing the imgrid might bite if she continued to disrespect the creature. She elected to keep her mouth shut
while she came upon an empty desk from the clutter of
books. Reaching her hand out, she tried placing the imgrid
on the flat surface. Her eyes closed as she tried to control

the fear she had for the creature, she gave a slight tilt of her hand. Nothing happened, the weight still clung to her. Merridayn peaked through her lashes to see the imgrid staring up at her still.

"Go on, sweetie." Merridayn encouraged, tamping down her fear with a facade of gentleness.

The imgrid tilted her head at the words, climbing Merridayn's forearm instead. Merridayn's free hand came to slam over her eyelids, her whole body shaking. She almost fainted as a warm, large hand came to rest over her opposite shoulder.

"Relax, Merridayn. Kinley is harmless, she prefers to curl around shoulders." Hansen's voice caused Merridayn to calm down marginally. Her eyes opened to look at him as tiny claws continued to crawl up her.

"Kinley?"

"I have not yet found a way to communicate with them. Therefore, I do not know if they even have names. I named them when I first came to the sanctum long ago." Hansen responded to Merridayn's question before letting go of her shoulder and returning to his desk.

"How did you come over here without making a sound? Let alone without your cane?" Merridayn questioned him as Kinley reached her destination, Merridayn's neck.

She followed him to his desk, an ample space almost identical to the ones the healers use, as if a trunk came out of the ground to create the space for him. Books, pens, and paper were scattered around. There was a look of disorganisation at first, but Merridayn recognised Hansen's knowledge of the location for everything.

"I have been here for some time, child. Nobody but me and the imgrids traverse these halls anymore. Those who do, however, know never to move an object from where it currently resides. I have learned how many steps I need and in which direction I need from various compass points around the room. Look at the desk in front of you." Hansen's hands brushed across a raised portion near the front. Merridayn spotted a compass, true to his word, with an arrow carved more deeply into the wood, indicating north. "The imgrids put these in for me when they first realised I was blind. Eventually, they began recognising how things in the room needed to remain consistent for me to walk without using my cane. When patrons of the archives visit, the imgrids have been known to become violent if the patron disobeys the rules. Having accepted me as their own, they have become fiercely protective and are enforcers of maintaining my ability to continue coming here."

Merridayn noticed how Kinley rubbed her beak against the skin of her neck as if in affirmation of Hansen's words. Looking around the room, she saw the other imgrids visible had stopped what they were doing to stare at her. A silent warning to obey or be punished was clear. Merridayn slightly bowed her head, a gesture of willingness to ensure Hansen could continue to be in peace even with her presence in the room.

"How can I help you, Merridayn?" Hansen asked as he leaned against his desk.

"I need books on runes, preferably angelic, as well as any information we have on soulmates." Merridayn listed off, her mind rushing with all the unanswered questions. "Something isn't adding up with Verena, and I was hoping to get to the root of the problem."

"Very well, I will see about the imgrids collecting the books we have on the topics. Go, child, find a seat you are comfortable with. Kinley will accompany you however long you are here." Hansen waved her off, moving around his table to collapse into the plush oversized chair. His age made a small appearance as he rubbed his fingers against his temple.

Merridayn wandered the halls, coming to a stop beneath a high, pointed glass window. Overlooking the high plains of Gordfain, Merridayn took in a hefty breath. Kinley squealed at her, gaining her attention from the mesmerising sway of tall prairie grass. She turned to witness other imgrids floating towards her, books in their clutches. Merridayn counted at least ten books coming her way, a promising start to a daunting problem. Pulling out her notebook and pen, she got to work and settled in for a long evening ahead of her. Before taking a seat, Merridayn rummaged around her bag, looking for anything to tie off her hair. It needed washing and was bound to irritate her should it get in the way too often. She let out a shout, perhaps a bit too loud from the jab into her neck Kinley bestowed upon her.

"I'm sorry, I'm sorry." Merridayn weakly apologised. "I'll be quieter."

Taking up residence in the chair before her, Merridayn opened her notes, heading straight for the images Gracie had drawn of Verena's marking. Eyes skimming past all the variations Gracie had drawn and remembering the explanations she had given. Merridayn scribbled down the definitions Gracie had said. Her years as a nurse caught up with her as she compared Gracie's neat script with her rushed and barely legible one. Her heart fluttered at the sight, memories flooding her mind of her Vivianne learning to write. She wiped the tears from her eyes, attempting to focus on her notes again.

Marked and Promise.

Tracing her fingernail over the curves of the rune, Merridayn's head flew with endless possibilities. Kinley jumped off her shoulder, landing next to her hands. The imgrid's head tilted back and forth before stalking over to the stack of books that had been dropped off by her kind. Merridayn watched Kinley insistently peck at one near the middle of the pile.

"What is it, Kinley?" Merridayn pulled off the books above the one Kinley was trying to tell her about. Having grown reasonably fond of the creature within a short time, Merridayn trusted Kinley's opinion.

Merridayn reached the book, her heart racing. A large, leather-bound book greeted her. Hesitating to touch the book, Merridayn observed the impressions of faint lines decorating every inch. Large letters took front and centre in a dark red font: *Runics of the Fallen.* No author was listed, and nothing documenting anything else about the book besides the name. Merridayn gently reached for the book, her hand coming in contact with the soft material. Her mind questioned where she had felt such a material before. Upon opening the first page, she nearly dropped the book. There before her eyes stood a sentence of nightmares.

> *Rest the one thousand souls required to create.*
> *Their donations have been remembered.*
> *As readers are touching their skin, their memories should remain.*

"What in Goddess' grace is this?" Merridayn whisper yelled at Kinley, the poor creature looking at her as if this was an everyday occurrence.

Kinley nudged the book further, using her claws to flip

the pages gently. After successfully getting to the first page, Kinley stared at Merridayn. The imgrid looked annoyed as if Merridayn had never seen a book before. Rolling her eyes, Merridayn glanced at the first page. Her breath hitched at what she saw before her.

> *Over the span of my lifetimes, only one in particular has given this author reason to believe the world deserved to be bestowed the knowledge of Angels. Contained in this book is the magnitude of Angelic knowledge over Runes.*
>
> *Runes hold significant power over the universes, as this author knows it. This author has compiled a working list of all current known Runes in the Angelic language.*
>
> *Use the information at your own haste, as this author cannot guarantee the outcome of those sacrificed to produce this collection is amicable.*

Merridayn delicately flipped the page over, her stomach rolled at the notion of touching skin. The countless lives taken to have created such monstrous works battled against her morals. The logical part of her knew she needed the answers this book might contain, while the human part of her told her to burn the disgusting scrap of flesh. Kinley looked at her, choosing to climb back up Merridayn's arm to return to her perch around Merridayn's neck.

"You believe the information I need is in here?" Merridayn flicked her head towards the book sprawled open in front of her. Kinley's answering chirp confirmed Merridayn's suspicions.

We are diving into the skin book, Merr. Thank the Goddess, we haven't eaten yet.

Merridayn wished she had gloves or tongs—anything other than her bare hands to turn the pages. Fighting back vomit, she aimlessly flipped through the pages. Her eyes skimmed as she read through countless runes with variable meanings. She learned there were runes for anything and everything, from essential heating to storage, defensive to combative, and many in between.

Angels cannot do anything with their hands, can they? Always resorting to magic.

"I found one, Kinley." Merridayn rested her head against the back of her chair after a seemingly long time resisting the urge to puke while flipping the pages.

Promise: In 14970 BF, the day of the Great Fall, the Creators of Time bestowed the Rune of Promise to the Archangel Ariel. A sign of keeping a promise in which her sister, Archangel Azrael, would return to their realm.

Promise is signified by a distinct set of symbols, namely, the exterior stroke remaining straight instead of curving in any direction. The initial stroke is an elongated upside-down 'U' shape with a straight line on the left underneath the 'U'. Similarly, beneath the 'U' and to the right of the straight line is an 'L'. Starting above the elongated 'U', running through the top of the 'L' to the middle of the straight line is a secondary line.

This rune has been appointed to two others since the day of creation, and this author knows not who has them or the reasoning behind.

Gracie was wrong.

Merridayn's first reaction was shock, which was beginning to morph into confusion. If Gracie had lied about the markings, what else could she be lying about? With renewed vigour, Merridayn jotted down her findings and continued on, eagerly searching for the second rune Gracie had mentioned: Marked.

"Why would she lie to me?" Merridayn questioned out loud, not expecting an answer. Kinley cooed, her soft fur coming to rest upon Merridayn's clavicle. "I do not know either, Kinley. It is suspicious, though, isn't it?"

Merridayn's skimming of each page slowed as she began coming across battle and defensive runes. She wholeheartedly believed the 'Marked' rune should be between this section, she read various runes for ambushing and erecting wards. A neat rune about creating duplicates to confuse the enemy caught her attention.

Archangel Azrael was a renowned strategist, General, and assassin. Having been granted the title of Archangel of Death, Azrael achieved many combat feats. According to this author, one of her most impressive feats was her creation of the Duplication Rune.

As the name dictates, this rune can duplicate, specifically the user. Each duplicate is capable of its own thought process so long as it is within a certain distance from the caster. Azrael created the rune for combat

purposes when The Creators would deny
the Archangel reinforcements to battles. Before the rune was cast, legend dictated that
the Archangel would be battle-locked for
months. Her skill was outmatched due to the
sheer military size of the opposition.

Archangel Azrael is the only one known to
have the ability to use this rune. This author
suspects Azrael used higher portions of her
soul to create the rune.

Merridayn continued to read about the vague descrip-
tion of the rune, skimming the portion where the author
mentioned having only seen it once for a fraction of a
second. She tilted her head, her hand absently running
over the marking. Her stomach lurched into her throat
before dropping, she had seen this marking before.

But where? Where? Where? Where?

Merridayn looked around the room, her eyes darting
anywhere and everywhere before fishing her phone from
her bag. Ignoring her notifications, she opened her camera. Her eyes scanned the room one last time before she
snapped a photo. Kinley growled, her beak coming to jab
her in the neck again, rougher this time.

"Will you quit it?" Merridayn swatted at the imgrid, irritated. "For the love of the Goddess, I've seen this marking
before, Kinley. I'm only trying to reach out to my husband
for confirmation I am not going crazy." Kinley ignored
her, jabbing at her again.

"I swear on my life, Kinley. Look, you can watch me."
Merridayn showed Kinley her cellular screen, pulling up
messages between her and her husband.

[Text]: Merridayn? Love? I haven't heard from you all

day, is everything alright?

[Text]: Yes, darling. I dozed off for a bit, but I'm in the archives now. Can you look at this photograph and tell me if I am looney?

[Text]: Photograph Attachment

[Text]: Of course, darling.

[Text]: This does look familiar. Let me ask the boys. I cannot quite put my finger on it.

[Text]: How is Aven doing?

[Text]: Aven is anxious, which is to be expected. Since we left, he has refused to leave his room, barely eats, and blames himself for Verena's situation. I've got Cav now. Let me ask him.

Merridayn impatiently tapped her fingers against the edges of her screen, the feeling of hours flowing by as she waited for his response. She knew she had seen the rune before. Her mind flashed with little glimpses of it. The damned thing toyed with her emotions, the recognition on the tip of her tongue. Merridayn was about to message her husband again, but her patience was running out. Just as she was about to open her phone again, the relieving sound of an incoming message sang in her ears.

[Text]: Photograph Attachment

[Text]: Photograph Attachment

[Text]: Cavanaugh recognised it.

Merridayn's eyes immediately flew to the attachment, opening the file and enlarging the picture. Her heart stopped as she took in the familiar sights of her own home, her eyes coming to rest upon the painting in her dining room. She took in the Angel Cavanaugh had painted years prior, the painting having been placed there after he had completed it. The Angel had their back to the viewer, their massive black wings unfurled and dripping. Their red eyes peeked over their shoulders. Merridayn flipped to the second photograph Elion sent her. She dropped her phone at the sight. Elion had taken an up-close photo near the top of the painted Angel's spine. The duplication rune appeared carved into the Angel's skin, painted near the base of the neck.

Cavanaugh has been painting Azrael.

"Cavanaugh..." Merridayn whispered out loud, a silent tear running down her face.

Exiting out of the photograph, Merridayn typed out a message and then erased it. Having gone on for a few minutes, she composed one she hoped would be adequate to send. Pressing the button before she could talk herself out of it, she put her phone back in her bag to continue her search for the rune on Verena's shoulder. Her search reinvigorated after the gloomy recognition of Azrael displayed in multiple places within her household. Merridayn skimmed the rest of the pages until she stumbled upon the second rune Gracie mentioned, 'Marked.'

Finally, we've made it somewhere.

> Marked: The day of the Great Fall, the Creators punished those who have partaken in the war with this rune. Those bestowed with the rune are unable to return. Their lives are perpetually held outside of their home realm. Many choose to wander the universe, while others settle on various planets. A life of solitude and self-reflection.
>
> Marked is unique in form, a box created by opposing 'L' shapes. The top loop signifies eternity, while the bottom loop signifies regeneration. The rune was explicitly designed

as a bind, and the holders could not take their own lives, forever tormented by the inability to end their solitude.

This rune has been appointed to many, namely, Archangel Azrael, The Morningstar, Archangel Uriel, and Archangel Marcelle, as well as Demon King Asmodeus of Dremorta, Prince Kieran of Dremorta, Succubus Sylvia of Grafton, and Prince Torvan of Mordinian.

Holy shit.

Merridayn stared at the words again, her mind re-reading for the millionth time. Her pen dropped from her hand, startling Kinley. The imgrid rubbed her face against Merridayn's neck as she awoke.

Holy shit. Holy shit. Holy shit!

"We were wrong, Kinley." Merridayn grabbed the creature, bringing her to her face and kissing the imgrid's forehead. "We were completely and utterly wrong."

Kinley tilted her head in confusion but cried at the loss of affection. Merridayn absentmindedly continued petting her, her fingers burying in the soft fur along her spine. Her mind raced as everything she knew about the Great Fall, the War, the Angels, it was all altered. If this account was accurate, it changed everything.

"Jerifeyn was never going to marry Torvan at all, Kinley. Which means the Fae War was started over a fraud." Merridayn searched the table for her dropped pen, collecting it to begin jotting down every detail she could remember about what she had been told caused the Fae War. "Kinley, do you know what this means? It means the Mordinians possibly lied about Torvan's mysterious death. Nobody could confirm how he died or where he went. But according to this, he was given the Marked rune. He couldn't die even if he wanted to."

Wait a minute.

"Oh God!" Merridayn shouted, ignoring the looks she knew she gained. "Jerifeyn's contract would have been violated because of Torvan's participation in the War. There was no plausible way her parents would not have an exit clause, perhaps many if I were to guess. And according to this, the bearer of the rune cannot die. Which means he is still alive..." Merridayn trailed off. Her pen was digging into the paper.

Fuck. If he is still alive...

"So would be the prophecy." Hansen's deep voice startled her out of her chair. The loud crash as she tumbled to the ground, her head slamming against the seat. Kinley's irritated grumbles sounded from her shoulder.

"Hansen!" Merridayn squealed. Her heart felt as if it was seconds from jumping out of her chest.

"My apologies, child. I often forget the training I received from the Monks to quiet my steps. Most can determine my approach from the sound of my cane. However, when I do not need it, I forget I am not always alone in the archives." Hansen grimaced, the snippets of Hansen's life were intriguing. She heard rumours of his previous lifestyle before coming to the sanctum but could not determine which were true and which were fabricated.

"You're sure you aren't some sort of assassin in disguise, Hansen?" Merridayn joked, his stealth was unparalleled. Having been raised by Hunters her entire life, being taught to mask her steps. She had never seen anyone be able to walk soundlessly.

"Perhaps." Hansen laughed, his hand running over the

table to find the secondary chair. As he attempted to sit down elegantly, it became an ungraceful fall.

"Are you alright?" Merridayn rushed to her feet, worried about the elder wolf.

"Quite, dear child, I am getting older. These old bones would complain about breathing if they could." Hansen waved in Merridayn's direction, signalling her to sit back down.

"Hansen, can I ask you a question?" Merridayn began, wondering if she should involve him.

"Of course."

"If Torvan is alive but Jerifeyn isn't, wouldn't the prophecy change?" Merridayn felt like she was bursting at the seams, the questions reeling in her brain. "If the prophecy is voided due to Jerifeyn passing, Verena should be safe."

"Or it could have changed." Hansen supplied, confirming Merridayn's suspicions.

"Do we have a copy of the prophecy?"

"I believe so. The imgrids should be able to find it for you." Hansen answered, a pensive look about the elder wolf as he stared forward. Anyone else would have assumed the male could see, but Merridayn could only wonder what he was thinking or if the elder was listening to something she could never pick up on.

"Hansen, do you know anything about soulmates?" Merridayn wondered what knowledge he held. "Verena was held in stasis for almost one hundred years, correct?"

"Correct, she was brought here by Heathrow close to a hundred years ago." Hansen paused. "Perhaps more than a hundred years ago?"

"What do you mean? Was it more or less than one hundred years?" She could believe Verena was alive for as long, the knowledge of Fae longevity was well-known. Though, she had to have been assigned to someone to care for her. Someone who was capable of protecting her here, in their world. Someone who would be able to live as long as she. But who?

"I do not remember the year she was brought here. You would have to ask him yourself. However, he becomes irritable when the subject is breached. I do believe it was around one hundred years ago." Hansen was shut off. There was something about Verena and Heathrow's story they were not fully disclosing. There was more to it, and Merridayn felt it was important.

"Okay..." Merridayn left the topic momentarily, circling back to her original question. "What about soulmates?"

"It is said soulmates are your destined partner, a tether your soul was always going to find. Mates have this internal feeling when they have found their partner, while soulmates show a visible marking. We know soulmates have special capabilities regarding each other, but this is limited to one known pair in history. They were capable of sharing pain between the two. Their journal states it was convenient during childbirth." Hansen added in an attempt to lighten the atmosphere. He was stalling, that she was sure.

"Visible marking," Merridayn repeated, remembering the gold thread between Verena and Aven. "Like the one we witnessed? It was gold and incredibly bright, going between Verena and Aven."

"Exactly like the one you witnessed. Though, did you not mention there was a second one, only fainter?" Hansen veered their conversation away from Heathrow. Merridayn cocked an eyebrow, studying the elder carefully.

Interesting, what are you hiding about Heathrow, Hansen?

"Yes, it had gone off into the woods and then disappeared, which is what is confusing me. If Aven and Verena are soulmates, why the second? Where did the second go? And who could it have possibly led to?" Merridayn pondered, her fingers tapping anxiously.

"As Heathrow mentioned, she could be mated to two." Hansen offered an answer to the problem, one Merridayn did not want to consider. Thinking solely about the welfare of her son, and how heartbroken he would be should he have to watch Verena fall in love with another.

"Perhaps. Something just feels off about this whole situation." Merridayn felt uneasy, questioning why life could not have been easier. Why did it have to be her son involved in this? A selfish thought, but a thought it was.

"A common feeling we elders share with you." Hansen nodded in agreement. Merridayn felt secure knowing he shared her concerns.

"Do you think her being placed in stasis has anything to do with having a second mate?" Merridayn wondered, the only logical reason she could think of to put a baby in stasis. A practice human medicine has not yet been able to figure out, though the benefits if they could would be substantial.

"I'm not sure I am following your thought process," Hansen spoke, confused at where her line of questioning was headed.

"High Fae live an exceptionally long life, right? What if Verena was mated to one who she was meant to outlive? So fate was bound to give her a second mate at some point in her life. But, because she was in stasis, fate became blinded." Merridayn threw out the theory which plagued her from the moment she heard about Verena's stasis, wondering if fate had a hand in it all.

Hansen closed his open mouth, his response dying on his tongue. Merridayn rested her head on her palms, the start of a migraine forming. Hansen's fingernails tapped on the table, reminding Merridayn of Morse code. Kinley rubbed her beak against her ear before nipping at her earring.

"What the hell?" Merridayn swatted at the pest, rubbing her irritated cartilage.

Merridayn looked up, preparing to scold the creature, when she caught sight of what appeared to be a glass cabinet moving. She was dreaming, this was all some dream she would wake from. Cabinets couldn't move on their own...or could they? Stranger things had occurred since she joined Elion's family. Kinley nipped at her again as if she'd heard Merridayn's internal monologue and was calling the female ridiculous for discounting the imgrids who had been sent on a task. The extra nip brought her back into reality, and she saw the vast array of creatures struggling with a glass case that was easily seven feet tall and possibly four feet widest in diameter. It almost sang in its aura as the case was brought to the centre of the archives floor. A grimace crossed her face as she realised the one rule of not moving furniture was broken due to the size of the object.

"Perfect timing, lovelies." Hansen perked up, his irritating tapping resolving. "Would you do the honour, Merridayn? I'm afraid I am not much use when it comes to reading things anymore."

"Are you making a blind joke?" Merridayn could not control her snicker at the jest Hansen made on his behalf.

"Life becomes boring when one is unable to embrace

their complications." He shrugged, the corner of his mouth turned upward.

Merridayn restrained herself from laughing, only just. Pushing up out of her seat, she looked into the case. Her elbow came to wipe off the gathered dust. Her eyes squinted. She leaned in closer and found it hardly helped. Turning towards her chair, holding her bag, she rummaged around inside.

"Where are those bloody glasses?" Merridayn mumbled to herself, Kinley squeaking behind her. "I swear to the Goddess if you nip me again right now, Kinley." Kinley squeaked again, more insistent this time as the imgrid leapt off her shoulder. Merridayn looked back to see Kinley clutching her glasses in her claws.

"Ah, I knew where they were the whole time." Kinley glared at Merridayn, the beast's head tilted in contemplation and disbelief one could lose an object so important and right under their nose. "I did, I swear it." Merridayn took her glasses from Kinley's clutches, fixing them on her nose before returning to the case.

"I'm going to presume I cannot take it out of the case, Hansen?" Merridayn rubbed against the glass again near the top where the beginning of the parchment began.

"Unless you prefer to read from the dust particles, no." Hansen laughed, finding himself amusing.

"Alright, here goes. I will preemptively apologise for any mispronunciations." Merridayn cleared her throat as she prepared to read the script.

Chapter 23

VERENA

Verena had no concept of time, her mind unusually blank as she vaguely heard voices around her. Her body felt confined with chains as her brain raged to get up. She couldn't make out words, only registering sounds near her. Occasionally, a feeling of warm, soft hands on her, changing her clothes, she assumed, was processed in her mind. Verena felt embarrassed. How long had she been asleep? Her legs spasmed, she thought, as she felt pressure pushing against her thighs. A sharp sting contrasted on her arm as the high-pitched sounds faded. Drug-induced sleep, her mind quieted while the bright lights faded into darker tones. The high tones swapped to deeper, melancholy and rough.

"Verena?" She could feel hands cupping her face, gently shaking her. "Verena?" The voice asked again. She recognised it, but in her drugged state, a fog still enveloped her mind. Her eyelids were heavy as she tried to blink them open.

"H-h-h." Verena coughed, her throat sore and dry as her stomach wheezed from the pain of coughing. "Hello?" She tried again, her tone still coarse, her oesophagus angry, and the rasping from her vocal cords.

"One moment, my love. Give me a fraction of a second." Hands lifted from her face, and the weight beside her shifted.

Kieran?

Who else would it be, love?

I'm in your head again, aren't I?

Shh, darling, let me grab you water before we speak.

"Kieran?" Verena voiced, her lips cracking as she fought against the dehydration.

"Stay still; I'm coming," Kieran ordered. She felt him sit next to her again.

Attempting to rub her eyes, she noticed her body resisting. The drugs she was given must have been blocking her, even in her head. She felt his strong hands snaking under her shoulders, dragging her to his chest. Holding her to him as she imagined he recognised she was battling herself.

The drugs...Kieran...I can't move. I can't move. I can't.

She panicked; memories of Colin holding her down rushed to the front of her mind. Her body shook as tears fell down her cheeks. She tried her best to will the reminder of the scumbag away and tried to remind herself she was safe. She felt Kieran's body go taut. She knew in her soul he was witnessing everything through her eyes. With their mental connection, Verena had little chance of hiding her memories from him. She realised she was crying more, not from the shame of what Colin had done to her, but knowing she wasn't strong enough for him. She felt as if she didn't deserve him. Her demons told her she was damaged, worthless, and useless. She wasn't strong enough to protect herself from him; how would she survive being the mate of a Demon Prince?

You are not worthless, my love. You are not useless. The things he did to you do not define you. They define him. They define the type of person he is, a man who does not deserve to be anywhere near your presence. You are strong, you are powerful, you are so much more than everything, more than everyone. You have survived and will continue to survive.

How can you look at me? I am broken.

I look at you not because of this soul bond we share, but because of you. Your body might be phenomenal, but your mind is angelic.

My mind?

You are in my head, Verena. Every emotion you feel, I feel. Every memory you see, I see. Every thought you have, I know. I know you, Verena. Inside and out. I have waited decades to meet you. I knew who you were the moment you stepped out of Lothaire.

You watched me kill Abigail.

I did, and Verena?

Yes?

Kieran moved her in his lap so his chin could rest on her shoulder. Her mind cried to be able to open her eyes, to see his red irises staring back at her. To witness his face as he looked at her. Her only condolence was the brief look at herself through his eyes, which he granted her. The brief seconds she witnessed herself from his point of view. She looked beaten and battered, thinner than usual and unusually pale. Her hair was braided in a neat french braid, and her elongated ears poked through the strays. She had bags under her eyes, or would they be suitcases at the point they had reached?

"You were magnificent, my love," Kieran whispered against her forehead, his honied breath reaching her nose as she inhaled deeply.

Verena held back tears, her heart skipping from his words. Buried in her subconscious, she felt the demon rear its head. Whispering how unworthy she was regardless of Kieran's affirming words. The Demon's voice was the same one which grew in her head from her younger days, it constantly repeated she was only good if she was silent. She was only to be seen and not heard for those better than her. She hated the voice, hated how she couldn't fight back. Her mind remembered the words Kieran said. He could see what she was seeing, feeling, and hearing. All the thoughts were in her head where Kieran had open access.

Anxiety washed over her. Worry about the things he would see overwhelmed every sense she had. She didn't want him to, didn't need him to, terrified of his reaction to the things she was subjected to. Verena fought; she fought so hard against the memories of her abuse. Memories of being shared with his friends. She tried to replace them with memories of her fight with Abigail. Ripping her apart, tearing her to shreds and exacting vengeance even temporarily. Her thoughts turned dangerous, bloodthirsty and wanting. Verena dreamed of the things she would do to her tormentor. Hoping the emotions distracted Kieran from questioning.

She was wrong.

"Who is he, Verena?" Kieran growled, angry and seething.

"He's nobody, nobody of concern. I can handle him." She attempted to calm him.

"I am aware you can handle him. The question still stands, Verena. Who is he? Where is he?"

"Kieran..." Verena started, her eyelids getting heavy as her body was beginning to lose the battle against the drugs coursing through her veins.

"Verena." Kieran held her tightly.

"Can we talk about this later?" Verena laid her head back, her eyes closing, and her breathing slowed. She had lost the battle with the drugs.

Kieran looked down at the beautiful High Fae snuggled in his virtual arms. The urge to fall asleep coursed through him. It was hardly an hour past his morning meal, and he knew he needed to get some of his paperwork done, plan how he was going to bring her home out of the wolf's hands, figure out how to bring her out of her coma and end the damn war. He laid her head down gently on his pillow, fighting himself to return to his conscious self. Kissing her head, he stared down at her one more time. His heart stuttered at the thought of her being heavily sedated. His thoughts ran amuck, ideas flowing on why she was drugged. What they were doing to her. Was she being taken care of properly? And most importantly, why was she with the wolves? He rubbed his temples, stress skyrocketing.

"I will bring you home, Love. I promise." He whispered against her temple before slamming himself back into reality.

Verena incoherently mumbled in her sleep shortly after he left, her dreams varying from memories of her ripping Abigail apart to her meeting with the Angel. It felt as if hours had passed before Verena began to open her eyes again, the dim room she occupied a stark contrast to the brightness of her memories. She rubbed her eyes before stretching, her hands brushing against soft fabric.

Kieran? She whispered in her mind, remembering he could hear her in her temporary residence in his head.

There was no response. She began to worry, wondering if she was alone in her mind again. Back in her unresponsive, drug-filled body. Unable to move or speak, at the mercy of whoever was in possession of her.

"Kieran?" Verena whispered, praying he would answer her this time.

Laughter sounded from her right, and nobody was

there to produce it. Her panic increased. She was terrified. Pulling the covers around her tighter, she searched the darkness. Searching for answers, someone, anyone.

"Kieran?" She cried out again, her fear present in her voice.

"Yes, Love?" His voice was soft as if he was miles away.

"Where are you?" She relaxed, relieved she was still with him.

"I am in a meeting at the moment, darling."

"I heard laughing..." Verena paused. "Your laughter. I thought I was back in my own body." She forced herself to stop, not wanting to anger him for where her thoughts were taking her.

"I understand, Love. You are safe. I have been checking on you the entire time."

Verena sighed in relief, thankful he was so understanding. She chastised herself; she barely knew this man, yet she felt an instant connection. The feeling of protection enveloped her the second she met him. Or, rather, when he entered her mind for the first time on the day of Abigail's execution.

"Are you almost done?" Verena asked him, feeling slightly embarrassed she was talking to herself.

"Almost. We have some things to go over when I am done. I want to give you my full attention rather than split it with others. Are you fine with waiting?" He sounded sincere, apologetic, but genuine.

"Okay."

Verena swore she could almost feel him leaving the pocket of his consciousness she was in. Her eyes wandered around the room, a nearly exact style of the room she had been in. However, this room felt different. It felt more intimate, more relaxed than the other. It was as if the previous was a sitting room for guests, and this was his private bedroom. Verena took in his taste, a style many might consider modern gothic. Dark and drab but contrasted nicely with the accented furniture. She felt comfortable in the space, a smile coming to her face as she pictured her home someday decorated in a similar style but with shades of blue instead of green. Imagining a royal blue setting with white oak furniture, somewhere in the mountains where the scent of pine trees would fill her nose. Remembering her grandmother's cabin was a smaller version of her dream home. She made a mental note to ask Merridayn what would happen to the house now.

Is she even my grandmother?

Who, Love?

I was just wondering if the woman I knew as my "grandmother" was actually my grandmother or if she was a random nobody Abigail used.

"Ah, we can look into it together if you would like." Kieran appeared before her, standing in a full charcoal suit. A charleston green turtleneck underneath his charcoal vest and a matching pocket square tucked into his breast pocket. Silver cufflinks, a silver watch with a black interface and a silver necklace with a strange symbol graced him beautifully.

Oh my...

"Like what you see, Dear?" Kieran chuckled, the right side of his mouth curling upward in a smirk.

"No." Verena turned her head away as her cheeks turned pink.

"Liar." He stalked towards her as he began to unbutton his jacket. Verena turned her head, a retort on his lips that she immediately forgot. She watched the way his fingers clenched around the buttons, his veins protruding from the action.

"Perhaps sometimes." She admitted, her eyes glued to him, and her hands gripped the sheets closer.

"Oh my sweet, you'll soon figure out exactly how liars are punished when they grace my bed," Kieran growled, fixing his red irises on her as she bit down on her lips. He watched a small drop of blood drip past her lips, landing on her chin.

Verena's eyes widened as she took in what he said, her legs squeezed together in controversy. Something about the way he presented himself, his words, and his actions had an immediate effect on her libido. She could have gone years without sex had it been her decision, but around him, she might as well have been a prostitute. The sheer desire she felt for him raged against all sense. Her cunt quivered at the thought of him every single time. She knew she should feel a bit of remorse, perhaps some self-control but all she could think about was the weight of him on her. How his skin would feel against hers, the brush of his hair down her arms.

He reached her, she gasped, her hands came to her chest as he leaned over her. His long white hair tickled against her cheeks as his eyes burned into hers. She shivered from the look, wishful thinking of the things he could do to her. Verena watched him raise an eyebrow, the perfectly shaped white hairs pointed upwards with a matching half smirk gracing his full lips. Those lips came to breathe against her ear softly, and her breathing stumbled and ultimately stopped. Her brain forgot how to inhale as it was focused entirely on him.

"Breathe," Kieran whispered against her, flicking his tongue out to run up the side of her earlobe. As if on command, her body obeyed as she gulped in the air. Her eyesight cleared from the oxygen deprivation.

"Good girl." Kieran praised, watching her cheeks flush with blood.

Verena looked away from him, her earlobe catching his teeth, nipping her skin sharply. Her hand automatically came up to cup the blood already dripping down her. She didn't notice how soaked her clothes were from the rising need. Verena was strictly focused on the blood overflowing her hand, the red droplets pouring onto his perfect cashmere comforter. So focused, she didn't see the way Kieran looked at her with desire. She was frantically trying to stop the bleeding. Kieran's patience had run out. "Verena." He growled, low and needy.

"I'm sorry. I didn't think your teeth were going to cut me." Verena cried out, her pulse racing. "I'll clean it!" She tried to get up, but his arms forced her to stay.

"Verena." He tried again, softer this time, as her fear showed through his voice. He gently gripped her chin and brought her eyes to meet his. "I don't care about the bed, Darling. It washes. You did nothing wrong; it was entirely my fault. Would you like to get cleaned up?"

"Are you sure?"

"Absolutely." Kieran brushed his thumb against her cheek, his eyes softening at her. "Would you like to continue this excursion of ours, or would you like to stop and get cleaned up? The choice is entirely yours, my love."

Verena pondered momentarily, chastising herself for ruining the moment with him because her insecurity was rearing its ugly head. She took him in, searching his face for sincerity or whether he would take her choice away from her.

"I'd like to continue..." She reached out for him the second the words left her mouth, silencing him as her lips slammed against his.

She moaned against his mouth, his hands coming to rest on either side of her. Verena could hear the sheets crumpling against his weight as her fingers deftly ghosted over his taut back muscles. Feeling the strain of them against the soft fabric of his turtleneck. Their tongues fighting for dominance, Verena decided she wouldn't play fair. Hooking her index finger at the top of his vest, she pulled downwards, divesting him of another layer of clothing. Her fingers lingered around his belt, fingering the soft leather, tempting him further. Kieran's growl of impatience reached her ears while the majority of her knew he would not do anything she didn't want. A small, devoid portion of her wanted him to do anything and everything to her.

"Are you okay, Red Eyes?" She jested against his lips.

"I feel like I'm drowning with you at the centre," Kieran said, shocking Verena to the point that she pulled back to look at him.

"What?" Her head tilted at him, curious at what he meant by his words.

"You, my love. I'm drowning every day you are not with me. Every passing second without you physically here in my arms feels as if I sink lower and lower into the water." His hands caressed her face, sadness filled those beautiful red eyes of his.

"Red..." Verena began, she didn't know what to say. Didn't know how to ease his worry.

"Say my name, Love." A plea came from him, he needed to hear her say it.

"K-" Verena stopped, the word foreign on her tongue. She licked her lips, soothing the dry ache in them.

"I need to hear it on those delicious lips of yours." He

was desperate, begging her. Cupping her neck with his hands, staring down at their significant height difference.

"Kieran," Verena whispered.

"*Oh tesoro, sei squisita.*" He purred in content, the strange words coming from him rocked through her.

"I don't know what you said, but say it again. It was scrumptious." Verena mewled, her fingernails digging into his hips, causing him to jerk into her hands.

"You like when I speak in tongues, do you?" Kieran smirked, a growl coming from him

Verena hesitated, debating on her next move, similar to a chess player faux studying the board before landing the checkmate. Looking at him, committing to memory every hard line. The way his jaw clenched at each inhale of her breath, his fingers tightening around the sheets. Each beat thumped in Verena's enhanced ears as his heart rate increased. It was then she struck, her hand striking out to pull him to her. Crushing them together, letting his weight fall onto her and causing his hands to release from where she had been pinned. She heard Kieran take in a startled gasp, but didn't hear the release. Ever devious, taking her free hand to grab ahold of his own. She tugged it free of the sheets, guiding his lithe fingertips to her core. The centre of her was already soaked with need, desperate for attention.

"You little minx." Kieran's tone was laced with the sensual vibrato Verena recognised when she was with Aven.

The same tone he had used to push her over the edge, an accomplishment only he had succeeded in, shook her body in anticipation. She knew the man above her could push her to her limits before releasing the dam inside her. Her core tightened, causing her legs to squeeze his hand in response, the action partially involuntary. Verena had not felt this overcome with need in her life; the desire for this one person was overwhelming.

What other languages do you speak?

Oh, my darling, I can speak many, but I can guarantee you my tonguing linguist skills are superb.

Tongue. Linguistics?

Correct.

Verena's legs twitched at the idea, her hips bucking into his involuntarily. Their groans echoed each other, the sound vibrating across the room. Kieran took the moment to roll them over, placing her astride his hips. His head rolled back as he took her in, his fingernails ripped into her flimsy clothing.

"Look at you-" Kieran emphasised his words with a quick thrust into her, his need for her evident by the enormous bulge pressed into her. "-so fucking perfect above me. Where you belong."

"Where do I belong?" Verena ran her sharp nail down his cheek, a raging red mark flushing to the surface in the wake.

"Above me. Sitting on a bloody throne with the entire world at your feet." Kieran purred, catching her trailing fingernails and cupping them to his face. Bringing her broken nails to his lips, he proceeded to kiss every single one.

"I like the sound of the pretty words coming from your lips." Verena watched as he paid close attention to her battered hands. "But, I thought you said your tonguing linguistics were superb. And so far, I have yet to see any of these skills besides the pretty words your mouth has formed."

Red eyes flicked to her green ones, darkening. Filled with emotions Verena couldn't place a name to. She held his eye contact, a silent challenge passing between them. The atmosphere dampened, filling the room with the fiery smell of him. Burning cedar and hints of oranges wafted intensely to her nostrils. Verena sucked in a deep breath of him, the scent rushing straight to her cunt. She wasn't sure how much more teasing she could take before bursting like some wanton whore.

Are you positive you are entirely High Fae, my love?

Now, of all times. Really? Right when it was getting all hot and heavy, you decided to start asking about me.

Calm down, my little hellfire. I only ask because your pussy is clenching around me like a damn succubus.

Verena blushed at her outbreak, smashing her lips together. Looking anywhere but his face, she hoped the air could swallow her up. Vanishing into nothing would be preferable to the embarrassment she had just caused herself. The silence broke between them, and only their heartbeats and lungs created noise. Kieran's eyes never left her, waiting for the petite Fae to look at him again. Wondering how long she could pretend she didn't exist before her curiosity became the best of her.

I have waited centuries for you, Love. I can continue waiting if that is what you want. However, I would rather not if it's all the same.

Kieran's plea for her to forgive herself cracked any resolve she may have had left, her attention snapped back to him. Levelling him with a look she saw Merridayn give her sons when they threw an attitude, she raised her eyebrows in emphasis.

"When are you going to show me these skills of yours?" Verena bluntly questioned him. "Or were they made up to get me hot and needy for nothing?"

"You really are a little hellfire, aren't you?" Kieran

smiled, his pearly white teeth shining brightly.

Before Verena could react, Kieran took hold of her blouse and ripped it apart. Her bare breasts were perky, and her nipples were hard against the sudden change in temperature. Verena blinked at him, looking between the smirk on his face, her ruined shirt and her bare upper half. Her mind was stunned at what happened, her arms unable to react, but her core cried in excitement.

"You were looking a bit too covered, Hellfire." Kieran's large body flipped them over again, gently placing Verena's head on the silk-covered pillowcase.

Still too stunned to speak, Verena just stared at him, awaiting his next move, as if her brain was a computer and he was forced to reboot it. His plush lips descended on her pebbled nipples, the warmth of his mouth eliciting a soft moan from her. Kieran's eyes looked up at her, his mouth never leaving her breasts. His tongue swirled around her left nipple before biting down softly. Verena's chest arched in response, the slight pain sending tingles down her abdomen and straight to her pussy. Clenching around thin air, Verena groaned. The need for him grew as each second passed. She watched, silent, as he placed a sweet kiss atop the breast he had just lavished, then moved to the other. Her nipple began to cool rapidly as the warm saliva he left from his ministrations became exposed to the atmosphere. As an involuntary shiver coursed through her, Kieran took it as a sign he was succeeding.

"Are you alright, Hellfire?" His words vibrated against her teat, and her eyes closed.

Immensely.

Kieran stopped, his mouth instantly removed from her. Moving away from her body, he looked down at her. A look of disappointment crossed his beautiful features, one

Verena didn't see. Moments passed before she opened her eyes again, wondering why he had suddenly stopped.

"What's wrong?" Verena sat up to meet his eyes, worried.

"Verena, when I ask if you are alright, I need you to answer me precisely. I want to push you to your limits but never push you past them." Kieran took hold of her hands gently. His skin was burning, though, and disappointment still coursed through him. "Do you understand, Love?"

She tilted her head, contemplating what he was telling her. An unexplainable feeling burst through her, starting at her heart. An emotion she couldn't name, an emotion she'd never felt before. Was this what it felt like to be respected? Cared for? She didn't know, couldn't say. Her entire life has been to please or serve. Go to school, Verena. Pick up the groceries, Verena. Check the mail, Verena. Make dinner, Verena. Be quiet, Verena. Yet to hear this powerful male in front of her plead with her to tell him she's fine every step of the way. What exactly would you call such an emotion?

"I understand, Kieran." Verena smiled at him, rubbing her thumb across the back of his hand. "I promise to answer you truthfully next time."

Kieran didn't need to be told twice, his mouth pressed against her lips as if she was the life support and he was drowning. Their hands were still between them, Verena fought to free hers, Kieran fought to keep her there. Ultimately, Verena won though, she knew, he probably had let her. Winding her arms around his neck, she felt him lean her back down gently. Her nails came to hook under the collar of his turtleneck.

"Take it off."

Verena pulled her head back to watch him. Her mouth

dropped as he slowly divested himself of his top. Each inch he pulled up revealed more of his toned stomach, the stereotypical washboard abs mixed with white stubble. Verena hesitated, reaching out carefully to touch him. Waiting for him to throw the garment on the ground to answer her silent question. A groan of relief flushed through her when he took the damn thing off.

Can you be any slower? I'm only getting older.

I could put it back on and do it again, slower this time, if you want me to.

Don't you dare. I'll be dead by the time you finish at this rate.

Fantastic thing you High Fae live a horrendously long life, isn't it?

You wouldn't dare...

Not today, no. But perhaps in the future.

Kieran.

Hellfire.

Kieran.

Hellfire.

Will you shut the fuck up and fuck me already?

"Yes, ma'am." Kieran bit his lip, attempting to hold onto his boisterous laughter. His face scrunching in amusement as he saluted her.

"You did not."

"I did."

Poised with a retort, Kieran took advantage of her distraction to dive head first onto her exposed breasts again. Lavishing them with unbridled attention, Verena gently laid her head back on the pillow, wrapping her legs around him. She could feel his fingers teasing her hips, lightly tugging on her bottoms before letting go. He did it a few more times, waiting while she writhed under him.

May I?

Yes, please.

Verena moaned loudly and then slapped her hand over her mouth. Gaze flicked between the door and the devious man lapping at her breasts.

Don't hold yourself back.

What if someone hears?

Verena, Darling, we are inside my head. While I can make you feel as if this is happening to you physically, I am merely manipulating the neurons in your brain to produce hypothetical sensations.

You make my brain hurt sometimes, you know? Let's skip the scientific talk for a tad and get back to where you show me how skilled you are with your tongue. Because so far, I'd have to say you were maybe conversationally fluent.

Kieran didn't have to be told again, ripping her bottoms off in one smooth motion. Hiking her legs over his shoulders, and dived right in. His tongue swiped from the bottom of her slit to her hooded clit, the little bundle of nerves alighting. Verena's hands flew to the back of his head, where she could grasp his hair near his neck. She was positive she had pulled a few out in the process. Her gaze left him, looking straight up as her eyelids fluttered closed. Surprise overtook her as she noticed the mirrors above them reflecting the scene below. His massive torso mostly covered her lower half, her pale legs in stark comparison to him. Spreading her legs around him, dragging them down his shoulders and interlocking around his middle. Her head tilted as the movement exposed a web of scars between his shoulder blades, closer to the right shoulder than the other. She made a note to ask him about it later and gave in to the pleasure he was giving her. Her eyes rolled into the back of her head, her hands periodically fisting his hair.

Kieran...

Not yet, Hellfire. Hold it in.

His hands gripped her thighs harder, the sheer size difference evident in how his hand encapsulated her thigh. Verena cried out, her body raging against his demand. She felt his teeth graze her clit, causing her muscles to flex around his torso. Anyone other than him might have walked away with broken ribs. But not Kieran. Not the giant of a man he was. No. He enjoyed it. He encouraged it. His teeth were biting down the next time. Taunting her to do it again, try to strangle him with just her thighs.

Kieran... I can't hold on much longer.

Almost there. Just a bit longer.

His shoulders shoved into the crevice of her thighs, her pussy lips swollen, her back arched, and her legs constricted around him. Kieran's tongue increased in pace, ensuring her bundle of nerves never stopped crying out. Verena's vulva gaping open and closed, desperate to be filled. Desperate for attention, any attention at all. Her body craved him; her mind needed him.

Kieran, please.

Now, Hellfire.

Kieran's fingernails punctured her inner thighs, his teeth sinking in around her clit as her body rocked against him. Her orgasm passed through her so violently she screamed. So loud, her scream echoed through to reality. Her eyes snapped open to meet him, watching as his tongue licked at his lips. He was savouring every taste of her, even if this was merely a variation of a dream. Verena smiled at him, her vision fading rapidly.

"Sleep well, Hellfire. I will see you soon."

Chapter 24

VERENA

Soft morning melodies from unseen songbirds filled her ears, a light breeze wafted through her hair, and sunlight shone in her eyes. Verena squinted against the brightness, a hand coming automatically to cast shade against it. The hand, tanned and heavily tattooed with white patterns running along every inch of visible skin past the elbow, continued moving closer where she could make out more details. Whoever the hand belonged to had extremely dainty fingers. Delicately upkept, manicured nude almond-shaped nails protruded from each, with no chip or crack visible. A silver hand chain connected at her wrist by a solid silver cuff, silver chains spiderwebbed to dainty rings on each finger, littered with small diamonds here and there. It draped across the skin, obscuring some of the tattoos, stemming from a silver quarter moon ring on their middle finger to a wide silver cuff on their wrist. Diamonds inlaid in the chain from ring to cuff scattered rainbows against Verena's cheeks. She could make out an intricate pattern in the cuff, giving the appearance of astrology signs, but Verena didn't know enough about them to make her theory concrete.

Nearby, a door opened, and the tell-tale sound of creaking hinges gave the intruder away quickly. Nearly silent footsteps strode over to her. So distracted by the unknown hand blocking the sun from blinding her, Verena didn't notice her presence in a bed made of stars. White sheets sparkled at each minute movement. Looking above her, Verena took note of a glass dome showing an array of colours, they reminded her of a sunrise. Wistful clouds floated meticulously around the top, throwing shadows about the room. In front of her, a wide arched balcony entrance sat with no doors to be seen. Tall, intimidating white stone columns stood on either side of the entrance. Moon phases carved into both sides, starting at the waning crescent near the top and ending at the waxing crescent near the bottom. Verena noticed the peak of the archway. A realistic new moon, its shadows dulled in comparison to the sun shining through the glass dome above her. She caught glimpses of a shimmer around the doorway, assuming some otherworldly capabilities were at play. Had she not learned magic and monsters were real a week prior, she would have checked herself into an asylum.

"Prophetess." A high-pitched, unnaturally melodic voice came from her right, startling Verena as she visibly jumped. "My apologies."

"Is it time, Nelvira?" Verena's tone was higher and softer, but most definitely not her own.

Wait. Prophetess, she said Prophetess. This must be another memory, then.

"It is, ma'am. We must be on our way."

Verena searched for a mirror to confirm her suspicions. If she was right, the hand she initially thought belonged to another was true. But not in the way she first thought. No, the hand did not belong to another body entirely. It belonged to the body she was in or whoever she was in. There was one person Verena knew was called the 'Prophetess,' and it was her mother. As the memory continued, Verena took note of the bed she was in. The bed appeared to be made of stars floating above the ground while little sparkles poured into the floor below. Looking down, she noticed her bare feet, taking stock of the similar white ink marking the skin shown there. The only problem, Verena wasn't walking. Granted, she was walking as if anyone would if one would call walking on air a form of transportation.

What the fuck?

Attempting to keep herself from internally panicking, Verena looked at the person named Nelvira. Noticing how their feet were actually touching the ground. Their small stature clothed similarly, but it dulled in comparison. While Verena's clothing twinkled against the movement, cashing an array of light with each passing step. Nelvira's garments lacked the shine, lacked the energy. Verena could only conclude the difference, chalking it to visible societal status. Her skin was married in white ink, Nelvira's was a blank canvas, as far as she could tell. Her footfall was non-existent, Nelvira's were practically soundless, the slight echo of her cotton slippers trailing after them.

Did she usually walk like this? As if she was floating?

Verena forced herself to look away at the attendant before her to take in the details of the room she was leaving. An identical archway from the balcony marked the entrance, this one also sans doors. The same shimmery magic encased the framing, and they headed right towards it. Nelvira didn't hesitate; she walked through it without a second thought. Verena watched as the body she inhabited followed suit. Magic from the doorway felt like she had walked through a thousand feathers before popping out on the other side. The magic knew her, accepted her, warmed her body, and electrified her blood as if saying goodbye without words. Wide pearlescent walls greeted her on the other side. If Verena were capable of controlling where her feet took her, she would have walked back through the magic. Astounded by the change of scenery, a change she hadn't noticed on the other side.

Definitely would have checked into a mental hospital.

Verena let out a soft sigh, sad and wistful. The sound caused Nelvira to stumble in her confident stride forward. She watched as the tiny Fae fought with herself to ask what was wrong. In the end, Nelvira continued, defining she would follow her duties regardless of her morality. Verena could respect it, or perhaps it was Jerifeyn who respected it? The feeling erupted inside of her, the originator unable to be determined. Bare walls greeted her gaze; lacking anything, not even a single sconce decorated the blankness. It felt like a hospital as if they were walking to a morgue. Sterile and without feeling, an execution to be presented for. Their walk continued, or in Verena's case, float. She could see the shimmer of another warded archway coming up. Focusing on the doorway, she determined she could only see the shimmer. Nothing else, only the shimmer. Revealing nothing on the other side.

Where are we headed?

"We are almost there, Prophetess." Nelvira chirped over her shoulder, her hands clasped behind her back.

But where, though?

"Very well." An uncomfortable silence passed between the two. "At least tell me he is handsome, Nel. Anything. Please." The memory begged, pleading with the servant to give her any information.

The short woman stopped, and Verena almost ran into her. The jingling of the excessive amounts of jewellery adorning her body groaned their annoyance. Verena watched as Nelvira turned around, catching a glimpse of a smile before Nelvira wiped it away. Verena's face smiled in response, the sheer look on the other woman telling.

"Jer..." Nelvira hesitated, looking around her and then back. You know I shouldn't say."

"I know, Nel, but we've been friends since birth." Jerifeyn scrunched her face up, the one she gets when she tries to convince someone to do what she wants. "At least tell me I am not walking in there, to someone who would turn the stars into dust, Nel."

Nelvira laughed softly, rapidly covering her mouth as her eyes frantically looked around. Jerifeyn burst out laughing, the musical sound vibrating off the walls. Nelvira joined her, clutching at her sides almost bent over.

"He's decent looking, Jer." Nelvia blurted out in between a fit of laughter. "The stars should be safe from your wrath, though I'm not sure about his mother."

"His mother?"

"Holy Mother, forgive me for the words I am about to say." Nelvira stared at Jerifeyn thoughtfully. "His mother is a nightmare, Jer—an absolute nightmare. None of the others want to even come near her. I heard she made Hinley lick her shoes clean. Sinclave's top healers have monitored the poor child since then." Jerifeyn watched as Nelvira looked around nervously, making sure nobody else but them heard what she had said.

"She did what?" Jerifeyn grew angry, and the hallway darkened.

"You didn't know?" Nelvira whispered, panicking. She did not mean to anger Jerifeyn with the truth, another reason why she did not want to tell her.

"I have not heard, no." Jerifeyn sighed, angry still but helpless. "Have my parents been informed? Somebody would have let them know of the treatment our *guests* have taken upon our clanmates."

"I am not sure. I assume they have, but you know how I feel about assuming anything anymore." Nelvria learned her lesson about making assumptions, the scar on her back evidence of such.

"Interesting. And she is waiting, I presume, with her son behind the archway?" As her anger entirely subsided, the hallway lightened again.

"You already know, Jer." Nelvira wanted to hide in a corner and hope she could disappear from observing the interaction she knew would occur shortly.

"Fantastic." Jerifeyn clasped her hands together. "Let us go greet our *delightful* guests, shall we?" Sarcasm laced Jerifeyn's words, causing Nelvira to roll her eyes before following her friend toward the archway. She knew her friend was about to make a scene, being wholly dissatisfied with having to continue to entertain the pompous houseguest who would soon be her mother-in-law.

"Let's hope her son has better manners and looks than those of his incubator," Nelvira whispered to herself, knowing Jerifeyn could hear it regardless.

"Don't hold your breath, Nel." Jerifeyn's voice carried to Nelvira and Nelvira only, the High Fae utilising her powers to do such.

As the pair gracefully strode through the ward, the accompanying room materialised before her eyes. Similar to her bedroom, the ceiling pitched tall, showcasing the now early morning sun. White marble floors shone brightly against the sunbeams, the harsh light diluted in the long, occasionally dark spotted clouds in a group of waves around the room. Identical pillars from her room spread out evenly in the octagonal shape parlour. A common place where her parents often took tea with fellow

Naedian's. Their favourite spot was near the back, where a spacious sunroom resided. Her mother frequently told guests the room had a certain aura as if it took a mind or life of its own. Jerifeyn personally hated this room; the implications and negotiations that had taken place here created unease for her. Her arranged engagement was one of those negotiations. Jerifeyn hated how one of the most essential life choices she could ever make had been taken from her. Her ability to choose the one she would stand with until the end of time was ripped away—all to satisfy some ancient woman and her incoherent words.

"The guest of honour graces us with her presence." The nasal tone was all too familiar to Jerifeyn and put her on edge; it was just like Jaquiryn to have a snide comment as a greeting. "And an hour late. Were you lost in the starlight, Jerifeyn?"

"Holy Mother, you haven't lived until you've had the experience of being lost in our starlight. I do recommend you try it sometime."

Jerifeyn could feel her accompanying clanmates attempting to contain themselves. Curtsying gracefully at the Mordinians attending Monarch, Jerifeyn continued towards the centre of the room. The place her parents and her, unfortunate, betrothed stood awaiting. His back was turned away from her, actively conversing with another. A taller male, darker in comparison to her father. His hair black versus Aurelius' silver strands. Whilst her father was tall to her, this man was flirting with a giant. Jerifeyn suspected him to be Alrain, the father of Torvan. Meaning the man whose back was turned to her must be Torvan himself. Jerifeyn took the time to study Torvan. His backside was broad, as most Mordinians were. His golden hair, a direct copy of his mother's, was neatly cut

short. A massive longsword sheathed on his right hip indicated he was left-handed.

What an exciting change—left-handed. Verena was
shocked at the additional voice in her head. She realised
she could hear her mother's thoughts and was almost convinced she could listen to others if her experience with
Kieran was genetic.

His house colours were proudly on display, the black
and red gifted by the Archangel whose blood was used to
create them. Torvan's frame alone made the colours look
good—great, even if she were to tell the truth. Though Jerifeyn decided she wouldn't admit it when asked, this was
supposed to be a day she detested. Yet she felt an inkling of
attraction to him, and she had only seen his backside thus
far.

I'm glad you think so.

Jerifeyn jumped, her shock falling from her lips, casting
everyone in the room's attention upon her. She could feel
herself blush. The blood rushed to her face before she had
a chance to stop it.

"Is everything alright?" Her mother's voice, Inessa Naedian, was commanding yet soft-spoken.

"Quite, mother. I was not expecting His Highness Alrain to be in attendance," Jerifeyn curtsied towards the
older Fae before looking at the younger. "And I presume
his eldest son, Prince Torvan, am I correct?"

Perceptive, I like it.

Jerifeyn noticed the Prince's lips discretely curl as he
bowed to her. Confirming her suspicions and solidifying
the Mordinian line had more secrets than they let on. Years
prior, when her parents informed her of their impending
marriage, she was assigned to learn everything she could
about the family. The Mordinians having inter-married

for millennia, it was a shock to all the houses when they inquired about her hand to marry. Jerifeyn tore through the information between her father and mother's side. Both libraries held little about their protectors. Only the bare minimum of their creation from their Archangel, and then the rest was mere speculations.

"At your service, Prophetess." Torvan's low voice vibrated through her chest even though he was not close.

You are telepathic?

It would appear so, wouldn't it?

But how?

All in due time.

"Isn't this..." the same nasally tone interrupting their thoughts as Jaquiryn had to make the moment about herself "...lovely."

"They make such a gorgeous couple, Aurelius!" Inessa gushed, her hands coming together in front of her. The smile on her mother's face was worth the years of torment Jerifeyn knew would come from her soon-to-be mother-in-law.

"I am but a dying star compared to the moon your daughter exudes, Your Highness." Torvan's smooth words made his mother's disappear.

"Shall we retire to the sunroom for a toast? Allow the youngsters the time to acquaint themselves?" Aurelius questioned the room. He may not have been as old as the elders, but he carried their older charms, and occasionally, this was most evident through his speech.

"Father!" Jerifeyn exclaimed, her cheeks reddening again.

"I would be honoured to take her for a stroll. Any opportunity to be in her presence is a gift from the Mother." Torvan bowed at their combined parents. He returns to his upright position and holds an arm out for Jerifeyn to take. "Shall we?"

"We shall." Jerifeyn took his extended arm and allowed him to lead her out of the room from the exit opposite the sunroom.

The warded archway revealed a beautiful sky bridge. Jerifeyn knew the bridge led them towards the Naedian library, a haven she had taken sanctuary in for the previous years. Many late nights reading, escaping reality into the fantasy books she hid from her parents. Strategy notes Nelvira snuck her stashed away in the pages of biographies. Her most precious book, the one about Angels and their Creators, remained hidden behind a false cover. Had her parents found out about her procrastination in her studies, she'd have been jailed in her room until further notice. Inessa was slight and soft-spoken, while Aurelius was grandfatherly. Every Naedian knew while Aurelius was a force to be reckoned with, Inessa held the power. Jerifeyn shivered at the thought of it. Torvan, having taken it as a sign of her being cold, proceeded to doff his outer coat and drape it over her shoulders.

"Cold, moon?" Torvan's lips brushed against her ear, closer than she had expected.

"Partially," Jerifeyn confirmed, the blush rising to her cheeks again.

Torvan paused their stroll halfway, electing to turn them towards the railing. Jerifeyn knew the surroundings well. Before them, she knew the grounds of medicinal greenhouses, a favourite of her mothers. Beyond the greenhouses were the fencing grounds, where she would often find Nelvira watching wistfully. Even farther was the Lourad Mountains, the divide between Naedian territory and Nightingale territory. Torvan looked out, his face stoic and calculating. Jerifeyn wondered if the man knew what it felt like to laugh. She couldn't see any laugh lines around his lips or under his eyes. The centre of his brow creased enough to leave a permanent indentation. She wondered if he knew how to relax but subconsciously was grateful he didn't, his body a testament to his training.

"I can feel your mind racing, Jerifeyn. Would you deign to enlighten me?" Torvan asked her without taking his eyes from in front of him.

Not particularly, no.

"Outloud, Jerifeyn."

"Demanding, aren't you?" Jerifeyn glared at him. "You recognise we hold the same station. I need not submit to your every whim, Torvan."

"You will learn." Torvan snapped back at her. "All in due time."

The tone instantly put Jerifeyn on edge, her senses screaming at her something was off about the man she would be required to spend her life with.

"What do you want from me, Torvan?"

"You are nothing but an object to get me what I want, little dove." Torvan looked at her, her skin prickled with goosebumps. "An object I intend to use."

The surroundings faded, and bright colours lightened until they were white. Torvan became blurry, his features dimming until they, too, were gone. Verena had been in a room surrounded by people, items and sounds. She was now standing in a white room with nothing, just whiteness. Her eyes searched for anything to give away where she was, but there was just emptiness. Her mind was racing; thousands of thoughts hit her all at once. One stood out among the rest. What had she experienced, and when could she find out more?

Chapter 25

MERRIDAYN

"Oh my god." Merridayn's eyes squinted, attempting to focus on the barely legible writing. What she saw staring back at her caused her to rub her eyes and then rub the glass again. Her mind went into overdrive, and she rushed to grab the nearby chair to stand on. Hoping the angle might provide better clarity, she could feel Kinley's beady eyes staring at her from the table. Hansen pushed himself away from the table, the legs of the wood chair casting a groan into the otherwise silent halls.

"Impossible," Merridayn whispered to herself. Gathering her wits, she hopped off the chair. Turning around, she met Kinley's gaze and flicked her attention to Hansen.

"Yes, Merridayn?" Hansen questioned softly, not knowing where she was, but looked in the direction she had just come from regardless.

"Does the council have a translated copy of this any-where?" She rushed around the table, flipping through her notes, searching for one thing.

"We should." Hansen tapped his fingers on the table, sounding like a modified version of Morse code. "Kinley, will you go check to see if we do?"

Kinley squealed as she took off, her wings stirring the pages of Merridayn's research. Conveniently, Kinley's downdraft changed the page in her notebook to the page she was hunting for.

"Impossible," Merridayn repeated, turning to rummage in her seemingly endless bag. "Thank God." She pulled out a black ballpoint pen, popping the cap, and shaking the ink slightly.

"Merridayn?" Hansen's fingers tapping on the table some more, an unknown melody Merridayn didn't have time to figure out.

"Hansen." Merridayn started, scribbling rough notes on the edge of her pages. "Who has the capability to unlock this case?"

"Which case? The one holding the prophecy?"

"Yes."

"I believe the other elders, the head Druids, and I all have the capability. Is there something I should be informed of?"

"I'm not confident at the moment, but I believe the prophecy is a replication, an altered replication even. At least this one is."

The room became silent once more, the only sound of their breathing and the light flaps from the imgrid's wings. Hansen's insistent tapping halted, and Merridayn buried her hands in her hair. Her head came to rest upon the palms of her hands. She knew the implications of her accusation and the potential outcomes of claiming the prophecy was false. Merridayn was prepared to take on the consequences of her actions should they prove her wrong. She knew what she saw and was optimistic she could prove it.

"How do you know?"

"On the parchment, it's old. Dirty. It looks like it was written on paper from centuries ago. But, in the lower right corner, near the bottom. Far from the original text.

There's the indentation of a pen marking. One someone would make on a separate piece of paper when trying to get their pen to work." Merridayn watched him, his expression changing from confusion to understanding. "Hansen, pens weren't invented until recently."

"Go on." Hansen probed Merridayn to continue, curious on how her mind worked through the problem.

"They used quills in the age this was made, correct?" Merridayn knew she was asking a redundant question: pens were made in the last century.

"As far as I am aware, yes." Hansen agreed with her, impressed how she had deduced it far faster than he expected.

"And who made the prophecy?" Merridayn was not naive enough to believe Jerifeyn made this prophecy.

"The information about its origin is not confirmed. Though, we understand the prophecy came from the... oh Goddess." Hansen abruptly stood up. His chair clattered behind him as it fell.

"Hansen?"

Hansen didn't say anything but began running off towards the centre of the room. Merridayn didn't hesitate to follow, her bag, notebook, everything left behind in her pursuit after him. She began to lose him; for a blind older man, he was definitely swift on his feet. Her heart began crying out, pained. She wasn't in shape and she knew it. She cursed herself for always putting her husband and children before herself. Her lungs burned, and she gasped between each inhalation. Her sides cramped, and she watched Hansen get farther and farther from her.

"Hansen!" Merridayn gasped out as she tried to get his attention. She couldn't keep up and feared she would collapse if she kept running after him.

After what felt like an eternity, he slowed, coming to a

stop before his desk. Merridayn's ire began to rise. Nothing was so important that he had to practically sprint off, leaving her behind with his unfinished thoughts and her question unanswered.

"For crying out loud." Merridayn coughed, her body doubling over in exhaustion. "At least tell me I nearly died trying to keep up was worth it."

"Merridayn." Hansen began, fumbling around his desk drawers. The noise irritated Merridayn progressively as time continued. "The prophecy came from House Mordinian."

"Oh God."

Hansen continued to rummage in his desk, item after item dropping to the ground from his rapid search through the drawers. Each trinket clattered but was wholly forgotten or ignored by Hansen's determined pursuit of whatever he sought. Merridayn peaked over the desk, internally debating whether she should ask him more questions, or wait for him to explain.

"Found you, you little bugger." Hansen held up a small key, delicate and floral looking. The key was ordained with a large copper flower, intricate in design and somehow familiar and foreign all at the same time.

"Hansen?" Merridayn questioned him, her curiosity winning as the elder took a seat. His age caught up with him after the copious energy he must have spent rushing here.

"Merridayn, take a seat. This is not something we have told many." Merridayn obeyed, watching him closely. "The alleged prophecy came from a self-proclaimed 'Prophetess' from House Mordinian. According to records, the only known true Prophetess was Jerifeyn Nightingale. Therefore, when this imposter became known, they began proclaiming prophecies. We-" Hansen paused, pointing to himself. "The Wolves, Druids, House Naedian and House Nightingale, we all speculated House Mordinian executed the prophecies to ensure their 'Prophetess' was seen to be true. She would create prophecies about certain weather, fortune being bestowed, citizens recovering from illness, these sorts of things. Prophecies House Mordinian was able to fulfil with relative ease."

"So she was a sham, creating plots the Mordinians would fulfil to ensure she was taken seriously? For what gain, though?" Merridayn whispered to herself, not expecting an answer from Hansen.

"When she created the Prophecy, we all know that many believed there could be a small possibility it could be real. However, House Mordinian would release snippets of the Prophecy over many years. There was only one problem." Hansen added to her confusion, the details of Verena's past becoming more apparent with each passing second.

"What problem?" Merridayn could not handle another momentous problem today, her head was already swarming with possibilities.

"They didn't add up. I'm not sure who caught the discrepancies, but they did. And when they put together enough evidence to take to their equivalent of a council, they disappeared." The other shoe dropped, Merridayn wondered how she was going to break this to Verena when the time came.

"How do we know there are discrepancies if they disappeared then?" Merridayn was afraid of the answer.

"Jerifeyn Nightingale," Hansen stated it like it was obvious.

"Pardon me?" Merridayn felt she should be offended though she couldn't find the energy to care at the moment. The overwhelming amount of information and contraindicating stories were becoming too much to handle.

"Jerifeyn Nightingale left extensive journals with her daughter, Verena. Heathrow brought them and Verena back over a century ago. With the help we have gotten from the Dremorta, we've been able to translate them. It's why Orla has been sending volunteers to the Demons for years. Asmodeus and Kieran Dremorta are the only ones alive who can read their language and don't intend to harm us."

"Wait a minute, Hansen." Merridayn's mouth dropped at what he had just revealed. "Did you say Verena was brought here, to Alusso, a century ago?"

"Yes."

"He's correct, Merridayn." Heathrow's low, exhausted voice sounded from behind her. Merridayn jumped from her seat in surprise, clutching her heart and whipping her head around to see the haggard wolf standing a couple of feet away. She hadn't heard him enter, nor had she heard him walking up towards them.

"Goddess, have mercy." Merridayn gasped, trying to calm her racing heart back down. "You practically caused me to have a heart attack. My heart rate."

"My apologies." Heathrow apologised, walking up the rest of the way before leaning against Hansen's desk. "Hansen."

"Heathrow." Hansen nodded his head in Heathrow's general direction, Merridayn watched the imgrid's slink away from the imposing figure of Heathrow.

"How much have you told her?" Heathrow snapped, sounding angry and irritable. Though, Merridayn figured that was a common occurrence for the man.

"We were just getting started." Hansen tapped his cane

against the ground, waiving for them to make their way towards a table.

"Very well." Heathrow moved to place his hand on Hansen's shoulder, offering him a hand. Merridayn watched as Hansen reluctantly wrapped his hand in the crook of Heathrow's elbow.

Merridayn watched the exchange between the two men, looking between them nonchalantly, discussing her right before her eyes. She felt uneasy, wondering if she was asking questions that could prove to cause her harm. But she needed to know and figure out how all this could help wake Verena back up. She owed Verena as much as she owed her for putting the young woman into this position, to begin with.

"You knew he was here this whole time?" Merridayn accused Hansen, catching the blind wolf smirking at her accusation.

"I did." Hansen did not seem to take offense to Merridayn's accusatory tone.

"And you weren't going to inform me he was here? Greet him? Nothing?" Merridayn pointed her finger at him, annoyed at him but more annoyed he couldn't see her annoyance. "You were just going to let him scare me to the point I almost keeled over?"

"You didn't, however." Hansen snarked playfully.

"I could have." Merridayn rolled her eyes at him. She walked towards the table nearest them, gracefully seating herself in the farther seat to allow Heathrow to escort Hansen to the nearest ones.

"Goddess, will you two stop? Last I checked, Verena is still in a coma, and the Druids are nowhere close to figuring out how to wake her." Heathrow snapped at the two, his patience gone from the chaos of the day. "I brought Verena back when she was nearly a year old. She was put into stasis before we went through the portal from Lothaire to Alusso. Her mother had sent along five journals. She was insistent we read the third one first. The only problem was I do not speak Old Fae. It was then I began searching for someone who could. As I was not from Alusso, it proved to be difficult. After almost a century, I was found by the previous council and taken here. Against Jerifeyn's, and my own beliefs, Verena was taken from me and placed with Abigail." Settling Hansen into a seat before taking his own, he looked at Merridayn for her reaction to the news. Shocked when the only reaction she had was confusion, a blissful change to what he was used to.

"You're not a werewolf?" This was news to Merridayn, the man never gave off any signs of being anything other than wolf.

"I am only half wolf," Heathrow admitted reluctantly.

"Only half?" Merridayn looked at him, questioning who was standing in front of her. Her knowledge of him had been wholly stripped away in the last few minutes. "What's the other half?"

"Fae."

"Hold on. You're part Fae? And you knew about this, Hansen? The council knew about this? Yet you still serve on the council?" A hybrid was allowed on the council? Merridayn wondered what the other clan leaders would say if they knew one of their elders was a half-breed.

"This is not relevant right now, but yes, Merridayn. Just as you are a human mated to a werewolf. I am part wolf and part Fae. This is exactly why Jerifeyn chose me to watch over Verena. My wolf side could mask her from trackers, while the Fae side gave me their longevity. I would still be alive for decades, while a human or normal wolf would pass after a handful. Verena would have had consistency with me instead of the obscene abuse she suffered from Abigail." Heathrow was defensive, something here was not right. Something he wasn't telling her about their circumstances. If he was to be Verena's guardian, why was she placed with Abigail?

"I understand. Let's continue, shall we? Jerifeyn left you, for Verena, journals. She told you to read the third one first. Why? Did you? What was in it?" Merridayn tried to defuse the situation. She needed answers, and she wasn't going to get them if the man who had them was angry.

"I believe Jerifeyn knew the Mordinians would not give up once she had passed. She must have seen Verena's future should she have stayed in Lothaire, which is why I was tasked with bringing her here. To keep her safe until the time was right." Heathrow sniffled, clearly trying to stop himself from crying. "The third journal detailed every discrepancy between the Mordinian's' prophetess and her interactions with Prince Torvan and his family. It took us about ten years and dozens of wolves to convince Prince Kieran to translate the journal. Even so, we can only take the translation with a grain of salt." The way Heathrow said Kieran's name was with distaste, Merridayn presumed he hated the Demon. Rightfully so, if he is as old as she suspected, Heathrow must have seen the way the Prince was in the war.

"If what you are saying is true, what's with the 'prophecy' in the dusty large case?" Everything led back to the prophecy, Verena's life a never ending circle around a false piece of parchment.

"A failsafe to keep the population calm. If they knew the prophecy we had was fake, chaos would break out.

Everyone would panic, believing the end of days was near. The previous council created it, specifying that Jerifeyn's death completed it. Jerifeyn was actually the one who suggested we write a false prophecy of our own, claiming once she died, the prophecy had come to an end." Heathrow strung his words well, leaving Merridayn with answers and a plethora of more questions.

"If the prophecy is fake, what did the Mordinians want?" Merridayn leaned back in her seat, looking up at the tree branches above her. Trails of sparkles flittered between the branches, playfully. There was always a margin of truth behind every lie, Merridayn learned that lesson the hard way. If this prophecy was fake, what was it hiding? Looking back at the men, Merridayn settled herself to getting all her questions answered this time. There would be no room for negotiation. She might be human but she was still raised with Hunters.

Hansen and Heathrow shared a look between the two, as much as a blind man could. Merridayn watched the two, seemingly appearing to communicate telepathically based on Heathrow's facial changes periodically. Merridayn tapped her foot impatiently and irritated. Mostly irritated, they would try to keep her in the dark when she had deduced everything thus far from a simple ink stain.

"I'm still right here. You both know this, right? Whatever you want to keep from me, I will eventually find it on my own." Merridayn snapped, her patience fully drained.

"Our apologies, Merridayn." Hansen broke the awkward silence between them all.

"I do not require your apology, I require a damn answer. Everything you have held back from the rest of us, commoners, only hinders a solution for the problem." It was times like these where she wished she was born a wolf, to be able to demand respect like her husband and sons could.

"We do not know what the Mordinians wanted, but we can presume it had something to do with Jerifeyn. And since she is now deceased, we can assume it has been passed onto her daughter." Heathrow was lucky Verena needed him, Merridayn fantasised about ripping his tongue out of his mouth.

"Didn't you say you had Jerifeyn's third journal translated? Did she not have any theories at all?" This was getting ridiculous, it was almost as if she was speaking to children. Did she have to pull the answers from all of them or would they finally just tell her everything she needed to know.

Goddess, I finally understand what my children have been telling me all these years.

"She did, a few of them." Evidently he was choosing the second option, the option where Merridayn had to drag every inkling of information out of him.

"Do I have to continue asking, or will you both unanimously decide to trust me? Clearly, I can offer some assistance. Perhaps being human has advantages instead of being a weak liability." She said it as nice as she could, with the limited patience she still held.

"Very well." Heathrow stormed off to grab a chair from nearby. Merridayn could tell he was not pleased. Nearly slamming the wooden high back down, the legs cried from his sudden weight being dropped into them. "Sit."

Merridayn obeyed silently, not wanting to anger the halfbreed any more than she already had. She didn't care, though; there wasn't any inkling of sympathy for them at the moment. They kept all these secrets from everyone because they were scared, or believed the general public couldn't handle the truth. They'd been forced to live their lives in some falsity, solely based on the lie fed to them by the council they were told to trust. Merridayn didn't say a word, her anger palpable and evident on her face. Heathrow let out a long groan, his fingers massaging the bridge of his nose.

"Out of all of Jerifeyn's theories, only one made sense. We have exhausted all our resources to gather more insight into this particular issue. The theory was based on a glimpse of a rune she had seen on Torvan. One she spent most of her time during her engagement trying to understand. Most runes had angelic origins or were created for angelic purposes. You read about this particular one, and Hansen has taken the liberty to inform me. The 'Marked' rune." Heathrow looked at her for confirmation. Merridayn slightly nodded, her thoughts bouncing around in an attempt to figure out where the conversation was going.

"Jerifeyn mentioned she had only seen the rune in passing when Torvan returned exorbitantly late one night from training. Bloody and battle-worn, his sleeve was rolled farther than she had ever seen him keep it. Jerifeyn was precise when she said Torvan kept himself extremely well dressed; she claimed it was almost obsessive. He never left his chambers without being completely presentable. He never strolled the courtyard without, at minimum, a frock coat. Jerifeyn mentioned she had not once seen a valet, either."

"So how had she seen it then?" Merridayn was confused about whether what Jerifeyn said was true. The man would not have let a small mistake happen.

"She wasn't positive about the coincidence. Blaming fate entirely for being in the area as Torvan. We do have a theory, though, based on context clues. Jerifeyn mentioned he had just returned from training. Based on

Heathrow's knowledge of Fae training, we believe he was, in what humans consider, 'tunnel-vision.' His probable only goal was to return to his chambers, wash and then rest. Heathrow believes Torvan did not expect anyone to be awake, or on the pathway he chose. Jerifeyn mentioned she had awoken randomly and was compelled to take a nighttime stroll." Hansen supplied, his voice sounding distant.

"Okay, she had seen it, chalked it up to random fate, and figured out the general meaning. What does this all have to do with some prophecy?"

"If Torvan has the rune, he cannot be killed." Heathrow supplied.

"I know, but it doesn't add up. So what, he can't be killed. Wouldn't anyone want to be practically immortal?" Merridayn's face scrunched up. She couldn't comprehend why this would be a problem for anyone.

"He also wouldn't be able to go home either." Hansen whispered, his face turning towards the sound of imgrid wings approaching them.

"You aren't making any sense. He cannot go home, and he cannot die. I do not see where this has anything to do with Jerifeyn." Merridayn tapped her fingers against the wooden desk, hoping someone would explain something before she left. At this point, she thought they were all bloody crazy.

"Merridayn, High Fae draw life from their homelands. Not only were the High Fae given blood from their respective Angels, but the Angel poured their essence into the land as well. They need the land to heal properly and regenerate their magic stores." Heathrow stated. Merridayn gasped as the information clicked into place.

"If Torvan cannot go home, he cannot draw the power

from the land. And since he cannot die, he could essentially be in perpetual pain, weak, and helpless." Merridayn stood up, her brain in overdrive. "If he is injured, the injury wouldn't heal correctly. He wouldn't be able to use magic because he would have no way of regenerating it again. He is basically immortal but the equivalent of a babe. A dead battery with no way of recharging."

"Go on, Merridayn." Heathrow leaned in his chair, watching the human woman assemble the pieces. He was impressed that she had come up with the conclusion faster than any of the wolves had.

"If he's weak then he would be excommunicated from his House. His title stripped away and given to someone else. Or his entire house could be challenged by someone else." Merridayn stopped, looking between the two wolves. "Can more High Fae be made? If so, anyone could become a High Fae and challenge the Mordinian's right to lead. But this is all presuming more can be created. Someone would have figured it out, though. Modern genetics would tell you breeding between a limited gene pool would eventually cause anomalies. Or what if a generation only had all females? What then? Would they pull a random male? Draw someone from a bloody hat and hope the two different genes would create a High Fae child?"

Heathrow and Hansen stared at her blankly, their expressions matching, awed by the human. The men had not considered the possibility of a new High Fae being made, not born. This information opened up new thoughts and theories, and this human Luna was figuring it out at lightspeed. Surpassing the generations of research, the wolves had done in the past hour. Heathrow felt a tinge of pride at Elion's mate, knowing the segregation the alpha suffered because of her. If only those who doubted Merridayn could see her now.

"Assuming new High Fae could be created, the Mordinians would be forced to ally with a strong House to solidify their place." Merridayn squealed, her excitement boiling over. "Oh my Goddess!"

Heathrow and Hansen both jumped slightly, not expecting and not prepared for the yell. Their hands came to rub their sensitive ears, catching the attention of Merridayn, who blushed apologetically.

"Sorry." Merridayn blushed again as Heathrow grumbled something under his breath she couldn't quite understand. "You both said the Mordinians had their own 'Prophetess', right?" She didn't wait for their response, continuing at full pace. "This prophetess created prophecies the Mordinians would execute to give the prophetess credit. What if they also used her as a scare tactic to keep whoever was about to challenge them at bay? Think about it. The general population put their faith in House Mordinian. If the oldest son could no longer return home, it would leave the house in disarray. A challenger could come up and take their place, promising all sorts of things to the commoners, to win their favour. Ultimately, they would have the citizens backing. Mordinians wouldn't be able to succeed if they lost the commoners' trust. Even if they did, those commoners could resist their lead." Merridayn wished she had took notes of all the information she had learned, a problem she was going to rectify at a later time. She was going to create a book, a timeline, for Verena to use when she begins to learn about her heritage.

"You have a good point, Merridayn." Hansen agreed, wondering how they had been blind to such a simple explanation.

"But it still doesn't explain why he needed Jerifeyn.

Unless there was something special about Jerifeyn's line which could prove useful to Torvan?" Things did not add up, what was so special about Jerifeyn the Mordinians had to have?

"Ah, and we have now come to the point where nobody has been able to piece it together," Hansen admitted ashamedly. "We were beginning to hope Verena might have an answer when she begins to figure out her abilities."

"This leads back to her; she is still in a coma. And as we all know, we have no idea how to wake her. What we do know is this: she is dying, slowly, extremely slowly. But she is definitely dying." Merridayn dropped her head as Kinley landed on her shoulder, a piece of paper in her beak. "If what you said about High Fae needing their homeland, do you think it could be the same case here? Does Verena need to go back to her homeland to wake up?"

"We were wondering the same thing, but you mentioned your son, Aven, healed her after the encounter with Abigail." Heathrow turned in his chair to look Merridayn in the eyes.

"Correct, we could all see their bond and then her injuries were gone." Merridayn had a feeling she knew where Heathrow's line of questioning was leading.

"You also mentioned there was a second, right?" Heathrow's hand came to rest on his chin, his long, calloused fingers scratching his stubble.

"Yes, it was faint, but it looked like a second bond extending from Verena somewhere else. We were unable to determine its destination." She felt ashamed to say she did not put much stock in the second line they saw that day, now she felt she should have.

"If she has two mates, perhaps if both were in the same room together, they could provide enough energy to wake her?" Heathrow smiled, watching as Merridayn's confusion flooded her features.

Merridayn opened her mouth to speak and promptly closed it again. The process repeated a handful of times, and she was unable to collect her thoughts. Heathrow began to smile, clearly having figured out the solution to the problem without any assistance—as if just speaking the question out loud was enough. She looked at him, waiting for the burly half wolf to share with the rest of them. She observed Hansen's mouth beginning to curl as well.

"Orla," Heathrow stated, his tone leading to no room for argument.

"Orla mentioned Prince Kieran was distinctively angry when she asked for their information on High Fae." Hansen grinned, his hand silently coming out to stroke the nearest imgrid's head.

Kinley decided she had waited long enough, harshly pecking Merridayn in the cheek. She dropped the parchment she was carrying onto the top of Merridayn's blouse. Angrily, Merridayn fetched it from falling farther down, shooting daggers at the pigeon fox. Kinley pecked her again as if the imgrid could read Merridayn's mind. Irritated Merridayn had called her a pigeon fox. Stuffing the parchment into her hand, Merridayn looked back at the two gentlemen.

"She also said Kieran had figured out who we were hosting. He already knew when Orla had come through the portal." Heathrow growled, angry at putting his mate in a situation where he was in no position to help.

"Do you think Kieran could smell Verena on Orla?" Hansen reached to place his hand on Heathrow's shoulder, missing drastically as his hand came in contact with Heathrow's face. The men chuckled together, Merridayn watched Heathrow move Hansen's hand into his own.

"It is a possibility. Especially if Verena is who I think she is to Kieran." Heathrow was calming down, the contact from his friend working to subdue his anger.

"No." Hansen stumbled, leaning back in his chair. "You think so?"

"It would make sense, Han. Wouldn't it?" Heathrow questioned him, squeezing Hansen's hand anxiously.

"Goddess. It really would." Hansen agreed with him, the veins in his hand protruding as he returned the man's anxious grip.

"Why else would Kieran help us translate Jerifeyn's journals after all these years if he didn't have a smidgen of an idea Verena was here, in Alusso? The cunning Demon was biding his time before he eventually figured out where she was." Heathrow's lip curled upwards, Merridayn could safely say there was no love lost between the hybrid and the Demon.

Merridayn watched the men exchange earnestly, catching up to what they implied. Her heart broke, knowing her child could potentially get hurt, especially if Aven had to share Verena with a Demon prince. There was no possible way her son could compare to a Demon prince. Merridayn's brain abruptly shut down the train of thought she was on, changing her path towards helping Verena. If Kieran was Verena's second mate, was there a possibility of them being in the same room as Verena they could wake her?

"Oh shit," Hansen whispered.

"Oh shit, indeed, Han." Heathrow agreed.

"He's coming here, isn't he?" Merridayn asked out loud, instinctually knowing the answer already.

"It would explain why we were put on a lockdown,"

Heathrow explained to Merridayn, confirming her suspicions from earlier when she watched the guards running around chaotically.

"Are you going to allow him to pass through the wards to get to her?" Merridayn's heart stopped, waiting for their answer. If he was Verena's mate, and he was coming here, he would have to be given access through the wards. Merridayn worried the council elders would refuse, effectively signing Verena's death certificate.

"Depends on Kieran." Hansen's answer scared Merridayn even more. The anxiety she felt caused her to begin running through contingency plans.

"Depends on him. How?"

"Well, it depends on whether he comes through wanting to slaughter anyone in his path."

"Let us pray then, pray Kieran is willing to listen to reason," Merridayn whispered; Kinley decided to peck her in the throat this time. Aggravated at the woman for refusing to read the note she had diligently brought. "What is it, Kinley?"

Jumping down from Merridayn's shoulder, Kinley roughly snatched the parchment in Merridayn's hand, cutting Merridayn in the process as the imgrid flapped the paper in her beak. Understanding the signal, albeit an angry signal, Merridayn took the paper and opened it. She read and re-read the note, her face blanched as her eyes read the note for the fifth time.

"Is everything alright, Merridayn?" Heathrow reached out, gripping Merridayn's upper arm gently in concern.

"Verena's vitals are crashing." Merridayn's breath hitched, her breathing almost stopping completely. The men watched, stunned, as her chair crashed to the floor behind her. Their eyes hastily followed the woman, and they began sprinting towards the entrance. "Kinley! Grab my stuff!" Merridayn yelled over her shoulder before the giant archives door flung open. Both men shared an ominous groan when the door slammed shut in Merridayn's wake.

Chapter 26

MERRIDAYN

Merridayn's sides burned as she sprinted towards Verena's room, cursing herself again for her lack of athleticism. Merridayn promised herself she would get into running when everything settled down. The people in her path jumped out of her way until she realised they were moving for the guards trailing after her. Suspicion rose, curious about the plan concerning the sanctum. Merridayn shook her head, chastising herself for veering off target. Verena was crashing; Verena needed her at her peak. Merridayn's nurse training kicked in. Her feet pounded against the moss-covered ground until she burst through Verena's room. A slim-cut figure, kneeling next to Verena as healers rushed in and out of the room, gave her pause.

Aven?

"Aven?" Merridayn got closer, her son's features becoming more precise, and her heart filled with joy. "When did you get here? Where's your father? How long have you been with Verena? When did she start crashing?" Merridayn spits out the questions rapidly, trying to assess the situation.

"Hello, mum. We all got here about an hour ago. Dad is with the others at the defence meeting. I heard we might be getting a visit. I've been sitting with Verena for about-" Aven looked down at his watch. "-twenty minutes or so?

They wouldn't let me see her initially. I've been trying since I got here. It took me forcing myself in, and I was too big for them to kick me out. All the guards were summoned to the meeting, so healers and Druids were left. Druid Nora gave the order to leave me alone. She said something along the lines of 'the bond between you could prove useful.'"

"I see." Merridayn grabbed the arm of the nearest healer, not looking at who she grabbed ahold of. "Tell me what Verena's status is."

"Her vitals began crashing approximately an hour and a half ago, Merridayn." Merridayn recognised Gracie's soft tone, pulling the healer into a crushing embrace before letting her go. "We tried finding you, but nobody knew where you went. It wasn't until Kinley showed up that I knew where you had gone. I sent her off with a note. Did you not receive it?"

"I did. I admit I was distracted and did not read it until a few minutes before bursting through the door. Kinley should be bringing my belongings, which I left behind. I hope." Merridayn squeezed Gracie's arm once more, affectionately and caringly, then made her way to the opposite side of her son. Kneeling next to Verena as the poor child was randomly writhing around, Merridayn's eyes pooled. Small cries released from Verena's lips caused more tears to gather.

Merridayn listened to Druid Nora barking orders; it was all hands on deck, and Merridayn felt as if she was in the way. She didn't care though, as nothing in the world could move her from Verena's side. Her regret forced her to stay by Verena's side even if she made the tasks of those trying to save her more difficult. Merridayn noticed Aven felt the same way, his head resting on one of his hands. She could barely see Verena's small, pale hand dwarfed underneath her sons. A loud sound erupted from the hallway, and Aven's head snapped up. When he looked out the doorway, the hair on Merridayn's skin prickled. Goosebumps lined her arms and neck, and a low growl sounded from Aven, giving way for even more worry to burst through Merridayn's composure.

"Aven?" Merridayn whispered, trying to gain her son's attention. "What is it?"

"I'm not sure," Aven growled again, standing up reluctantly. His hands gripping Verena's again before letting go. Walking towards the doorway when the familiar rude healer whom Merridayn encountered at Verena's admittance barreled into Aven.

"He's here. Oh, Goddess, he's here." The healer cried out, grasping hold of Aven, tears running down her face. "Oh Goddess, help us."

Shit. Shit. Shit.

The healer's words struck a chord in her son. Merridayn knew all hope of convincing him to stay with Verena was gone. His morals would not allow him to remain when those he saw needing protection were crying for help. Merridayn's head rested against Verena's arm. She whispered a prayer to whoever would listen as she steeled her nerves to follow Aven.

"Gracie." Merridayn's voice, laced with command, echoed throughout the room.

"Yes, Luna?"

"Stay with Verena. Do not leave this room. All of you. Do not walk past the wards from the Willow. Do not look out the door. Keep her alive. I may have figured out how to bring her out of her coma. But I need to convince the elders first." Merridayn looked each person in the eyes. Making sure her orders were understood and followed. The wolves' biology could not disobey an order from a Luna, regardless of whether they were their Luna or not. Merridayn only hoped the Druid would listen.

"How long do you need, Luna?" Druid Nora's raspy voice broke the silence.

"Long enough to convince the elders to let me test my theory." If who Merridayn believed was here, she knew she'd be racing against time. She wished she had more to convince the stubborn elders, but fate had decided to douse everything in flames, to hell with everyone else.

Druid Nora nodded her affirmation to Merridayn just as Merridayn had left the room. Carefully walking towards the sound of the commotion, she instantly regretted not knowing much about the Willow's warding: how strong was it, how far did it reach, and could it keep an extremely angry and old Demon out?

"Where the fuck is she?!" Pure, unbridled rage reverberated from the entryway, the place Merridayn considered as the 'Circle.' All pathways merged at this central room, an empty area with an open roof.

Here we go, Merr. Let's hope your theory is correct, or many people might die.

"Kieran." Armand began. Merridayn drew closer, shuffling her way through the crowds of guards. In her peripheral vision, she caught the top of her youngest son's unruly hair, but there was no sign of her husband or eldest.

"You will regard his Highness with respect, animal." An unknown, deep, voice Merridayn didn't recognise. His exceptionally pale skin and bright green eyes was a testament of Merridayn's lack of Demon knowledge.

"My apologies, Apsephion." Armand quipped; Merridayn could see the elder bowing as much as his body allowed him to with his age. "Prince Kieran, what can we do for you?"

"Yes, what can we do for you? Besides executing you for trespassing." Islabell sneered. Kieran's two guards flanking him placed their hands on their swords, shifting their feet into a defensive stance.

"I would enjoy seeing you try to touch our Prince." The man Armand called Apsephion stepped forward, defensive.

Wolves everywhere began growling, the rattle of metal clanking as they all took offence from Apsephion's words echoed in her ears. She could only assume the sound was deafening in the more sensitive one of wolves. Though, she suspected at this moment, nobody cared about the sound. Only the three Demons standing before them, their Prince at the front. Merridayn took a moment to look over the legendary Dremorta Prince. His tanned skin seemed to glow unethically against the bright light of the moon above them. White hair was stark against his black armour, gracing his lethal form from head to toe, with no visible expanse of skin beside his neck and face. Red eyes swept the crowd opposite him, behind the protective warding of the Willow. Merridayn spotted Aven edging near the front. Steps from the barrier, steps from potential death.

"Now, now, Islabell, Prince Kieran, there has to be a way we can come to some sort of peaceful compromise?" Armand spread his arms out, trying to calm the room down.

"I will not ask again, Armand. Where is Verena?" Kieran grumbled, his voice sultry and sensual. Completely throwing Merridayn off, she wasn't exactly sure what she expected from the terrifying Demon Prince. "Do not attempt to lie to me, either. I know she is here. I can *smell* her on you all."

"Why do you need to know where my mate is?"

Oh, bloody hell.

"Aven." Elion and Cavanaugh hissed simultaneously, attempting to reach him from where they stood. Many bystanders blocked them, and Merridayn's fear ever closer to coming true as Aven took another step towards the boundary.

"Your mate?" Kieran laughed, signalling something to his companions; one of them left immediately. Fading into the unnatural darkness behind them as if the moon itself were snuffed out. "Such a cute little wolf. Stop talking about things you know nothing about."

"Things I know nothing about? I'm sure Verena could attest otherwise." Aven stood up straighter, his chest puffing out.

"Until you come out from behind those wards, you are irrelevant." Kieran barely gave Aven a second glance, fixing his red eyes back on Armand. "Bring her to me, and no one will be harmed."

Merridayn watched, astounded, as Kieran reached out with his armoured hands. He ran the tip of his forefinger down where the wards ended, sparks flying at the contact point. He was toying with them, messing with their minds, and causing the room to tense.

"Let me go! Help! Please! Anyone!" A young female screamed out. All heads turned in the direction it was coming from.

Being dragged behind Apsephion by her hair was a small, fragile girl. She appeared physically fine; there was no evident bruising on her, but the fear in her eyes terrified all the bystanders. She was kicking and screaming, tugging at the arms of the burly Demon. Kieran smirked, his face

taking in the fear on everyone's faces. Based on their reactions, Merridayn assumed most in the room knew the
individual who had been dragged in. The entirety of the
situation did not bode well to Merridayn; her hope of
convincing the council members to allow Kieran to see
Verena diminished with each passing second.

"Your Highness, surely there is no need for this." Armand waved towards the woman, his face contorting
painfully. "We sent her to you as a bargain. We did not
mean for her to be humiliated like this."

"I warned you not to make me ask again where my
mate is." Kieran looked down at the screaming wolf who
was brought to his side, his piercing red eyes quieting her
instantly. "Since you have decided to ignore my question, I
will ignore your plea for this pup's survival." At this, Merridayn watched Kieran pick the child up as if she weighed
nothing, her feet coming off the ground as tears began
streaming down her face.

Merridayn watched the poor child, imagining how she
must have felt abandoned by her pack. The realisation
that nobody would be coming to her rescue showed on
her face as if she had accepted her fate. Without hesitation, Kieran snapped the girl's neck with one hand. A feat
many could not do, let alone with one hand and the hand
which was holding her in the air. Merridayn could not lie
to herself, the feat was impressive, yet at the same time,
utterly terrifying. There was no doubt Verena would be
safe in his protection; however, she could not help but
fear for the child's safety. Kieran dropped the corpse onto
the ground, the body crumpled against the moss-covered
dirt, the dull thud still echoed in everyone's hearts. At this
moment, Merridayn questioned the leadership abilities of
the elders.

"What have you done..." Orla began, her sentence broken and stopped by the sobs which shook her entire body.

"You fucking monster!" Islabell yelled, her foot mere centimetres from the edge of the wards.

Kieran's secondary Demon appeared instantly on the opposite side, his devilish white teeth a confusing contrast to his dark skin. Fangs sharp and bloody, head tilted sideways, one hand on the hilt of his dagger while the other caressed the wards. A shiver ran through Merridayn as she watched the Demon eying Islabell. She prayed Islabell didn't step past the one thing protecting her.

"Come outside the wards and say it, pretty girl." The beautiful Demon's sultry voice caused another shiver to pass through Merridayn.

"Your choice, Armand. Let me see Verena, or I will kill another wolf every five minutes." Kieran leaned against the closest wall. The sight could have been mistaken for a model posing for a photoshoot.

"Aven, keep your ass right there." Elion's command boasted through the silence.

"Aven!" Merridayn screamed, watching her son cross the border, right into the awaiting Demon's hands.

Kieran pushed himself off the wall, his white hair flowing backwards from the sudden movement. The motion an example of sheer swiftness and ease; Kieran showcased a miniscule amount of mastery of his form. There was a deliberate difference after Kieran pushed himself up, and now, a game of predator and prey began. He was gracefully walking towards his accomplice, whose hand was wrapped around Aven's throat. Merridayn fought internally against her mother-bear instincts but concluded it would not be wise. What could a human do against a centuries-old Demon?

"What do we have here, Orias?" Kieran taunted them all, his third pulling Aven off the ground. The young testosterone filled wolf fought meagrely against him. "Tsk, tsk. Were you not taught your place, little wolf? What was your name? Aven, was it?"

Aven mumbled something incoherently, his oesophagus constricted by the Demon's hand. Orias laughed hauntingly. Merridayn watched her husband's fists flexing, closing and opening as he processed what his next moves might be. She pushed her way through the crowds towards Elion and placed her hand on his shoulder. Elion's tenseness calmed partially, but not enough to satisfy Merridayn, not sufficient to show her he wouldn't go after their son.

"Sorry, I can't hear you." Kieran mocked, Apsephion and Orias' laugh joining him. "Put the wolf down, Orias. Let us see what the runt has to say."

"Don't hurt him." Armand began, his voice cracking in trepidation.

Merridayn wondered if Armand was worried Elion would cross the wards and start a war if his son was killed due to the elders' stubbornness or if Armand was concerned about Verena. Either way, Merridayn knew she needed to act. Not only did Verena's life depend on her being correct, but now her son's life depended on calming an angry Demon.

"Verena does not belong to you," Aven growled.

"Shut up, son," Merridayn whispered, her body freezing at his words.

"Really? And she belongs to you?" Kieran taunted him, Merridayn cursed them both.

Goddess, they couldn't be any more egotistical, could they?

"She is my mate." Aven fell for the bait, his fists clenching repeatedly.

"You're what? Eighteen? Nineteen?" Kieran looked at his clawed gauntlets, showing Aven he was of no importance to him.

"Why does it matter?" Aven bit out, inching closer and closer to the barrier.

"I've existed in this realm for a few years shy of a thousand, child." Kieran stared at Aven, an eyebrow raising. "Verena has been my mate since the day she was born. When I felt her existence being brought into this dreadful life, she was mine."

"Excuse me?" Aven bristled, unsure what Kieran meant.

"Who do you think got her off when your pathetic attempts to pleasure her failed? Whose voice does she hear in her head besides her own?" Kieran smirked. He could tell he was under the young wolf's skin and was dutifully emasculating him in front of his entire pack.

"He's taunting you, son; don't listen to him" Elion's voice was lost in the sudden commotion. No words could stop Aven from jumping towards Kieran. Apsephion and Orias watched from the sidelines. Knowing Kieran would not want them to interfere. The wolf had played right into his hands, and Kieran found himself delighted by the chaos. Aven swung haphazardly with no concern for his safety. Even with all his force behind it, the blow was best described as glancing. Kieran showed no reaction to the pathetic attempt from a male he knew was lesser. Merridayn could only watch from behind the safety of the wards, trying to devise a plan to ensure nobody else died.

"Are you done? Already?" Kieran taunted again. Aven's rage was visible on his face.

"Fight me, coward!" Aven roared, unable to understand the discongruity between the two of them.

"Are you sure? I wouldn't want to harm the pretty face

you have. It does seem to be the only thing going for you. We both know who Verena will choose. I would hate for you to be alone with no other options if I were to take your looks from you." Kieran flourished his hand in front of his face, indicating the softer features of the wolf.

"She chose me." Aven was at a loss for words, hoping he was correct.

"Initially, when she didn't know she had better options. A temporary mistake on her part from being without me." Kieran took advantage of Aven's irrationality and slammed him against the wall, holding him off the ground by his throat. Kieran gave a deadly grin as his sharpened gauntlet nails pierced into Aven's skin, crimson blood poured from the punctures and down Aven's front.

"Armand, please." Merridayn begged as they all watched her son being bested. "Verena needs them both."

"I do not want to kill you, pup." Kieran looked at Aven, his grip tightening slightly as more blood spilt. Aven's hands struggled to pull Kieran off him. "My little hellfire would be upset. I'd have to hear about it. You know High Fae live for an extensive amount of time. You wouldn't want me to deal with her anger over you for the rest of my life, would you?"

"Armand!" Merridayn screamed, gathering the attention of everyone surrounding her. The guards flinched, their hands going straight towards their weapons. "She needs them both. Let him in before you sign all of our death certificates because of your damn choices."

"What did you say about Verena?" Kieran's head snapped towards Merridayn's voice. Unable to find her in the crowd, he scanned everyone, waiting for Merridayn to speak again.

"She needs you both, you and Aven. The soulbond you

three share could wake her." Merridayn admitted, hoping
he would see reason and drop her son.

"If you are lying to me, I will kill the boy here. Slowly."
Kieran growled.

"I'm not. I promise." She hoped her hypothesis would
be correct and not misconstrued as some falsehood if it
did not work. "He healed her before when she was injured
in her fight with Abigail. Theoretically, she should be able
to pull enough energy from you both to come out of the
coma." Merridayn quickly rattled off her hypothesis, and
almost clinically, all emotion vanished.

"Theoretically?"

"Well, it's not been done before, but I assume it should
work. It has to work. She's dying." Desperation plagued
Merridayn's tone and expression; she was at a loss and
knew Kieran was the key to saving Verena.

"What do you say, Armand?" Kieran pushed Aven
higher up the wall in emphasis. "Are you going to let me
in, or do I need to kill a few more wolves to get my point
across?"

"Armand..." Elion growled, his body signalling he was
ready to cross the wards to save his son.

"We promised the volunteers they would be safe, Armand." Orla piped in. The tears dried from her face; evident now were the stained streaks where they had been.

"They will kill us all, Armand. Don't make me your
enemy." Islabell threatened.

"Prince Kieran," Armand cleared his throat of worry, his
authoritative stature returning. "If we allow you, and only
you, to cross the wards, what guarantee do we have you
will not cause anyone harm?"

"I suppose you just have to trust me, right?"

"Your Highness, do you understand our predicament?

You have already killed one of our own right before our eyes. Even now, you hold another by the throat with clear injury, and yet you expect us to allow you inside the wards keeping us safe?"

"I'm going to let you in on a little secret. Armand, your wards would take me less than a minute to burn through. Though it would anger my Lady, it is a consequence I will accept with a smile on my face. If I did not want to give you an option, not even she could stop me."

"Armand. Either let him in, or I am bringing Verena out." Merridayn could barely finish the threat before an audible gasp broke through the crowd. The mass seemed to split, causing a pathway where Heathrow could be seen carrying Verena to the edge of the ward. "I'm sure she would rather be back in her bed. Make the right choice, Armand."

With bated breath, everyone watched as Armand reached his hand out of the wards, inviting Kieran to take it. He flicks his eyes between his hand and Aven, removing his gauntlet-covered talons from Aven's throat. Unceremoniously dropping the gasping pup onto the ground, everyone could see Kieran debating on killing him regardless. Merridayn released the breath she held as Kieran took the proffered hand instead. Being pulled through by Armand, she watched the wards shimmer and stretch as they fought against his entry. Once Kieran was safely on their side, he immediately took the fragile Verena from Heathrow. Curling her to his chest cautiously, his red eyes filled with many emotions.

"I've got you, Hellfire," Kieran whispered, leaning to kiss her forehead. "I told you I was coming, didn't I?"

Chapter 27

MERRIDAYN

"Gracie!" Merridayn yelled out, hoping the healer could hear her over the chaos. "Her room is this way, Kieran. Can I call you Kieran? Actually, I don't care right now. Verena is more important than titles, would you not agree?"

"You're a feisty one, aren't you?" Kieran smirked, nodding his head. His height rivalled only by Heathrow, he was easily nearly a foot taller than the rest. Merridayn held his attention, it was strange for a small human to command him.

Human?

Kieran discreetly inhaled deeply, pinpointing the one before him. She was covered and surrounded by the wet mongrels, but underneath it all, was definitely human. The revelation surprised him, though he didn't think about it too long. It was something they could circle back at a later time, when his hellfire wasn't dying in his arms.

"Will someone please tend to Aven? We will need them both for this to work." Merridayn shouted over her shoulder. "My name is Merridayn Belmont. I know yours; I feel it is proper for you to know mine."

"Interesting. You say Aven with distinction, I assume he is your son? Therefore you are the wife of Elion Belmont, no?" Kieran glared at the guard standing a few feet before them, clearly debating on defying orders from the wolf leader. "I would reconsider your actions, little wolf. Your, what do you call them? Alpha? He has allowed me through your wards. Continue to block my way and I will show you no mercy whilst Verena is in my arms."

"Let them pass, son." Armand calmly ordered from behind Kieran.

Kieran watched, eyebrow raised, visibly shifting Verena's weight in his arms to free his right hand. As he flexed, the metal clanked as it clashed against itself. A silent challenge, one Kieran hoped would scare the young wolf into backing off. He wasn't sure if he could hold his anger back after getting to hold Verena. The young wolf growled, verbally dissatisfied with the predicament he was in.

"Listen to your Armand, little wolf. Test my patience and you will be yet another name on my list." Kieran warned again, a few feet away from the challenging wolf. "This is your last warning. Step aside so I can return my heart to her bed, or my face will be the last you ever see. Which will it be?" Kieran levelled his opposition again, nearing a foot and a half taller than the wolf, Kieran had to look downward. Moments passed, an eerie silence slithered through the crowd. The wolf moved, still debating with himself as he reluctantly obeyed.

"Her room is right around the corner, the healers and Druid should still be in the room awaiting her." Merridayn's smaller form parted the lingering crowd, Kieran watched as they jumped out of the way of them. He was taken off guard by how fast the tiny human could walk, having to elongate his stride to match her.

"Very well." Kieran was brief, his worry for Verena apparent based on the change in his voice, Merridayn peered at him from over her shoulder, she knew instantly how much he cared for the girl. "And your son? Is he following?" Merridayn barked out a feeble laugh before shutting her mouth forcefully. "Is there something amusing?"

"No," Merridayn answered with no hesitation. Kieran's mouth ticked upward marginally.

"Are you certain?"

"Fine. Yes, there is something amusing." Merridayn rounded the corner swiftly as if she was running away from the conversation. Kieran followed her blindly, Verena tucked safely in his arms.

"Go on."

"Verena's room is the second door on the right." Merridayn threw out, confirming Kieran's suspicion she was trying to distract him.

"Very well." Verena's roomplate began to come into clarity, her name listed at the top. Underneath listed what Kieran assumed was her assigned healers and Druid, he took considerable time to memorise the aforementioned names. Should anything happen to his hellfire whilst he is present, he had a decent place to start the massacre. He watched Merridayn walk through the opened door, sensing multiple presences within the room. A Druid, a handful of wolves, and one tiny human. There was one scent in the room reminding him of someone, the scent tickled his memory. Their name within arms reach yet flitted away every time he was about to remember.

"Place her on the bed please." The Druid motioned towards the white cloud-like bed in the middle as Kieran ducked under the door to cross the threshold of her room. "I am Druid Nora, Your Highness."

"I see my stature is known without the need for introductions." Kieran snipped though he obeyed the Druid's direction. Gently setting Verena in the middle of her bed.

As he stood, Kieran realised his head would be exceptionally close to the top of the ceiling. "Is there a chair I can occupy so I will not be courting the ceiling?"

"Yes. If it'll shut you up so we can get on with this." There it was again, the scent he recognised but couldn't place, teasing his subconscious memory.

"Elder Islabell!" A meek wolf hiding behind the Druid whispered harshly. Kieran watched her step out from behind Nora. His eyes took her in, flashing over to Merridayn and back again.

"Islabell, is it? What was it you said earlier?" Kieran brought his armoured gauntlet fingers to tap against his chin, looking like a seductive mercenary.

"Hmm, I believe it was 'execute you for trespassing.' Am I correct?" His fingers stilled, and his red eyes flashed with rage as he stared into Islabell's soul. "Do you still believe you hold a chance?"

"Leave her alone, Demon." Aven croaked out behind them all, leaning heavily against the doorframe. The blood on his neck from Kieran's punctures dried and blackening. "Verena is our priority. So remove your head from your ass and start doing what you were allowed past the wards for."

"I can see the family resemblance." Kieran chuckled, shuffling carefully towards the chair on the other side of Verena's bed. As he studied the chair, he sincerely hoped the fragile looking thing would be able to withstand his weight. Taking the chance, he sat gracefully with minimal complaints from the toothpick seat.

"What do we need to do to assist, Luna?" Nora addressed Merridayn, Kieran awaited the brilliant plan Merridayn claimed to have pieced together.

"We all know Aven healed Verena with their soul bond. There was a second bond present, and until today, we could not understand why. Today, we uncovered the possibility Verena could be bonded to two: Aven-" Merridayn pointed towards her son. "-and Kieran. I suspect her body shut down after the blood transfusion due to lack of previous exposure to her own kind. Which is entirely my fault, and I will take any and all consequences for it. However, from my understanding, High Fae need to be connected to their land to heal and regenerate their magic stores. Since we are not capable of taking Verena to her home, theoretically we should be able to use the two soul bonds to infuse her with magic. The same way Aven healed her when her body was distressed and injured, we should be able to use the soul bond to transfer energy from both Aven and Kieran, as well as magic from Kieran."

"You're under the impression Kieran has magic at all, Merridayn. He's a Demon. All his kind knows how to do is kill." Islabell rolled her eyes, snarky and disrespectful.

"We also know how to fuck, don't forget that little tidbit." Kieran matched her sass, enjoying the reaction he garnered from the aggravating wolf. "But you would be incorrect, Demons do have magic. Though Merridayn, Verena carries the bloodlines of Archangels Haniel and Ariel. Demons were created by Archangel Azrael. Would infusing her with magic gifted from my Archangel not interfere with the bloodline magic she carries?"

"We do not have the time to research. It's now or never." Merridayn glumly replied, unable to hold back her worry from his valid questioning.

"Let's get on with it, shall we?" Islabell examined her perfectly manicured nails, her indifference to the situation palpable from the bored expression on her features. It was as if the elder thought herself better than the others in the room and did not care if the girl passed.

"Do you not have anywhere else you can disgrace the presence of? There must be someone who enjoys the whole 'Bad-Ass, No-Fucks Given, Better-Than-Thou' attitude?" Kieran snapped, his patience depleted. His only grounding element was currently asleep and rapidly losing the fight to stay on their plane.

"Damn, man, if you weren't a Demon, we might have been friends." Aven's lighthearted jest echoed through the room, everyone at a standstill, waiting for the temporary accord to break.

"I do not befriend children." Kieran shifted his weight in the tiny chair, awaiting Merridayn's direction.

"I'm throwing in the dark here, I didn't have enough time to research how to activate the bond. Perhaps if you and Kieran touch Verena?" Merridayn offered, kneeling at the end of the bed to give the two men space.

Everyone besides the two mentioned stayed where they were. Islabell muttered something under her breath, resulting in a warning growl from Kieran as he gracefully vacated his seat. Electing to follow Merridayn's lead and kneel on Verena's left side, opposite to the door. Aven followed suit on her right. Looking between Aven and Merridayn, Kieran took the initiative. Shucking his gauntlet off and dropping it on the ground next to him, with his now bare hand, he reached out to take hold of Verena's delicate hand. Interlacing their fingers and nodding towards Aven, insinuating the wolf to follow suit. Silently, Aven laced his own with hers, bringing the back of her palm to his lips to kiss. With bated breath, everyone's attention turned towards Verena.

Her body spasmed, and her back came off the bed eerily before slamming back down. The vitals floating near the head of her bed triggered alarms which screamed loudly.

Her body arched again, the alarms continuing to scream in Kieran's ears.

"This isn't working, Merridayn." Kieran snapped.

"I know. I know. I don't-" Merridayn desperately kept herself from sobbing as stress caused her to stutter. "-I don't know what to do."

"Fuck this. Alctra-Vez." Kieran yelled into the air, holding out his left hand. Black smoke covered his hand, fading out to reveal a silver bound book.

"Kieran?" Merridayn questioned, curious but hesitant.

"This is the book Orla had fallen through the portal unannounced wanting. All the information the Dremorta have on High Fae." Kieran flipped through the pages, knowing precisely the section he was looking for. "Let's see... Soul Bonds... Triggers... Ah, there it is."

"And?" Merridayn leaned forward on the bed, desperate to get a glimpse of the book and was highly disappointed she was unable to make out the lettering.

"Interesting." Kieran hummed to himself, shifting the weight on his knees to his heels.

"What is it?"

"I see." Kieran cleared his throat, removing his attention from the page he was on and snapped the book closed, the force of which revealed how aged the bound document was when a puff of dust could be seen lingering in the air. "My little hellfire, I apologise in advance for the pain I must cause you."

"Pardon?" Aven forced out, his face twisted from concern to confusion and back to concern within a fraction of a second.

"Verena is only capable of activating the bond when she is conscious. Our information states when one of the bonded is incapacitated but not injured in a physical sense of the word, the partner can activate the bond from severe injury. When there is potential for the bond to become broken, it forces the uninjured partner to sacrifice a portion of their life to heal the other. Life demands equilibrium, and each partner has a shared fate once the bond is accepted. Until their time has run, the bond will continue to play healer."

"Which means?" Ever the scholar, Merridayn was almost leaping at the chance to learn more information.

"Verena is not physically injured, or so the bond believes. Therefore, we have to cause bodily harm to awaken it." Kieran looked down at his hellfire, the way her skin became perpetually paler than possible. The state of her was identical to how she was in their shared mental bond. A state he would immediately rectify once she returned home with him. "Hence why I apologised to her."

"Absolutely the fuck not you will," Aven growled.

"So you want her to die? Because I can do this with you conscious or not."

"Over my dead body will you harm a single hair on her."

"I'd be happy to oblige when my mate is not seconds from greeting my Archangel!" Kieran shouted, drawing his dagger from his ankle sheath. "Make your choice now, whelp. Are we doing this the easy way or the hard way? In case you forgot, I am a Demon. I have no morals."

"Son, we do not have the time. If what he says is correct, the bond needs to be activated. It would make logical sense, considering you healed her - or you both did? - irrelevant. She was direly injured after the fight with Abigail, and then your soul bond activated." Merridayn reached out to place her hand on her son's shoulder, hoping the contact would calm him.

"Very well. But if she dies because you are wrong, I will

not hesitate to kill you." Aven grumbled, upset about the circumstances they were presently in.

"I would enjoy watching you try. I am rarely wrong, however." Kieran angled his dagger near Verena's abdomen, analysing the least fatal area he could injure with enough impact the bond should hopefully activate. "I'm sorry, my love. I will take every single ounce of your ire once you wake. But you have to wake. There are still so many sights and so much I want to do with you." Without further hesitation, Kieran struck. His dagger landed in the upper right quadrant of Verena's abdomen. Puncturing her right kidney and liver as his knife went in and was dragged downwards. Blood immediately poured out of the wound, spraying on Kieran's face, hands and chest. Everyone watched as Verena spasmed once more, then stopped altogether. She stopped breathing, her heart stopped beating, the vitals alarms began a whole different series of sounds. The room went silent, nobody moved, nobody breathed. The scene before them was confusing, alarming, invigorating, a strange mix of emotions no one person could quite name or explain.

Verena screamed.

Chapter 28

VERENA

Everything hurt. Every part of her wailed. The agonising sound echoed in her head. It was annoying and high-pitched. She couldn't figure out where the screaming was coming from, and maybe it was herself. She really couldn't tell in the moment. The darkness she had grown so accustomed to flashed red and then a bright white. Was this the end? The white light people say they see before death? Was she dying? The empty sterileness began shifting. It wasn't noticeable at first. Verena thought her mind was playing tricks on her. Then the shadows formed, outlines of objects or people. Verena couldn't tell. She recognised the beginnings of a memory. Having witnessed a few now, she was beginning to recognise the pattern they took.

"Verena?" Familiar, but so distant, Verena's head turned on a swivel, trying to locate the voice.

Aven?

Where are you, Hellfire?

Kieran?

"Verena!" Aven hollered, and Verena simultaneously clutched at her figurative head.

"Enough, whelp. Lower your tone. You'll hurt her even more." Kieran's outline began materialising in front of her, overshadowing a smaller form next to him.

"Me? Hurt her? You're the one who stabbed her, and then she screamed." Verena could feel Aven's anger, as if he was there, in her mind. "Where are we?"

"My Lady, why must I have been fated to walk life with this impudent child?" Kieran's form materialised even more, Verena could see Kieran rubbing both sides of his temple. "We are inside Verena's mind, she must have been overwhelmed and the bond forced us inside."

"In her head? As in, she can hear us?"

"Yes, and feel the headache you're giving me from screaming every five seconds, prat." Verena spat, rubbing her ears in a feeble attempt to rid the headache she could feel coming on.

"Goddess!" Aven jumped, Verena's physical form startling him as she became visible.

"Are you alright?" Kieran rushed to her side, lightly gripping her shoulders. The stark difference in height had Verena looking up at him.

"You stabbed me?" Verena's mouth set in a line. She was unsure if she wanted to murder the man before or after his explanation.

"I can explain." Kieran pulled his hands off her, raising them in front of him, a sign of surrender.

"Verena... you're alive?" Aven interrupted her before she could formulate some sort of response to the knowledge of being injured.

Around the three of them, a particular room began to take shape, a room Verena had seen a handful of times. This was the same room she had a fascination with for having doorways without actual doors. Within the vision was a floating bed formed from clouds and stars. Above them, a glass dome which showcased the sky. The memory of her feet being unable to touch the space around her, even in this, made her feel comforted by the room. There was some solace in the cool marble flooring, which seemed to help ground her. Before her eyes, a familiar person took shape. Identical eyes and angular face greeted Verena upon a woman with long, braided black hair. Her skin was paler than Verena's own as if the moon shone through the woman's flesh. Delicate drop moon earrings swayed against an imaginary breeze.

Her mother's room.

"Mum?" Verena whispered, ignorant of her companions attention snapping towards the area Verena was glued to. Verena could hear Aven gasp as Kieran stepped closer to her, protective and dominating. Kieran's aura was a dead giveaway, the reason Verena knew who had stepped behind her.

"Hello, my darling girl." Jerifeyn smiled, one Verena had seen many times before in her recent flashbacks and was now directed towards her.

"Prophetess." Kieran stepped forward once more, standing next to Verena and slightly bowed at the waist.

"Prince Kieran Dremorta, I have long awaited to meet you. And you, Aven Nathaniel Belmont." Jerifeyn nodded in their direction. Verena looked behind her to witness Aven closing his mouth and attempting to regulate the shock on his face.

"Who are you?" Aven, still shell-shocked, stumbled forward to join Verena and Kieran. The latter trying to cover his sign of indignation.

"I am Jerifeyn Amelia Nightingale, High Fae Princess of House Nightingale and House Naedian. Secondarily known as the Prophetess. I am also the mother of Verena." Jerifeyn relayed gracefully. Verena noticed her mother's feet still did not touch the floor.

"How is this possible?" Verena stepped forward, itching to be closer to the woman she never knew.

"A small portion of my consciousness was locked away in your blood, just enough for us to have one conversation at the proper time."

"But how?" Aven spoke out, unable to understand the capability behind it.

"All will be explained to the best of my ability, though my time is limited whilst your bond heals you, my child." Jerifeyn waved her hands and the entire room changed. It changed to one Verena knew well, the one she had seen the first time, when she had witnessed her mother losing a child and Verena flinched.

"I'm right here, hellfire." Kieran took hold of her hand, recognising the signs of pain rearing in Verena. Aven still staring at everything around him, all his training has not prepared him for this.

"Around two hundred years ago, your father and I were on the run. A decision Francis begged me to agree to in a last attempt to flee from Caine Mordinian and his elitists. Despite what history may say, Torvan never died. He physically couldn't, having been bound by the Angelic rune: Myithathyce or Marked. The rune was created for the Morningstar and his followers after their rebellion against the Creators. Torvan was unable to return to his home, unable to heal his wounds properly and regenerate the blood magic from his Angel. Forever forced to become a nomad despite his royal upbringing." As Jerifeyn spoke, the room inside Verena's mind shifted to mimic Jerifeyn's words.

Verena watched as the man Jerifeyn named Torvan materialised before her. Taller than her mother by at least half a foot and with short golden hair. His piercing emerald eyes, sunkissed skin, angular facial features, and heavily pierced ears which ended in a high point, gave him the look of kind-heartedness as if he was someone to be trusted. The man before her stood dressed in deep maroon slacks, a white collared shirt, a black suit jacket with a matching vest and a deep maroon bow tie. If Verena had no prior information on the man, she would presume him to be fairly attractive; however, this attractiveness diminished from the memory she had seen of his deceitful side.

"I broke the engagement with Torvan the day I realised what he wanted from me, namely, what he believed I could do for him. In fear of retaliation, I ran to the neighbouring House, House Nightingale. Where I met your father, Francis Nightingale. He was my saviour and the love of my life. We concocted a plan with the help of my mother and his parents. My father, your grandfather, was utterly destroyed by the severance of my engagement to Torvan. So much so, he rejected me as his daughter, the only heir apparent to House Naedian." Jerifeyn paused, looking off into the distance. "The plan was simple: Francis and I would elope. Sealing two of the four Houses together and hoping the Mordinians would accept this as final. We didn't plan on their retaliation. Torvan faked his own death, causing his mother, Jaquiryn, to seek revenge. She blames me for her son's 'death', claiming had I married him, her 'baby boy' would still be here."

"She still would have blamed you regardless," Verena spoke up, hardly knowing the woman who gave birth to her but understanding how these types of people function. "She needed an excuse and you were the closest target." Jerifeyn smiled at her, the smile warmed Verena's heart knowing her mother saw her as intelligent.

"You've grown to be so wise, my child." Jerifeyn smiled

again once more. "Yes, she most likely would have blamed me regardless. Torvan's death began a civil war between the Houses, House Mordinian and Sinclave, against House Nightingale and Naedian. It became a living nightmare. One the Fae had not seen in decades since the Red Gaylewen War. Our own people fighting against each other, slaughtering one another, it was chaos. It was exactly what Jaquiryn wanted. A war. One her husband's House was guaranteed to win. House Mordinian was gifted in strength and agility. Created by the Angel's to be the warriors of our species and yet they turned against their own at the command of Jaquiryn Mordinian. All she wanted was to have unlimited power, believing the Mordinian house should be elevated into complete control over the rest. There was only one problem: her greatest warrior and General was believed to be dead."

"Where does the Mordinian Prophetess come into play?" Kieran questioned, the pieces he was missing began to fall into place.

"I am not surprised the Dremorta knew about the fake prophetess." Jerifeyn chuckled, the sound music to their ears. "I believe she became a public figure due to the influence of House Mordinian. Giving these grand prophecies of marginal feats, such as someone's loved one would make a smooth recovery. Though the loved one would be poisoned beforehand by Mordinian shadowhunters and healed by Sinclave healers. Creating the illusion the prophetess was not a sham. Or a family going through hardship would find a box of gold in their fields on this specific day, which was placed beforehand by the Mordinians. These are the sort of 'prophecies' she would create, and the Mordinians would carry out. It was from this prophetess the alleged 'Great Prophecy of Kylune' came about. Where it was said, Torvan or I would have to die for the boundaries between our three universes to become obsolete."

"The boundaries between universes to become obsolete..." Kieran repeated, his face scrunching and arms crossing as he was lost in thought. "No."

"I'm afraid so," Jerifeyn confirmed, completely confusing Verena and Aven.

"Can somebody explain what is going on here? No to what?" Aven blurted before Verena could get the chance to.

"She means the Mordinians wanted to combine the universes. As in, merge our three universes into one. Which means they wholeheartedly believed something in your blood could complete such a feat." Kieran brought his hand up to massage the bridge of his nose, an action Verena found so endearing she cracked a small smirk. "Fuck, it all makes complete sense now."

"Well, come on then. Because I got lost about five minutes ago." Verena sighed, the pressure in her head increasing drastically.

"This faux prophetess was created by the Mordinians to ensure the citizens would be compelled to listen when they spoke. By setting up fake prophecies, they created trust between the prophetess, and when she released the 'Great Prophecy of Kylune', it endeared the citizens to believe this must happen for peace to occur. Therefore, the citizens would feel obliged to assist the Mordinians in finding Francis and Jerifeyn. As Torvan was declared deceased, the prophecy would rely solely on Jerifeyn to complete. Do you believe Torvan planned his death beforehand? As relatively close Torvan and Jaquiryn were, I find it suspicious Jaquiryn did not know her son's plan to fake his death." Kieran questioned Jerifeyn, pulling Verena into his arms as the bond between them minutely relayed the sheer pain Verena was feeling.

"I believed the same. Their relationship was strong. I found it doubtful the plan was not concocted together." Jerifeyn agreed with him, waving her hands in a sign for him to continue his train of thought.

"It all makes sense now. House Mordinian not only wanted to rule the Fae, they wanted to rule everyone." Kieran rested his chin on top of Verena's head, contemplating his next words carefully. "This leaves us with one question unanswered, what is in your blood House Mordinian wanted, Jerifeyn?"

Verena, Kieran, and Aven all looked at the woman in question, awaiting her answer. The pounding in Verena's head increased, causing her to become dizzy and lean heavily against Kieran. The information she was presented with was overwhelming, in addition to the raging headache she had. Aven looked like a lost puppy, with his doe eyes and blank expression. Verena questioned momentarily how she found him remotely attractive. Kieran was intrigued and irritated, if his body language against hers and breathing patterns were to be believed. She watched as Jerifeyn looked up at the night sky from the glass dome ceiling. Mesmerised by the image, Verena took a moment to take her mother in. Jerifeyn was beautiful, similar to the Archangel Haniel she had conversed with. Jerifeyn's skin was covered in what Verena could only describe as a phosphorescent ink. What would normally have been white anywhere else gave off an eerie blue glow, which contrasted against her midnight black hair. Verena was familiar with the ink, having seen it in first person.

"House Mordinian believed I contained the blood of all

four Houses Archangels. Whilst it is mostly true, my blood only contains three. They believed I was capable of releasing Torvan of his runic bondage. An ancient book was found by the Nightingales describing the angelic runes, within the margins of one page was a theory Mordinians became obsessed with. This theory said one with the blood of all could break any runic marking." Jerifeyn looked back at the three standing before her, her eyes filled with sorrow.

"Blood of all? As in the blood of all the Archangels which had gifted the Fae?" Verena questioned, the pain in her head radiating towards her heart.

"I never figured out the answer. However, there is only one person I am aware of who has the blood of all four Archangels, Verena." Jerifeyn stared directly into her eyes, as if she was seeing Verena's entire life through her eyes. "You, my child. You bare all four Archangel's blood in your veins."

"Excuse me?" Verena almost fell. Kieran's reflexes were fast enough to keep her from collapsing.

"Your father and I struggled to procreate. I presume from the long history of intermarrying between the Houses created a small selection, which is why one hundred and fifty years ago, two more Houses were created. Though they were not gifted by the Angels, they were selected by the populous to enhance our gene pool. After my first loss of child, we had been on the run for almost a year. I prayed daily for the Angel's help, cried myself to sleep many nights and was on the verge of taking my own life to end the misery of running. We continued to run, we did not dare to stay in one place too long until we reached an abandoned temple of Azrael. I begged Francis to stop, and every cell in my body alighted the closer we reached the heart of the temple. It felt as if I was meant to be there, as if Azrael herself was calling out to my cries. Francis stayed at the entrance, allowing me to retreat into the heart alone. He knew something extraordinary was happening, the feeling present in the air around us. Once I had reached the heart, I knew I was meant to be here. As Azrael herself had walked out of the shadows before me." Jerifeyn paused, a smile coming to her face from the memory.

"My Lady came to you?" Kieran was baffled, awestruck at her proclamation.

"She did, and she was magnificent, Kieran. House Naedian stemmed from her sister, Ariel, and while Ariel is beautiful. Azrael is pulchritudinous; she is the epitome of death and chaos, but it does not control her. Azrael heard my cries and offered a bargain to assist in having you, Verena, as well as placing this small portion of my consciousness into your blood to be activated at a later time. Without any hesitation, I agreed to her deal."

"What was the bargain?" Kieran's voice darkened, his arms surrounding Verena tightly.

"I am bound by my contract to be unable to speak on the bargain. Just know, my dear child, I would do it all again in a heartbeat if it meant I could give birth to you."

"What do you mean when you said this part of you had to be activated, Jerifeyn? What did you do?"

"I'm so sorry, my child. I am so sorry for the situation I have put you in." Tears actively streamed down her mother's face, her pale skin causing them to look almost like diamonds when they fell. It was as if there was true beauty within the sorrow her mother felt over the predicament they were all in. "I had foreseen your bond with Kieran and knew his blood held Azrael's. When I informed the Angel of my request to be able to converse with you once, when the situation was dire enough, I told her of your bond.

She bound the piece of my soul needed for this to Kieran's blood. Requiring the miniscule amount of Azrael's blood within Kieran to re-activate my soul."

"I see." Kieran's rage was palpable now. "You knew she was my soulmate, yet you still sent her into stasis."

"I did."

"Why?" Kieran's teeth clenched, Verena could hear them grinding together.

"Because I wanted them to forget her. To forget she was ever born. Because I wanted to give my daughter a fighting chance at survival."

"I just had to fucking stab her to wake her from a coma because her alleged caretakers infused her with blood she was not ready for! Do you still call this a 'fighting chance?'"

Jerifeyn sobbed, her elegant voice cracking as the sobs shook through her violently. Verena felt a desperate need to reach out to her, to embrace her and yet she didn't. She didn't know the woman in front of her, she only knew what the memories had shown her, even then those were shades of rose coming from the eyes before her now. What was to say this woman had her best interest in mind?

"I didn't know. I couldn't have predicted. My foresight was not something I could call on command, regardless of the rumours. It's why I sent her through the portal with Heathrow! He swore to protect her. We sent him with four of my journals so you could read them when you were older, Verena. Along with our entire fortune to ensure you did not live in squalor."

"Heathrow? The Werewolf elder?" Aven spoke up, his voice startling Verena as she forgot he was in the memory with them.

"Yes, he's a hybrid. Half Fae and half Wolf. He promised to protect her, his lifespan was confirmed by healers to be equivalent to the Fae. You were not aware of this?"

"Aware I was supposed to be with Heathrow instead of the narcissistic, money hungry, abusive ass I killed, which resulted in needing the damn blood transfusion in the first place? Which apparently caused me to go into a coma. Who knew? Certainly not me because apparently I'm in a bloody coma right now talking with the ghost of my mother, the person I've had a crush on forever, and a man who got me off in my head." Verena lost her composure. Her feet gave out beneath her, and despite Kieran's best efforts, she slumped to the ground. "I really need to get checked into an institute because this is crazy."

Kieran crouched behind her, wrapping his legs around her and pulling her into his lap. Verena's will broke, tears cascaded down her face before she could stop them. The pain in her chest and head began to overwhelm her to the point she curled in on herself. Kieran attempted to soothe her, whispering sweet nothings in her ear as Aven twiddled with his hands, attempting to figure out some way to comfort her without angering the ancient Demon. Jerifeyn watched the scene unfold, her face melding into a familiar expression, one Verena herself used constantly.

"I'm sorry, my child. I wholeheartedly believed Heathrow would not have given you up without an extenuating circumstance."

"How is it Verena has two mates?" Kieran questioned, attempting to understand the possibility of her having two soulmates.

"Theoretically, because she was placed in stasis, it could be believed she was not technically alive to complete her bond with you, Kieran. Therefore, fate gave her a secondary mate as a second chance." Jerifeyn looked at her daughter, curled into a ball on the Demon's lap. "We do not have much time left."

"Tell me how you put her in stasis," Kieran demanded, the last question he had before his hellfire had to drop the connection.

"Francis and I sacrificed our lives to create the portal Heathrow took her through as well as put her into stasis. By using our entire magic stores, we essentially burned ourselves up using too much magic at once. When Verena had passed through the portal from Lothaire to Alusso, Francis and I were gone."

"And the transfusion just put Verena back on the Mordinian's radar."

"Unfortunately so." Jerifeyn agreed, the image of her fading as Verena clutched her head.

"It hurts so much. Why? Why does everything hurt so much?" Verena cried out, the world around her spinning and fading, to the darkness she became accustomed to. Kieran and Aven's presence within her mind could no longer be felt, and a multitude of voices she didn't recognise started teasing her ears. Beginning as small, faint sounds which erupted into loud and aggravating, her head felt as if it was about to explode. Bells were ringing, pens were scratching against paper, someone was crying in the corner, and it all became too much. Verena fought against the crust built upon her eyes as she opened them to an exceptionally large amount of faces above her. Their faces were hazy and unrecognisable except the two pairs of eyes she knew in her soul belonging to Kieran and Aven staring back at her.

"Will you all just shut the fuck up? Your voices are making my head hurt." Verena snapped. Kieran burst out in the melodic laughter she recognised as Aven joined him shortly after.

Chapter 29

VERENA

"Hello, my little hellfire." Smooth, seductive, and sitting right next to her was the man she had only seen in her dreams. Verena reached out to him, believing this moment to be fictional, another encounter in her head. Expecting to barely feel him, her fingertips brushed against the stubble on his chin. The surprise she felt caused her fingers to jolt backwards, her nails cutting him in the process. As a singular drop of blood began to seep from the wound, Verena knew this was reality.

"You're really here..." Her voice was scratchy and harsh, a sudden cough overwhelmed her body. Pain erupted in her abdomen, causing her to curl inwards, her face pressed against Kieran's metal covered torso. Her nostrils filled with the sweet, iron smell of blood. Verena revolted backwards marginally, her empty stomach rolled as she gagged. "You really did stab me."

"I did. I'm so sorry, it was the only way to activate the bond between us." Running his hands through her hair, Kieran silently summoned one of the rags he saw when he first entered the room. Rushing to remove some of Aven's blood which had dried against his armour.

"Your Highness, I need to examine her. If you will allow-" Druid Nora began, her sentence interrupted by the piercing growl Kieran let out. The sound reverberating in his armour made it sound more menacing than he intended.

"You will wait until she gives you permission, Druid. Lest you forget, Verena is royalty in her own right. Regardless of her mate bond with me, she is still the sole surviving heir to both House Naedian and House Nightingale. Once our bond is solidified, she will be Princess of Dremorta." Kieran snapped at the Druid, asserting his position over Verena, depicting himself as her protector.

"She will also be my Luna once our bond is solidified." Aven popped up as if he couldn't allow Kieran to outdo him, his head propped against his hand. Verena took in his appearance, dried blood staining his throat and upper torso. Along with darkened bags underneath his eyes told Verena something amiss happened while she was allegedly napping.

"How long have I been asleep?" She croaked, sitting herself up to take in the countless amounts of bodies looming in front of her. "Will someone please find me a glass of water? My throat feels like sandpaper and speaking is torturous."

"Almost a week, dear." Merridayn's voice filled her ears from somewhere, Verena turned to find the familiar woman. She found her stepping away from the far wall near the door, Merridayn's small figure overshadowed by the Druid standing in front of her.

"A week..." Verena paused, her throat feeling like thousands of cuts ran the length. She grew more irritated in the passing seconds her request had not been fulfilled. Just as she was about to ask again, Aven's hand stretched out with a crystalline cup filled halfway with bubbly water. Bringing the delicate, lavish glassware to her lips, Verena's eyes rolled into the back of her head as the liquid battled the demon fires of her oesophagus. "I've been asleep for another week? There went any and all chances I had at Heaven Sight." Verena attempted to joke. The soft laughter coming from the room assured her she was just being humoured.

"At least you are awake now, so your pet Demon can go back home." Verena was not sure who spoke, but she already hated them. She had just unceremoniously awoken and was immediately met with autocratic tones plummeting her mood.

"You would do well to remember, Islabell, I am on the same side of the wards as you. I would be more than happy to stain my armour again. Nothing better than blood to grease the old girl. She gets cranky when she isn't lubricated properly." Kieran growled, reaching for his gauntlets, warning of his intentions.

"Tsk." The irritating woman voiced, Verena couldn't see her, covered mainly in shadows against the far wall. "You would go to war with the Wolves because of some words?"

"I have gone to war for less, Islabell. Bloodlust is in my genetics. As you said, I am a Demon."

Gone to war for less? Verena hoped the mental bridge between Kieran and herself was still intact.

I killed a man because he sneezed on me.

Oh...

Are you afraid, Verena? Kieran's stunning red eyes caught hers. A shiver ran down her spine.

No. Should I be?

You? Never, hellfire.

Are they?

Them? They already are. Look at how her hands shake, she's trying so hard to control it. How her eyes cannot meet mine. Listen how her heart rate spikes every time a word falls from my lips. She is terrified, she's old enough to hear the stories of my prowess in battle. The bedtime stories they tell about me are all meant to embrace the fear I bring.

Why?

Because, my love, I was bred to kill.

Their silent conversation went on, oblivious to those in the room awaiting an answer. Holding their breath until one brave, or unquestionably idiotic, healer stepped forward. Exhaustion written on her face, the dark circles under her eyes and the way she was barely capable of standing without swaying. Verena's attention focused on her, she was beautiful, and something about her tickled in Verena's memory. The memory on the tip of her tongue vanished, as if she was not meant to remember.

"Your Highness, if you permit us to overlook you, I would be eternally grateful. I fear tempers are still high. It would be in everyone's best interest to be able to retreat to their stations." The healer's voice was soft, soothing to Verena's ear, easily gaining her trust.

"Very well. The faster you finish, the faster I can leave. Though I need a chat with these alleged council members, particularly one named Heathrow?" Verena flinched away from the healer's frigid hands as they came in contact with her. The healer's wrist was ordained with a red insignia. Various sounds beeped next to her before Verena yelped from sudden pain erupting in her upper arm. Glancing over, she watched the healer draw a small vial of blood. She was fascinated, struggling to turn away despite the dizzying sensation she felt as she observed her own blood in the vial. What originally was sanguine turned into a brilliant iridescent silver.

"A chat with us about what?" The same imperious voice from earlier spoke. Kieran had called her Islabell. Each passing word drew more of Verena's ire, accentuated with a scoff from the younger woman.

"With you? Absolutely nothing. Your voice alone aggravates me, are you on this council?" Kieran scoffed, looking affronted this irritating blonde had the audacity to look at him, let alone address Verena in such a manner.

"Unfortunately for you, I am." Islabell held her head high, pompous and egotistical.

"Unfortunately? Please, do you realise Kieran is practically foaming at the mouth to kill you? The only reason he has not is because of me. If I were you, I would mind your thoughts before responding. I've already killed one wolf. Her intestines tore like paper under my fingernails. Would you like to be my second?" Verena snapped, her pearly whites shone with saliva.

"I fucking love it when you talk dirty, Hellfire. I cannot wait to see you with a dagger in one hand and the blood of your enemies running down your armour." Kieran practically purred.

Verena watched as Islabell stalked out of the room, her shoulder length, platinum blonde hair bounced in rhythm with her steps. The healer, whose name Verena had not caught, smirked next to her as she wrapped up whatever it was she was doing. Before the female could step away, Verena felt a small folded piece of paper slip into her fingers. The healer shook her head, Verena was not to open the missive yet. Attentive, Kieran caught sight of the passed note and nonverbal gesture. As he glanced about the room, Aven was asleep, some protector he would be. The innocent inaction further solidified Kieran's hate for the male.

What happened to Aven?

Nothing, wolves being stubborn and hotheaded.

And?

I may or may not have punctured his throat in a last attempt to get through the Druid's Mother Willow wards...
May or may not have?
He really twisted my arm there, Love.

"Gracella, how is the Princess?" Verena rolled her eyes at Kieran, watching the healer she now knew was Gracella approach the Druid cautiously.

"Her vitals are stable. I need to examine the blood specimen I extracted and compare them to our databases. I would recommend that Aven and Kieran stay next to her, at least for a few days. Their mate bond seems to be assisting Verena's magic stores if her blood reaction is anything to go by. She is still weak. Ultimately, it would be best if she could return home. Though I know it is not an option at this time." Gracella bowed her head respectfully at the Druid. "If I may take my leave, Druid Nora?"

"Proceed." Druid Nora, a fitting name for the Druid. Verena watched as Gracella left, and Nora stepped farther into the light before her.

Verena's eyes widened, taking in the sight of her. Nora's red hair, graced with flowers and leaves, fell down to her calves. A crown made from branches sat delicately atop her head. A fitted, v-neck tunic of earthy green with draped sleeves and matching ballooned trousers hugged Nora's features. The one interruption was the brown, stitched leather near her hips she wore as a basic armour. Her trousers were tucked into knee high brown boots sporting a tipped point protruding from the front, gold florals embroidered in an intricate pattern. To complete the ensemble, Nora tied a brown leather waist corset with gold rings fastened to leather pouches in various locations. Around Nora's neck, a key black as shadows hung from a brown cord. Verena had the urge to reach out for it, the key called to something in her blood, every inkling of her whispered to take it. The Druid smiled, knowingly.

"I am Druid Nora, Princess Verena. You have been my charge since you were brought here. I am thankful to Mother Willow for your recovery. Though, I am afraid, Prince Kieran." Nora shifted her attention to Kieran. "You should take your leave. Since you passed through the wards, Mother Willow has been furious. Her anger can be felt in the air we breathe and in the hearts of all Druids. We will be forsaken should we continue to allow you inside our sanctuary. For this reason, I beg of you to return home."

"And what of Verena? Leave her to grow weaker without my presence?" Kieran stood, his height easily dwarfed the Druid.

"I will personally arrange for a better solution to be present within the next hour after your return to Perdytion. It goes against my nature to allow my patient's health to decline when there is a viable solution present. If you will, I can see you back to your men." Druid Nora looked up, unafraid of the Demon, and held her hand out towards the door. Kieran hesitated; Verena wished a part of him would fight to stay. Kieran bent to gather his effects and snuck an unexpected kiss before he departed her room.

I will be back to bring you home, my hellfire.

Verena blushed as Nora's small frame became obsolete to Kieran. His broad shoulders easily blocked out the door. Metal creaked with each footstep he took. Verena took advantage of her newly enhanced hearing, following Kieran's movements until he was beyond the grove. Soft snoring came from her right. While Kieran had noticed Aven's sleeping, Verena was now aware. He was in such a deep sleep drool dripped over his palm as his head rested there. She lit up with a smile at the innocent man before her, daydreaming about their potential life together if her life had been normal. The renewed quietness of the room and the daydream which filled her head made Verena's eyelids heavy. She had been asleep for a week and yet still welcomed the rest as she leaned her head back into the cloud pillows behind her. The folded piece of paper was forgotten and fell to the ground as the warmth from the blankets covering her body helped lull her into sleep.

Chapter 30

VERENA

Hours passed before Verena awoke to her stomach growling angrily. A quick visual search of the room revealed nothing she could consume. Pangs of hunger ate at her, and she pushed the blankets from her body. Her legs swung over the side of the bed, and a static-like tingling ran down her toes from her previous inactivity. As she pushed herself from the bed, what she expected to be a cold, solid floor was hot, movable flesh. Verena peered down; Aven had, at some point during their sleep, sprawled himself next to her bed.

Typical, it seems every man you know snores, Verena. She rolled her eyes at herself, stepping over him carefully. The tingling sensation faded slower than she would have liked as each step towards the doorway radiated the feeling up her calves.

I do not snore, Verena.

Electing to ignore Kieran's ever-present voice in her head, Verena continued on her mission, one step gingerly in front of the other until feeling returned to her toes. Reaching the doorway, Verena looked left and then right. The sounds emanating from each direction further confused her and did not help ascertain exactly which way she should go. Choosing to go left, Verena looked out the door frame one last time. She would have to sneak about if she wanted to avoid being doted over. Following the twists and turns of the corridor, Verena eventually hesitated; footsteps sounded before her. Her only way of remaining hidden was through the door a few steps behind her. Slight panic ensued as she raced backwards to the door she had seen. Her attention was drawn to everywhere and nowhere, all at the same time. The few feet it took her to crash through the door felt like minutes, though it only took her seconds to reach the safety of concealment. Verena's heart stopped as the door slammed shut behind her. In her panic of being caught in a well-lit hallway, she had been careless and reckless and now was confident she had damned herself. No light pierced the darkness but for the eerie red glow emitting from behind her.

Verena turned meticulously toward the glowing light. She checked behind her with every step, almost sure she was being followed. Before her, a partial doorway rippled. The rectangular frame appeared to be cut diagonally. Fiery crackles and pops paired with the faint sounds of crumpling paper exuded from the frame. Verena could discern voices from within the doorway, but not enough to tell what was being said. It was as if the doorway called to her but was muffled like she was underwater. The bright red ring around the exterior, darkening to almost black in the middle, called to her. Verena wanted to reach out to it, to touch it, to inspect it. A sudden slamming caused her to jump, her fingers brushing the intriguing frame ever so slightly.

"Huh..." The room began to shift. Objects rapidly melded together, and previously coloured shapes merged into blackness. Verena's thoughts were immediately halted as every fibre in her body stretched apart. Her lungs cried out as if the weight of a car had sat upon them. She could have sworn her heart stopped, momentarily at least. The pain suddenly stopped, and Verena was sure she was floating, peaceful, and calm. Verena had not noticed she closed her eyes. Her heart raced in her chest, and the sounds of fire sounded around her. She expected to smell smoke but instead was met with the sweetness of vanilla paired with cinnamon.

"Well, child, you do not belong here. Yet, I can smell my son upon your skin." The voice was smooth, velvety and delicate. Verena spun towards it, taking an unconscious step back as she came face to face with a white-haired, dark-eyed woman. Wait, were those wings? Verena rubbed her eyes again, glancing back at the woman.

I'm really not hallucinating right now?

The woman smiled, four sharp and prominent canines stared Verena back in the face.

What in the fuck? Verena, calm down. Calm down. But holy fuck, she has wings and four goddamn fangs.

"You must be Kieran's mate. Princess Verena, isn't it?" The woman held out a hand, and Verena's eyes flashed straight at the pointed black nails reaching out to her. "I am Sylvia Grafton, Kieran's mother. However, Princess, you should not be here right now."

"Kieran's mother?" Verena questioned as she allowed herself to be herded backwards towards the crackling fire she had heard. "Kieran is here?"

"No, not at the moment, darling. Which is why you should not be here. It's not safe for you with him absent. Go, get back to bed. We shall meet again soon." Sylvia smiled, her words repeating in Verena's mind.

Where is Kieran?

Chapter 31

VERENA

Sylvia gently shoved Verena backwards. Her body went through the same stretching, pulling, and squeezing as it had her initial trip through the mysterious doorway. The wait to enter her plane took an eternity before she was released into the darkened room she had taken refuge in. Facing the odd frame, she heard a throat clear behind her.

She'd been caught.

Shit.

"Verena..." The voice was rumbly and hoarse. Verena looked behind her shoulder, and an innocent smile was plastered on her face. "You're all grown up now."

"Um..." Verena turned around, facing a giant, burly man primarily covered in the darkness except for one lone, small, pointed ear. "Well, yes, I am. But, who are you, exactly?"

The man before her chuckled, opening the door behind him leading back to the hall. As he stepped through it, Verena stood dumbfounded by him. Why make a statement to confuse her and then walk away? While the door shut, Verena internally debated chasing after him. Who was he to her? Was he expecting her to go after him? The more she argued with herself, the more her common sense depleted, and she ran out the door chasing after the mysterious man from the room.

"Hey!" Verena called out as loud as she dared, hoping to only draw attention from the man she chased. When the man didn't stop, Verena picked up the pace. Her steps only covered a fraction of his. She was losing him. "Excuse me!" Verena yelled, precautions be damned.

He huffed, amused, and glanced back at her before he rounded the corner. Verena broke into a jog, her limbs groaning from their recent immobility. When she rounded the corner, he was nowhere to be found. The hall drifted quiet, excluding a soft creaking of a door hinge. Wistful and exhausted, Verena carried on, coming upon a door still closing. She cautiously pulled the bronze handle, opening it. Initially scanning the room, she met his gaze. He leaned against a small stone table with four chairs around it. As she took in his features, he held an apple in one hand while the other contained a familiar crystalline glass filled with a shimmering blue liquid. His features were soft, kind, and grandfatherly in many ways. The smile on his face was one she was sure a father would give his daughter.

"Hungry?" He extended his hands toward her, a straightforward benign offering at which her stomach growled loudly. He burst into laughter, stepping closer to force the items into her hands. He would not let her pass on the offer. "Apparently so."

Leary of the male, Verena took a cautious bite of the apple. The tart taste created a moist explosion in her mouth. Verena couldn't stop the soft moan which escaped her, her body and mind grateful for the nutrients. While her body begged her to drink, she was suspicious of the liquid offered.

"I didn't poison it, you know." He laughed again, picking up his glass from behind his broad form and downing the entirety in one gulp. "It's a type of flower tea from

your home world, Verena. Drink it. Many said the Naedians bred the flower over many centuries." Hesitantly,
she brought the glass to her lips. The smallest amount
of liquid flowed onto her tongue. A faint tingling sensation spread over her body, the epicentre of which was her
tongue.

"Why was it bred? What does it do?" Verena took another sip, this time taking more liquid than her initial taste
test. Those tingles she felt grew steadily in magnitude.
"Who are you?"

"The flower was created for the High Fae, like yourself,
to harness the energy around them, supplying their magic
stores without the need to return to their homeland."

"Okay..." Verena finished the glass, contemplating her
next question. Clearly, the man had something to hide.
"Still does not answer who you are."

"Your mother had me bring the flower here to cultivate
in preparation for you when it was time to awaken."

"My mother..." Verena dropped the glass. The revelation of her mother caused an instant connection between
the man before her and the man her mother informed
her about. "You're Heathrow." She whispered, growing
irritated by the tears forming in her eyes.

"I am." Heathrow stepped closer to her, visibly fighting
himself, then abruptly pulling her into his arms. The top
of her head barely reached his shoulders, his face buried in
her hair. She could feel his chest heaving from unreleased
sobs. "I failed you, Verena. I am eternally remorseful for
losing you."

Verena stood still. Did she hold onto him as he did her?
Should she cry tears of happiness for reconnecting with
the one her parents trusted her to? She felt as if she wanted
to do all those things: put the past behind her and create

a new life with the guardian she was meant to be with. But she couldn't bring herself to lie to him, to the sobbing giant holding onto her as if she were his lifeline. She felt betrayed, anguished, and ignored. All the nights she cried herself to sleep and the early mornings wishing she could disappear. All the lies she told when those around her asked about the bruising, the cuts, the broken bones. All the times she said she was fine, just clumsy. When there was a person her parents trusted, a guardian who wanted to help her, was there, waiting. The person breaking his heart into pieces before her because he believed he had failed her. One question remained, one question which haunted her.

"Why?" Verena forced out, her tone meek and cracked. The emotions threatened to overcome her.

"Verena." Heathrow began, his tear-filled eyes looking down upon her. A single drop crashed upon her cheek. Her skin absorbed it hungrily, and her genetics recognised another Fae. "We will talk about this. But not today. Not here. You need to rest to regain your strength. The others in the council will want to test your abilities."

"If not here, not now, then when? You left me, Heathrow. My parents, they entrusted me to you! And you left me. You left me with them!" Verena spat, her rage encompassing all rational thought. "I do not give a single damn what the council wants, and they do not own me. I do not owe them anything. My entire life, I have been beaten, starved and ignored because why? Because some person, somewhere, at some time believed I was their property? Because someone told you to give me away when my parents gave their lives so you could bring me here, just to let someone tell you to let me go?"

"Verena..."

"No, do not 'Verena' me. You could have fought,

Heathrow. I've seen the way my mother looked to you as her only hope, my only chance at survival, at a life I could have enjoyed. But here we are." Verena huffed, exacerbated by the thoughts running rampant in her mind. "They tell me I was on the cusp of death. My genetics rejected the blood infusion because my High Fae side became dormant." Verena broke free of him, shaking her head at the burly man, her eyes spilling with tears. "Because of you."

"I know." Heathrow sighed, his head dropping, hands clutching the air where she had been. "I know, Verena. There is nothing I can say or do to justify my inaction."

"Find me when you are ready to talk because until then, I have nothing left to say to you." Heathrow watched as she stormed out through the doorway, her footsteps fading the further she walked. Once he could no longer hear her, he let out a wail.

Chapter 32

VERENA

Days passed, and all Verena saw of Heathrow were the glasses of blue tea and apples on her bedside table each morning. Verena knew he had stopped by when she was asleep. She could smell him in the air every morning. It had been a fortnight since Druid Nora first told her she'd be released, and she was still trapped within the medical bay. Verena knew Aven remained in the complex. His days were spent doing Hell knew what, but his nights were spent in bed with her. He was always gone before she woke and returned well past supper, but at least he was there.

Kieran had consistently been refused access to her since he had been forced back beyond the wards. His absence caused Verena to believe she was going mad when she began to see the golden thread, representing their bond. It had started faint, and she thought it was a reflection of light at first. She was dismissing it until this morning when she woke to Gracie bringing in the glass of tea instead of Heathrow. The healer was shrouded in a red aura, so bright and distracting that Verena rubbed her eyes a few times, hoping she only had something in them.

"Gracie?" They were not deceiving her; the healer was surrounded by a glowing aura that seemed to emanate from the same red marking Verena initially noticed on her wrist.

"Yes, Verena?" Gracie had yet to look up from placing the glass down. Over the past few days, the two have assimilated something close to a friendship, having forgone the formalities and occasionally sharing stories.

It felt nice.

In her lifetime, Verena had not made many friends, pushing them away when many got too close to the truth of the horror at home. Gracie made her feel wanted as if the girl was just happy to be around Verena without pushing to know more. Without pushing her to open up before she was ready.

"What's on your wrist?" Feeling confident in their friendship, Verena asked plainly. Hoping Gracie would not take offence to the question. Evidently, she was wrong. Gracie paused in her daily routine of checking Verena's vitals floating above the bed, nearly dropping her clipboard in the process. "I'm sorry, you don't need to answer if you don't want to. I thought I was going crazy, but you are red. Legitimately red, Gracie. Everywhere around you," Verena waved her hands in the air, outlining Gracie from a distance. "It's like you are glowing, but it's all red."

"Verena, how long have you been able to see it?" Gracie whispered, rushing to close the door to the room. Verena watched as she stuck her head out of the doorway, looking both ways. Then, she shut the door softly, flinching as it still creaked.

"Since I woke up," Verena admitted, curious about the secrecy. "Why?"

"Because nobody should be able to see it. Nobody. I can't even see it. If I didn't know it was there or weren't present when it was put on, I would have never known." Gracie rushed her words, and Verena could hear her heartbeat increasing. She was nervous, possibly scared, but why?

"What are you hiding, Gracie?"

"I can't tell you. Not yet." Gracie admitted, scribbling something on her pages. "Did you read the note I gave you?"

"Oh hell." Verena scrambled off her bed, desperately searching for the paper she had forgotten about. She had found it under Aven the morning after Gracie had given it to her, then wholly erased it from her mind. "Where did I put that blasted thing?" Ripping open the drawers beside her, she found it stuffed inside one of her socks. Slumping onto the bed in relief, she looked at Gracie. The healer nodded and then turned to watch the door.

They are coming, Verena. It's not safe here.
Find Heathrow and get to Kieran.
I will let you know when it is time to move.

"Who are you, Gracie?" Verena whispered as she read over the note for the fifth time. Her anxiety increased with every pass over.

"A friend." Gracie reached her hand out for the paper Verena was holding. Verena obliged, handing it back to her. Gracie had replaced it with another, nodding again as she returned to watching the door.

Let Heathrow know about these developments.
Do not, at all, tell anyone else what you can see.
We will try to move you at the next full moon.
When the rest are honouring the Goddess.

"What about Aven?" Verena asked; she should be able to tell him. He was fated as her mate.

"No, he's connected to the pack bond." Gracie snapped, her face flushing red, more profound than the aura surrounding her, as she realised what she did. "I'm sorry. I shouldn't have been as aggressive when answering."

"Don't apologise. I should be thanking you for letting

me in." Verena offered weakly, attempting to connect with her. There was a feeling Verena couldn't describe, as if the Angel's had placed Gracie in her life intentionally.

"He is sorry, by the way," Gracie whispered. Verena caught it in the nick of time.

"Who is?" Verena picked up her tea, getting used to how the tingles felt after days of drinking it.

"Heathrow."

"You do not address him in the way everyone else I have talked to does." Verena noticed it earlier: Gracie addressed Heathrow without his title added as if the two were on familiar terms.

"I owe him my life." Gracie was reluctant to admit it, only speaking after an awkward silence fell between the two women.

"Do you want to talk about it?" After many weeks of being in a coma and occasional memories of her parents plagued her when she slept, Verena started to notice her speech patterns changing. Reflecting the graceful way her mother had spoken to others, though her temper was still a work in progress.

"He saved me from myself, took me in when I needed it, taught me so many subjects, and is the reason I became a healer. His knowledge of High Fae healing is why I was assigned to you when you showed up on our doorstep. I helped him grow the flowers he grinds every morning for your tea." Gracie smiled, Verena assumed from the happy memories of her time with the grumpy elder.

"How do you know he is sorry when he himself has not come to see me?" Verena could feel the jealousy creep up. She attempted to force it back down.

"He talked about you all the time when I was young. He mourns failing you to this day, Verena. Having grown the same flowers for over a century, ensuring you would have enough to survive here, in Alusso." Gracie must have been intuitive, reassuring Verena's insecurities without barely a thought.

"He did?" Verena whispered, doubting her decision to push him away.

"He just doesn't know how to tell you without blaming himself for everything you went through because of his failures." Gracie took the empty glass from her hands. Verena had no recollection of finishing it in her guilt-ridden state. "I convinced him to come see you today. Can you promise me something, though?"

"Anything, Gracie." Verena was not sure why she said it. Something about the way Gracie held herself reminded her of Elion. There was an air about the two of them which sang to her soul.

"Let him finish before you get angry. Just listen to what he has to say. He already blames himself enough, especially after Merridayn informed him of what you endured at the hands of the Saxons." Gracie pleaded with her. She wondered if the woman would have gotten on her knees and begged if it meant Verena would agree.

Verena couldn't bring herself to agree, almost verbalising her response before changing her mind and closing her mouth again. Gracie looked at her knowingly, giving Verena a weak smile, one which didn't reach her eyes. Verena watched as she left, still unable to voice her answer as she couldn't admit she was wrong. She couldn't admit she had hurt Heathrow when she met him when she could see he was sincerely sorry.

"I will..." She whispered to nobody, curling into a ball on her bed. All desire to explore had vanished, guilt ridden and unmotivated, she fell back to sleep. Her dreams of interacting with Heathrow showed her what she could have had if she had only controlled her temper.

Verena awoke when a weight sank onto the edge of her bed. Blinking away the sleep, she saw him. Hunched over, a glass of the same blue tea she knew he had grown specifically for her in his hands. Verena sat up, hoping not to disturb him. Heathrow looked behind his broad shoulder, and Verena could see the dark circles under his eyes. Silently, he placed the glass in her hands, standing back up once he did. Verena dropped the glass, the tea spilling everywhere as she grabbed hold of his wrist.

"I'm sorry..." The words fell from her lips before she could stop them. Wondering if he would forgive her with such a meagre apology. He didn't say anything, didn't move. Verena's heart began breaking again. It was too late. He didn't want anything to do with her. "Heathrow." Tears formed in her eyes, her anxiety whispering nasty things in her mind. He didn't want her. She betrayed him. He's only doing this out of duty. He never cared about her.

"You have nothing to apologise for, Verena. It is I who should be begging you for your forgiveness." Heathrow turned around, witnessing the tears falling down her cheeks. As he sat back down, he pulled her to him, and Verena felt the dam break. "Oh, honey, don't cry. I never left you, not willingly. Never willingly."

"Why was I with them then?" Her lungs hitched, she wiped her nose with her sleeve. Not caring if her shirt got dirty.

"When we came through the portal, Verena. I was almost sixty-two. I lost my mate long before, having no children of my own and no one else to help me. I found a little village a couple of miles past where the portal dropped us. They were welcoming, hearing your cries caused all the older women to come forward to help. I was covered in blood from killing my way to the room your parents had taken shelter in. The Mordinians nearly breached it. I was barely in time. I had just enough to take you into my arms before Jerifeyn pushed us through. I watched her fall as our passage home closed. We were safe in some unknown place here, in Alusso. I watched as she took her last breath, knowing you would survive." Heathrow squeezed her tightly, holding Verena as a lifeline from the memories.

"Was our coming here planned?" Verena angled her body towards his, relishing in the comfort he gave.

"Yes." He looked at her, his lips pressed together roughly. "Yes, it was. After you were conceived, Francis reached out. Using every single person we had known, he got a letter to me within the Mordinian's estate without them knowing. It was risky. If they had found out, everyone who colluded with Francis would be dead."

"What did the letter say?" Verena had to look up at him, his height casting a significant difference between the two. She could see he was struggling with the memories, but she also knew he needed to tell her.

"He asked to meet. He gave a date, a time, and a location. I didn't know what to think at first. The man had been my friend. Before the war began, we were inseparable." Heathrow paused, looking up towards the ceiling of her room. He listened to the beating of wings from passing birds, the sound of water rushing, and the gentle breeze flowing through the leaves. Taking the time to centre himself again before looking back at Verena. "It was difficult to refuse. Here I was, stuck across the country. The farthest away I could have been, with an army of Mordinians, Sinclaves, and a few vampyre clans tearing everything apart to find them." Verena watched as he shook, trying to contain the mountain of emotion swelling. Trying to get through the hard points of his past that led to her birth. She deserved to know, deserved to understand. She remained silent, allowing the emotions to pass through him on his own.

"I couldn't convince myself to refuse. He was my best friend. It would have been impossible, should have been impossible, had I been a full-blooded Fae. Everything seemed to work in my favour. To this day, I still thank the Goddess. Being part wolf, I could shift, blending in with the wolves in Lothaire. They knew something wasn't right but left me to my own devices. I stayed with them, ensuring the pack covered my scent. Until the last second, I stayed, waited, and migrated with them as we travelled from southeast Lothaire to the north." His free hand took hold of his loose-fitting trousers. The cotton blend crinkled in his tight grip. Verena was heartbroken; she wished she could see the memory like Haniel had shown her instead of forcing Heathrow to live through it.

Verena was saddened, wistful for a map of Lothaire to keep up with him, her mind unable to understand the hardships of his journey, the terrain of a place she had never seen. As he continued, her guilt increased, and she blamed herself for not allowing him to speak last time. Considering everything he had done to get to her, every sacrifice he had made, his decision to answer her father's letter despite his safety was enough evidence Verena needed to believe him, to forgive him.

"We were to meet at the temple of Archangel Azrael. The laws forbade entering a temple to the Angels with the intention of desecrating it. We were safe and Francis knew it, but for how long, I couldn't tell. The Mordinians were ruthless in their search for Jerifeyn. Some say it stemmed from her refusal to marry their second son, while others say it was because she was the reason Torvan was dead. They killed anyone they marginally believed was against them. Why would they stop at the temple of an Angel if they had no mercy for the innocents?" Heathrow stopped. Verena could see the anger pulsing around him, his Fae blood creating the energy in the room to sizzle.

"I made it a day early. They were not there, so I waited. And waited. The second night had passed after the proposed meeting day. I began to worry, began to pace, still unwilling to shift back until I knew they were there. It was getting late. I was about to return to the shelter I had found inside the temple when I smelled them. I could smell the sweat as if they were running for their lives. It was so distinctive." He pulled her in closer to his chest, resting in the proximity of the child he swore to protect with his life. Her presence gave him comfort. She reminded him of his best friend. Her eyes sparkled like Francis's when he was up to mischief, and her smile tilted to the right as Jerifeyn's had when she was truly happy.

"Were they?" Verena whispered, desperate for answers. "Were they running for their lives?"

"Yes. A unit had spotted them the day we were to meet. They had no choice but to hide, taking shelter within the high water pond of Kytran. Its foul, murky waters hid their scent from the hellhounds well enough. They stayed until Francis' familiar, Noxx, cleared them to return to their path. They ran the entire way there. Your mother was far along in her pregnancy by this point. She was exhausted, worn out, and sickly from overexertion. We dared to stay for three nights to allow her to rest. It was on the third night we were found. Being a temple to Azrael gave us more protection than I expected, many fearing the wrath

of the Angel. We were surrounded, outnumbered and dis-
advantaged; Jerifeyn was a powerful magic wielder but
heavily pregnant with you. You were burning through her
energy stores faster than she was able to regain them. While
they dared not step into the temple, they knew we would
eventually have to leave. Our food supply was limited, our
water rapidly draining, and Jerifeyn was becoming sicker
and sicker the longer she could not bask in the moonlight.
Drawing the majority of her magic from the moon, the
longer we stayed in the dark, the sicker she would become."

"What did you do? How did you get out?" Verena
scooted towards the edge of the bed, angling herself towards Heathrow even more. So engrossed in the story she
forgot, momentarily, this was her parents and not some
strangers she did not know.

"Francis and I knew we maybe had a day or two left
before Jerifeyn became too sick to travel. He didn't know
what to do, didn't know how to get her out safely. They
wanted her and only her. They didn't care about us. We
were collateral to them, easily dispatchable and forgotten.
It was my plan to fend them off while Francis got Jerifeyn
to safety. My wolf, easily a head taller than them, was
something they were not expecting. I knew I could run
faster than them, but they would not follow because I was
not who they wanted." Heathrow chuckled; an inside joke
between himself and Francis came to the forefront of his
mind. Verena thought the man insane but stayed quiet, an
odd time to laugh.

"The plan was formed: I would shift and carry Jerifeyn
out of the temple. Hide her in the wolf pack until we can
reconnect with Francis. Noxx would always be able to find
me once he had my scent. Francis would stay behind. They
would send the bulk of their unit after us; he only had

to wait. Wait within the safety of Azrael's temple until their unit dispersed enough to ensure he could win. By the following night, Jerifeyn was strapped to my back with shreds of my discarded shirt. I ran. Through the awaiting, unexpecting Fae and I didn't stop. Even when every muscle was aching and burning, I refused to rest. Not until we were safe within the pack, on the border of the previous Naedian territory." He could feel his lungs burning from the memory, remembering the way his body screamed. What he would give to never feel that again in his lifetime.

"What then?" Verena prodded, she needed to know they were safe. Needed to know her father made it out alive.

"We waited, crossing from Naedian to Nightingale and back again before Francis found us. Jerifeyn had made her recovery days prior, occasionally begging to walk. Francis insisted they could hide in Jerifeyn's father's old cabin, the Naedian territory having been combed through already. I left them as close as possible without straying too far from the pack. Afterwards, I began completing the list Francis requested. Finding those still loyal to them and those willing to turn against the Mordinians. We began moving Francis and Jerifeyn to safehouses across Lothaire, never staying in one place longer than a week until you were close to being born. Francis and Jer returned to the temple then, hoping the Mordinian forces wouldn't cross the boundary just as before. I was a day away when I found Noxx circling above me. I knew something was wrong the second I saw him. I broke from the pack and rushed to the temple. I saw them trying to breach the door, a simple wood door. It should have been easy. But nothing involving the Angels is easy; I suspected Azrael had a hand in their inability to pass. Unable to involve herself, she still slowed them just enough to buy me time to get there. I tore them apart and broke through the door like a sheet of parchment. It was then I knew Azrael was watching." Heathrow looked back towards the ceiling, clutching a pendant Verena never noticed he had worn around his neck. She watched as his lips moved, a wordless prayer to the Heavens above.

"Why would an Angel help, though, Heathrow? Aren't they forbidden from interfering?" Verena recalled her questions to the Angel Haniel, where Haniel confirmed Angels were not allowed to interfere in their affairs.

"I do not know, honey." He pressed his lips together, pondering her question. A question he asked himself countless times over the previous decades. " I do not know. It is a question I ask myself often, one I know she must be being punished for." He said slower, a tear forming in the inner corner of his eye. Whatever the reason for Azrael stepping in, Verena swore she would ask the Angel someday.

"What happened after you got through the door?" She wanted them to get back on track, her anxiety pushing to get to the end. To where they came to Alusso and how she was given to Abigail, of all people.

"Your mother handed me a bag filled with food, journals, and a clipping of the flower I use to make your tea. You were asleep and wrapped up so snuggly in your father's arms. He didn't want to let you go. Jerifeyn had to convince him, and even then, he didn't want to. Not until we heard the rest of the Mordinian army marching towards the temple. Francis thrust you into my arms, joining his wife to create the portal. I didn't know what Jerifeyn did before we were pushed through. It wasn't until after the first night we spent in the little village I had found that I figured it out. By morning, you wouldn't wake up. Your skin was glowing like the moon shone through you.

I knew then, having seen the Sinclaves do it to patients with severe injuries. She put you in a stasis. I had to sneak us away from the village. I didn't want to alert them of our non-human descent." Verena looked at him, her eyes narrowed and brows furrowed. What did he mean, didn't want to alert the villagers?

"Why not?" Surely her mother would not send them through a portal to an entirely new world without knowing where she was sending them, right?

"I was under the impression humans killed those they didn't understand. I wasn't going to take the risk, so we left. We kept moving. I have never brought you into another village since. Always finding a native wolf pack to harbour you while I would restock the bag Jerifeyn gave from the nearest market." Heathrow questioned the words leaving his mouth the second they left, knowing Verena would have a fit with him leaving her with the wolves.

"You left me alone with wolves!" Verena shouted, disbelief at what he had just said but proved him correct. "Wolves, Heathrow. I could have died. I could have been eaten." She internally debated if she still needed to check herself into a psych ward for examination after that revelation.

"They wouldn't have. I would always bring you in wolf form; you smelled like me. While I couldn't communicate with them like I can with Werewolves, the pack alpha understood what I needed well. Unmated females would curl around you, keeping you warm and protected until I returned. I was never long, hardly ever more than a few hours." Heathrow stumbled over himself, trying to convey to Verena that she was perfectly safe when they got here. "Then, we would continue again until I came across a werewolf village on the outskirts of Gwendolyn, where I met Elion's great-grandfather, Nathaniel. He allowed us safe harbour, able to derive my wolf from the sweet smell of Fae blood. We stayed there, in a cabin Nathaniel owned, as far away from the pack as possible. We feared they would catch your scent, Verena. A tad over three-quarters of a century passed at Nathaniel's cabin. I had integrated with their pack as their combatives instructor. My knowledge of Fae warfare tactics gave me an advantage over their traditional fighting style. It wasn't until we were found that all hell broke loose, and I failed you." A tear did fall down his cheek this time, guilt taking over as he fought himself from crying.

"What happened, Heathrow? What happened that caused you to give me up?" Verena asked him as gently as she could, fearing the worst.

"The elders at the time found out about Nathaniel harbouring a hybrid. Their laws were strict back then. Wolf hybrids were seen as a disgrace to the Moon Goddess. They were supposed to be killed on sight if they passed the age of maturity. Technically, they should have been killed at birth. I was not from Alusso; therefore, I was not subject to their laws, nor a part of their world. My mother was from Lothaire, and my father was an ambassador from Alusso who lived in House Sinclave. However, Nathaniel was an Alussian subject, forcing him to abide. He was given an option: surrender us to the council or execution. I begged him to surrender us. He did not deserve death because he gave us sanctuary. He refused, saying he was nearing one hundred. It was his time. And I watched as my friend, head held high, walked to his execution." She leaned in to hug him; the awkward angle made it more difficult than it should have been. But she hugged him nonetheless, burying her face into his chest and wrapping her hands around his waist.

"He did what he thought was right. You cannot take the blame for his actions, Heathrow." Verena felt his massive hands squeeze her back before gently pushing her to her upright position, using a hand to wipe the tears falling down his cheeks.

"I know, and I knew then, too, but it didn't stop the pain I had felt. The anguish I caused his family, all because he didn't believe I deserved to die for being born a hybrid. The council didn't stop at him. They threatened every single person in the pack until I gave myself up. They didn't know about you, not yet anyway. I couldn't stand by as they killed off one by one while I stayed safe in our little cabin. So I did what I had to; I went before them." Heathrow grew angry, cursing the damned council for every decision they had made.

"And? What happened when you stood before them, the previous elders?" Verena sniffled, using the handkerchief Heathrow silently passed her to wipe her nose. She raised an eyebrow, curious as to when she started crying.

Heathrow remained quiet, bursting into tears. They streaked down his face faster than Verena could see, one after another, as the memories he was subjecting himself to caused the anguish she could see. She reached out, grabbing his hand, finding comfort and safety in the action.

"Armand challenged his father, the alpha, to a warrior's challenge. He didn't believe I should die as I was not Alussian, but Lothairen. He didn't know about you yet, either. I had not brought you along. You were still in the cabin; a female wolf volunteered to stay with you while I was gone." Heathrow looked towards Verena, wondering if she was going to lose it on him again for leaving her with someone she did not know. Surprised when she didn't question his choices, he smiled at her.

"Geirden couldn't refuse, and it led to his death. He knew he did not stand a chance against Armand at his age. Once Geirden passed, Armand became the new alpha. His first decree was my sanctuary. I trusted him enough to bring you to him, to beg him to help me keep you safe. He could not decide without consulting the rest of the elders; you were not a wolf. Therefore, he needed them all to agree. I suspected later that one of the elders was colluding with the Saxons, having found out about the wealth I had carried for you from your parents. The day of our meeting before the rest of them, the Saxons provided the council with a letter claiming Jerifeyn would have wanted you to be with them. I couldn't believe it. They weren't alive when we came through the portal. I couldn't figure out how they knew her name, let alone forged her signature on their alleged document. I didn't have a choice; Armand and I both knew it. We either had to let you go to them, and they would grant you sanctuary. Or leave, and we would never be allowed near another wolf pack again, for they would give the order to kill us on sight." His lips curled in disgust. The distaste he had for being chained to this life weighed heavily on him.

"I understand now, Heathrow. You didn't fail me; you did what you had to do for us both to live." Verena smiled back at him, fully understanding him now. Accepting he had not given her up without a fight. She did not blame him anymore, did not see him as someone who wanted to use her for their own gain.

"I did, though, don't you see? I could have run. We could have kept running. I could have kept you safe until it was time for you to wake. But it would have been selfish of me. You were growing slower than you should have, but you were still growing. At some point, you would outgrow the clothes you had. I didn't know how to care for a child, let alone a female. So I gave you up, allowing you to go with Abigail. When Merridayn told me about the abuse you suffered from their hands, I wanted to kill them myself. The pride I had when she told me you ripped Abigail apart was reinforced by the memory Elion showed us when you were brought in unconscious." Heathrow reached out to cup her face between his hands, his partially pointed ears flickering between the movement in his hair.

"It's not your fault." Verena squeezed his hand, leaning into him. "What they did to me wasn't your fault."

"No, but the things I will do to him when I find him would make a Demon even blush," Heathrow growled, an unspoken promise. He would find Colin Saxon and put him in the ground himself. He owed it to Verena, to his friends, to himself.

"No." Verena blurted out, looking up at him, his puzzled face meeting hers. "He's mine. I want to be the one to kill him. After everything he has done to me, I want my face to be the last he sees before he goes to Hell."

Chapter 33

VERENA

"I can see magic in the purest of forms, I have since the transfusion Merridayn gave me, and I have no idea what to do." Verena spits out after a few moments of peaceful silence with Heath. She didn't know how else to put it, how else to say the things she needed to. Even after her conversation with Gracie, she didn't know how to ease him into the conversation. So she did the best next thing: she blurted it all out in one go.

"You what?" Heathrow was flabbergasted, staring at Verena as if she had grown two heads and a tail. The sudden shift from the previous talks of revenge to this was twisting his thoughts into a knot he didn't know would come undone.

"Gracie," Verena stated matter-of-factly, as if it was the answer to every question he could have had. When his face never showed any clarity, she continued. "I told her I could see the red marking on her wrist, the way it created an aura surrounding her. The way I can see the blue glittering line connecting you and I. It's different from the golden ones between myself and Aven, even more so with Kieran. I can see how your golden one leads away from here. The way Druid Nora has green ones between herself and the healers. I can see the energy floating in the air around us, how the tiny molecules float towards me after I drink the tea, and how they get absorbed into my skin. I could see the blue band forming around Aven's wrist, disappearing after Abigail died. I can see all of it. And I don't know what it means. I don't know what to do, and I'm terrified." Verena rushed the words out of her mouth so quickly Heathrow had to take a moment to process everything she said.

"I wondered if this is why Jerifeyn sent you away." Heath reached out for her, grabbing her hands and engulfing them. "I believe it is time you read your mother's journals, and we begin your training."

"Training? What training?" She was giddy at the thought of getting to know the woman who had given birth to her. All her memories led to this moment.

"You're in danger, Verena. The war hasn't ended, and if Jaquiryn finds out, she will send the Mordinian's entire fighting force to find you. You grew up in a world you were not meant to be in. It's time you came home. You need to learn how to defend yourself. I might not always be around to protect you, little cub."

"I never was the greatest at sports... or any physical activity. Abigail did not let me pursue tennis in primary school. Afterwards, I focused on studying to get into University and leave. Flee as far away as I would be able, and never look back."

"Well, there's no better time than now. Let's get going then." Heathrow stood, and the weight of his lifting from the bed almost caused Verena to fly off the bed. Once her balance was restored from the near fall, Verena stood, twiddling her hands as if she were back in primary school, unsure what to do next.

"Where are we going?" She asked him once they left her room, but she was still in the hospital wing. Druid Nora claimed she wanted to keep watch on Verena's vitals.

"Where all the wolves go during the day." Heathrow cracked a smirk as if he knew something she didn't. Verena assumed he probably did, and she was clearly about to find out.

True to her suspicion, Verena walked through the right side of an oak double door, the left covered ground to ceiling in vines. When Heathrow moved to the left before her, Verena's mouth dropped. In front of her were countless men and women, paired, solo and grouped alike, and they were all staring at her, baffled, except for the one pair of stormy eyes looking at her as if she were his next meal. Aven bloody Belmont was shirtless, sweating and walking right towards her. Verena could feel the anger pulsating in the room from women and men alike. She didn't blame them in the slightest. He was delectable and entirely hers.

What she was also not expecting was the way her blood boiled when she saw who he was walking with. The woman could have been formed by the Goddess herself. Her features were soft yet striking. Her hair, the colour of melted caramel, formed waves over her shoulder, framing her nauseatingly perfect face. Her training outfit left little to the imagination. It hugged every curve of her hips. Her crop top barely dipped below her breast. Verena knew she was staring, but who wouldn't?

"What the fuck is she doing here?" One of Verena's brows quirked upward as she leaned to one side with her weight, her hip jutting slightly as she rested one hand on it. Her other hand indignantly pointed to Kessa.

"Woah, calm down, Love. She's here because we were all called to gain training from Heathrow." Aven held his hands up like a guilty man would after being caught.

"When in the history of being told to 'calm down' has it ever worked?" Verena snapped. The magic around her crackled in response.

"Okay, point taken." Aven looked at her with widened eyes, submitting to her, backing away slowly and away from the sudden shift of static in the air.

Heathrow cleared his throat, and an amused smile graced his features. Everything would have been great, fine even, until little Miss Perfect strutted, too perfectly, over.

I really do not have the patience for this bitch today. Verena's lip curled, her eyes narrowing as she watched Kessa sway her hips with exaggeration towards them.

Which bitch, Hellfire? I am aware it rhymes before you say anything.

Miss perfect at everything, looks great in everything, can't do anything wrong. Kessa Lane. If she could bleach her eyes and still see, Verena would. Every inkling of her brain wanted to douse the room in it, and even then, it would not be enough to cover the stench of Kessa.

Would you like me to kill her? Kieran asked seductively, too seductively for her taste, an offer she had to think twice about.

Is it an option?

Anything I offer is an option. He was making this exceptionally hard to refuse, Verena almost gave in.

Perhaps later, I want a round or two with her first.

Oh, darling. Speak to my heart some more.

"Aven! You left so abruptly!" The tone of Kessa's voice grated at Verena's nerves. It was flirty and filled with an air of temptation. Verena rubbed two of her fingers against her temple.

"Do you ever shut up?" Verena was fully aware of her actions.

"Verena..." Heathrow started to scold her, shrugged, and walked off as if he had no desire to be part of any portion of this right now.

"I said it out loud, didn't I?" Verena looked smug.

"Sure did," Heath whispered from a few feet away, knowing Verena could still hear him.

"Oops." Verena feigned apologetic, placing her hand delicately over her mouth and fluttering her eyelashes.

"You are going to stir up trouble, aren't you?" Aven pulled her more petite frame into him; he was sticky, and the smell, she almost gagged.

"As much as I love seeing you..." Verena trailed her fingernails down his chest. "You smell. Bad. Like a wet dog mixed with stagnant pond water."

"I'm hurt." Aven feigned actual offence and allowed her to pull away as he brought a hand dramatically to his heart as if he had been shot.

"I have one word for you." Verena held up her index finger at him. "Dramatic."

"Learned from the best, Love."

"What did you learn, A?" Verena's light expression dropped, her lip curled in disgust at the want to be succubus before them.

"How to see himself out of a conversation that doesn't involve him."

"Oh, such a bite from the prissy princess just off bedrest." Kessa rolled her eyes at Verena before turning her attention back to Aven, a move that made Verena more agitated. Verena seethed at the sight of her perfectly manicured white nails running down Aven's arm.

"Do I need to say it slower? Aven is mine, has been mine, and will continue to be mine. So, fuck all the way off."

"He wasn't always." Kessa smiled. It was too perfect; her teeth were too white and too straight. "He was mine before you." Dropping her hand from him, she leaned towards

Verena.

"Are we reaching your point sometime soon? He's not now, is he?"

"Did he show you how he digs his fingers into the little divots at the base of your spine when he's going down on you? Or how he likes to take you while you are up on a wall? How about how he wraps your legs around his shoulders and brings them to yours? No? How sad."

"Kessa, enough. We have been over for months." Aven snapped, getting between her and Verena. "You knew there was a possibility we were not compatible. You knew when we both reached maturity, there wasn't a connection. You knew. And now you want to torment her, the one the Goddess gave me, out of what? Jealousy? We aren't meant for each other. It's time for you to move on."

"She's not even one of us, Aven! She doesn't have a single drop of wolf blood in her. It's all Fae." Kessa spat the last word, disgusted by the thought. "You're willing to defile yourself with halflings? You know as well as I that your potential children will be slaughtered for what they are."

"So what, Kessa? Defile? If the Goddess meant for us to be together, then this is how it will be. Who are you to question?"

Verena wished she had brought a chair, some tea and a camera to record this so she could watch it again later. She was still thinking about Kieran's offer earlier. Perhaps she would take him up on it.

Just tell me a time, Hellfire.

Eavesdrop much?

Little hard not to when you practically scream your thoughts into my head.

"She can not be our Luna if she is dead, Aven."

"What did you say?" Aven growled. The height difference between them made him seem more intimidating than ever.

He's still a baby compared to me.

Oh, shut it.

"I said she cannot be our Luna if she is dead," Kessa repeated confidently. Verena would not stand a chance against her. Kessa was sure of it.

"And who is going to kill me? You?" Verena laughed; the audacity of this bitch was slightly impressive.

"What, is it so surprising? The Goddess chooses our mates, but anyone can challenge it if it involves an alpha pairing. Sometimes even the Goddess is wrong, and sometimes there is a better wolf to become the leader." Kessa backed up, holding her hands out to the side. "Scared, little Fae?"

"Of you?" Verena pointed at her, and the entire room fell into a silent stupor. She wondered how long they had been watching the interaction. "My shadow is scarier."

"Prove it then, fight me. A true battle, no interference. It does not end until one of us is dead or incapable of continuing." Somebody handed Kessa a set of daggers, small and dainty. She flipped one the opposite way.

"What are you going to do? Stab me?" Verena walked forward, calm and collected. Merridayn told her about the unsolicited research she had conducted during her extended coma. Verena knew the blades Kessa had would be useless against her skin, and her magic stores were nearly full over the days she consumed the floral tea Heathrow made her. This fight would be easy. Kessa? Not so much.

Chapter 34

VERENA

K essa was predictable, easily angered and utterly full of herself. Verena watched how she flipped her daggers around. Was it for show, or was this actually how she used them? There were better ways to go about it. Verena was untrained, purely basing this off straight instincts but damn, was she really about to get into a pissing match with another woman over a man? She had two options: fight her and win because death was not on her agenda for the day, or walk away and listen to her constant whining for the rest of her life. If Heathrow's age was anything to go by, and he was only half Fae, she would be ancient. After a few years of this from Kessa, she would likely launch herself from the nearest cliff.

I'm really about to get into a fight... over a man... with another woman. This bitch is too much.

"Are you coming, Princess?" Kessa's pronunciation of her title caused a roar of laughter from the ever growing crowd.

Where the hell do they keep coming from?

"What's the rush? Do you have a hot date later, or are you always this pushy? I'm not shocked Aven left you." Verena stepped towards the sparring circle Aven had abandoned, looking down at the sweat drops. Were they soon to be replaced by blood? Verena did not know if she had the mental capacity for this right now. Especially over a man, one clearly hers. She solidified her resolve, knowing this was going to happen regardless. At this point, she might as well enjoy the outcome she knew would play in her favour. Verena took the final step into the ring, and the game began.

As Verena expected, Kessa launched at her the moment she crossed the boundary. Anger was written on her face, and she was out for blood. Verena's blood, to be precise. Acting on instinct, Verena narrowly dodged the tip of her first dagger but missed the second. The sharp blade ripped through the side of her long sleeve, exposing the expansive white intricate tattoo on her abdomen. Little sounds of affirmations came from the crowd. Verena could hear them yet maintained focus on the angry wolf rounding on her again.

"Damn, Aven, you didn't say the Fae had ink, man."

"I had a feeling she was just like her mother..." Heathrow whispered, distracting Verena just enough for Kessa to swipe at her again. This time, when her knife caught fabric, the entire lower portion of Verena's shirt dropped to the floor.

Low whistles sounded, and many more onlookers came closer. Verena's ink was now mostly displayed for the crowd to see.

"You'll have to try harder, Kessa." Verena smiled at the lack of blood pouring out of herself where there should have been. The look on Kessa's face was priceless when the impudent child realised her blades wouldn't puncture.

"What the fuck is wrong with you, you freak!" Kessa wailed, thrown off guard and forcing herself back into the fight. Verena caught on to her fighting style, each move coming slower and slower until it looked as if Kessa was pre-planning all of her moves. "This is who you want, Aven!? She's a freak, a bloody fucking freak."

"She is, indeed. Funny how it works, isn't it? The Goddess might have a thing or two about mates and who would work out the greatest and who wouldn't. It became clear we would not work out the second time you cheated on me, Kessa."

This seemed to fuel her rage even more, causing the poor girl to de-escalate rapidly into a frenzy. Verena narrowly missed being tackled to the ground, losing her footing and stumbling about. She needed to figure out a way to end this quickly. Her instincts were only good for so much. Kessa growled, ditching her daggers as she barreled right into Verena's midsection, her back slammed on the hard ground. Shooting pain fluttered to her toes. She tried to push Kessa off and failed.

Fuck me, she looks like a damn twig but weighs like a box of rocks. What the fucking rugby player.

Who's a rugby player?

Kessa.

How would you know this?

Ah...well - about that.

Verena. How would you know she's a rugby player?

I am currently on the ground with her fat ass on top of me. She ran through me like a train.

Verena swore she could feel Kieran's eye roll from there, and he didn't even say anything. She needed to think. There was no possible way she was getting Kessa off her. Not with the woman continuously pounding into any part of her she left exposed. Verena knew the knives couldn't hurt her, but fists, they most definitely were going to bruise later.

Think, Verena, think.

Your nails, love.

What?

High Fae nails are sharper than most blades. Dig them into her sides. Right under her hips, bury your thumbs, hard. The pressure point being punctured will cause her to go into defence immediately.

Do I want- never mind. I am not asking.

Verena did as she was told, moving her arms away from protecting her face to bury them as far into Kessa's hips as she could. Just as Kieran said, she went into self-preservation mode, pushing Verena off her with as much force as she could muster and retreated to the farthest portion of the ring she could. Blood stained her abnormally perfect skin. Verena was a bit giddy and excited. She wanted more.

"Give up so soon? Did you realise your knives wouldn't work on me and then switched to an All-Star linebacker? I have to say, you look skinny, too skinny, but you hide the weight well. I'm impressed." Verena was not trying to antagonise her anymore. She wanted this petty fight to end and get on with her day. Clearly, this wasn't in the cards for today, probably not even tomorrow.

"I don't need compliments from you, slut." Almost on all fours, Kessa charged at her again as if she were an animal.

I guess she is actually an animal.

"Slut? How rich, coming from the person who, according to Aven, not even five minutes ago, announced to the entire room you cheated on him. Not once but twice! Twice! And I'm the slut?" Verena was done; she had enough, and her body sizzled with power. A power she didn't know was there, power she didn't know how to use. Yet it answered, it obeyed. Because one second, Kessa was on her way to making the rugby player's tackle look like child's play to being pressed against the farthest wall, clutching at her throat. Verena was furious and bored; now, she'd had to deal with bruises. She was over this whole ordeal. "You are done, Kessa. Done. Touch Aven, look at him, fuck, if you even think about him, I'll kill you."

"Verena, honey, put her down." Heathrow's hand gripped her shoulder. There was no mistaking his mixed heritage from how the fur-like hair extended past his wrist and onto the back of his hand. Kessa choked, her coughing raspy, and her hands hadn't left her throat. She was paling from the lack of oxygen in her bloodstream, and all Verena wanted was to see her take her last, pathetic breath. To watch her life tortuously drain away. She deserved it, didn't she? She challenged Verena's position, challenged Verena's bond with Aven, the rules dictated until one is dead or incapacitated. "Verena, you're killing her." Kessa coughed roughly, blood spraying out of her mouth. Verena snapped out of it.

"Fuck, Heathrow, I don't know how. I don't know what happened. How do I stop?"

"Focus, dear. Focus on me; don't look at her. Don't think about her. Just focus on me. Calm your magic down. It's lashing out because you are angry. It's only responding to your desires. Look at me. Close your eyes if you have to, but I need you to think about something else which could calm you down, such as your favourite memory, place, Aven, or Kieran. I don't care who or what, or frankly even where. I just need you to focus on something happy or calming." Heathrow turned their bodies so Verena couldn't see Kessa, couldn't see anyone actually; Heathrow's body was wide enough that all Verena could see was his small patch of hair peeking out the top of his shirt.

Verena inhaled; Heathrow smelled of basil, pine trees, tobacco, and a hint of jasmine. The combination was bizarre, and then she began thinking about how Aven always reminded her of horses, the ocean and summer storms. While Kieran was a mixture of lava, burnt oranges and caramel. Her anger subsided, dissipated. She could hear Kessa coughing, which was softer this time. She wondered if Kessa was down; she didn't dare look backwards for fear of irritating her magic again. Heathrow pushed a few of her stray hairs out of the way, reminding her of her Nan.

"Good, you are doing wonderfully, Verena. Keep concentrating. We want your magic to go dormant for now. We will practise, you and me, where the only things you could harm are the trees."

"Okay." Verena yawned. Heathrow pulled her into a big hug. She felt safe there, and she didn't want to leave it. "Can I go take a nap now? I think I overdid it."

"Of course." Heathrow searched for Aven, who was already standing there waiting. "Aven, can you take her to her room? Inform Nora she might have overdone it today."

"Yes, sir." Aven did not hesitate as he scooped her into his arms, her head resting against his exposed pecs.

"You smell heavenly." Verena purred, halfway lucid. She met Kessa's eyes.

Aven hummed, remaining silent—a wise choice to avoid the anger pulsating from Verena.

"I will kill you next time. I don't want to except for a small part inside begging me to rip you apart. Blame it on the Angel of Death's blood flowing through my veins at a higher rate than normal." Verena laughed to herself, hiccuping. "I will actually kill you, Kessa. So learn from this because the next time, I'll rip your heart out of your chest and make you watch as it beats in my hand while your brain dies without it."

"Sometimes you scare me, my love." Aven peered at her, not paying attention to where he was going, as evidenced by the way Verena's foot bounced off the entryway door.

"Keep your eyes on the road there." She draped her arms around his neck, and her stomach grumbled in protest. "But you should be."

Chapter 35

VERENA

Verena overdid it. She knew the second Nora came in, yelling about how she was supposed to be resting. Her magic stores were depleted, and she looked like a walking vampyre from the purses under her eyes. Or perhaps, at this point, they were luggage and not purses. Either way, Nora alluded to her looking like absolute shit. Nora was terrifying, and Verena did not want to anger the Druid again. Which is how she found herself sneaking out of her room with Gracie's help at three in the morning to meet Heathrow. Scandalous, she knew, but she needed answers, and she needed them before she accidentally killed someone who didn't need to be on the opposite side of uncontrollable sentient magic.

"Gracie, are you sure you know where we are going?" Verena whispered, surely the sheer amount of turns they had taken was leading them back towards her room. "Because it feels like we are going in circles right now."

Gracie chuckled, nodded in response, and pointed towards the doorway ahead of them. She rolled her eyes at the woman, finding her reaction amusing with the lack of verbalisation. Verena could feel her magic, just under the surface of her skin, waiting to be released. Ever since her accidental outburst against Kessa, Verena felt as if she was constantly on edge. Someone could light a match, and she would explode.

They approached a charcoal coloured door, the deep grey easily mistaken for black to a human eye. Gracie pushed it open gently, yet her face still scrunched when the eerie creak of the ageing hinges betrayed her caution. The sound echoed off the walls. Verena looked around, and the room darkened to match the hallway they were in. She felt the petite hand grip her upper arm and yank her sharply. Verena stumbled through the doorway, crashing into Gracie in the process. Before a snide comment could leave Verena's lips, she was silenced by Heathrow's seemingly neon green aura, seated in the centre of what she could now tell was an otherwise empty, circular room.

"Heath?" Verena whispered, but he didn't respond. "Heath?" She whispered again, louder this time. The door had closed, though it didn't mean their conversation could not be overheard from the other side.

"You do not need to whisper, dear. They cannot hear us once the door is closed. Can you see the runes, Verena?" Heathrow stood, using an odd looking stick in his hand to indicate towards the door. Verena's gaze followed where he was showing, her eyes taking in the runes on the backside of the door she had missed, too distracted by the new sight of Heath, the aura she had never noticed before.

"What are they?" Verena subconsciously walked toward them, her fingers ghosting the stroke marks. They were calling out to her, edging her to touch them. "They are calling to me. I don't understand what they are saying, but there is buzzing, like someone is whispering words across a busy street. Should they be Heathrow? Should I be able to hear them?"

"I cannot see them, Verena. I only know they are there because I drew them. The first one is near the top. Focus on it. Your hearing is more advanced than a wolf's. Block everything else out and focus solely on the buzzing you hear from only the top one." Heathrow joined her, his green aura indicating his nearness without having to look behind her.

Verena momentarily doubted herself because Heathrow's hand touched her shoulder, and the gesture boosted her motivation. She focused on the rune, the one he wanted her to study, taking in the strokes of each line and the colour it emitted. Closing her eyes, she tried to focus on Heathrow's slower, steady heartbeat, deep inhales, Gracie's faster heart and shallower breaths, the ants she could hear scurrying around the ground. Verena tried to focus on the buzzing, focusing on one particular sound instead of the multitude which invaded her senses. She pictured the rune in her head, the colour, trying to force herself to pick the one she wanted. The second she visualised the rune, her magic snapped into place. The whispering voice became louder, and nothing around her existed. She was alone with the sound she wanted, and a barrier formed to keep everything else out. She could hear it, hear the whispers speaking.

Kyrnnix

"Silence." Verena blurted out. "What the hell? Heathrow, it wasn't in English, yet I knew what it said."

"Try the next one."

Verena did, following the same steps she had done for the first rune. She was faster this time. The magic within her knew instantly what to do.

Intrym

"Ignore."

"Good, and the last?"

Verena hardly needed to focus before the words jumped

out at her.

Uilusym

"Illusion." Verena opened her eyes, turning around to face him. "Right?"

"Right." Heathrow was distant, as if he was a million miles away, lost in his thoughts.

"Heathrow? What is it?"

"Nothing, apologies, I was lost in a memory. To answer your question, Verena, the runes are Angelic. They were created by the Angels, using their language. When you told me you could see magic, I wondered if you would be able to hear magic, as well. You carry the blood of four Archangels."

"What do you mean, hear magic?"

"You should have noticed the energy particles around you, specifically after your tea. You must have noticed how they come to you, appearing to be absorbed into your skin. The feeling you get afterwards like you are on a caffeine high?"

"Yes, I thought everyone could see the energy, though."

"We cannot, Verena. I can drink the same tea and feel the same energetic high, but cannot see the physical manifestations entering my body. But you, you can. Therefore, you should be able to hear it as well. Runes are alive; they require not just magic but your soul to create them. The Angels used their souls to create them; the voices you are hearing are the creators of the runes. Many Angels are predisposed to certain types of runes. For example, the Archangel Azrael could only create runes of death: Odykstaz, known as the Death Call; Pitustra, Bloodlet; and Givianchi, or Soul Stealer. Each Angel can create runes outside of their particular affinity, though it is said to be much more difficult. The first rune, Kyrnnix, was created by the Morningstar. The second rune, Intrym or Ignore, was created by Archangel Gabriel to be used during meetings where they needed confidentiality. The third, Uilusym, was created by Angel Sathariel, the Angel of Deception."

"I am hearing them? The Angels?" Verena was dumbfounded. The explanation made sense; however, as she thought about it, each rune whispered to her in a different voice. All three were not the same.

"You are, which is good information for us to know so we can tailor your training." Heathrow jotted down something on parchment she didn't notice he had. It appeared out of nowhere, or perhaps Gracie had given it to him.

"Tailor what training?" Verena raised her eyebrows at him. Tailor her training? What did he mean?

"When you were fighting with Kessa, when did you feel your magic lash out at her?" Another question. Was he reading them off a script?

"Probably after she called me a slut, I was getting angry then. I just wanted the childish bullshit over with so I could leave. I felt I had no choice but to accept, or she would never have left it alone." Verena could feel the magic in the room swirling around her, responding to the rise in her emotions.

"And what did it feel like?" Definitely a script, did her mother write these questions for Heathrow to ask her when she was older?

"It started here," Verena said, placing her hand on the opposite side of her heart. "It felt like a muscle pain at first, one you would get if you didn't stretch before doing something strenuous. Then it moved, rapidly, outwards towards my fingers."

"What were you thinking about after it started reaching your fingers?" Heathrow indicated towards her hands.

"I wanted her to suffer, to shut up for once. Next thing, she's against a wall with her hands around her throat, coughing up blood." Verena remembered the fight and saw how Kessa was coming at her. Moments later, she was against the wall. Looking at her as if she was an alien, something foreign. Verena now recognised the look Kessa had on her face; she was scared.

"Because your magic reacted to your desires, you wanted her away from you and silent. Your magic responded." He was writing down more notes on the booklet Verena recognised as one of Gracie's, which answered her question about where he got the parchment.

"But Heath..." Verena started. She tried to forget what happened after Kessa coughed up blood. She didn't want to admit how it made her feel. "There was a part of me which wanted to continue. Even after you told me to stop when you told me she was dying. I didn't want to. I wanted to keep going."

"But you didn't, honey. You didn't, and I am proud of you for fighting your base instincts to kill her." Heathrow said the words she did not know a part of her needed to hear. Her heart fluttered.

"Why was it there, though? Why did I want to?" Verena questioned, if her instincts were to kill, why couldn't she oblige?

"You have the Angel of Death's blood running through your veins, and when Kieran was near you, Azrael's blood within him called yours to the surface." He was making sense and Verena didn't like it.

"Will this happen every time we are near each other then? Will I become some type of bloodthirsty monster?" She was terrified of herself, terrified of hurting anyone else who remotely angered her.

"Not necessarily. I believe you were murderous because of the intense emotions you were feeling and your inexperience controlling your magic." Heathrow was throwing out ideas, Verena could tell in the way he tapped the booklet anxiously.

"So what do I do?"

"We practise; this is why we are here. This is why you were snuck out of Nora's eyesight at three o'clock in the morning." Heathrow walked back towards the centre of the room. "We will start by calling on your magic, getting it to respond to you instead of your emotions."

"Um, how? I don't know where it started to begin with."

"Come, sit down in front of me." Heathrow was much more graceful than Verena gave him credit for. Following suit, she gasped at the change of colour his aura presented, switching from a light green surrounding him to a dark green near his chest. "I know you can see it. Focus on where my magic is stemming from."

"Your chest?" Verena touched precisely where she could see the light emitting from.

"They say our soul is located here." Heathrow cupped her hand, smiling gently at her. "Look inside yourself now. Try locating your magic stores."

Verena did as she was told, trying to duplicate the feeling she had in the fight. The room grew quiet, except for the steady breathing of the two others with her. It felt as if hours had passed, and she still couldn't find it. Frustration bubbled to the surface. Self-loathing and anger kept her from following Heathrow's instructions.

"I can't do this."

"You can. You deciphered runes you had no prior knowledge of. You are capable of controlling your magic.

It is a part of you, Verena. It has always been a part of you. Try again. See if you can hear the energy calling to you."

She huffed; this entire thing was pointless. But to appease her guardian, she tried again, listening for any spark or sizzle she could find. She tried again, and still, she couldn't hear anything. There were no whispers like the runes, no visible colours she could see, just emptiness. She almost gave up again. Her self-depreciation was smug, telling her she couldn't do it, so why keep trying? Just give up already until she heard *her* voice, faint and weak.

Keep trying, Verena.

The voice sounded like it belonged to Haniel, but different; Verena wouldn't have noticed the slight difference if she hadn't been paying attention.

Haniel?

Silence. Verena waited, hopeful for a response. There was not one, yet Verena felt like someone was dragging a feather down her chest. She heard the buzzing then. It had been soft, exceptionally so, missed by her attention drawn to the feathering feeling. The faint buzz turned to a roaring cascade the longer Verena focused. Her eyes flew open to see Heathrow smiling at her.

"You did it."

"How did you know?" Verena looked down. Her chest glowed a bright blue, exactly in the spot Heathrow's is, the place he claims holds her soul.

"I can feel it in my magic. I can feel yours reaching out towards mine."

"Why would it reach out to you?" Verena fluttered her hands through the light, proud of her accomplishment.

"High Fae can accomplish great feats of magic with others. Think of it as if you went to pick up a heavy table by yourself. You could do it, but it would be difficult.

Now, you and I can pick up the table; it becomes easier, right? By adding more people and more magic, the strain is spread out between the many instead of one. Your magic is reaching out to connect; it's not a bad thing, Verena."

"I see. So what is the next part?"

"There is no next part until you can call upon your magic independently, consistently, instantly." Verena was disappointed. She wanted to continue but didn't argue. He had probably been through the same training he was putting her through. "Don't give me that look. It took you eight minutes to call upon it. You need practice. Secondly, I pulled a few books I want you to go through from my library. The first one, however, is this one." Heathrow handed her a book bound in what appeared to be skin. She nearly dropped it in disgust. "This one is the full extent of runes we currently know about. I want you to study them, learn their uses, who they were created by and why. This is important, Verena. You are the only one I know who can see them. You need to be able to harness your ability. It might come in handy at some point."

Chapter 36

VERENA

"The Princess presents herself to us. The delay is unbecoming of your station." Islabell's snark was already pushing Verena's patience. The past few days had been filled with constant practice. Verena rose in the wee hours with Heathrow and studied the skin-bound book, which still gave her an unsettled feeling each time she touched it. From there, she was met with constant lecturing from Nora, the Druid's voice too slow for her liking.

"We're already off to a great start, aren't we?" Verena mumbled to Merridayn. Having not seen the woman since she woke from her coma, Verena was surprised when Merridayn came to her room to accompany her. The two planned to have more time after the meeting with the council; they both had much to share.

"Princess Verena Halliwen Nightingale, you've grown much over the years. I remember when you were brought here with Heath as a babe. I find it interesting that you are well over a hundred years of age and yet appear to be no closer to an adult." Verena assumed the speaker was Armand; his appearance and eloquence in speech fit how Heathrow had described him in the stories from their arrival in Alusso. She remembered he had been the one to save them from what could have been their demise. A smile graced his features, quickly reaching his eyes. There was no doubt to Verena that he was genuine in his sincerity.

I see where Heathrow said Armand didn't believe their elders should be able to dictate over people not from their world.

"I should introduce myself. I am Armand; you could consider me the alpha of the elders. I see you have already met Islabell. She oversees the healer's quarters. The red-haired man to my right is Hansen, our records keeper. He is blind, but don't let this fool you. He studied as a monk for many years of his youth." Verena took in the blind man; his features appeared soft and kind, yet at the same time, he looked eerily at her for someone who was blind. She already knew Islabell, or more so Islabitch, as she and Gracie liked to call the irritating woman. This left one person Verena did not know. The woman was smaller, petite, and ethnic in appearance. Her hair was long and dark, coming well past her shoulders, which blocked some of the ornate designs on the colourful, floral robe that covered her body. "The woman next to Hansen is Orla. She is our linguist master. Her language skills encompass seven languages and multiple dialects within each language. She is also the mate of our Heathrow here, your godparent, as the humans like to call them."

"It is nice to meet you all, but I believe we have some pressing matters to attend to before I can return to Gwendolyn." Verena was curt, possibly too much so, though her point stood. She wanted answers, and the ones who had them were those standing before her.

"You waste no time, do you?" Hansen jest. His smile lit up his face, making him appear younger and happier than his prior emotionless appearance. "It's nice. I am not making fun of you, Verena. I can hear your anger rising. Take a few deep breaths, dear. It is not good for your health to consistently be pent up."

"He is right, you know." Heathrow leaned to whisper to her, a smirk tugging at the edges of his mouth. Verena rolled her eyes at them both, focusing her attention towards Armand. She was hopeful her next question would be answered without irritating comments from the rest.

"Let us get to the point: your council gave me to a woman who used me, used the money my parents left for me, allowed her partner to physically beat me whenever it fancied him, and occasionally made me starve. I grew up thinking this was just the set of cards I was handed, wishing I could have lived a better life. I grew up envying the Belmonts every time I passed by their home, wondering why I was given this life. What did I do to deserve this? In reality, it wasn't fate which had given this life. It was you and your damned council members. This useless group believed they had authority over someone outside their own species. This group decided to hand me the worst deck of cards possible while looking the other way at the abuse I suffered at Abigail's hand. Over a note she had forged, one you all believed. Now, I want this all rectified. Heathrow informed me you took control over my inheritance. You will give it back to me today. You will also return any other property my parents left Heathrow to give to me when I was old enough." Verena looked each and every single person before her in the eyes.

She was furious, and every passing second added to her rage. The audacity these people had over their kind was enough. Verena wondered if the rest knew what freedom looked like. But the audacity they had to believe they had any sort of dominion over her, a High Fae, a completely different race, Verena would see them killed if they tried refusing. The leash she had on her magic was still feeble at best. Bloodthirsty at worst.

"Who do you believe you are to make demands of us?" Islabell stuck her nose up, and Verena fisted at the material of her pants, her last attempt to maintain control over her magic.

"Islabell..." Heathrow started, rubbing the bridge of his nose. "Really? Are you really going to start this again today? Have you not had enough drama lately to fill your thirst for it?"

"What of it, hybrid? She was brought here in a coma by the Belmonts, the same family who sacrificed their lives to harbour you, demanding our healers and Druids' help. Now, she is here demanding more from us?" Islabell held her head high, reminding her of the stuck up popular girls back at her school. The ones who believed they were better than the rest purely based on their parents.

"Insult him again, Islabell." Having kept quiet this entire time, Orla spoke up with a heavy accent, but the message was clear. Islabell would be at her own risk by continuing her verbal assault.

"Enough, Islabell. Verena is well within her rights to demand her inheritance back; after all, it is the money her parents gave her. Her parents are not wolves and should not have been dictated to by wolves." Armand snapped. Power radiated off of him in visible waves to Verena as she stood there awestruck by the sheer amount of energy he commanded. Armand's power was the most she had seen since she began to see magic in the world. "You are right, Verena. I will personally oversee the transfer of your assets back to you today. If you come to see me in my office after the last light today, I should have everything arranged by then. Now, there is another matter we need to discuss."

Verena had not expected them to fold so easily. She had

been prepared to fight for what belonged to her back. This entire process seemed too easy; it gave Verena an uneasy feeling, like a sword was hanging above her head, one that stood ready to cleave her in two. Armand surprised her with the second matter. One Heathrow knew nothing about based upon the look he gave her. "Armand?" Heathrow questioned, taking the initiative to figure out what was going on. He did not like being surprised either, making the three of them. Verena could hear Merridayn's irritation in the way her breathing had changed.

"The lily, Heathrow. It does belong to her. She should have it back."

"Lily? You're giving me a flower back?" Verena laughed, amused.

Are they really giving me a flower back?

Who is giving you a flower, Hellfire?

"Not just any flower, Verena. A Tenestell Lily Ilium Stellarum, commonly known as an Onyx Whispers Lily." Armand clarified proudly. Verena started. Was she supposed to instantly know what the hell he was talking about because he listed off some fancy name for a flower she had never heard of?

An Ilium Tenestell something or another. Onyx Whispers? Mean anything to you?

A Death Flower?

I need you to imagine the eye roll I am giving you right now. You are making as much sense as they are.

"A flower. What exactly am I supposed to say? Thank you for some odd flower and the vague explanation for said flower like I should know what you are talking about."

"I believe you and Heathrow should speak privately; he knows more about the flower than anyone else here." Armand nodded, looking at everyone, then walked towards an exit Verena had not noticed, hidden behind the tree trunk pillar.

"After you." Heathrow motioned towards the main entry, signalling the end of the meeting. Verena seemed happy with the outcome, yet she still couldn't shake the feeling something wasn't right.

The three of them walked in silence, following Heathrow as he led them in the opposite direction of her room. Verena should have felt excited to be able to explore the place she had called home in the previous weeks. Areas outside her training space and bedroom, but she couldn't shake the sense of impending doom which now plagued her mind. The feeling interrupted her pride, pride at how much she had grown from the timid, malnourished delivery girl into a High Fae Princess able to yield magic she still didn't know the bounds of. She was on the precipice of the edge in her mind. A subtle wind could blow her over.

Merridayn interlocked their arms, pulling Verena into her. She momentarily sunk into the motherly love the woman exuded, wishing for a split second she had grown up with them. Perhaps her life would have been different if she had. Maybe she would have different circumstances, different opportunities. Perhaps she could have seen life in a better light than the dark, dreadful one she had grown accustomed to. Verena watched as they approached two large oak doors covered in foliage and birds. Their beady eyes looked into her soul and smiled as if they had found one of their own. Verena shivered, weary of the animals' leering caws and hoots and how they seemed to watch her every move. Until one, a larger black and red bird, pushed off its perch to fly directly at her. Verena ducked, horrified and covered her head. She felt a sudden sharp pain in her right hand.

"Did this damn bird just bite me?" She straightened up, taking an overview of the tiny droplet of blood on the top of her hand. The evil looking avian cackled back at her, coming to land on her shoulder. "You bastard. What did you do that for?" Clearly, it was the wrong thing to say as she felt the sharp pain in her neck. "I swear to hell, you do it again, and I'll kill you."

"My name is Acheron, little Fae." A smooth yet airy voice came from the bird's beak. Verena snapped her neck to the side just to see it. She needed to lay off the tea, apparently.

"Did it just speak?" Verena tried to shake off Acheron, earning herself another stab in the hand. "I warned you, now get off of me."

"No, you are my bonded."

"How fun!" Heathrow was all smiles, and Merridayn joined him, yet her face betrayed her confusion. "It would appear you have found your familiar, and they have completed the bond."

"What the absolute hell?" Verena eyeballed Acheron. The bird was exquisite, she had to admit.

"You are my Fae, Verena Nightingale. I will always be able to find you no matter where you go." Acheron nuzzled her hair, making himself comfortable on her shoulder.

"Acheron took your blood to commit the smell of you to memory. Wherever you go, Acheron can find you. He will be your eyes and ears, delivering parchments to any realm. He is a Death Falcon. He gains magic from you and his originator, Leliel, the Angel of Night. So long as you live, Acheron will always be with you."

"Wonderful, I have a pet bird." Verena rolled her eyes, walking towards the now opened doorway before them. "Anything else you all want to throw at me today, or can we get to the part where you tell me what this bloody flower I'm supposed to have is?" Verena felt Acheron's claws dig into her shoulder. "What was that for, Acheron?"

"I am not a pet. I am a familiar."

"Okay... familiar. Do you have to keep stabbing me every time I piss you off?" Acheron dug into her shoulder again. "Take it as a yes. Got it. Don't piss off the bird." Another stab. "Falcon. I meant Falcon."

Bloody birds.

Another stab.

"You can read my mind too?" Verena shouted at him, and his responding cackle confirmed her question. "Of course, you can. Can we just move on? I'm over all of this already."

"After you." Heathrow stepped back, motioning for the two women to lead onwards. Merridayn knew where they were heading as she leaned closer to her. Acheron glared at the offending avians leaning closer to Verena. His chest puffed out, and talons dug into her shoulder, prepared to strike should another come closer. Verena took in the beauty of the enormous library before her, how the earth seemed to meld with the bookshelves, how the foliage swayed back and forth. The library appeared as magical as it felt. Tiny trails of light flew before her. Had her eyesight been as it was, she wouldn't have seen the odd looking animal: half fox, half bird. The creature landed gracefully on Merridayn's neat chignon.

"Hello, Kinley." Merridayn smiled. The fox bird nuzzled itself into her forehead, causing the woman to laugh softly. "It's been a handful of hours, Kinley. You can not be this dramatic? You could have come with me."

"Kinley?" Verena questioned, though she had a feeling she already knew the answer.

"She is my familiar, though it baffles me as I am human." Merridayn continued to lead them towards a table towards the middle of the room.

Archeron and Kinley settled on the table when they approached. It was clear this was where they were meant to be. Merridayn grasped Verena's hands in hers, a smile on her face as the two women took their seats.

"How have you been? Are you eating well enough? I can have Elion bring you food from Gwendolyn if you want. Aven told me about the fight with Kessa; she has been appropriately reprimanded and will no longer be a concern. How have your studies been? Are you sleeping well?" Merridayn swarmed her with questions.

"I have been well. The food they bring is fine, but Heathrow insists on bringing me tea every morning. I am unsure how I feel about Kessa, though I desperately wish she would leave me alone. I cannot change fate; she cannot change who she is. My studies are good. I have learned about many Angelic runes, their origins, who created them, and who they were meant for. My sleep has been fitful. Heath has requested that we practise in the early mornings to ensure we are alone. It is a bit daunting, honestly."

"Do not hesitate to ask for anything, dear. We will be right behind you the whole way." Merridayn squeezed her hands and then looked towards Heathrow. "I believe a few things need to be discussed."

"Indeed; however, Verena, do you remember when I told you about the conditions regarding your conception? Do you remember your mother asking the Archangel Azrael for assistance?"

"Yes." Verena felt sceptical. She did not like being left in the dark or being told mere portions of the truth.

"Your mother begged the Angel to protect you, allowing her soul to be damned in exchange. Azrael gifted your mother one of her feathers, designated to be absorbed by you. This feather turned into the lily Armand referred to. The same one you have seen, Merridayn, behind the healer's station."

"I am supposed to absorb it? How?"

"Each High Fae was gifted a particular set of abilities. Yours is the ability to syphon magic, including magic created by Angelic Runes. I believe this is the reason Jerifeyn hid you here, in Alusso. It is the reason she fought to ensure the Mordinians would forget you were born."

"What do you mean?"

"Torvan Mordinian was cursed with the Angelic rune: Marked. Do you remember your mother talking about this in the memory she planted in your blood?" Heathrow looked at her, waiting for her to answer.

"Vaguely, I remember his face, and now, I think about it. I remember seeing a small black rune on his wrist." The memory of him floated to the front of her thoughts, focusing on the slight edge of the rune she assumed was the one Heathrow mentioned.

"Have you gotten to this rune in your studies?"

"Not yet, no." Verena read as much as she could in the previous days, staying up until her eyes couldn't stay open any longer.

"In a simple version, Torvan cannot go home. He cannot heal; once his magic stores are depleted, he cannot restore them. He's been forced to be a nomad for decades." Verena suspected there was a longer version that Heathrow would tell her at a later date.

"I am confused. What does this have to do with me?" Verena spoke too soon. She already knew what it had to do with her. Except she needed to hear it, needed to hear yet another person wanted to use her.

"You have the ability to remove his rune."

"Excuse me?" Verena rubbed her ears. Did Heathrow actually say that?

"Torvan can combine the universes by demolishing the barriers between them." He said it as if it was common knowledge, yet Verena looked at him like he was insane. A common feeling lately these days, it would seem.

"He wants to merge them? All of them?" Merridayn whispered.

"He does." Heathrow agreed solemnly.

"But why? Why would he want to merge them?" Merridayn recently learned about the time when all the universes were one. Before, the Archangels combined their strength to separate them. While the separation was documented, no one alive knew the reason for the Angel's action.

"Domination would be my guess. The Mordinians believe their control over the Demons of Hell would give them complete dominance over the rest." Heathrow did not look amused, knowing full well the contracts Demons made.

"They would not stand a chance against the Angels. They knew this, right?" Merridayn couldn't believe the words processing in her brain. Mordinians of all should know the Demons of Hell were the worst to call upon.

"The Angels cannot interfere, Merridayn." Contrary to other times where they have intervened, on principle the Angels would not be able to this time. They would have to watch as the Mordinians command the battlefield with bloodshed and depravity of Hell.

"They would have to watch as hundreds of innocents

die without the ability to assist." Merridayn wanted to cry, scream, hold Verena to her close, and never let her out of her sight.

"The Mordinians would have a complete dictatorship."

"Oh, my Goddess." She prayed someone was listening, someone cared enough to protect them.

Verena watched the conversation. She tried to pull her knowledge of the situation from her various sessions with Heathrow to keep up with the two.

"They need me to remove his rune so he can go home. Once he can return, his magic will be revitalised. He will tear the barriers between the universes apart, creating a totalitarian state with them on top."

"Precisely, Verena."

"Over my dead body." Verena seethed. "I am tired of being a pawn on a chessboard."

Kieran?

Yes, Hellfire?

I need you to teach me how to defend myself.

Oh, my flame, I never thought you'd ask.

"This is why your mother requested the feather." Heathrow looked towards Verena now, the room stagnated, everyone on edge.

"What does it do?" She could not picture a feather doing much but being a decoration, perhaps a necklace.

"It gives you the ability to escape death. But only once." Heathrow knew he had her attention now from the way Verena turned her entire body to face him, curious.

"Escape death? Why would I need to?" Did he mean what she thought he meant?

"Jerifeyn must have seen a moment in your future where she deemed it necessary."

"Great." Verena leaned toward Acheron. It was always

death and destruction in her future. The falcon moved closer, nuzzling her cheek. "How do I absorb it?"

"I believe I can answer that." Merridayn piped up, cheerful she could be useful for once. "I was reading about Angels gifting feathers, it has only happened three times. From what I read, the feather must be inserted into your spine."

"Excuse me? Inserted how." Verena reeled back, her face twisting in disgust.

"Um, I'm not sure, but I theorise it physically gets put into your spine."

"As in, cut me open, insert feather?" She felt her stomach roll over, putting a hand over her mouth in an attempt to stop from vomiting on the floor.

"Yes."

Verena felt faint. Her head spun at the idea someone would be surgically inserting a feather into her. There was no way this was sanitary.

"Can we move on to a different topic, please?" Verena begged, wanting to escape from the thought of a feather, lily, any sort of surgery, the whole lot.

"Armand should be finishing with the transfer of your assets soon. Once he is, bring the documents with you to our meeting tonight." Heathrow stood, the table shaking as he accidentally bumped against it. "I am being summoned to the training quarters if you will both excuse me." He brushed Verena's shoulder as he passed by her. Verena took the opportunity to excuse herself as well.

"I feel a tad faint. I am going to lay down for a bit if you do not mind." Verena looked towards Merridayn, hopeful she understood her plea.

"Of course, dear. I have some more research I wish to finish. I will have my son come to check on you," Merridayn said, looking at her dainty wristwatch. "Let's say two hours?"

"Please. I could use the comfort he brings." Verena stood, jostling Acheron, who was preoccupied with pruning his feathers. As she walked away, her familiar following close behind, Verena felt like someone was watching her. Eyes belonging not to Acheron, not to Kieran, eyes she didn't know, followed her subconscious.

Chapter 37

Verena

Death Call: Archangel Azrael created this rune using her blood and soul. Within a limited radius, the rune emits a shockwave. This shockwave rips the target's soul from their body to be collected by Azrael's bound sword, Givianchi. It was created during the First War against the Demons of Hell.

Death Call has the form of a 'V' shape with a line intersecting at an upward angle. A secondary perpendicular line intersects the previous one on the right side of the 'V'. The 'V' represents the action of ripping out the soul, while the sideways cross represents the limited radius of the rune.

It is said the rune was used twice in battle, cleaving the souls of Apollyon, Angel of the Void and Asbeel, Angel of Ruin. These Angels have not been seen since the War. It is rumoured their souls are still trapped within Givianchi.

*F*uck, she is ruthless.

Who is, Hellfire?
Azrael, I was reading up on the rune Death Call she created.
Ah, yes, My Lady is legendary for her vengeance.
My Lady?
Yes, love. Archangel Azrael created my lineage of Demons with the assistance of the Morningstar. We were born of their blood.

Clarity: Eistibus, the Angel of Divinity, crafted this rune to help him see prophetic visions clearly and contort his visions into a context that made the most sense. This rune is widely used by Seers, Prophets, and Prophetesses in many universes.

Clarity begins with an 'F' shape. The intersecting middle line is downward facing instead of straight across. At the bottom of the 'f' is an upward-facing line coming from the bottom to the left. Lastly, there is a connecting line from the left side of the middle line to the downward slope of the 'F.'

It is said Eistibus placed this rune upon one person to assist her, Princess Jerifeyn Naedian, who was given the Clarity rune when her visions began at an early age. The Princess is currently the only one this author knows of to be one of the most gifted Prophetess of the era. Her ability to determine every variety of the future was unparalleled, even by the Angel of Divinity himself.

Verena put the skin book on her end table, closing her eyes briefly to realise how exhausted she felt. She leaned back against her pillows, pulling the blankets up and around her as she fell asleep. Verena dreamed of her life and how different it would have been if her parents had raised her. She dreamed of the stories Heathrow told her and the views he had described. She dreamed of her parents being there for her when she became stuck on homework. Did Fae have schools like the humans do? Would she have been given homework if so? Would she have had to attend classes to teach her how to be a proper royal? What felt like an hour in her dream, reality had moved ahead twelve. When she awoke and rubbed her sleep-crusted eyes, she took in a gigantic stack of documents resting above the rune books. Along with a full glass of tea, Heathrow must have delivered it at some point.

Bringing the documents closer to her, Verena skimmed through the various pages. From deeds to houses in locations she has yet to hear of to bank accounts with variable amounts. Within an envelope sat an ominous black key, one she tossed to the side to circle back to later. The final pages listed all transactions since the beginning of the accounts creation. Verena noted many transactions of the same amount to a bank account she didn't recognise. Every single one was over twenty thousand placed at different times of the month. No date was the same.

"Odd." Verena flipped through the pages again, wishing she had a highlighter to make note of each transfer.

"Is everything alright?" Aven's voice came from the doorway. Verena looked up to see him covered in sweat, a half cocked smile on his face, as he bounded right towards her. She put a hand up to stop him in his tracks.

"Absolutely not. Go take a shower." She aggressively

pointed towards the bathroom door, waving her other hand over her nose, indicating he smelled. He laughed in response but headed towards the room she directed him to regardless.

Verena pulled the rune book from her end table, depositing it beside her while tidying the documents Armand left her. Flipping the book open, she began to study the different types of communication runes to the sound of the shower running. The runes fascinated her. She started lightly drawing them on her thigh with her fingers, memorising them. When Aven stepped out of the bathroom, Verena had gone through a handful of runes. A towel wrapped around his waist, and remaining water beads ran down his chiselled chest, hair damp and in disarray. Verena mindlessly shut the book, dumping it on the ground instead of the end table. Her eyes took him in, the picturesque man she had crushed on for the majority of her school years, standing before her, a towel away from naked. He met her ogling eyes with a sassy smirk, his hand resting where he tucked the towel.

"Like what you see?" Aven purred, twirling in a slow circle for her viewing pleasure.

"Are you asking?"

"No, I know the answer. I just love hearing it come off your lips." He was cocky, sometimes arrogant, but he was not wrong. Verena loved what she saw.

"Confident, are you?" She toyed with him, a smirk tugged at the edges of her mouth.

"With you? Always." Aven walked over to the side she was closer to, leaning down to put his hands on either side of her. His face was inches from hers, and water droplets from his hair splashed across her cheeks. "The way you look at me, the way your eyes light up, how your heart races, even the way you nearly stop breathing. I see every detail, Verena, and I want - no, need, you to know I feel the same way. You have given me a higher purpose than I had before. The thought of becoming alpha was dreary, something I never looked forward to. I never thought I would have the love my parents shared, how my father looked at my mother as if she were his entire world. I wanted it too, Verena. I wanted a mate who depended on me, one I could lean on when times were too hard to handle alone. Someone I could look forward to coming home to, watching them grow our children and raising them together. I had sanctioned myself to be alone. Most males my age already found their mates. I almost lost hope, yet here you are. You'd been here the whole time. Driving to my house weekly upon my father's request, you were right under my nose this whole time. But now I have found you, Verena, I will not let you go. Ever."

Verena was speechless, tears coming to her eyes at his confession. She never had someone feel this way about her. Someone who genuinely cared about her wellbeing. Verena was on the brink of coming apart thinking about his confession. There was nothing she could say to convey her thoughts properly, so she did the only thing she could think of. Verena reached to lace her hands behind his neck, crashing their lips together. Conveying how much she appreciated him as their mouths battled one another. Aven sank a knee into her mattress, the towel loosening deliciously. Letting his neck go, she found herself wandering towards the teetering fabric. Toying with its edges, she ran her nails across his barren waistline. Collecting the groans, he gave her into memory.

"We should get some sleep..." Aven dragged, a groan stopping him in his tracks when she dug her nails into his hips. She wanted more, needed more, she needed to feel a modicum in control of her life. "Verena..."

"Not now." Verena pleaded against his lips. "I need this. I need you."

"Verena, Love. As much as I want to, we shouldn't right now." Aven growled, gripping the sheets in a meagre attempt to control himself.

Ignoring him, she dug her nails in harder, using the leverage when he jumped to push forward, standing them both up. His towel dropped to the floor from the movement, his entirety bare for her, her hands running down the slope of his rear, melting into his moans. Verena tested her newfound strength when she turned them swiftly, breaking skin on his hips and throwing them both onto the bed. She landed on top of him, straddling his waist, his erection pressed into her covered core. A cry left her, heady and wistful. Aven's hands came to cup her ass, massaging the cloth covered muscle.

"Verena, Love. You need to rest." Aven wrapped his knee around her waist, flipping them back over, one hand coming to protect her head and the other on her waist. "Trust me when I tell you there is nothing more I want than to sink into you, hear you crying my name, and feel the way your skin feels against mine. But right now, your health is more important to me than my carnal desires."

"You're right," Verena admitted, releasing him as she looked up towards the ceiling, her body crying out from the rejection. "Let's just get some sleep, yeah? I need to meet with Heathrow soon for my training anyway." Aven nodded, walking off towards a pile of his clothes. Those which she hadn't noticed he deposited on the chair in the corner. Slipping on a pair of boxers, he came back to curl up next to her under the covers. Wrapping an arm across her waist to bring her back into his warm chest, Verena shivered at the heat, ignorant of how cold she was.

"I have to return to Gwendolyn tomorrow, Love. Do you need me to pick up anything?" Aven whispered against her shoulder.

"No. Thank you, though." Verena answered him after a period of quietness, thinking about if she needed anything. His answering snores made her roll her eyes in envy at how easily he could fall asleep. She began watching the molecules of energy floating around, imagining the figures they made in the air. Only when she knew Aven was completely asleep, did she uncurl herself from his arms and placed a pillow in them instead. Taking hold of the documents Armand left her, she tiptoed to the door, looking back once to see his chest rise and fall softly. Ensuring the hall was clear, she darted out, sticking to the edges of shadows in her journey to the meeting room. She had met Heathrow every night since Gracie had led her there the first night.

Chapter 38

VERENA

Heathrow studied the pages Verena brought with her, suspicion rising with each transaction she pointed out to him. Something was amiss, and he realised her concerns warranted an investigation. He had his suspicions, but he swore to keep it to himself until he could officially find evidence against them.

"I will look into these, Verena. The frequency of the transfers does raise questions, but the infrequent dates open up different questions." Heathrow neatly deposited the documents on the floor near the door, returning to where she stood once completed. "Give me a few days to look into these."

"Who do you think is responsible, Heath?"

"There are a few, but it is too early for me to be conclusive. I do not want to accuse the wrong person should it give the person responsible enough time to hide their tracks better."

"Okay." Verena agreed that if anyone could figure out what was happening, it would be Heathrow. "What are we doing today? I am unsure how much time I have before Aven wakes to find me missing."

"You have made great progress summoning your magic at will. Let us see if you can do so today without hesitation, and then we will move on to test your ability to remove runes." Heathrow sat on the ground before her, and Verena followed suit. Focusing diligently on where she knew magic resided within her, calling it forth. Pride rose as she could call upon it faster than ever. Her eyes flew open to see her guardian smiling happily at her. "Well done, Verena! I think this is a new record for you." Heathrow clapped, happiness filling her with his praise. "Now, call your magic back into you." Verena imagined the magic flowing back into the little box she pictured it living in, feeling the resistance it gave as if her magic wanted to be used. She could feel the sweat forming as she wrestled with the power, trying to force it behind the lock. While it raged against her, she felt her magic slip back into its confines. Acheron cawed from the branches above them. His presence soothed her, knowing he was cheering her on as well.

"It gave me a lot of trouble this time. Is it supposed to?" Verena struggled to catch her breath, wiping the sweat off her brow with the edge of her sleeve.

"Your magic is a part of you as much as the blood running through your veins. I believe you struggled more this time as your magic felt it needed to be used. We have been practising control for days now. Your magic is angry at being called upon but not utilised, which we will correct today when we begin removing runes." Heathrow drew the Silence rune, one Verena recognised easily by its intricately shaped 'S'. "You know this rune?"

"I do. The Silence rune was created by Shateiel, the Angel of Silence."

"Good. Now, I want you to reach out to the rune. Feel the magic and attempt to dissolve the rune. Now, Verena, this is uncharted territory for me, so I will not be able to assist you through this process. I can only assume dissolving the rune will feel much like untying a knot."

Verena closed her eyes, reaching towards the rune with her magic. She felt the rune's power, a field of energy against her delicate wisp. Mentally, she imagined her magic running around the field, attempting to find a weakness. Around and around, she felt, searching for an entry point to no success.

"What am I looking for, Heath? It feels like an invisible wall with no entry."

"Perhaps instead of trying to breach it, maybe try melding with it?" Heathrow threw out, grasping at straws.

She tried again, feeling for the hardened wall of magic. This time, she opened herself up to the magic and offered it an exit, to merge with her power. Her body jerked when she felt the energy reach out as if trying to wrap itself around her. Squeezing her roughly before Verena could not determine where her magic started, and the rune began. Pulling, she felt blood rushing down over her lips and cheeks. Bound and determined to accomplish the feat, she pulled against the rune. Her sheer determination fought the anger of the mysterious magic, battling with it, she tried to call not only her own but the runes magic into her.

Each passing second grew harder and harder, more blood dripping down her face onto her hands. Vaguely, she could feel Heathrow trying to shake her out of the trance she found herself in. She could see his face splattered with worry as if she was an onlooker. Blood poured from her nose, her ears and her eyes, but she wouldn't give in. Wouldn't give up. Until the last portion of the rune's magic was pulled into her, she watched the angry rune begin to fade until it was gone entirely. Only then did she feel as if she was slammed back into her own body. Her eyes opened, and she fell backwards as if an invisible force had shoved her.

"Did I do it?" Verena asked weakly, attempting to push herself back into her sitting position. Heathrow's hands came under her arms to assist her. He looked like he couldn't decide if he wanted to strangle her or hug her.

"I swear to hell, Verena, you are going to cause me an early death." Heathrow looked over her face, producing a handkerchief from out of nowhere, dabbing at the blood on her. "You did it, though. Look for yourself."

Verena peered around him. The rune on the ground was gone, replaced by a small cloud of smoke as if there was a dying fire.

Chapter 39

VERENA

"Come with me, Verena." Orla startled her, creeping up behind her without making a sound. "I have been tasked with taking you to Borraine to see Prince Kieran." Orla did not wait to see if Verena had followed.

It has been days since she absorbed her first rune. She had spent multiple days after recouping from the strain. Being next to Aven helped, but it wasn't enough. She needed both to heal. Heathrow's ire grew. He'd failed once to protect her, it would not happen again. Verena could hear him arguing with the other council members. He demanded they allow her to go through the portal, even threatening to fight the entire council should they refuse.

Verena was not one of them. They had no reason to keep her from her other mate. She could hear how angry Islabell became, stating Heathrow would give up their safety for Verena. The comment Islabell made angered Verena to the point where Aven had to physically restrain her from stalking into their meeting to slit the woman's throat.

Verena remembered Aven chuckling at her attempt to break free. The struggle she gave him earned her a new nickname from him. One which made her heart spike and core shake.

"See you soon, Vengeance." Aven strolled in, wrapped his arms around her waist, brought her to him and crushed his lips against hers. "Try not to kill him, please. I would prefer having the honour."

"I'm not going to kill him, Aven. You are not the only person I am bonded to, crazy ass. He's my mate as well." Verena fluttered her eyelashes, only partially irritated at his implication.

He can sure fucking try. Kieran growled in her head. Verena clamped her lips together in an attempt not to laugh aloud.

Aven mumbled something under his breath, sounding eerily similar to 'for now.' Verena smirked as she followed Orla out of the room. A bag she borrowed from Heathrow slung over her shoulder containing extra clothes, shower supplies and dried tea leaves. She was meant to spend a few days with Kieran in Borraine. Something about her soul needing both mates to fully recover. As Kieran was not allowed past the wards, Verena had to travel to him. She understood the reasoning, though she did not like it.

"I heard time moves differently in Borraine. Is that true, Orla?" Verena caught up with the woman, the height difference between them assisting with the task.

"It does." Orla was short and well-mannered, but Verena could tell she was unhappy to be there.

"Will someone come get me when I need to return?"

"I will."

"Okay." Verena started, irritated at the woman's answers. Someone else could have taken her if she had a problem with this. "Is there a problem between us?"

Here we go, Verena. You don't know how to keep your mouth shut, do you?

Orla ignored her, storming off faster towards the room Verena stumbled upon accidentally. Her body buzzed in excitement, knowing her Demon was on the other end of the portal. Her exceptionally moody, often murderous Demon Prince. It had been days since he had thrust his dagger into her to force their bond to heal her, the healing scar on her abdomen a stark reminder of the event. Days passed since she had seen him, against her desires. Verena had to beg Heathrow to force the other council members to let her use the portal. Eventually, she said she would go through it regardless of their opinions. She was granted two mates for a reason, and if it took two to wake her, then fuck all if they were going to keep her away from one but not the other.

"We are here." Orla was curt, pushing her arm out for Verena to take as they stopped in front of the glowing, jagged doorway Verena now knew was a portal between dimensions. "Take my arm then we will go through together. Sylvia is waiting for you on the other side."

Verena took the petite woman's arm, and without warning, Orla threw them into the portal. The awful feeling she had felt once before slammed into her. The perpetual feeling of being stretched and pulled just to be pushed back together caused her stomach to flip in a multitude of circles. She felt as if she would be sick. The feeling subsided as quickly as it came. Her feet touched solid ground. Her head spun wildly. Cold fingers reached out to stabilise her, a soothing voice she knew.

Sylvia.

"Hello, Verena." Seductive and sensual, Verena knew exactly where Kieran got it from.

"Hello, Sylvia." Verena smiled softly at the beautiful woman before her, her stomach still spinning.

"It gets better over time. Drink this." Sylvia handed her a glass full of a dark burgundy liquid. One Verena missed was in her hand. Or did she summon it out of thin air?

Verena took it gratefully, carefully allowing the smallest amount to hit her tongue, the bitter taste almost instantly calming the raging storm inside her belly. "Good, I can take her from here, Orla." Sylvia absently dismissed the wolf. Verena could hear Orla huff in annoyance but vanished back through the portal.

"She doesn't like me," Verena admitted out loud, confused about why she felt comfortable enough to talk.

"She is not a fan of most people, especially concerning Kieran." Sylvia took hold of Verena's arm, leading her away from the opulence, unlike the sanctum's portal room.

"Why not?" Verena could believe why many would not like Kieran, yet Orla tended to become angry when he was even mentioned in passing.

"I should let him tell you the reasoning, my dear." Sylvia gave her a weak smile. Clearly, the story was not pleasant.

The two continued their walk in silence. Verena took in the various paintings and photographs lining the walls. A variety of voices were heard as they passed numerous closed doorways. The roaming guards all stopped to show their respects before continuing. Verena noticed they paid particular attention to her, her status as a High Fae on clear display with her waist length hair twisted into a messy braid.

Heathrow had gifted her a large moon pin. One Gracie looped through the beginning of her braid at an angle. The large crescent shape contrasted with her brown locks. Sylvia stopped them in front of a moderately sized mahogany doorway. Muffled sounds of metal against metal snuck through the cracks. Verena watched Sylvia gently push the door open. Someone stood between a circle of at least a dozen men. She recognised the armour.

Kieran.

And he was winning. Or so it seemed, considering they were flying against the opposite wall at various speeds.

"Son." Syvlia's voice rang through the room.

Kieran didn't hear her. The sound of bodies crumpling overpowered the soft spoken woman. It wasn't until Sylvia caught a rogue sliver of metal, before it hit Verena, that the chaos stopped. Someone spotted the two, instantly sinking to a knee before them. Verena was not sure if it was for her or Sylvia. Once one sank, the rest followed, enough to where Kieran noticed in his tunnel vision haze. Pulling his helm off, Verena's entire core flooded with heat, his piercing red irises practically undressed her from where he stood. The distance between them vanished faster than she realised, simultaneously walking towards the other.

"You're here..." Verena could hear his helm drop to the ground, his gauntlets following suit. Bare hands cupped her ass, sweeping her off her feet, Verena's leg wrapped around his waist. The metal of his tasset dug into her upper thighs. She didn't care. Her body sizzled with energy, waiting to burst.

"I am," Verena confirmed, staring at him silently. Being here, with him, it felt right. It felt like home.

"I shall leave you two alone then." Sylvia laughed in her sing-song pitch, closing the door behind her. Verena didn't need to see her to know the expression she must have held. Kieran had yet to put her down, intent on ensuring Verena was actually there.

"Are you going to put me down anytime soon?" Verena ran her nails down his sweat slicked jaw, committing every scar, blemish and dimple on his chiselled face into memory.

"No." Kieran walked them over towards the doorway, latching the lock. "So nobody disturbs us."

"Disturbs us?" Verena looked down, recognising how high off the ground she was.

"Yes."

"Are you going to answer me without one word answers?"

"No." Verena huffed, squirming in his arms. "Keep trying, hellfire."

"Heathrow informed me you are going to teach me how to fight? He said something along the lines of him being too soft on me because of our relationship. He could not bear to hurt me."

"He did?" Kieran raised his eyebrow, setting her down in front of him.

Ensuring she was stable before he let her go and took a step back. Seductively, bending to unclasp the fastens on his cuisse and poleyn. Verena bit on one of her fingernails as she watched the performance. With each section of his armour hitting the ground, the fire in her core burned hotter and hotter. Until he stood before her in a sweat slicked tunic, hugging every curve of his body. Along with a tight fitting pair of trousers, doing nothing to hide the raging erection he held.

"My eyes are up here, Hellfire." Verena blushed as she had been caught appraising him.

"I know." Verena was smug, but she wasn't ashamed.

Chapter 40

VERENA

K ieran tossed her a short dagger, not waiting to see if she caught it before charging at her. He lunged at her nearly faster than she could see, faster than she had seen when first entering the room. Unarmed and without armour, Kieran still terrified her. His blood red eyes sang with glee. He was born, raised, and trained to be the right hand of an Archangel. What could Verena, a newfound High Fae, do against him? Against a machine that lived and breathed war? She was too slow. The dagger sliced down the palm of her hand, dropping to the floor. It all happened in a flash; she was too stunned to speak or even move. Crimson blood poured from her hand and onto the mat beneath her feet.

She was bleeding.

"How?" Verena whispered. Absorbed with the stinging pain and newfound injury, Verena had no choice but to watch the ceiling come into view. Kieran's hand braced her head as they both hit the ground hard.

"Verena, Love, you were supposed to defend yourself." Kieran flipped the two of them over so she straddled his hips. "What happened?"

"I'm bleeding, Kieran." Verena had yet to take her eyes off the gaping gash in her palm. "I'm bleeding?"

"You are." His tone was unmistakable, yet, at the same

time accidental. He found her question to be ridiculous and he couldn't even hide it on his face as he quirked up a brow.

"How?" Verena could not understand how he managed to cut her when Kessa couldn't.

"I do not understand."

"When I fought against Kessa, her blades did not break the skin. But yours did." Verena showed him her palm. "How?"

"I understand now." Kieran brought her bleeding hand to his lips, kissing each section. His lips, stained with her blood, made her eyes roll momentarily. "Our blades are made from Merytra, the same ore the Angels use."

"What do you mean?" Verena unconsciously ground her ass on him. His laps at her hand sent chills down her spine.

"Human metals cannot cut through your skin, love." Kieran kissed her wrist again, subtly bucking his hips to meet her.

Interesting.

Verena pushed herself off his waist, using his taut chest as leverage. Holding her hand out for him to take, Kieran took her offered appendage, pulling himself to a stand. Licking the remaining blood off his lips, his eyes flushed with desire. Taking his lapse in attention, Verena shoved, hard. Sweeping down to grab hold of the dagger she had dropped, allowing her body to take control as she flung the blade at him. His focus on the knife soaring at him, Verena used the full force of her shoulder to body the seven foot killer. The air in his lungs audibly exhaled, and a curt laugh exuded from his voluptuous lips.

"Vengeful little thing, aren't you?" Kieran's frame hitting the stone behind him ricocheted off the barren walls.

"Shall I change your name from Hellfire to Vengeance?"

Verena threw him an innocent smile, jumping backwards out of arm's reach. She might not have the training he did, might not be stronger, might not be faster, but what she did have was her size. Heathrow drilled it into her many times over the previous days in their early morning meetings. She was smaller and more agile, so as long as she stayed out of her opponent's ability to throw her around like a rag doll, she would have a fighting chance. Kieran summed up her outcome faster than she expected, his eyes flying around the room, taking her position in, his position to her and Verena could only guess at the rest. He lunged at her. Verena felt it was half-assed, testing her and judging her reflexes. She needed to be quicker, sharper, faster. He lunged again, and Verena ducked, barely escaping his fingertips.

"Okay, Hellfire. Is this how you wish to play?" Kieran circled her, raising goosebumps on her skin.

"I'm not playing any game, Kieran." Verena managed to stay out of his range, failing to notice he was corralling her into a corner.

"Watch your surroundings, Verena." Kieran parried to her right, forcing Verena to step left straight into the stone wall she had pushed him into. His body was against hers faster than Verena could comprehend. He held himself back, it angered her to be treated as if she were breakable.

"Caught you." Kieran whispered, the scent of him eliciting a small moan from her. Verena hated the effect he had on her. She was meant to be training. Even then, every portion of her wanted to feel his skin against hers.

"Are you holding back?" Verena seethed, her hands coming to push against his upper abdomen, her anger increasing when he did not budge.

"Of course I am, darling." Kieran's eyebrows scrunched, confusion etched across his handsome features.

"Why."

"Verena, darling, look at me. I mean, really look at me." Kieran nudged his head downwards, edging her to look at him. "Look at the size difference between us. I am two heads taller than you. I am broader than you. Verena, I was born to fight, to kill. It is who I am at my core. I am not saying you are not a worthy opponent; however, I could severely injure you if I am not careful. I will end the entire world should you ask it of me, my love. But do not ask me to hurt you, please, Verena." Kieran's voice wavered, begging.

"How am I going to learn then, Kieran? When my enemies are all bigger, stronger, faster? How will I come out on top?" Verena dropped her head against him, feeling his heart racing in his chest, the sound soothing to her ears.

"I will teach you, Verena." Kieran sank a hand into her hair, holding her to him. "While you are not built for war, you are more agile. Stay out of your opponent's reach, toy with them from the edges, wear them down, and when they are slowing, land your final strike." Taking hold of her hand, he pulled them towards a rack against the perpendicular wall. Lined from the top to bottom, encasing a quarter of the space, were rows upon rows of various weaponry. Verena could perhaps name a handful, but she could only guess at the rest.

"What are all these?" Verena gestured towards the wall, noticing every weapon was made of the same metal as the dagger.

"These are all common weapons from the present to the past millennia." Kieran gently dropped her hand, reaching to pluck a curved, longer sword from the wall. "I believe this would work best for you."

"What is it?" Verena held her hand out to take it from him. The weight, or lack thereof, shocked her. "It's light, really light."

"This is a rapier. The design is meant to remain light. Mostly used by mounted warriors, the blade is designed to arc in the way your arm would when striking from a mount. Think of it as an extension of your arm, Hellfire. Keep your enemy on the opposite of your blade. Do not let them past the radius of your arm. Allow the blade to do the work." Kieran shifted to stand behind her, taking hold of her hands and raising their arms. Using his foot, he pushed her feet farther apart. Her left foot was pushed forward while her right remained where it was. His knee pressed gently into the back of her right knee, bending it slightly. "Keep the majority of your weight on your back leg. Only strike when you have a clear line. Always return to this position."

Verena allowed her body to go slack, letting him control her movements from behind her. She vaguely paid attention to the motions he was putting her body through. Her mind paid more attention to the way his body heated hers, the way his breath ghosted by her ears. Remembering the first time she met him in her dreams. The seductive way his voice sounded in her ears forced a roll of her hips against his. His instructions fell upon deaf ears, her attention captured by his sheer presence behind her.

"Focus, Hellfire," Kieran whispered, his lips nipping at her ears, shocking her out of her trance. "Can you do that for me?" Verena nodded, shifting her focus towards the rapier in her hands. "Again." She felt him let go of her hands. Her body went through the motions he had taken her through while she was distracted.

"Good, now apply it." Kieran snapped a different type of sword. Verena didn't know the name of the weapon off the wall, but the way he handled it told her he was familiar with it.

Kieran didn't wait, didn't ask if she was ready. His massive sword swung high over her head and was brought down rapidly. Verena barely had time to block it with her own, the force of the strike groaning through her joints.

"Don't think, Verena. Your body knows what to do." Kieran struck again, this time using a foot to sweep out at hers. She dodged it, leaping towards the side, coming face to face with the hilt of the sword at her throat.

"You're dead." Kieran gently tapped her, stepping back after. "Again."

Same as the last, he did not wait for her to be ready. Her pulse raced, her breathing became strained, her magic stirred. Thrusting his sword low, Verena parried it only to watch him toss the weapon to his other hand. Again, she was tapped with the hilt of his sword at her abdomen.

"Dead."

Verena growled. The unnatural sound surprised her. She was getting angrier with each passing second. Another parry, another tap with his hilt. She was dead, again and again. Her body would be heavily bruised from the amount of times he tapped her. After she lost count of the number of times he bested her, her patience snapped. Kieran lunged head on at her, her rapier crashed with his, and her control over her magic snapped. One moment, she was staring at his beautiful red eyes. The next, every weapon in the room surrounded him, inches from his skin.

"Well done, Hellfire." Kieran's face held a prideful smile.

"Well done?" Verena felt her magic slink back, the room

screaming with sounds as metal fell to the ground.

"You utilised every option within your abilities and won."

"But I cheated? I used magic."

"War has no honour, hellfire. You use everything you have to walk out of there alive." Kieran took the rapier from her hand, dropping it onto the ground with the rest. "You do whatever you have to." Kieran took her into his arms once more, ignoring how drenched in sweat she was. "Whatever you have to, do you hear me?" He gave her no option to respond as his lips crashed to hers for the first time. In reality, she felt like her whole body was lit on fire.

Chapter 41

KIERAN

His body crashed against hers, hardened muscle against hardened muscle. It was wrong; he knew it, she understood it, and they didn't care. She found her mate, taboo as it was, but she still found the one she was meant for. Only by chance, Kieran wouldn't say it was fate. He didn't believe in the damned thing. Fate had nothing to do with his situation, nothing to do with his life. He forged his path, the bullshit they called fate was for those who believed good things happen to good people. And he was most definitely not good. The countless bodies he had ripped through, the endless amount of blood he had spilt, the deals he had made, they rivalled his Lady. But with her, he forgot it all. She was as demented as he, killed as much as he. They found a mutual understanding in their carnage.

"Fuck..." Kieran panted, a hand dug into the bottom of her neck, entangling her curls. "We shouldn't do this."

"We shouldn't." She answered in kind, sinking her nails under his shoulder blades.

"I don't know how to stop." Another hand cupped her ass, heaving her up. She was a head shorter than he, but he would wager almost as ruthless. Her discarded armour was just as blood stained as his. Her dual swords, covered in various stages of drying gore, tossed against the wood beams of his tent. His own was a handful of inches away, where they were dropped in their haste. Pieces of their armour were thrown about as they had torn it off the other in need.

"So don't." Her sharpened canines sank into his lower lip, sucking it into her mouth with a delicious moan.

"Delaney..." Kieran's eyes rolled back, dropping her in the process. She took advantage of it, swinging her legs to hook them around his neck. Momentum took them, his close to eight foot height crashed to the ground. The laughter she released caused his empty heart to race in excitement.

"Kieran." Her voice wavered releasing him from his blissful hold, eyes focusing back onto her. A hand clutched against her abdomen, blood poured out of it. Concern and worry were etched on her face, but not for herself.

"Delaney!" Kieran shouted, scrambling to get up, to get help. "Healer!"

"Kieran..." One of her blood covered hands came to rest upon his face, his own cupping it to him harder. He couldn't lose her, couldn't let her go. Somebody had to be there to help her. Nobody was coming. Why weren't they coming?

"Healer!" Kieran shouted again. Where the fuck were they?

"It's alright, Kieran. I'm ready." She tried to comfort him. When did she move to sit between his legs? When had she placed her back against his chest?

"You can't leave me. Not yet." Kieran sobbed, his Del lashed against everything, setting the entire tent ablaze.

"Kieran..." She choked out. "You're hurting me."

"I can't lose you." Kieran cried, tears streaming down his face. "I can't."

"Kieran. Stop." She thrashed against him, clawing at his

hands. "Kieran. I can't breathe." Her voice came out in whispers.

"Verena?" The fabric walls of his tent faded to stone, and Delaney was nowhere to be found. Instead, Verena, his Verena, her body held her tightly against him. "Fuck, Verena. I'm sorry."

"Kieran..." Verena coughed. He released her, air flooding back into her lungs caused her head to spin. "Kieran?"

"Fuck. I'm sorry." He let her go, pushing himself away from her. Terrified of her seeing him. Terrified for her. "I'm sorry."

Verena looked at him, her hands clutching herself protectively, she was scared. He could see it written all over her, how she held herself from him. He scared her, he deserved every inkling of ire she threw his way. His head lowered, ashamed. He couldn't look her in the eyes. He didn't want her to see him like this. She didn't know what to say, didn't know how to say it. With each step she took towards him, he took one backwards, fleeing. She took another, and another, until his back was pressed against the wall with nowhere to run. Only then did she reach out for him, her hands shaking. Instinctively, she knew he needed her, needed the contact. So she gave it to him, wrapping her arms around his shaking torso. Her head barely came up to his chest as she laid it on him, rubbing circles into his back.

"What is going on?" Verena looked up, she wished she was taller so she could look into his eyes. He was pertinently ignoring her, looking anywhere but down. "Look at me." Verena demanded, pressing harder into him, trying to gain his attention.

"I can't, Verena. I don't know how to start. How to begin." Kieran admitted, though it sounded painful, Verena suspected he didn't want to let her in.

"How about we start at who Delaney is?" Verena tugged on his tunic, he looked down at her, tears filled his eyes.

"She was—" Kieran hiccoughed, stumbling over his words. "She was my best friend, my confidant, my lover, my top General, and I lost her."

"Okay." Her jealousy spiked, but she knew it was unwarranted. Verena knew this was a part of his past; she shouldn't feel jealousy over someone who was deceased. "How did you lose her?"

"It was during the war." Kieran sank to his knees. Verena followed, his head resting against her shoulder. She stroked his soft, white strands of hair, matted in sweat. "I couldn't stop it."

"Couldn't stop what?"

"We were at war. I couldn't stop the arrow coming. It was coming right towards me, and she stepped in front of it. She took the arrow coming for me instead. I lost something that day, something I hadn't found until you stumbled into my head weeks ago." Kieran's red eyes met hers. The look he gave her would haunt her for eternity. "You walking into my life, after all these years, is why I continue fighting. I need you more than you know, Verena."

"What happened on the battlefield was not your fault, Kieran." Verena wiped the tears falling down his cheeks away with the pad of her thumbs. "You were in a war, fighting. You knew the risks. You understood people would die. Delaney did what she had to. She did it for you. She knew what she was doing, and I bet she would do it again, without hesitation."

He did not respond, could not respond, surging forward to bring their lips together. Verena was shocked and unmoving. Her body reacted on its own as she fought with him for dominance. She knew he was trying to distract her, perhaps more so to distract himself. She didn't care, not right then. They could return to the conversation later, when he had calmed. Her nails ripped his tunic apart, his answering growl evident of his need. The way his tongue forced a mewl from her sent sparks down her core.

"I need you." Kieran's voice, deeper than ever, huskier, needier. "Now."

He left no room for negotiation. No room for protest, though she knew if she wanted to refute, he would obey without hesitation. Confident in his respect for her, Verena allowed his exploratory hands to grab hold of her fabric covered ass. He brought them to his feet. She weighed nothing to him, a porcelain doll. He didn't look around. His feet knew where they were taking him. Absently fumbling with the lock on the room's door, they groaned in protest at the force he exerted in opening them. Verena watched as those in the hallway eyes bulged, not expecting their respected leader to be emerging with her in tow. Her legs wrapped around his half bare torso, shirt torn in patches, hair tousled and the small Fae woman he held to him. Their immediate bowed heads answered Verena's unsaid question: the entire damn house would know about her momentarily. She couldn't find it in herself to care. Her mind was overcome with pure need for him as he strode down the hallway to a room she recognised from her dreams.

His.

Chapter 42

VERENA

His lips caressed every inch of her skin, running fire through her veins with each needy press of his mouth. Every nip of his teeth sent wave after wave of pleasure to her core, so heedy she could feel herself seeping through her leggings. Kieran's answering, feral, growl was the lid to her self-conscious jar. He wanted her, needed her; she was enough for him. The door behind them rattled off the frame, crashing to the ground. Verena could hear tiny little shouts of terror from above her. She could not be bothered at the moment. One second, her body was pressed against his, legs wrapped around his large torso, his hands holding her ass against him. Without warning, she was airborne, landing on her back in the middle of the bed. Pillows flew everywhere. She looked up at him. He embodied what Verena would later compare to a wild animal in heat, his red eyes sparkled with mischief, hunger and lust.

"Have I told you how utterly fucking perfect you are?" Kieran groaned, shredding the last remnants of his tunic off of himself. Verena drooled, catching the saliva with the back of her hand, blushing. "Oh no, Mia Cara, give me all of it." Stalking towards her like she was a pool of water and he was a dying man.

"Kieran..." Verena looked back towards the broken

doorway, the obvious passerbys peering around the corners, intrigued. "People are watching." Verena nudged her head in their direction, blushing.

"Let them." Kieran gripped her ankles, giving her a quick pull towards him, her legs dangling off the edge of his bed. "Let them watch, Mia Cara. Let them wish to be in your place."

Verena watched in embarrassment as he dropped to his knees, hard. The reverberation of the drop she could feel in her bones, and the audible gasp from the hall confirmed the onlookers felt it too. She didn't dare look towards them. Couldn't let them witness her embarrassment. And Verena was exceptionally embarrassed. Kieran gripped the top of her leggings, hooking his nails into them and pulled. Hard. Her seams gave, splitting in two as her bare legs came into view. She couldn't find undergarments before going through the portal with Orla, so she went without. Verena was positive her cheeks could not have gotten any darker, yet here Kieran was, making her flush like a tomato.

"Fuck, Hellfire." Kieran dropped his head back, looking up towards the ceiling. His low rumble shook through her. His laboured breathing sent chills to her now exposed centre. She shivered. "You are heavenly."

"Kieran," Verena whined, squirming, trying to close her open legs at her knees. "They are still watching."

"You are my woman. In my bed. With my head in between your legs." Kieran grabbed the underside of her knees, pushing them outward and closer to him. His tongue flicked out, teasingly. Verena cried. The barest of warm flesh against her core sent her over. "Let them fucking watch."

He gave her no room to argue, his hands snaked under her hips, his tongue drawing circles around her clit, intensifying with each cry she let loose. Verena was so lost in her screams she didn't hear him, if he even said anything before he shrugged her legs farther around his neck. Heaving them both up from their position, Verena momentarily panicked. She was well over seven feet in the air, her legs sitting on his shoulders, his hands dug into her hips, holding her core into place at mouth level. He showed no signs of struggle, no sign of potentially dropping her. Verena laced her fingers into the base of his hairline and sunk in. She could feel the warmth of his blood pouring around her nails. He bucked roughly, startled, aroused; his answering smirk was enough of a warning to her as he sank his fangs into her clit. Verena hollered, head thrown back, her hair inches from covering the exceptionally large tent in his trousers. Her white tattoos began glowing, steadily growing brighter and brighter. Nearly blinding.

"Oh my, hell." Verena groaned, shaking as her body neared climax. One she was denied when he suddenly removed his mouth from her. Those devilish red eyes looking up at her, his lips smeared in her burgundy blood, gave him an ethereal appearance. Verena hadn't a damn clue how she ended up in this man's arms but fuck all, if she had an auditorium full audience, she didn't care.

"We haven't even begun, Hellfire." Kieran's full fanged smile was enough to send Verena into another coma. She would have, too, if her back had not slammed against the wall opposite the doorway. She reached up. Something metal hung above her. She couldn't be bothered to check. Grabbing hold, Verena looked forward as Kieran resumed his unrelenting onslaught. Standing near the edge of the doorway were the most eerie looking black eyes, staring at her. And they were seething. Verena looked them up and down, dramatically increasing her moans. Something overcame her, something she would chalk up to, claiming her territory when she smirked at them. Kieran's large frame had her hidden entirely, except for the wide expanse of ink snaking down her legs and the vague outline of them on her hips.

"I'm so close." Verena let go of the metal bar, one hand fingering his hair while the other grabbed his shoulder for support. "Oh. Fuck. Kieran." Verena screamed, teetering on the edge.

"Let go, baby girl." Kieran hummed; the motion sent her overboard. Her legs clamped around his neck, involuntarily squeezing. Eyes closed, body spasmed, heart raced, Verena tumbled over the crest. Her screams reached a higher pitch than she had ever heard her throat make, echoing his faint praises. "Good girl."

Kieran gently brought her down to his waist, tucking her legs around him and smiled. He was sinful, deadly, and just had his tongue shoved so far into her she almost orgasmed from the thought of it. She pressed her cheek to his chest, panting hard. Kieran looked behind him, staring down the onlookers until Verena could hear the sizzling crackle of a fire. Peaking around his bicep, she blinked rapidly at the sight of an entire wall of blue flames covering the entryway where the door should have stood. Except it was now sitting on the ground, but in cinders.

"Verena." One of Kieran's hands came underneath her chin, directing her face to look at him. He didn't drop it. "You are delectable."

She almost fainted.

Did he just say that?

"I did. Indeed." Kieran chuckled, walking them over to his crumpled bed.

"Stop reading my mind." Verena blushed again. At this

point, she might as well be a tomato.

He didn't respond, only placed her on the bed, stepping back to watch her scramble towards the headboard. Verena watched him edge his fingers into his waistband, teasing her with his little seductive pulls downward. More and more of his skin became exposed. The edges of black ink she hadn't noticed played peek-a-boo on the side of his ribcage. Verena only noticed it due to a small portion of it wrapping around his hip.

"Like what you see?" Kieran did a slow turn, showcasing his ink proudly. An enormous, continuous black design ran from the top of his left shoulder, down his rib cage and disappeared into his waistband. Verena recognised some of the runes she had been studying back at the sanctum, noticing the most prominent one located near the pit of his arm: Death Call. Between the runes were various intense shades of ink, like whispers of the shadows, paint spilled on paper. As he began to reach for her, Verena caught sight of the glowing black rune on a gold cuff. She must have missed it before. She swore it wasn't there. She knew the rune well, having seen it in the vision of Torvan, her mother had shown her.

Chapter 43

VERENA

*M*arked.

"Kieran." Verena pushed up against the bedding to sit up straighter. "Kieran. Look at me."

"What is the matter, Hellfire?" He turned to her, worry etched in his stance and tone. Striding over to perch on the edge of the bed nearest her, his head tilted, trying to assess if she was hurt.

"You were Marked..." Verena trailed off, remembering the information on the rune from her book. "You were in the war."

"I was."

"How are you able to be here?" Verena waved her hands around the room, confusion written everywhere. "The conditions of the rune. Kieran. How the fuck are you able to be here?"

"You know about them." Kieran sighed, rubbing his temples. "I am Marked. Many of us in the war were. At least those of us who fought under the Mordinians were."

"Why?" Verena's anger rose, and she pulled a pillow to cover herself. She thought about throwing it at him. "Why would you fight for THEM!" She seethed, the people responsible for her entire fucked up life, and he fought for them. Killed for them.

"Verena..." Kieran reached for her, flinching as she slunk

away from him. "I deserve this. I do. But give me the chance to explain?"

"Why should I?" Verena snatched his wrist with the rune etched upon the cuff. "This tells me everything I need to know. You were punished by the Creators for your actions. So what is there to explain?"

"There are multiple answers to the same question, Verena. At least let me tell you mine before judging too hard?" Kieran begged her, desperate for her ear. Hoping she would at least listen to him. Why should she, though? The voices in her head argued. It was her mothers she listened to. The one telling her to give him a moment to explain. As if her mother knew this would happen and was prepared.

"Okay. But I cannot promise I won't be judging you." Verena was being childish, petty, whatever they called it. She didn't care. She would listen. She couldn't promise she'd like what he said, though.

"I deserve that, too." Kieran shrugged his shoulders lightly, a smile tugging at the corners of his lips. "What have you been told about the war?"

"Heathrow has vaguely told me how it started, how I came to be and how he managed to escape to Alusso with me in tow." Verena eyeballed him, waiting for him to tell her it was all a damn lie, and she couldn't trust him. It wouldn't surprise her if he did.

"Okay. It's at least a start." Kieran got up, and the weight of him leaving the bed shifted her marginally. She watched his toned back walk away from her towards a doorway. The fire cackled angrily where his bedroom door had stood, still burning brightly. Keeping the onlookers at arm's length, their curiosity peaked. She watched him open the door, step in momentarily and then return with a piece of fabric in his hands. As he approached, Verena saw they were a pair of pants. For her? "Put these on, please. The sight of you drives me rabid, and I believe you would prefer I could tell you the truth without being distracted." He placed the oversized trousers on the bed next to her, turning around to give her a sense of privacy. Or perhaps so she could put them on without him losing control. She did as he asked, clearing her throat when she sat back down. Tucked under a red throw blanket he had across his headboard, her back against the fluffy pillows.

"The Mordinians started the war when your mother rejected Torvan. She refused to marry and bond with him. I believe she saw something that gave her pause, or perhaps he showed his true self at the wrong time. He and his mother concocted a plan to 'kill' him. If he died, they could demand Jerifeyn marry his brother to fulfil the contract between the families. If she refused again, it would give them cause to declare war." Kieran took a deep breath, ashamed of his actions in the war. He wouldn't leave anything out. She deserved the truth. Verena waited, impatiently, but she waited nonetheless. "How much do you know about Demons and our creation?" Kieran threw her off with his question. She didn't want to admit she knew little.

"Only what you have told me," Verena admitted, blushing.

"Demons were created by the Morningstar and our Lady, Archangel Azrael, to be warriors, fighters, killers. We were created without emotion, without the capability to feel, we were the perfect weapons. We followed orders, and when we died, we were reborn at the lowest level of Hell: Koth. Once reborn, we would spend millennia rising through the levels to return to Borraine. It wasn't until our

Lady fell that she granted us the ability to feel, to be able to love and marry, procreate and mate. We do not know the specifics of how. There are many theories, but none of them make sense." Kieran twisted to face her, looking Verena in the eyes. Those beautiful red pupils flickered with a sense of magic.

"She gave you a soul…" Verena whispered, the words flying out of her mouth before she could register what she said.

"She did." Kieran nodded, a prideful smile on his face. "Demons with a soul—it was unheard of. It also opened up an entirely new set of problems. Not only were we given the ability to feel and make our own choices, but the Sinclaves figured out how to summon us. Previously, only the Morningstar and our Lady could do so. With Demons possessing a soul, they have found a way to do the same."

"Hold on. You're telling me High Fae were able to summon Demons? As in, like what you read in storybooks? The whole 'Know Their True Name' and bind a Demon into a pact?" Verena was amused; the entire thing could not be real. Kieran laughed. For real, this time, a full-bodied laugh shook through his large frame.

"No, my love. Not even close." Kieran chuckled again, finding her hilarious. "Demons were able to be summoned by the Morningstar and our Lady due to the blood running through our veins being the same as theirs. We were created through their blood; therefore, we were a part of them. I theorise the Sinclaves, in their medical expertise, were able to pinpoint the exact portion within the blood the Mordinians share with us to mimic a summoning by our Lady." Kieran took her hand, pushing her fingers down until her index was left. Verena nearly jerked her hand back when he dragged her nail across his palm, splitting the skin open.

"Somewhere within my blood and your own, our genetics match. We both have my Lady's genetics coursing through us. And the damn Sinclaves figured out how to extract just hers. Once we were summoned, we were stuck, trapped in their plane until we agreed to their conditions. Only then did they release us from our bloody prison so we could return to Borraine. This is how the Demon army was bound to the Mordinians." Kieran stopped; Verena saw a singular tear breaking free and running down his cheek. She wanted to reach out to comfort him, to show him it was acceptable to cry. But she didn't, couldn't.

"How does this mean you had no choice? You just said if a Demon dies, they are reborn. You had a choice, Kieran." Verena's voice increased; there was no way he was telling her this right then.

"If it was up to me, Hellfire. I would have rather taken my own life than subject my people to this." Kieran ran his hand down the right side of his body. A shimmer of magic flushed through her as rune-like markings appeared before her eyes. Hidden by magic, not even she could have sensed, thousands upon thousands of small markings littered his right rib cage. Wisps of inky shadows flitted between them, a language she couldn't decipher. "They summoned my father, binding him to their plane for centuries until he agreed to their demands. Only after summoning my mother and torturing her for years did he cave. Forcing everyone under him to servitude." He was crying now. The tears streamed down his face at the memory. Verena knew this would haunt her for eternity, the way he looked at her as if she wasn't there. Like he was living in his own personal hell, and she was a figment of his imagination.

"What are these?" Verena tentatively reached out, her fingertips ghosting the ink he revealed to her.

"Every single Demon's name I have lost since we were forced into this hell." Kieran gently took hold of her wrist, pulling her fingers to his skin. Allowing her to explore the ink, he moved as she pushed and prodded, giving her full access to see them. "Every Demon who has died because of my father I have inked onto me, a promise their death would not be in vain."

"Kieran..." Verena looked up at him, an apology on her tongue. One she didn't get to say when his finger pressed against her lips.

"I know what you are going to say, but it is not necessary. I deserve every inkling of your hatred, of your anger. Because of my father, yours is dead, and I will never be able to formulate an apology worth your forgiveness." Kieran rubbed his thumb against her cheek. She leaned into it. Knowing he was right, yet wanting him to be wrong.

"Their deaths are not on you, Kieran. They died protecting me, fighting for me, to give me a chance at life. You did nothing to them." Verena laced her hand with his, trying to convey how her heart felt through the smallest of gestures.

"But I did, Verena." Kieran gave her a weak smile, continuing his massage of her cheek with his thumb. "I am why your parents did not stand a chance at survival. Because of me, your parents' defences were obliterated. I am a killer, Verena. I was created to kill, and Verena, I am extremely good at killing. I was selfish, Verena. I did what I was told, and I did it well."

"You were forced into it, Kieran." Verena insisted. "I don't blame you."

"But you should. I could have done something. I should

have done something."

"What could you have done? If you didn't obey, would more people have died? If you didn't follow orders, what would have happened?" Verena shook his hand off her, her own coming under his chin to push his head towards her. To make him look her in the eyes. She didn't know when the roles were reversed. When she started to care. When the anger, the hatred, the fear, subsided. "If you didn't obey, more names would be on your list, Kieran. How many more would be inked on your body? If they could kill your mother, who else would they have killed until they found someone who would obey? Did you send oblivious men, women, and children to war? Those who were not trained to fight? Or did you send those who knew the consequences, knew there was a chance they would be punished or killed? Because if it wasn't you who didn't follow those sadistic fucks orders, someone else would have, and more would be dead. Right? You fought for the wrong side, yes. But you fought to protect your people as well. Did you not?"

Kieran looked at her, seeing the way her mind was set. Seeing how he knew she held no hatred in her heart at his confession. The unbridled love he had for her flourished into something more, something concrete. With every action he had made and every life he had taken, he swore to his Lady that he would do it all over again if it meant he would get to be here with her, again and again. To know she saw him, saw his past and did not judge him for the path he had been forced on. Her acceptance of him was the catalyst he needed to heal, to forgive himself and his father for being the reason he was a murderer to begin with.

"I did." He admitted, something he never thought of in this way. Always blaming himself for the things he has done and never seeing the outcomes. Never seeing those he was protecting by doing what he was told when he was told. He had only seen the death and destruction, the lives of his foes vanishing beneath his blade.

"Then, I do not blame you. Because I would have done the same." Verena whispered, her answer concrete.

"I don't deserve you, Verena."

"You don't, you're right." Verena leaned forward, inches from him. "But you can earn the right to."

Chapter 44

VERENA

K ieran extended a hand towards her, levelling her with a suspicious look, one Verena didn't know him well enough to place. The crackling of the fire in the doorway stopped, and Verena could see the flames subsiding, dying down. Scorch marks scarred the surroundings but didn't veer farther than the fire's location. Verena was impressed. He snapped his fingers, a litany of profanity left his mouth when a team of men and women rushed into the room in answer. Verena slunk behind his large frame, embarrassment filling her. Meeting the eyes of some, they were filled with a variety of emotions: envy, rage, sadness, and the most confusing, lust.

"Find Verena something to wear and get cleaned," Kieran ordered; his command was revered, and everyone in the room held him in the highest regard. "Also, in her bag are dried tea leaves. Process them and make her a cup. She is still recovering and requires it twice a day while she is here."

"Of course, sir."

"Right away."

Various sounds of affirmation filled Verena's ears. Nowhere could she hear a single person being disrespectful.

"Verena, Darling, the door to the left is the bathroom. Illiria will follow you to get the facilities in order. She will assist you while you are here. Things here may be different than in Alusso; let her help. She nearly took my head when I attempted to refute earlier." Kieran motioned towards the door he referred to, then the tall, beautiful, milk chocolate skinned woman he called Illiria. She was stunning, her gold eyes rimmed with full, dark lashes. Her hair was wild and free, and white smooth silk fabric accented with sparkling red jewels pulled the look together completely. Large gold cuffs decorated her arms, and her dainty fingers were littered with gold rings to match her well-manicured nails. Jealousy flooded Verena at the stunning woman walking towards her.

"Your Highness." Illiria's voice sounded of hummingbirds, soft and sweet, perfection.

"Verena is fine." She choked out, stumbling on her words at what to say. "You are gorgeous." Illiria laughed. Verena blushed when she heard the remaining attendants in the room laugh as well.

"Thank you, Verena." Verena's name was a question on the woman's lips like she was not used to addressing people by their names, as if it was taboo. "Have you seen yourself, though?"

"I think I'm going to like you just fine." Verena bounced off the bed, happy to have found someone who could match her quirkiness. "Shall we? Any longer, and I might have to fight Kieran for your attention." She stuck her elbow out towards Illiria, hoping the woman would take the offer. Using her thumb, she indicated where Kieran was still, baffled, sitting on the bed.

"No, thank you. He has the wrong parts and way too much attitude for me." Illiria laughed again. The sound was musical. She linked her arm through Verena's, pulling her towards the bathroom.

"I do not have an attitude!" Kieran protested, but his words fell on deaf ears as he watched the pair stroll off towards his bathroom.

"You do." Verena and Illiria said in unison unexpectedly, bursting out in laughter afterwards. The door slammed shut after they crossed the threshold.

"They are going to be the death of me." Kieran rubbed the bridge of his nose, as a headache was incoming.

"Most likely." Apsephion slunk from the edges of the room, his ability to manipulate the shadows a unique gift in his familiar line. One Kieran had taken advantage of many times throughout their lives.

"When did you get in?" Kieran did not need to glance at him to know where Apsephion was, knowing the man's signature well enough after all these centuries together.

"A few moments before you broke the door down." Sep admitted, albeit reluctantly, he knew Kieran would recognise what that entailed.

"Oh."

"I turned around." He rushed to get out before Kieran's infamous anger got the best of him, Sep did not know how Kieran would react should his Demonic side take over.

"I hope so, Apsephion. I'd hate to have to kill you for seeing her in such a state." Kieran growled jokingly to his second in command.

"You could try, old man." Apsephion twirled his fingers tauntingly, the shadows around him inching closer.

"Who are you calling old?" Kieran raised an eyebrow, pushing off the bedside to rise to his intimidating height.

"You." Illiria's voice broke through the two, and both men's heads whipped around to where she stood. "Also, why didn't you tell me High Fae were so damned beautiful?" She crossed her arms, demanding an answer from the two of them.

"Because of that." Kieran pointed at the way she was standing. "Right there. Exactly that. You'd try to slither your way into stealing my mate."

"I would not." Illiria protested, moving out of the way of Verena, who gently tapped on her shoulder.

"You definitely-" Kieran's sentence was cut off as Verena moved into his eyesight. "Thank you, My Lady." He praised his Lady for sending the absolute powerhouse of a woman standing before them.

Her long hair twisted into an elegant updo, strands fell loose to frame her face. His extraordinary mate was dressed in a daringly low-cut, deep burgundy dress, the bodice sheer except for the top, where the outline of stars covered her breasts. Falling to her ankles, the dress flared to expose a high slit. The fabric looked as if the seamstress captured the stars and forced them into submission for the dress. Various astrology signs were sewn in with gold thread, twinkling from the gems used to create the stars. Verena's white astrology tattoos were highlighted by the deep red of the fabric against her skin. She looked like the walking night sky; her eyes flared with life. To bring it all together, Kieran could see the Meklatine gem necklace nuzzled between the tops of her silky breasts. The gem glowed happily as if it had found its owner.

"Verena, Darling, you take my breath away." Kieran walked to her, dropping to his knees before her, looking to meet her gaze. "I cannot believe you are mine, but I am eternally grateful you are."

"Your Highness." Apsephion dropped to a knee, following Kieran, lowering his head in submission.

"Who are you?" Verena tilted her head at the strange man who dropped to his knees behind Kieran.

Are all Demons this damn good looking?

He was tall, by the looks of it, but he didn't come as close to Kieran's height. The man looked as if he hadn't seen the sun in years with how pasty his skin was. His loose fitting tunic ended around his elbows, exposing black ink. Verena couldn't quite make out the details from where she was. Dark, almost black, curly hair sat atop his ridiculously angled face. Bright, nearly white, blue eyes met hers as he looked up at her. A nervous and toothy smile showcased his equally scary looking fangs.

"This is Apsephion, Kieran's second-in-command, Borraine's greatest spy, and the third most deadly Demon alive," Illiria answered her, stepping towards the man and pushing against his shoulder.

"And who is the second then? If Kieran is the first?"

"Well, me, of course." Illiria pointed towards herself.

"Ah, of course. Of course." Verena smiled.

"Well, are you going to get up anytime soon, Sep? Or are you going to be on your knees all day? I think I can find a sponge for you to make yourself useful down there if so." Illiria bent down to look at him, stumbling backwards when he stood up.

"Over my dead body, will I ever scrub the floors after you again." Apsephion mumbled, glaring at the Demon woman.

"I can arrange it for you." Illiria punched him playfully.

"You two never stop, do you?" Kieran sighed again, following suit to stand next to Verena. "Where is Orias?"

"He said he would meet us at Tyvarn's." Apsephion ignored Illiria, who pushed on him as he walked towards the balcony. "Shall we?"

Illiria took the hand offered gingerly, as if she couldn't stand being touched or perhaps couldn't stand needing assistance. Verena couldn't tell, but she almost had a heart attack when the pair jumped over the railing. Rushing over to peer over the side, Verena watched as the two landed gracefully on the blackened ground below. Illiria looked back to wave at her, encouraging?

"What the hell?" Verena looked back at Kieran, baffled, scared and slightly amused at the prospect of jumping. "They jumped?"

"They did. We are."

"Wait, what?" Before she could react, Kieran surged forward faster than she could see. Her previous feet planted on the floor were suddenly in the air and falling. Falling?

"Oh, my hell. KIERAN!" Verena pressed her face into his shoulder, eyes firmly closed, and she was definitely screaming. She was going to kill him once they were on the ground.

"You can open your eyes now, Hellfire." Kieran was amused. Verena was still screaming.

"Are we dead?" She opened one eye, looking over his shoulder. When had they landed?

"No." He laughed, setting her down softly.

"What the fuck were you thinking?" Verena punched him in the shoulder as hard as she could muster. She was positive that it probably felt like a child was hitting him based on his lack of reaction. "You just fucking jumped. JUMPED. Off of a balcony. JUMPED, KIERAN. YOU JUMPED. WITH ME IN TOW."

"I did."

"Why?" Verena wanted to hit him for almost putting her in the grave early.

"Verena, darling, look behind you." Kieran took her by the shoulders and spun her around. "How else are we to get out of the house?"

Verena opened her mouth and then promptly shut it when she noticed there was literally no entry to the home. The house sat upon a bloody mountaintop with no access to the damn thing except for the various windows and balconies.

"Oh."

"Oh, indeed." Kieran took her hand, softly pulling her towards where Apsephion and Illiria stood waiting for them. "Are you fine to continue towards the city, or would you like to hit me again?"

"I am still trying to decide if I want to push you off a mountain currently."

"Well, when you come up with an answer, let me know. I can take you to the nearest one for you to push me off of. Until then, let's go, shall we? I'm starving, and there are some shops I'd like to show you."

"We are stopping at Hel-Vanity, Kieran. You're buying." Illiria snatched Verena's hand away from him, taking hold of it with both of hers, tugging Verena towards the city below them.

"I expected nothing less, Illiria." Kieran rolled his eyes, joining Apsephion in the back as he watched his mate get dragged forward. Her head turned back towards him, and her eyes practically screamed, 'Where are we going?' She followed the energetic Demon dragging her forward, closer and closer to the bustling city, the buildings growing larger and larger as they drew closer.

Chapter 45

VERENA

Dark, ominous buildings made from obsidian loomed all above her and around her. Kieran's mountain-top home at her backside, Illiria and Apsephion bickering to her right. The man in question stood behind her canted on her left, silent as can be, while she took it all in. It was not what she expected, granted she didn't know what to expect, having grown up in Gwendolyn. Where the only opulent buildings were the city hall, a select handful of shops and the Belmont's home. Yet standing before her were gigantic, almost gothic in architecture, shops of various markets. People were bustling around, carefree and happy. There were balconies full of them, sitting, walking, strolling, with a plethora of bags and boxes in tow. She hadn't seen anything like it before, a city, alive and thriving. Strings of lights strung between the buildings, old looking lamp posts with flickering lights placed around gave off an eerie but not unsettling glow.

"It's..." Verena stopped, trying to think of a word to describe the scene, but she just couldn't find one.

"I know." Kieran wrapped his arms around her from behind. Their height difference meant his arms wrapped around her upper torso.

"I can't describe it. There isn't a word in the dictionary to convey it." Verena leaned her head back against him, his pectorals cushioning her.

"I know." He said again, Verena could tell he was nodding his head without looking at him based on his tone. "Shall we join them?"

Verena had no idea when their companions left their side until Kieran pointed them out a few metres ahead, talking to someone slightly taller than Apsephion. Illiria's laughter easily pinpointed in the cacophony of sounds around them, clearly something was funny. Verena smiled, carefree and, for once, completely happy, not a single thing to be stressed over. Hand in hand, they walked towards the laughter. Verena spotted a bookstore that caught her attention, one door before the one their companions were standing before.

"Kieran?" Verena stopped, pulling him to a halt as well.

"Yes, Love?" Looking down at her, her heart skipped a beat.

"Can we go in here after we eat?" Verena used her eyes to indicate the store she was standing before, a quaint little bookstore which sang to her.

"Of course. Do you want anything in particular?" Bashful, Verena blushed and looked down, embarrassed to admit her darkest secret to him. Kieran was having none of it as he crouched down to look at her, curiosity crossing his handsome features. "What is it, Hellfire? There is no need to be bashful; we will get you whatever it is you desire."

"Don't judge me." Verena poked him in the chest. "Promise?"

"I swear it." His free hand was placed above his heart, and a promise made would be a promise kept.

"I can't cook. Like at all." She whispered, hoping he wouldn't hear her.

"Are you wanting to buy some cookbooks?"

"Yes." She looked at him, expecting him to be laughing at her admission.

"Okay." Kieran stood up, his hands cupping her cheeks as he leaned to kiss the top of her head. "Would you like me to teach you?"

"You can cook?" Shock, surprise, and a marginal bit of jealousy flooded her.

"I can." He lightly guided her back towards where his friends stood, waiting on them.

"But you're male?"

"I am, yes." This time, he laughed, but not at her, only at the fact that she was stating the obvious.

"I've never met a man who can cook."

"Well, Darling, when your life revolves around the battlefield, you tend to have to learn some skills necessary to survive." They reached his companions. Illiria linked her arm with Verena's while the unknown male and Apsephion briefly bowed their heads.

"Do not let him fool you, though. His cooking was absolute shit for the longest time until Illiria here made him help the house cooks for a year." The same unknown male spoke up, his voice rough and deep. As he stepped out of the shadows cast by the building, Verena met his green eyes, giving Verena's own a run for her money. They were contrasted starkly by the deep colour of his skin, almost as dark as Kieran's armour but looked as soft as a newborn babe. His hair was short and neat but held an edge about him. An angry scar under his left eye ended just above his chin, pulling the look together. Dangerous, a skilled assassin, Verena could feel the magic oozing off him in waves, yet it was soothing as if it was trying to say she was safe around him. She was more surprised she could feel his magic when she could barely detect Kieran's or even

Apsephion, something else she would ask him about later.

"Really?" Verena smirked, imagining tall, dark, and deadly Kieran in the kitchen, wearing an apron, assisting the staff.

"Can we reminisce inside, where I can at least try to drown out my embarrassment of the stories with a glass of ale?" Kieran grumbled, tugging Verena through the door. She subconsciously noticed how the other patrons had stopped speaking and moved out of their way while he dragged her towards a table near the back.

"A round of the usual, Bal, with an extra," Illiria yelled at someone while she sat across from where Kieran had sat. Appearing as if this was an everyday occurrence, Apsephion slid in next to Verena. At the same time, she assumed the man who had yet to introduce himself was Orias and sat next to Illiria.

"Sure thing!" They responded, the atmosphere returning to normal afterwards, chatter picked up, and the musicians in the corner returned to their instruments.

Once everyone was seated, Verena took the time to look around the place. A luxury she didn't have while her grumpy mate dragged her into the building. The interior matched the exterior with its gothic charm. Obsidian floors, deep red plush chairs littered around obsidian clawed tables, lamps with the same glowing flames strung from various points in the high vaulted ceiling. Upon closer inspection, however, she noticed the fire was not a fire but a person? If they could even be called a person that is. The one nearest her stared at her intently with its creepy bug eyes and elongated claws, opening its mouth to showcase rows of sharp, pointed teeth.

"What the fuck are they?" Verena blurted out, her companions pausing their conversations to look in the direction she was. Kieran was the first to speak when he noticed the object of her curiosity.

"Ah, those would be Sargynx. Nasty little devils, they are."

"Why are they in the lantern?"

"It is their jail, Verena. They have been imprisoned." Kieran stated this as if he was doing them a service, as if there was nothing wrong with the fact that these creatures were imprisoned like light fixtures.

"Excuse me?"

"They are in there because they committed a crime of some sort, most of them have committed murder. Some twisted offspring of an imp and a pixie, they are cannibals by nature. A handful have been able to survive on animals, but those imprisoned have been tried and convicted of murdering Demons, Succubi, Incubi and the like."

At this moment, the bartender decided to walk up with a tray full of intricately carved obsidian mugs, filled to the brim with a sparkling red liquid smelling of cinnamon and something Verena couldn't put her finger on. They left without a word once their delivery was complete: each person with a mug in front of them and a basket full of various coloured breads in the middle. Without hesitation, all three men at the table scooped their mugs up and took an exaggerated gulp, their sighs of contentment done in unison like they had practised it many times before.

"Careful, Verena." Illiria covered her mug with her hand when she went to follow suit. "It's a bit, ah, how do you say it? Spicy?" Illiria looked towards her friends. They shrugged again simultaneously. "Yeah, I would say it is a tad spicy, so maybe baby sips until you get used to it."

How bad could it be?

Try it and find out, Hellfire.

She didn't need to be told twice, bringing the mug to her lips and taking a mouthful, ignoring the woman's advice. Cool liquid washed over her tongue and throat, settling in her belly. Verena couldn't see what Illiria was saying about it being spicy.

"It's not as-" Verena coughed. Her throat was on fire. "Oh hell." Waving her hand in front of her face, she reached for a slice of bread. Kieran replaced the one she had taken with a different one.

Chuckling the entire time, Illiria gave her an 'I told you so' look. Verena wanted to flip her off but was too occupied with the raging fire in her oesophagus. Scarfing down the piece of honey-coated, lavender-smelling roll, she glared at every single person at her table. Their answer was to burst out laughing simultaneously.

"You could have warned me." She mumbled, her throat still screaming but subsiding as she continued to go through the honey bread Kieran kept passing her. His laughter was barely contained as his hands shook slightly.

"We did." Illiria shrugged, her plush lips squeezing together to keep from laughing at her.

You ass.

She warned you, Love. You were a bit too stubborn to listen, though.

"How do you all stomach this, this? I don't even know what this is. Liquid fire?" Verena fluttered her hand about the table, indicating their empty mugs.

"We are Demons, Princess. The fire that runs through our veins almost completely dulls. What did you call it, Ria? Spice? It dulls the spice in the ale." The same un-named man's laughter gave his sentence an amused lilt. "I am Orias. I apologise for neglecting to introduce myself earlier."

"This isn't hot to you all?" She was baffled, accepting his apology in stride in the face of his admission.

"Not even in the slightest," Kieran whispered against her temple, pressing a kiss afterwards. "We are Demons, after all. Our bodies are perpetually burning with fire."

"I hate you all."

"No, you don't," Illiria smirked, waving at the bartender for another round. "Hold for the Fae here, Bal!"

"You want a Lorfi instead, Ria?" They shouted back, already filling up new mugs to bring over.

"Sure thing!" Illiria looked at her, shrugging innocently. "Let me tell you about when Kieran here nearly burnt the entire forward camp down because someone put a Sargynx in his tent."

Verena sat back, curled into Kieran's chest as she listened to his friends' numerous embarrassing stories, from his tantrums as a child to walking into the Incubi sector on accident. She joined in with their laughter when he groaned as each person told their own story.

How are you doing, Hellfire?

I'm fine, why?

Just checking on you, making sure you are alright.

"Alright, boys. Enough drinking." Illiria clapped her hands, each male exuding a differing level of mumbles. "Shopping time." She beamed, bouncing out of her seat and approaching Verena's side. She watched as the excited woman pushed Apsephion to the floor to grab hold of her hand. Apsephion moved just in time as Verena came out of her chair faster than lightning, almost like she weighed nothing or perhaps Ria was exceptionally strong. Were all Demons this strong? Was Verena the weak one in the group?

"Let's get this over with. I already can feel my pockets

burning, Ria." Kieran growled, jesting with the woman, placing some coins down on the table, the type Verena had never seen before. A handful of large black, gold, and a singular silver. Verena could only make out a face on the large black one, eerily similar to the face Cavanaugh painted.

It is our Lady, Azrael, on the coin, darling.

What are the others?

The Morningstar are on gold, while our Lady's sword, Givianchi, is on silver.

"Come on, boys. We don't have all day!" Illiria sang over her shoulder, skipping out of the entryway with Verena in tow. The bystanders moved out of their way, heads lowered and lips sealed. "Hel-Vanity awaits!"

"Hel-Vanity?"

"Oh, darling, only the absolute best clothing store in Borraine. You'll love it! Especially with those daring white tattoos you have going on, Kieran will be drooling on his knees by the time I'm done styling you."

"You are mistaken, Ria." Kieran, low and seductive, sending a wave of fire straight to her core.

"How so?" Illiria quirked, egging him on.

"I don't need a reason to get on my knees for her."

Chapter 46

VERENA

"Ria!" A blonde, tall, slender and ridiculously gorgeous woman screeched when they entered the unbelievably luxurious building, which took up almost six shops' worth of space. Verena had to rub her ears from the ringing and buzzing. Kieran's hand was laced with hers, pulsing roughly.

What's wrong?

You'll see. He was already irritated, about to bite someone's head off, irritated.

"What do we have here? Our elusive Prince Kieran? Before my eyes?" The woman sauntered, literally sauntered over, dragging her well-manicured nails down Kieran's chest, batting her eyelashes, and completely ignoring Verena, standing not even a few inches away. Verena already hated her, and the pounce reminded her too much of Kessa.

Oh. She gritted her teeth. She wasn't going to hit someone today. She wasn't going to hit someone today. The mantra repeated over and over until Verena vaguely believed it.

"Kat." Short, sweet and to the point. Verena smirked. Surely the woman wasn't so oblivious to blatant rejection?

"It has been such a long time since you have come to see me, Kie. What has taken you so long?" Kat pouted, and Verena did a double take. She was pouting. It wasn't a figment of her imagination.

"Kat, we've been over this. Take your hands off him, or I'll cut them off." Illiria snapped, twirling a blade in her hands. Verena had no idea where it came from until Orias raised an eyebrow. His arm shifted slightly to reveal an empty holster on his torso. "It's so simple. Though, it doesn't surprise me that you haven't been able to understand after all these centuries."

"Don't be jealous, Ria. We all know you want me. Unfortunately for you, I don't play for your team." Kat snarked. Verena was starting to wonder if she could hit her and get away with it. Surely, Kieran wouldn't mind?

"I would rather die." Illiria faked throwing up. Verena caught herself from laughing with a quick hand over her mouth and hiding her face in Kieran's arm.

"Who's this, Kie?" Kat dropped her hand from him, placing it on her hip, accusatory.

"This is Princess Verena Nightingale, High Fae from House Nightingale and Naedian. Our Prince Kieran's soulmate." Apsephion stepped closer, anger palpating off him in waves. Verena could feel his magic riling up her own. "I would suggest getting back to your job, Kataryna."

"What can I do for you all today, your Highnesses?" They watched Kataryna's face switch rapidly between so many emotions and many centred solely on Verena. The sarcasm from her, though, was evident when she bowed, a shallow, disrespectful and pissing Apsephion off even more if his answering growl was to be believed.

"We need at least five sets of fighting leathers for Verena, preferably in hellhound skin. I was thinking a handful of evening gowns, ten to twelve, would suffice, in the traditional colours. But also, bring some in the Nightingale and Naedian House colours. She will also need undergarments, bathing garments, a few robes, jackets, cloaks, and enough everyday wear for a month." Illiria rambled off like she was reading an imaginary list. "Oh, and shoes to match the gowns, riding boots, some sandals, maybe a few with lace and some fighting boots in Demon scale. We also need to see the weapons master for some new Merytra blades for Orias, Apsephion and Kieran. Verena will also need to get fitted for her main, a secondary and a bow."

"Anything else?" Kataryna was blunt, smoothly switching back into work mode.

"I don't believe so. Wait, we need the jeweller as well. She needs, at minimum, a dozen hairpins and matching jewels to go with her gowns. Along with daily wear jewels. This should be all. I will let you know if there is anything else as we continue." Illiria has already headed away from them. Verena looked towards Kieran for direction. He shrugged, following the energetic woman and the rest of their group was in tow. "Verena, come stand on this platform for me to get your measurements. Boys, you can sit there." She indicated a black leather couch opposite the platform and what appeared to be dressing rooms. Verena did as she was told, marginally embarrassed to be in front of everyone.

Winged women who resembled Sylvia appeared out of the woodwork, tape measures, pins, fabrics and other instruments. Verena had yet to learn what they were for. Measuring, taping, pinning and flying through fabric colours with murmurs of yays or nays. Her arms were pushed this way and that, up and down. She was turning in circles, told to squat, sit, jump, bend and more. The process was exhausting, and she knew they were just getting started. Kataryna had brought them all glasses of off-white bubbling liquid. Verena deduced it was a form of wine the moment she tried it. Handing it off to Illiria, Verena wanted a level head while she was showcased as a mannequin. A few winged women left, returning with stacks upon stacks of pieces. Corralling her into the dressing room behind her, Illiria entered promptly, all smiles and laughs, while Verena eyeballed the offending mountain of clothes perched on the dressing room table.

"There is no way I'm getting all these, Ria," Verena whispered, her arms coming to cover her exposed chest when Illiria unzipped the gown she was currently wearing.

"There is, and you will, Verena. Kieran has been waiting centuries for you. Let him spoil you." Illiria motioned for her to step out of the dress, now around her ankles. She did, standing nearly naked while waiting for the first piece to be ready. "Alright, first one. Step in, and then I will let the ladies finish the look before you step out to show it off."

Verena felt ridiculous, not because of the dress. No, the dress was stunning. A gorgeous ice blue A-line reminds her of falling snow and Kieran's blue flames. No, she felt ridiculous because of the women surrounding her, pulling her hair this way, slipping earrings on, clasping a ridiculously large diamond necklace around her neck, bracelets and cuffs. The worst portion? Verena loved the matching sky-high heels but knew she'd be a newborn giraffe. What would have taken Verena hours to prepare took them mere minutes.

"Alright, gentle-Demons and Prince, I present our own, Princess Verena," Illiria announced like she had been waiting her whole life to do so as she pushed the curtains back to reveal a wobbly Verena. Verena gave them a weak smile, praying desperately as she stepped up to the platform.

Good job, Verena, you didn't fall on your face.

"Hellfire..." Kieran stood, aimlessly handing his glass off, his eyes never leaving hers.

"Ah ah, Prince." Illiria rushed over, pushing him back onto the couch. "Sit your ass back down. You can drool from your seat."

The remainder of the outfits she tried on elicited the same response from him. She could tell he was hanging on by a thread. His desire for her was visible in the way he had to cross and uncross his legs, how he had broken three glasses already. Orias had to stop him from ripping Kataryna's head off when she rolled her eyes. Since the first dress, Illiria had her try on various ones in different colours. Deciding she couldn't pick a few, Illiria placed them all in the purchase pile. Her return pile was non-existent, and the woman had too much fun dressing up Verena. They had just finished the fighting leathers when Kieran had to stand up and pace behind the couch.

You're trying to put me in an early grave, Hellfire.

This is nowhere near my fault, Kieran. Illiria keeps insisting I show you. I would be fine trying them on myself and not coming out.

You better not. I want to see every single piece on you. If only to remember what they were for when I have to replace them because I ripped them off of you.

Kieran!

"Your Highness, the weapons master and jeweller are here." Kataryna announced, showing the two elderly looking Demons behind her. Both had an army of people carrying boxes, totes and cases behind them.

"She needs a rapier, no longer than forty five inches, swept hilt, made from Merytra. She also needs six stilettos. Have the sheaths sewn into the back of her fighting leathers at an upward angle. As well as a recurve bow, no

shorter than fifty six inches, metal frame, gargoyle string."
Kieran spoke up after remaining quiet during her fashion
show. "She will also need matching hair pins sharpened to
match her gowns, along with no less than ten for everyday
wear. Use Merytra for her everyday ones, whatever else
you need to match her dresses. These all must be done by
tomorrow. There will be no exceptions."

"Very well, sir." The two elders bowed, their companions following, and then shuffled out of the room. Verena
stood, her mouth agape at what had just transpired. Everything he had said went in one ear and out the other.

"What was all that about? Rapier? Stilettos?" Verena
stepped off the platform carefully, and the softness of the
leather she had on made the transition easy.

"Yes, Hellfire, a rapier. While decent with a dagger, you
would be best suited with a rapier. You are not built for
close combat. The rapier is thin, lightweight and will be an
extension of your arm. Keeping your enemies at a distance
gives you the best possible chance of winning. I will train
you how to use it, and Orias will train you on the bow and
Apsephion with your stilettos, a type of thin but deadly
dagger. A last resort should your rapier break or you be
disarmed." Kieran sat on the backside of the couch, looking her up and down, licking his lips. "Now, I believe we
are done here, Illiria?"

"We just need to pay and have the purchases brought to
the house," Illiria confirmed.

"Great. I will be taking my mate with me now." Kieran
vaulted the couch elegantly with minimal effort. Verena's
eyes widened at his athletic ability. "I promised to take you
to the bookstore you wanted to go to, Love. And I am
a Demon of my word." Sweeping her off her feet again,
Verena meekly waved goodbye to their companions over

his shoulder. Illiria gave her a thumbs up while Apsephion and Orias strolled over to Kataryna, passing her over a few sacks full of what Verena believed were coins.

"Be gentle with her, Kieran!" Illiria shouted. Kieran shifted her in his arms to flip the woman off.

Chapter 47

VERENA

Verena's time in Borraine came to an end. Kieran informed her the prior night that he was needed to quell some civil unrest in their farther colonies. He sent a message to Orla about retrieving her shortly after Sep told him the unfortunate news. She wasn't ready to leave; the time here with him felt right in her heart. The memories of the past days flooded back while she waited for the set time Orla would be returning to help her return to Alusso.

"Add in the flour once the eggs have been mixed." Kieran stood behind her, watching as she whisked vigorously. He had contained his amusement to a minimum when a flour cloud puffed up, coating her shirt, hair, hands and face with the white substance. "Or you can do it like that."

"Are you amused?" Verena looked at him, her face still covered in flour, inching closer and closer to him.

"Very." Kieran used his thumb to smudge some of the flour off her nose. "The flour is supposed to go in the bowl, Hellfire."

"I know." Verena looked at him deviously.

"What is with the evil look, Love?" Kieran backed away, his hands raised.

"Oh, no reason." Verena scooped some of the remaining flour into her hand and threw it into his ungodly posh face.

"You little devil." Kieran huffed the flour out of his nose,

levelling her with a look Verena learned was him plotting revenge.

The way he took his revenge for the flour escapade that night made her legs shake the following day. He had yet to penetrate her with anything more than his tongue or fingers. It was driving her mad. But the way she screamed his name made it to the point Illiria asked her if she had seen a ghost when the woman came to help Verena get into her fighting leathers for the day's training session with Apsephion, and her recurve bow. The entire house knew what transpired in their room if everyone snickering as she passed was to go off of.

"It's time to go, Verena." Sylvia entered Kieran's study gracefully; she was always put together so well, her gait proper, as if she was almost floating. "Orla is waiting for you. I have Illiria keeping her occupied from bursting in here to allow you your time to say goodbye."

"I guess I must return." Verena trailed off, trying to hold back the tears that came out of nowhere. Her heart hurt at the prospect of being away from him for too long. She grew comfortable in the limited time she had been there. The house felt like home. He felt like home—something she never felt before, and now she was having to give it all up again.

"You do, indeed, Hellfire." Kieran sounded just as depressed as she. His armour was already polished and ready to be put on once she left. "It pains me to see you leave, it is not safe here for you without me present, currently."

"I know. I don't have to like it, though." Verena wrapped her arms around his abdomen, not able to touch her own hands due to the sheer size of him. His arms snuck under her legs to pick her up.

"It should only be for a handful of days. When I return,

I'll come get you personally from the wolf den." Kieran promised her, nuzzling into her neck, inhaling the scent of her deeply, ingraining it into memory. "Let's get you to Orla before Illiria tries to kill her."

He didn't put her down, refusing when she tried to walk on her own. Instead, he picked up her bag and slung it over his shoulder. Containing a handful of the fighting leathers he bought her, her rapier sheathed and strapped to the top, along with some hairpin daggers and stiletto daggers tucked into their unique sheaths sewn to her tops. After her first attempt failed, Verena did not dare to argue, concluding he needed the contact to calm himself. Their stroll to where Orla awaited her was short, considering his legs could cross the distance faster than her shorter ones. Orla's short stature stood in the middle of the room, a few feet before the portal, her foot tapping angrily. Illiria and Orla were arguing about something, the wolf's accent thickening with each sentence while Illiria seemed to be enjoying herself.

"It's about time, Verena. We must go." Orla snapped, surprising everyone else in the room with her attitude.

"She will go when she damn well pleases, pup and not a moment before." Kieran handed Verena's bag off to Illiria to hold onto while he placed her on the floor. Hooking his forefinger under her chin to make her look up at him. He leaned down, slowly, too slowly, showing Orla his lack of respect for her impatience. His lips felt heavenly, soft, and plush; the way he dominated her attention and everyone else faded away and curled her toes. Their kiss lasted an eternity, and even then, it wasn't long enough. She yearned for more when he pulled away. Pressing the straps of her bag into her hands and stepping back, a tear escaped his eye, holding himself back from keeping her here with him.

"Go, love. You'll be safer with them while I am gone. And once I return, I'll bring you back home. I promise."

Verena frowned, turning to face Orla as the shorter woman took hold of Verena's arm, tugging her towards the portal. Verena was able to give Kieran one last longing look when the portal sucked her in, striking hell upon her stomach and body and then spitting her back out on the other side. The familiar room became clear, and Aven's arms steadied her as she regained her footing. His arms were nice, but they felt different, stand-off-like. They weren't home. They weren't his. And for the first time, Verena felt like an ass. She knew Aven was also meant for her, but her heart didn't seek out his as much as it fought for Kieran's. Aven's affection and love for her felt wrong, forced, and she hated herself for having those feelings.

Chapter 48

VERENA

F our days passed since she returned to Alusso, and four days passed since she talked to *him*. Ninety six hours. Ninety six hours of pure fucking torture. Their mental connection had been silent, no matter how hard she tried to get him to respond to her. Aven drove her up a wall with the obsessive amount he has clung to her from the moment she returned. To the point where she begged, literally begged, on her knees, to Gracie to make up some sort of condition to keep him away from her while they 'evaluate' her. Just so she can have some semblance of peace.

"I'm unsure how long I can keep him away, Ver. He's been hounding us all morning asking for updates, asking what you came down with, threatening to kill Kieran if he infected you with anything." Gracie sat on the edge of Verena's bed, rubbing her temples of the headache Verena could imagine stemming from Aven.

"I don't know what has gotten into him, Gracie. He has completely been stuck up my ass for the past ninety six bloody hours, and I'm about ready to kill him." Verena groaned, scratching at a spot on her spine she couldn't reach, which had been bothering her for the past few hours. Her hair was a mess. She had not had a chance to wash it since her return, Aven managed to hog every inch of the shower each night. The knots she knew were growing in size were about to push her over the edge. She wanted to bathe and relax, maybe read a damn book in silence.

"Druid Nora is meant to discharge you today. She stated this morning during the changeover how your magic stores have recovered and opened. But she wants you to continue to drink the tea Heath makes you until we can figure out a way to get you into Lothaire so you can absorb your home magic." Gracie skipped over to her, pulled her brush from the drawer and began running it through, working the knots out of Verena's hair. Verena scratched again, this time drawing blood from the roughness. "What are you scratching at, Ver? You're bleeding."

"I have no damn idea, but it itches so badly." Verena's hands shook as she tried to pull herself away from itching.

"Let me see." Gracie's cool hands pulled on the loose fitting tunic Verena had nipped from Kieran; the scent of him was fading faster than she liked. "Oh, Goddess."

"What? What?" Verena twisted, trying to see what Gracie was panicking over. The location of it is in a spot blocked by Verena's shoulder. "Gracie, what the hell is it?"

"It's another rune, Ver. I think. I'm not sure, but it looks like it."

"A what?" Verena stood, throwing the chair around as she rushed to the mirror. Lifting her shirt to see a bloody marking, which did indeed look like another rune to her, bleeding and irritated from her insistent scratching. "The fuck?"

"I don't know, I've never seen it before. How long has it been since you started scratching?" Gracie leaned in with a warm towel, dabbing at the blood to get a better look at it.

"A few hours, I think? I'm not sure. It wasn't there

when I woke up." Verena looked at it again, her back nearly a pretzel as she tried to get a better view. "What does it say?"

"I've never seen it before," Gracie admitted, jotting down the rune on her hand with a pen to look up later.

"Great." Verena rolled her eyes. "Just another thing to add to my list of irritating things today. Can you put something on it to stop it from itching so badly?"

"Yes, we have some ointment I can get you. Let me grab it along with Druid Nora so she can officially discharge you." Gracie began walking out of the room, stopping before she opened the door. "You can return to Gwendolyn by tonight if you would like."

Oh, yay, so I can return to thinking about my shitty life there.

"I'll think about it," Verena said to her, Gracie left, leaving Verena with her thoughts.

Kieran...

No answer, as usual. Her worry increased as the seconds passed.

Are you okay? Are you still alive?

I miss you.

Please come back soon. Everything here doesn't feel right. I feel like an outsider, like I shouldn't be here.

She felt like she was talking to a wall. Her concerns were brushed aside. A small portion of her self-consciousness sneered at her, telling her Kieran had left her. He was never coming back. Yet their bond was more vital than ever, her ability to see it grew with each passing hour. While her bond with Aven began to fade, the intensity paled compared to where it was before she met Kieran. Her self-hatred ate her alive for it every day. She assumed it was why she didn't want to see Aven. Currently, she couldn't face him and see how in love with her he was, while her feelings for him were depreciating. He was the good boy, the safe boy, the one where life with him would be simple and straightforward. In contrast, Kieran was the Demon, quite literally. Kieran gave her a sense of adventure, excitement, and unknown. Kieran was the man every woman lusted after, yet he only had eyes for one. Her. According to everyone who didn't know him, he was the villain in the story, while Aven was the hero. Aven was the one everyone expected her to be with, the one every Princess fell for in the stories she was told growing up.

Fuck the fairytales.

She didn't want to be saved. Didn't want to be helpless. She wasn't a damsel who needed saving. She wanted to feel power. She wanted to be capable of saving herself. She was a force to be reckoned with. The eye of a storm. The fire from a dragon. The sharpened edge of her sword.

A knock on her door shook her from her thoughts, and Nora and Gracie entered after Verena had voiced her permission. The Druid still took Verena's breath away, similar to Sylvia. Nora had an air about her that oozed with grace. Verena could see it in how the plants around them seemed to reach for the Druid, wanting to touch her.

"Verena." Nora delicately bowed, the courtesy Verena could not convince her not to. "Healer Gracie informed me you have a new rune needing to be looked at and treated. May I see it?"

"Of course." Verena turned around again, shifting her shirt to expose the still bleeding marking on her back near her right shoulder blade.

"Interesting. I have not seen this one before, either, Gracie. Have you taken the necessary notes to research this later?" Nora's frigid hands traced the outline of the marking.

Verena shivered from the sudden change in temperature. "I have, Druid." Gracie passed the Druid some sort of pink hued ointment in a glass jar.

"Good, let me know what comes of your research. Until then, Verena, Gracie will apply this salve twice a day. Once it stops bleeding and the inflammation is gone, we will re-evaluate. But, other than this new development, I am officially discharging you from our care. I have taken the liberty to speak with the council on your behalf. Should you wish to remain here, a room is being made up in Heathrow's sector of the sanctum. It should be ready within an hour or two." Nora hugged Verena gently, taking care to avoid the irritated rune. "If you need anything, do not hesitate to come find me, you hear?" The Druid sounded like she was trying not to cry. Verena hugged her back hard.

"Thank you, Nora." Verena gave her a half smile, releasing her but keeping her hands on Nora's shoulders. "For everything."

"Always, Dear, always." With that, Verena watched Nora leave her room. Leaving Gracie and Verena alone once more.

"Alright, no waterworks, please. You start crying, then I'm going to cry. And I look like a drowned cat when I cry; it's not pretty." Gracie demanded, spinning Verena around again. The salve stung as her skilled fingers pressed it into the open wound, eliciting a hiss of pain from Verena. "Shall we go check out your new room, or have you decided to return to Gwendolyn?"

"I think I want to stay here a bit longer." Verena shrugged. She knew there was no way she could fib to Gracie. The wolf had a weird ability to tell when Verena was lying to her. She practically demanded all the details of her visit with Kieran when she returned, threatening to sicken Aven when Verena tried to tell her nothing happened. The two spent all night giggling and laughing at the stories Verena spilt.

"I was hoping you'd say that!" Gracie squealed, linking their hands together and dragging her towards the door. Verena silently watched as Gracie stuck her head out, looking in both directions and then tugging roughly. They scrambled down the hallways, stopping every so often. Gracie would sniff the air and then pull Verena in all sorts of directions. Most likely attempting to skip past Aven without alerting him of their escape from the healer's wings.

After many dives into doorways, clamping her hand over her mouth to keep quiet, and Gracie barreling them into a random male wolf from her inattentiveness, they stopped before an ice blue door. Wolves were going in and out of the room, moving furniture, plants, and various other objects into the room. Utterly ignorant of the two standing there, watching, when a wolf carried in Verena's rapier last seen in her old room.

Damn, they move fast.

"Careful, it's ridiculously sharp." Verena stepped forward as the wolf began to slide her rapier out of its sheath.

"Your Highness!" The girl screamed, dropping the rapier to the ground. It clattered angrily while the girl's hand came to clutch her heart. Verena frightened her, but Verena couldn't be bothered to care. She was irritated that her sword had been dropped to the ground so harshly.

"I'm sorry." Gracie offered the girl, her eyes flicking between Verena and the child anxiously. "We should not have snuck up on you so suddenly. We can get the rest. Thank you." Gracie dismissed them effortlessly, the helpers bowed their heads respectfully to Verena as they passed her, scattering out of sight.

"She could have damaged it, Gracie!" Verena muttered, delicately placing her sword on her new bed. Plopping down next to it, she took in her room. It was almost identical to her previous one; the only exception was the massive in-ground tub in the corner and a glass ceiling that opened to show the midday sun breaking through the clouds.

"It's fine, Ver." Gracie rolled her eyes, joining Verena on the bed. "Where has Acheron been lately?"

"Somewhere, I suppose. Doing death falcon things." Verena shrugged. "Speak of the devil." On cue, Acheron plunged from the glass ceiling. Clearly, one of the glass panels was fake, Verena wondered if it would let a draft in. Her falcon landed on her footboard staring at her, a rolled piece of parchment clutched in his talons.

"The Demon sends his regards and apologies for ignoring you." Acheron squawked, allowing Verena to remove the paper from his claws. Unfurling the rolled parchment, she recognised Kieran's elegant scrawl. Her heart skipped a beat reading the singular line on the paper.

The Sun cannot shine without the Night, and the stars are never as bright without you to guide them.

Chapter 49

VERENA

Her peace ended with Aven bursting through the doorway, frantic and panicked. His phone was clutched in one hand and a satchel in the other. He didn't say a word, not a sound. His heart raced in her ears. His lungs fluttered roughly to keep up with the demand. He stalked towards her, angry and frightened. Verena sighed inwardly. She knew the explosion was bound to come when we set the light on the fuse. It was only a matter of time. Except, to her utter shock, it didn't go off. He wrapped her in his arms, the pounding of his heart subsiding to a slow, steady beat. Inhaling deeply, squeezing tightly. Gracie coughed and silently excused herself. Verena could hear she only stepped outside and didn't venture far.

Here we go...

"I thought you were ill." Aven broke the silence, the tension, Verena waited for the other shoe to drop. "Goddess, Verena, I thought I would lose you again."

I was expecting something else.

"I'm fine, Aven. A new rune appeared. It wouldn't stop bleeding. They wanted to ensure it wasn't contagious before releasing me. And when they did, Gracie was so excited to show me my new room we had completely forgotten to let you know. I always knew you'd find me, though."

A half truth, but truth nonetheless. Verena's guilty conscience raged against her fib, demanding her to tell him how she felt. Demanding that she be upfront about how his clingy nature recently has driven her mad.

She didn't.

She should have.

But she couldn't.

"Are you staying?" He sounded hurt, like a puppy beaten. It broke her heart again, what was left of it anyway.

"I am." She confirmed, knowing there was no manageable way to break the news to him softly. Not when he had asked so forwardly. "I want to spend more time getting to know Heathrow. By all intents and purposes, he is my guardian. He knew my parents. There is still so much about them I do not know and he refuses to leave here. Or cannot leave here."

"I understand."

"I'm sorry, Aven." She added hastily, not hearing his response and its finality. "Are you returning to Gwendolyn?"

"I will be, shortly. Yes." Aven held out his phone to her. "Though I need to investigate something first. Elder Armand received a missive from an unknown sender indicating a disturbance a few hundred kilometres from here. The council has dispatched myself, a tracker and a handful of Elites to check it out. We are set to leave shortly, but I wanted to tell you before I leave first."

It would explain the way he was dressed. Loose clothing, looser than she had seen on him before. Verena chalked it up to being able to remove the clothing easily before he shifted, having witnessed the aftermath of shifting in clothes before. She guessed it was a wise move on his part to try and save something for when he inevitably shifted back. It would be a sin, for herself, knowing others would see him walk around in the nude. It was a sin because Verena would have to carve their eyes out for even looking upon him. It was too early in the day to be so violent. She hadn't had the chance to eat yet.

"Kessa will be joining." Verena must have spaced because she did not hear a word he said until her name crossed Aven's mouth. "I know what you're going to say, Ver."

"Kessa. Is joining? We are talking about the same Kessa who tried to fight me over you, right?" Verena's eyebrow tweaked slightly, enough for Aven to notice. He threw his hands up submissively.

"Woah, Love. It wasn't my choice." Aven defended, scooting backwards from her. "The order came from the council. I didn't have a choice."

"Why is she coming?" She could make time today; it wasn't too early for violence. She could get a bit of anger out in the process in time for brunch. It sounded like a good plan to her.

"She's the best tracker we have; the others left yesterday for a different assignment." Aven sounded tense, almost hesitant to tell Verena. "I hoped to convince you to come home with me when I return." His puppy dog eyes nearly broke her. He wasn't playing fair.

"She needs to keep her hands, eyes, hell, even her thoughts to herself," Verena grumbled, irritated beyond imagination. Though she knew she had no say in his orders, she was not a wolf. She wasn't even human or officially mated to him. "While I would have loved to come back, Aven, I don't think I am ready to return just yet. I know I am not ready to go back to *that* house, to say the least. I need time. I fear I'll set the whole place on fire just to forget. I still might. The thought has crossed my mind a few times."

"I know, Love. It hurts, but I understand. Take as much time as you need. Heathrow is getting you a new phone. When you are ready to come home, I'll be there every second of the way." Aven cupped her face in his hands, his heart on his sleeve and love in his eyes crumpled her. She didn't deserve him, this kind, honourable, gentle soul. "I need to go now. I don't want to, but I can only keep them waiting for so long." He was leaning in, allowing her to move away if she wanted.

Letting her control the situation, knowing he didn't want to push her any farther than she was willing. She closed the gap, pressing her lips to his. It was great, fantastic even. Enough to make any other woman's heart melt, tear their walls down and help them rebuild. Enough to make anyone, literally anyone else, feel the pain of knowing he was leaving. Always having the potential of never returning home. Knowing a simple task of investigating a disturbance could be the last time she sees him. It should bring tears to her eyes. It should cause her to worry for his safety. She should be anxiety ridden as she watched him walk through the door. She should have run after him and begged him not to go.

She didn't.

She didn't because it lacked everything. There were no fireworks in her stomach. Her toes didn't curl inwards. It didn't make her heart stop beating. She didn't feel the brain numbing anxiety coursing through her. She didn't feel the need to run after him. She didn't feel what she knew logically she should have felt towards someone she believed she loved, at least at one point in her life. As his footsteps faded into nothing, she knew then and there.

She was so fucked.

Completely and utterly fucked.

Chapter 50

VERENA

Gracie broke her out of her internal damnation, bursting through the door like a rabid bear had chased her. She closed the door behind her quietly, locked it, and then double-checked that the door was locked. Verena could only watch, curious at what possessed her friend, her head tilted to the side like some sort of dog staring at their master. Verena knew the look on her face said everything Gracie needed to see. She was never good at hiding her emotions. Especially when she was so utterly lost on what the hell was going on.

"Are you good?" Verena asked when she watched Gracie throw everything around in her room, tearing through all the boxes the movers had brought in. Gracie ignored her, ripping everything apart, pushing Verena out of the way so she could search her bed. "What the fuck are you looking for?"

"Give me a moment." Gracie rushed. The room looked like a tornado had entered and sat for days. She still wasn't done, though, shaking every piece of fabric, every single piece of clothing, even boxes and picture frames.

"Okay, okay, stop. Gracie." Verena snatched the pillow Gracie had picked up again from her hands. "What crawled up your ass and died? Because no sane person would just come into someone's room and make it look like a damn storm blew in. So spill. Now." Verena snapped her finger, pointing at the only untouched, right side up, chair in the space.

"Remember when you told me about the rune I have on my wrist? When you woke up one morning and scared the absolute shit out of me because of it?"

"Obviously." Verena plopped on top of her now ruined bedding, eyeballing the woman. Trying to determine if she needed to grab Gracie or shake the ever loving shit out of her. "I was there, remember? I also remember you ignoring my question, too."

"There is a reason I didn't answer." Gracie played with the edges of her uniform, looking anywhere but Verena. Minutes went by, and Verena waited patiently. But even her newfound patience was still limited.

"Well? Spit it out." Verena snapped. She had waited patiently, and now she was done waiting. The shaking was still on the table.

"My name is not Gracie."

"Well, duh, it's Gracella." Verena levelled her with a 'no shit, Sherlock' look. This was not what she was going to tell her, was it? "What does your name have to do with a rune?"

"I'm trying to tell you, Ver. So shut up and let me finish."

"Fine. Fine. I'll shut up." Verena waved her hands in front of her, offering Gracie the floor.

"My name is not Gracie, and the rune has everything to do with it." Gracie peeked up at Verena, probably looking to see if Verena was going to keep her promise of staying quiet. Gracie continued when Verena nodded, showing she would do what she promised. "You know the Belmont's have a daughter, right?"

"Yes. Vivianne, I believe. I've never met her; there are no photos of her in their home, and they never talk about her."

"I am Vivianne, Verena."

"You- What?"

I was definitely not expecting it. Actually, I don't know what I was expecting.

Gracie stuck her hand out, pulling her sleeve to expose her wrist. Verena saw nothing except her unblemished flesh until Gracie used her nails to pull a piece of skin-toned tape, a band-aid, something, off to reveal the glowing red rune Verena had seen before. Verena leaned over, trying to focus on the rune itself, ignoring its angry glow like it was fighting being exposed.

Forget.

"Gracie, why do you have a forget rune?" Verena poked at the red aura lashing out at her. Verena's magic rose to meet the rune, practically forcing the rune back into submission.

"That's what I'm trying to tell you, Ver." Gracie sighed. "My name is Vivianne Marquess Belmont. I am Merridayn and Elion's third child, the youngest child of the Belmont's."

"Uh-huh."

"Fuck, Ver, will you try to believe for me a second? We don't have that much time. Something is going on, something big. I can feel it coming, but I don't know when, and I don't know how." Gracie - Vivianne? - shouted at her, startling Verena as she had never heard the woman raise her voice at anyone.

"Okay, hypothetically, if you are Vivianne, why do you have the forget rune? And why do they not talk about you? Why are there no photos of you around their home?

Why do they act like you died?" Verena crossed her arms, waiting to see what the wolf would say before jumping to conclusions. She had grown up since the day Merridayn infused her with blood. Verena mentally patted herself on the back.

I swear to hell, if someone else drops a bomb on me like this, I'm going to start second guessing everyone's identity.

"Since I was a child, I was different. I could always tell when there was danger, call it a hunch. Like a feeling in the back of my head, nagging, most people call it a gut instinct. Except for me, it was more of a roar than an unsettling feeling. I would get these intense dreams, worse than deja vu. I thought it was just me being a child, with an active imagination. My parents thought so until we were out and about one day. Have you ever wondered why they do not leave the house anymore? Did you ever ask why they hired you? A random stranger who just happened to drive by our home every day for school?" Gracie had a point. To this day, Verena still could not understand why Elion had stopped her and given her a job seemingly out of the blue.

She has a point, Verena. You have been wondering why he stopped you for years.

"Well, yes, I did wonder, but it wasn't my place to ask. I figured they just didn't want to deal with people. Hell, half the time, I don't even want to deal with people, especially those stuck-up snobs in Gwendolyn."

"When I was sixteen, we were supposed to go out for my birthday. Mom had an entire day planned for us. Our first stop was the Jones' bakery. I absolutely loved their croissants. I loved watching them make them, too, so Mom contacted them to let me come in and help make my own. Except before we were getting ready to go, I had one of those raging deja vu dreams. I screamed and shouted, and did everything I could to convince my parents I didn't want to go. Even locked myself in my room, barricading it with anything I could find to make it more difficult for them to enter." Gracie got up and paced the room, back and forth, again and again. Like the memory of what she was saying was causing her pain. Verena wanted to reach out to her, comfort her, and tell her it would be fine and that she didn't need to talk about it if she didn't want to. But she couldn't. Verena felt that whatever Gracie was going to tell her, she needed to know.

"You succeeded, didn't you? You didn't go." Verena asked gently, as gentle as she could muster. The answer felt right. She only needed Gracie to confirm it.

"I did." Gracie nodded, and her pacing stopped. "We didn't go."

"What happened?" Verena hesitated. Did she want to know what Gracie felt caused her to miss her birthday?

"The next day, we heard on the news that an out-of-control trucker had struck the Jones' bakery. He had lost his brakes coming out of the mountains and didn't use any of the emergency pull-offs." Gracie looked at her for the first time since she entered. Her eyes were puffy and red, tears barely contained. "It struck exactly at the time we were supposed to be inside, making croissants."

"But you weren't there..." Verena trailed off. She understood what Gracie was telling her. "A part of you knew it wasn't safe to go."

"I snuck out the next night, and found my way to the Druids after months of searching. Nora found me, led me to their inner sanctuary, vouched for me when the rest of her grove wanted nothing to do with me." Gracie came to sit next to Verena, laying her head on Verena's shoulder. The barely contained tears broke the dam holding them back. "Nora was the one who cut her soul in half to put this rune on me. Druids aren't supposed to do this type of magic. It is unnatural to them. She risked everything, Ver, everything for me."

"Why did she? Why 'Forget'?" Verena ran her fingers through Gracie's hair, trying to comfort her.

"I needed my parents to forget me. I needed them to not remember me. I knew there was a chance I would run into them. Druids and wolves work together all the time. I needed a failsafe if we ever crossed paths. They wouldn't know who I was. I felt it was the only way to keep them safe." Gracie stopped, sobbing now. The tears turned from a trickle to a raging waterfall. Verena pulled her into her arms, holding her there, letting the woman get it out of her system.

"We all do what we think is best to protect those we love, Gracie. I won't judge you for doing what you thought would protect your family." Verena rocked them softly, her hand still stroking through Gracie's hair. "Is there anything else you want to tell me? Can I still call you Gracie? Or would you like me to call you Vivianne?"

"Gracie is fine." She hiccuped, her tears drying. There is still something I need to tell you—two things, actually."

"Anything, Gracie," Verena swore she would do whatever she had to to help her friend. If Verena could do it, she would.

Please be something I can do.

Please be something I can give you.

"Something is coming, something big. I can't tell what it is. But I know it's coming. And when it does, I need you to promise me you will run when I tell you to. Run and don't look back. Ever. You run and run until you find Kieran. You run until you are back in Borraine with him."

Gracie's voice hardened, leaving no room for Verena to argue. "Promise me, Ver. Promise me you will listen to me when the time comes. I can't lose you too, not when I know there is a chance I can save you."

Verena struggled. She didn't want to promise to leave her friend, and she didn't want to swear to leave Gracie in harm's way. But she couldn't go back on her promise; she promised Gracie anything. And Verena hated people who broke their promises; she couldn't be one of those people she hated.

Fuck. Fuck. Fuckity Fuck.

Damnit, Gracie. Why do you have to put me in this position?

"I promise." Verena eventually bit out, snagging her lip in the process. "What was the other portion you wanted to tell me?"

"I need you to keep this between us. My parents cannot know I'm alive." Gracie begged, giving her the same puppy dog eyes she had seen on Aven not even an hour ago. There was no mistaking they were siblings. She could see it now.

Fuck me. Again.

"Okay, I won't tell a soul." Verena could feel the headache forming. Perhaps she might go for something more substantial than tea today. She knew Heathrow kept a bottle of whiskey in his study. Maybe she'd conveniently borrow it. Permanently.

Chapter 51

Aven

"We are almost upon the coordinates. Aven, Kessa, Tal, take the right. The rest will take the left." Their team lead, try as he might, Aven couldn't remember his name. He was efficient, ordering all of them to shift before crossing the sanctuary wards and instructing them to leave their clothes in a specific order to ensure maximum efficiency when they returned. "Understood?"

Everyone returned with their version of confirmation. Aven shifted into position in the front, his larger frame ensuring he was the first seen before Kessa and Tal. Kessa had been essential in finding the correct location. Her keen nose kept them on track. Telling the group when to change directions to avoid problems ahead. Namely, the rogues who stalked around picking off lone wolves. Tal was quick but a beta, better off as a messenger than a warrior. However, their team lead had informed him earlier that the smaller wolf was good. Their breakpoint was rapidly approaching, everyone began separating, shifting to their assigned groups.

The command to break was given, and Aven set off at a slower pace, guaranteeing the smallest amount of noise from his team. Kessa and Tal followed suit, mimicking his steps and watching their surroundings.

"One Kilo left. Keep it sharp." Aven used their pack

bond to communicate, the feeling as natural as speaking. The ability to command flowed through him, as was his birthright.

"Wait, Aven." Kessa hesitated, stopping abruptly, scenting the air. "Something isn't right."

"What is it?" Tal snapped his head in each direction, trying to catch whatever Kessa could smell.

"I'm not sure. It doesn't smell like a rogue." Kessa whimpered, coming to crouch near Aven.

"Tal, can you sneak up without being seen?" Aven questioned, knowing he would not be able to. His size was his weakness when it came to sneaking.

"Understood." Tal nodded. The sleek dark brown wolf darted off, and not a sound came. Aven was impressed, so he took note to ask how Tal did it when they got back.

Kessa huffed nervously, crouching down lower next to him. Aven moved to hover over her, hoping his presence would calm her. She shouldn't have been here. She wasn't trained for combat. He knew he didn't have a choice. She was their best tracker at the moment. He stood as close to her as he dared. Granted, he didn't want to piss his mate off, Jasper agreed, telling him he would throw them off the nearest cliff if he pissed Verena off because of Kessa. Minutes passed of pure silence. Tal had still not returned, and Aven was getting anxious for news, any news.

"Tal? Check in." Aven called out, pausing before asking again. "Tal?"

There was no response. Jasper considered all the options, deciding that their best bet was Kessa waiting where they were while Aven investigated.

"I'm sorry, Aven. It should have been me you mated with." Aven shifted to move forward when Kessa surprised him. One moment, he was walking towards where Tal went, and the next, a puncture in his hide. Aven fell to the ground, looking at a tranquiliser dart sticking out of his flank. Kessa's body hovered over him, someone else's shadow cast over her, and Aven tried to warn her. It was too late. His eyes drooped close, and darkness welcomed him.

Chapter 52

VERENA

Screaming woke Verena from the nap she involuntarily fell into. Gracie snuggled beside her, and her dried tears streaked her cheeks. They both sat up, looking around anxiously. The screaming increased closer to her room this time. Gracie pushed her finger to her lips, telling Verena to stay still. Verena whispered, protested, when Gracie got off the bed carefully, ensuring it didn't creak or groan as she did. Gracie ignored her protests, choosing to creep to the door and open it partially, only enough to be able to peek out. She shut it closed promptly, her hands shaking as she snuck back to Verena's side.

"Remember what you promised?" Gracie whispered, looking Verena in the eyes and then frantically searching the room for something.

"Yes, why?" Verena looked around the room for her rapier, spotting it against the back wall, next to her hellhound skin leathers. Gracie seemed to take stock of what she found, nodding to her to grab them.

"Because it's here." Gracie tiptoed to a corner of the room opposite Verena, shuffling things around and looking for something in particular. Verena didn't notice, couldn't, her attention solely on reaching her leathers and rapier, hoping her daggers were in this set. She didn't know if she would have time to find another set before the commotion reached her door. "Found you."

"Found what?" Verena snatched up her top, sighing, distraught that this set did not contain the daggers Kieran had custom-made for her.

Fuck. Fuck, where are they?

Verena searched the room again with her eyes. The room was in such disarray from Gracie earlier that she couldn't find anything. She spotted a hairpin on her end table, another tossed by the chaise, and something which looked suspiciously like her dagger near it. Verena looked at where Gracie stood, her hand clutching the weird black flower she allegedly inherited from her parents. Gracie was clutching onto it like a lifeline, making sure she didn't drop it or hurt it, like a new father holding their baby for the first time: delicately.

"Uh, Gracie." Verena stepped backwards, away from the woman, who was aggressively walking towards her. "What do you plan on doing with a flower?"

"You can hate me later, but I need you to take your shirt off and lie down, face first, on the bed." Gracie gently placed the lily on the nightstand, rummaging in her pockets for something. "Now, Verena. We don't have much time."

"What the hell are you planning, Gracie?" Verena snapped, obeying the crazy woman's instructions, however. Her shirt flew off, exposing her naked upper half, and her white tattoos flared. Verena could feel the new rune on her back, and it was angry. "Gracie."

"This flower was grown from the Archangel Azrael's wing feather. It was gifted to your mother upon her request to protect you in need. From my research, the flower has to be implanted at the base of your neck until the bottom of your shoulder blades. Almost as if you had wings yourself. Do you understand?" Gracie found what she was looking for. It clattered against whatever else she had in her pockets. Verena looked over her shoulder to see Gracie tear open a disinfectant wipe, using it crudely to clean a sharp looking black scapula. It was eerily similar to Verena's daggers, perhaps made from the same metal. Verena knew it would have to be. Human metals couldn't break through her skin. She wasn't about to do what Verena thought she was about to do, right? "This is going to hurt, and I am sorry."

Oh, hell no. Hell no.

"Woah, woah. Slow your roll, Gracie..." Verena bit down on her tongue, feeling her teeth break the skin, and blood flooded her mouth. Gracie had shoved Verena's head into the bed with one hand, using the other to press the sharp blade at the base of her neck. Verena felt woozy. One moment, she was there, and the subsequent intense pain had flared. As much as she wanted to squirm from Gracie's hold, she resolved to stop. If she moved slightly in the wrong direction, Gracie could cut wrong and leave her a heaping mess.

"I'm sorry," Gracie repeated it over and over, and Verena wondered if she was saying it to calm herself down or to calm Verena down.

"Fuck. Fuck. Fuck. Gracie, are you done? I don't know how much more I can handle." Verena bit through her teeth. It felt like an eternity had passed since she began, with no progress. The pain made her insides curl, her magic was furious, and the edges of her vision started darkening.

"Almost there, just a bit bigger." Gracie pushed down hard one last time. Verena could hear her skin and tissue tearing. "This might hurt, I don't know. This has never been done before." As soon as the words left Gracie's mouth, the crazy ass was digging her fingers into the gaping wound to pull it open.

Holy shit.

Verena's head spun, her nails ripping the sheets below them. Tears flooded her eyes, and the darkness grew. She was losing the battle against unconsciousness. Verena didn't think the pain could get any worse. There was nothing worse than someone's fingers in her spine, pulling it open, right?

Oh, how wrong she was.

For the second time in the span of the day, Verena mentally applauded herself for the mysterious amount of patience she seemed to have. Because there was something worse than someone's fingers in her back, tugging the tormented skin apart. What, one might ask? It was the lily being shoved inside said opened hole. The sensation caused her to black out, losing it just momentarily. When she came to, the pain returned in full force, as if it was waiting for her to come back to her senses to torment her again. The bloody lily burned. Everything burned. Her entire body felt like it was on fire, inside and out. The blood in her veins burned, her lungs, her brain, and it all stemmed from the damn flower Gracie planted against her spinal cord. She could feel it changing, wrapping itself around her vertebrae, if that was even possible. Gracie sucked in air, her hands left Verena's body as if she was burning. Then the pain subsided like it wasn't there to begin with. Verena couldn't feel anything. Not the open wound in her back, not the burning from previous, not even the weird sensation of the lily melding with her core. There was nothing.

And then it came crashing back, harder than before.

Verena knew the feeling now and recognised it from the new rune from earlier. She knew what was happening, knew the itchy, burning sensation for what it was. The lily was indeed burning her, burning another rune into her spine. Verena scrambled to get up, ignoring the pain it caused and rushing to the mirror. Desperate to see what was appearing on her back, needing to know if it was worth being flayed open on her bed by a woman who just recently told her everything she knew about her was a lie.

"Verena..." Gracie stopped herself when Verena glared at her, her magic demanding silence.

Reaching the mirror, Verena contorted herself to look at it. At the monstrosity she knew would be there, considering the size of the flower and the size of the wound she knew had to be made. Yet when she turned, there was no blood running down her back. No burn. No open wound. Not even a new tattoo to indicate the rune was there. There was nothing. Absolutely nothing. What Verena saw in the mirror was only her skin and the stark white tattoos she knew she shared with her mother.

Not even the new rune she had gotten that morning.

Verena rubbed her eyes, then looked again at Gracie and back in the mirror. The sight didn't change. The only thing staring back at her was herself and Gracie's shocked reflection at what she saw in the distance. Verena had no words, no witty comeback, no snarky retort. She had nothing. Her mind had vacated her. Her body went on autopilot as she located her leathers. Gracie was wise enough to stay mute because she was terrified of what Verena would say or her thoughts had gone wherever Verena's had. They both remained silent, mute. The screams from the hall increased, and the women didn't move. Once Verena had changed, her rapier within arms reach, hair pins in place, three daggers in their sheaths with the rest missing. They both sat on her bed, not daring to move or speak. Footsteps pounding closer and closer to her door, Verena poised and ready for whatever or whoever came through her door.

Chapter 53

AVEN

He ran as fast as his wolf could handle and continuously pushed harder. Faster, he needed to move faster. It was all a lie, the entire thing, an elaborate lie Kessa had fabricated to get him out of the sanctum. To get him away from Verena. Jasper was mad. Their body cried out, and everything burned. He had never run this far, this fast and never for this long. Aven didn't care, couldn't care, couldn't think. It was nearly dark when he awoke, and everyone had vanished. Kessa was gone. There was no hint of Tal or the other team members. They were all gone, their scents fading rapidly. He didn't have time to waste. He had to get back to her.

He knew the moment he crossed into the council's territory, something was amiss. There were no guards. No one was patrolling, no sounds of hearts beating nearby. Nothing. It was silent, still, except for the steady pounding of wings. And they were coming right for him. Aven ducked, his chest hitting the ground as the bird flew over him. The bird banked, coming at him again. Aven braced himself to snap, his muzzle opening wide, his mouth scrunching in anger. As it came closer and closer, Aven paused.

He recognised the bird. He knew the colouring. Acheron?

Acheron didn't stop, his talons gripping Aven's neck and ripped. Gaining Aven's attention immediately. Aven followed, Jasper was irritated and plotting how he would throttle the falcon later. But for now, he followed behind, avoiding any piles of leaves or branches which could give away his position. Once they rounded the corner, Aven knew something was wrong. An Elite's body, a handful of feet from the wall, ripped in two, with a spear he didn't recognise straight through the guard's heart.

Verena.

Aven picked up the pace, following her falcon. He knew the bird was leading him to her. They banked left again, and Acheron flew up over the wall. Stopping just at the crest, indicating that Aven should follow. He did. Backing up, Aven lunged at the wall, his front paw digging into the tree's bark while his back pushed as hard against the ground as he could. He didn't dare look down, pushing off the bark again a second time. He was almost to the top. Acheron waited, anxiously tapping his talons on his perch. Waiting for Aven to get to the top. Making it, Aven wobbled and hesitated. Less than two feet before him was a glass dome. He spotted fabric near him, suspiciously looking to be the ones he had discarded earlier to shift. Looking at the bird and back again, he snatched the clothing with his mouth, bringing it closer.

The change came faster than it ever had before. Jasper didn't fight him this time. They were both on edge, desperate to get to Verena as fast as possible. Whatever killed the Elite was not good news. He rushed to put his clothes back on, tossing the shirt aside when it became too difficult to get on quickly. Acheron cawed, flapping his wings over a section of the glass. Aven watched as he was above the glass for one second and then under it for the next. Was it actually glass?

"I guess there is only one way to find out," Aven grumbled, carefully testing the roof, praying to the Goddess it would hold. "Goddess, this is going to suck."

One step down, then another. He was before the windowpane Acheron went through. Crouching down, he tentatively reached out, but his hand disappeared through what should have been solid. Snatching his hand back, he let out a groan.

"Well, here goes." Aven stood and jumped through the fake glass without a second thought.

He was falling, surprisingly not screaming until he wasn't. The fall was over just as soon as it started, he landed on something soft, squishy even. Opening his eyes, he didn't know he closed, he patted around him. He landed on a bed, definitely a bed, though a messy one, and it smelled like blood. Looking up, he jumped out of his skin. Verena's rapier was centimetres from his throat.

"Ver, it's me." Aven inched his neck backwards, away from her blade. "It's me."

"Aven?" Verena pulled her rapier away cautiously. "What the fuck are you doing falling out of the fucking window? You could have died! I could have killed you!"

"Verena, keep it down," Gracie whispered, stepping out of the shadows behind her.

"I should be asking the same question." Aven stepped off her bed, looking around the room to see the disaster. There was blood on the bed, confirming the smell Aven caught of it. "Who died here? Where is everyone? Why are there dead Elites outside? And why is there screaming out there?"

"We don't know. We've been in here, waiting for someone to come and inform us." Gracie spoke up, slinking closer to Verena's side. "What happened to you? With the disturbance?"

"It was a set-up." Aven pulled Verena into his arms, and Acheron cawed from the armchair he sat upon. "Kessa set me up. I'm almost positive this was all her doing—at least partially her doing to keep me away from you. I just don't know why yet."

"Where is she now?" Verena was getting angry, vengeful. The bitch just didn't learn, did she?

"I'm not sure." Aven let go of her, kissing her forehead before he did. Jasper was calming down. They were both still pent up, wanting revenge. "Has anyone gone out to check the status?"

"Did you not hear what I said not even a minute ago?" Gracie huffed at his audacious behaviour. "Obviously not because I literally just told you we have been waiting right here. This whole time. We haven't moved."

"Stay here. I'll go check it out." Aven told them both, creeping towards the doorway where the screams had eerily stopped. He opened the door marginally, softly, silently, listening for anything near them before opening it wider. There was no sound, no noise. He saw the chance to step out and was about to take it. One foot passed through the threshold, and then another, the coast was still clear. Nobody had come running down the hall at him, no screams of pain. He turned to look back at Verena, gave her a thumbs up, and whispered he would be right back.

Her face was scrunched up; she looked like she was screaming, but no sound reached his ears. He stepped forward, trying to hear what she was saying, why was she yelling? His whole body froze, and pain erupted in his chest. Verena dropped to the ground, Gracie followed, tears streamed down both of their faces. Verena clutched her heart, and Gracie pointed at him, saying something. He couldn't make out the words, as if she was yelling them, but something was blocking him from hearing it.

He looked down when Gracie tapped her own roughly, multiple times. He looked down to see someone else's hand sticking out of his chest. His heart clenched between their bloody fingers. The last thing he saw and heard as they dropped it was Verena screaming as she tried to crawl towards him. He smiled, bloody teeth and all, looking up at the love of his life. There was only one thing left he wanted to tell her, one thing he hadn't dared to say before.

I love you.

* 9 7 9 8 9 9 2 3 4 8 4 2 2 *